Next to Love

Next to Love

a novel

Ellen Feldman

W F HOWES LTD

This large print edition published in 2011 by
W F Howes Ltd
Unit 4, Rearsby Business Park, Gaddesby Lane,
Rearsby, Leicester LE7 4YH

1 3 5 7 9 10 8 6 4 2

First published in the United Kingdom in 2011
by Spiegel & Grau

A CIP catalogue record for this book is available
from the British Library

ISBN 978 1 40749 345 9

Typeset by Palimpsest Book Production Limited,
Falkirk, Stirlingshire
Printed and bound in Great Britain
by MPG Books Ltd, Bodmin, Cornwall

MIX
Paper from
responsible sources
FSC
www.fsc.org FSC® C018575

FOR *André Bernard*

War . . . next to love, has most captured the world's imagination.
                                    —Eric Partridge, 1914

It's all so terrible, so awful, that I constantly wonder how 'civilization' can stand war at all.
                                    —Dwight D. Eisenhower, 1944

They fed us with all this crap about John Wayne and being a hero and the romance of war . . . They set up my generation, they set us up for that war.
                                    —Ron Kovic, 1986

In the last 3,421 years of recorded history, only 268 have seen no war.
                                    —Will Durant, 1968

PROLOGUE

July 17, 1944

In the year and a half Babe Huggins has worked for Western Union, she has been late only once before. Maybe that's why in the months to come she will occasionally persuade herself that some premonition delayed her this morning. But in her more rational moments, she knows her tardiness has nothing to do with a sixth sense, only an unsteady hand when she draws the line down the back of her leg to simulate the seam in a nylon. The odd thing is that before the war made off with nylons, her seams were rarely straight, but this morning she washes off the crooked line, starts over, and is late leaving for work.

The walk uptown from her parents' house, where she moved back after Claude shipped out, takes fifteen minutes, and by the time she turns onto Broad Street, the clock on the stone façade of First Farmers Bank says eight-ten. As she passes the open door of Swallow's Drugstore, the familiar mix of fresh coffee and frying bacon and medications wafts out to meet her. Later in the day, when

1

she goes in to get her Coke, the store will smell of tuna fish and grilled cheese and medications.

Late as she is, she cannot help slowing her pace to glance inside. A line of men sit at the counter, their haunches balanced precariously on the red leatherette stools, the backs of their necks strangely vulnerable as they hunch forward over their coffee. In the four booths along the wall, men lean against the wooden seat backs, polished day after day, year after year, by the same shoulders. Swallow's is not the only drugstore and lunch counter in South Downs. There are three others. But Swallow's is the best, or at least the most respectable. All the men there wear suit coats and ties, though this morning some of them have taken off the coats. Mr Gooding, the president of First Farmers, who lives in a large Tudor house on the western edge of town where wide lawns rise and dip like waves in a clement green ocean, is already fire-engine red with the heat. Only Mr Swallow, standing behind the prescription counter in his starched white coat with his fringe of white hair like a monk's tonsure, looks cool, or as cool as a man with two sons in the service can look.

Mr Creighton, the undertaker, waves to her from his usual stool near the door. She waves back and quickens her pace again as she digs the key out of her handbag with her other hand. The key feels greasy. The mayonnaise from her egg salad sandwich has seeped through the waxed paper and brown bag.

She unlocks the door and steps into the Western Union office. It's like walking into an oven. Without stopping to put down her bag, she crosses the room, switches on the fan, and turns it toward her desk. A heavy metal paperweight shaped like the god Mercury holds down the stack of blank telegram forms, but the breeze from the fan ruffles their edges. When she goes next door to get a Coke to go with her sandwich, she will ask one of the soda jerks to give her a bowl of ice to put in front of the fan. Mr Swallow never minds. Sometimes he sends a bowl over without her asking.

She walks around the counter where customers write out their messages, puts her bag in the bottom drawer of the desk, and takes the cover off the teletypewriter machine. Only after she folds the cover and puts it in another drawer does she turn on the machine. It clatters to life, quick and brash and thrilling as Fred Astaire tapping his way across a movie screen. The sound always makes her stand up straighter. She's no Ginger Rogers, but as long as she stands over that teletypewriter machine, she feels like somebody. She certainly feels more like somebody than she used to when she stood behind the ribbon counter at Diamond's department store. She never would have got the job if all the men hadn't gone off to war. Even then, her father laughed at her for applying. Who did she think she was? He said the same thing when she went to work at Diamond's rather than

3

at the five-and-dime. Who did she think she was? It is the refrain of her life. She has heard it from teachers, though not Miss Saunders in tenth-grade English; and nuns; and a fearful, suspicious gaggle of aunts, uncles, and cousins.

Rumor has it that, after the war, Western Union is going to install one of those new machines that automatically type the message directly onto the blank form. They already have them in Boston, but Boston is the big city, ninety-one miles east and light-years away. She is not looking forward to the new machines. She likes cutting the ticker tape and pasting it on the telegram forms. She takes pride in never snipping off a letter and in getting the strips in straight lines. Not that it will matter to her what kind of machine Western Union installs after the war. She had to promise, as a condition of being hired, that once the men started coming home, she would give up the job to a returning veteran and go back where she belonged. She wanted to ask the man who interviewed her exactly where that was, but didn't.

The ticker tape comes inching out of the machine. She leans over it to read the check. To most people, it's the first line, but since she started working in the telegraph office, she has picked up the lingo. The check tells where the telegram comes from. She lifts the tape between her thumb and forefinger.

WMUC200 44 GOVT=WUX WASHINGTON DC

She drops the tape as if it's scalding. Grace and Millie and the other girls she went to school with say they could never do what she's doing. They try to make it sound like a compliment, but what they really mean is their hearts are too soft, their skin too thin, their constitutions too delicate to serve as a messenger of the angel of death. She does not argue with them. She stopped arguing with them, except in her head, in third grade.

She picks up the ticker tape again to read the second line, the one with the recipient's address. In the cables from the war department, that's the killer line. Fear, hard and tight as a clenched fist, grips her chest as the letters inch out. If the first few spell MR AND MRS, she is safe. The dead boy has no wife, only parents. If they form MRS, the fist in her chest clenches so tight she cannot breathe. Only when she has enough letters to read the name and see it is not hers can she suck in air again.

She has never told anyone about the giddy relief she feels then. It's too callous. She has never told anyone about the sense of power either. As she watches the words inching out of the teletype-writer, she is the first one in town, the only one until she cuts and pastes the words, puts the telegram in an envelope, and gives it to B.J. to deliver on his bicycle, who knows something that will knock whole families' worlds off their axes. Sometimes she wonders what would happen if she did not deliver the telegram. Could people be happy living in ignorance and illusion? What if she delayed handing the telegram to B.J.? Is it a crime or a kindness to give some girl another day of being married, some mother and father an extra few hours of worrying about their son? Would she buy that extra day or hour if she could?

She has another secret about those telegrams from the war department, one she will never tell anyone, not Millie, certainly not Grace. Even if she still went to confession, she would not own up to it. Once, in the past year and a half, she read the name in the second line and felt a flash of relief, not that the boy was dead, never that, but that what he knew about her had died with him. She knows the penance for most sins. So many Hail Marys for lying or missing confession or sins of the flesh, which always sounds better to her than he-did-this-and-I-did-that, Father. But what is the penance for a black heart?

She looks down at the ticker tape again.

MRS

The fist in her chest clenches.

WALTER WOHL

The fist opens. Mrs Wohl is the widowed mother of a large clan that lives north of town. If you take the main road east toward Boston, then turn off onto School Road and keep going past the pond

6

where the town swims in summer and skates in winter, you reach the Wohl farm, though almost no one does. The Wohls keep pretty much to themselves.

She goes on reading.

THE SECRETARY OF WAR DESIRES ME TO EXPRESS HIS DEEPEST REGRETS THAT YOUR SON PRIVATE EARL WOHL

She cannot remember which one Earl is. Was.

The ticker tape comes to the end of the message. She picks up the scissors, ready to go to work, but the machine keeps clattering and spewing out tape.

She glances at the new check. It's from the war department again. This one reads MR AND MRS. She forces herself to look away and begins cutting the words of the first cable.

DEEP REGRET STOP SERVICE OF HIS COUNTRY STOP

She does not want to fall behind. It's bad enough she came in late.

She is still pasting the strips of ticker tape from the first wire onto the Western Union form when the machine begins spewing out a third message. By noon she has cut and pasted sixteen messages from the war department, enough to break the hearts of the entire town, more than B.J. will be able to deliver on his bicycle in one afternoon. This is nothing like the fantasies of hiding or holding up telegrams. This is real. All over town, people are waiting for bad news, only they have no inkling. She knows the worst, but she cannot stop to take it in. She has to get the telegrams out.

She thinks of going next door and asking Mr Swallow if she can borrow his delivery boy. Then she realizes. She cannot ask Mr Swallow.

Through the plate-glass window, she sees Mr Creighton pulling up to the curb. He'd be going into the drugstore for his usual ham-and-cheese sandwich. He would be happy – well, not happy, though who knows what an undertaker thinks about death, but willing – to deliver the telegrams. And, with his car, he could do it much faster than B.J. could. She pictures him driving up to a house in his big black Cadillac. She imagines him walking up the path with the pale-yellow envelope in his hand. This is not news an undertaker should deliver.

She tells B.J. to watch the office for a minute and walks quickly down the street to the hardware store. She is careful not to run. She does not want to alarm people. She keeps her head down so no one can see she's crying.

Mr Shaker is sitting on a high stool behind the counter, leafing through a catalog. There are no customers in the aisles. She starts to explain that she has sixteen telegrams from the war department and wants him to deliver some of them, but before she can finish, he is coming out from behind the counter. He says he will close the store and deliver all of them.

It is the worst day of Sam Shaker's life, until his wife dies eight years later. By three o'clock, he has delivered ten of the sixteen telegrams that came that morning and the three more that arrived afterward. By then, everyone knows what he's up to. He can feel eyes watching him from behind half-drawn blinds, tracking the progress of his truck driving slowly up one street and down another, praying he will keep going.

One of the telegrams takes him to the Wohl farm outside of town. On his way back, he passes the pond that serves as a swimming hole. The heat has brought out half the women and children in town.

He pulls off the road and sits watching them for a moment. Millie Swallow is sitting on a blanket with her little boy held in the embrace of her crossed legs. She's wearing a straw hat with a wide brim, but even at this distance he can see that her shoulders are pink and freckled. Grace Gooding is standing waist deep in the pond, her hands supporting her little girl beneath her stomach, while the child churns her arms and kicks her legs and sends up a spray that splinters in the sun like diamonds. At the water's edge, a group of matrons sit in low canvas chairs. Mrs Huggins is knitting, probably another sweater for Claude. Mrs Swallow is pouring lemonade from a Thermos. Mrs Gooding is watching her granddaughter splashing in her daughter-in-law's arms. The scene is as peaceful and perfect as a *Saturday Evening Post* cover. *What We're Fighting For.*

He takes the telegrams from the glove compartment and rifles through them until he finds the ones he's looking for. A sudden wave of nausea makes him lean back in the driver's seat and close his eyes. Which hearts break harder, wives' or mothers'? The question has no answer. Misery cannot be weighed on a scale. He slips the envelopes into his pocket, gets out of the truck, and starts toward the pond.

Awful as the day is, Sam Shaker never regrets volunteering for the job, though it costs him business, not just during the hours the store is closed that afternoon but for years to come. People still like him. They admit he carries a good line of products. But certain men and women in town cannot walk in to the store and see him behind the counter without remembering the day the bell rang and they went to the door and opened it to find him standing there with a telegram in his hand. For a while they feel guilty going to A&A Hardware two blocks away. Eventually they get used to it.

BOOK I

1941–1944

CHAPTER 1

December 1941

Babe does not take long to learn the dirty
little secret of war. It is about death.
Everyone knows that. But it is also about
sex. The two march off to battle in lockstep.

Her discovery is not original. Eros and Thanatos,
she will read later, when she is devouring anything
she can get her hands on that might tell her what
is wrong – no, that might tell her how to make
it right. But Freud did not have her firsthand
experience.

Sex is all over the war. Sex inspired by love. Sex
born of longing. Sex driven by loneliness. Sex out
of desperation. Sex fueled by rage. Violence
unlocked does not go docile back into its cage.
She has firsthand experience of that too. Or did
the war have nothing to do with it? Did she just
run across a bad apple?

Sometimes she thinks the whole barrel is tainted.
Once, before the men shipped out, she watched
Charlie Gooding cradle his baby daughter in his
arms, and even as something in her melted at the

13

sight, she remembered another Charlie, ten or eleven, one of the bigger boys she was afraid of, running along a line of daffodils with a stick in his hand, decapitating them with a single long murderous stroke. Because they were there. Even Claude, the gentlest of men, at six or seven threw a stone at a harmless robin. It was the only time in his life, he will tell her later, he was grateful for his pathetic throwing arm.

But at the start of the war, she knows nothing of the twinning of sex and death. All she knows is that the Japanese are evil and the Germans are almost as bad – this is before they learn of the concentration camps – and the men, the boys really, the ones who decapitated daffodils and threw stones at robins, are going off to kill. All she knows is the fear for those men, those boys.

They are all in this together, people say, only they aren't, because some will come through and some will not, and she is not thinking only of the men.

They are all in this together, so you try to worry about all of them, the boys you grew up with, the ones your friends married, but what you really worry about at three in the morning, and three in the afternoon, and all the moments between, is Claude.

They are all in this together, only she is still an outsider. She knows the logic. It is one thing for girls like Grace and Millie to befriend her. They are not snobs. It is something else for one of the

14

boys to marry her. Until it isn't. That is another irony of the war. It takes Claude away from her. It also gives him to her. Sometimes she wonders if he would have married her without the war.

There is one more contradiction, and it lights up those blacked-out war years like a firestorm. They live in fear, but they live. Misery and heartbreak and loss are just around the corner, so you might as well suck as much out of life as you can before you turn the corner.

No one admits that. Hypocrisy is the official policy. She does not understand how other people, people who are smarter and richer and more powerful than she is, do not see through it. At first she thinks she is missing some truth other people know. Then she realizes other people are the ones who are missing the truth, and it makes her angry. In movies, the stars on the screen crow for joy when they get their draft notices, while the lone character actor who is classified 4-F mopes in shame, muttering about how he wishes he could get his hands on those rotten Jap sons of guns. Once, she gets so angry that she mutters a furious *phooey.* The woman in the row in front turns around and gives her a filthy look. Then she stares hard at Claude, who fortunately is in uniform. Fortunately?

Newspapers run stories about Jews who managed to wriggle out of the Nazi grasp, but a sign in front of the hotel Grace and Charlie Gooding went to on their honeymoon said

NO DOGS OR JEWS. Babe knows, because Grace showed her a picture of Charlie and her standing in front of the sprawling white building with its big pillars.

'Didn't the sign make you uncomfortable?' she asked Grace.

'What sign?' Grace answered.

Babe does not blame her, not really. Grace was newly married, and the world was all soft edges and misty horizons. Only Charlie was in sharp focus, Charlie and the girl in the mirror, dressed in a trousseau of sundresses and tennis dresses and evening dresses, who was suddenly a wife.

Gene Tunney, the former heavyweight champion, now a naval commander, urges servicemen to pin what he calls the 'Bright Shield of Continence' on their uniforms, but Claude writes from training camp about sitting through films, again and again, showing festering body parts and pretty girls whose faces turn into skulls, and through lectures indoctrinating with doggerel. *If you can't say no, take a pro. Put it on before you put it in.* At her worst moments, Babe wonders if Claude would report on the films and lectures if he was writing to Grace or Millie or one of the other girls. At her best, she knows that Claude is writing to her because she is not like Grace or Millie or the other girls.

Nonetheless, people seem to be buying what Gene Tunney is selling, because suddenly everyone is getting married, as if a marriage license

16

is money in the bank against straying. During the last month of 1941, Babe puts on the awful home-sewn pink dress, which makes her feel like a wad of cotton candy, thirteen times. She is not super-stitious, but she cannot help wishing she were invited to one more or one fewer wedding.

For a time, it looked as if there would be no weddings at all. With American sea and air power crippled in a single Sunday, and the country at war on two fronts, surely the army and the navy would cancel Christmas leaves. But when the smoke of all those burning ships and planes cleared, someone high up in command decided this was exactly the time to send the boys home for the holidays. God knew when, or if, they would have the chance again. The government might as well have issued a mass marriage license.

The weddings are hurried affairs, conceived in a fever of hope, dread, and desperation; planned at the eleventh hour; carried off in a quick cere-mony at the bride's house or a church; followed by a slapdash though not necessarily unsatisfac-tory reception. Sugar rationing and champagne and whiskey shortages are still in the future. A few of the brides manage white dresses; most settle for suits. But all of them carry some kind of bouquet, and every one of them insists on throwing it. Millie Swallow – Millie Vaughn until four blissfully dizzying hours earlier – must have eyes in the back of her head to lob hers directly at Babe. There is nothing Babe can do but lift her arms to catch it. She always did have good hand–eye coordination. One of the first things Claude said to her was that she threw like a boy. He winced when he said it, because, as a boy, he was taunted for throwing like a girl. That was why he missed hitting the robin.

Some people cannot understand what Babe sees in Claude Huggins, except that he hails from above Sixth Street, the dividing line of respectability, or at least income, and she comes from below. Others cannot fathom what Claude Huggins sees in her. A few, like Grace Painter Gooding's mother, think they deserve each other, or would were it not for the Sixth Street divide. Claude's family does not live in the section of undulating green lawns on the west side of town, but Hugginses have been in South Downs since it was founded. The cemetery is full of them.

Babe knows Grace's mother's opinion even before she overhears her at Millie's wedding. Babe is in the small pantry behind the kitchen, putting away the plates she has dried – she knows how to make herself useful; more to the point, she knows how to hide her resentment at making herself useful – when Grace's mother comes into the kitchen for a glass of water. From where Babe is standing, she can neither see nor be seen, but she would recognize Mrs Painter's voice anywhere. She spent a good part of her girlhood being hectored by it. Wipe your feet, girls. Watch those crumbs, girls. I'd ask you to stay to supper too,

Bernadette, but you live way down below Sixth Street. We couldn't let you walk all that way in the dark, and I can't ask Mr Painter to get out the car to drive you home.

'I can't imagine what Claude Huggins sees in her,' Mrs Painter says now. 'Unless it's . . . well, you know what I mean.'

If the other woman doesn't know what she means, Babe does.

'Now, where do you suppose I'd find a glass?' Mrs Painter goes on, and Babe hears cabinets opening and closing.

'I think she's striking,' the other woman answers. Babe doesn't recognize the voice, but she's prepared to like the woman. No one has ever called her striking. 'With that honey-brown hair and those dark eyebrows.'

'That honey-brown hair, as you call it, is limp as a rag. I know she's poor, but there is such a thing as a home permanent. And that long upper lip. She always looks as if she's sneering. Not that she has anything to sneer about. Those Canucks are as bad as the Irish. Worse, if you ask me.'

Sometimes Babe dreams of moving to the big city, Boston or even New York, where everyone she knows does not know everything about her.

'Her legs are long and slim,' the other woman insists.

'Who would notice in that awful dress? A girl with shoulders like a fullback should not wear pink tulle.'

19

Babe hunches her shoulders and looks down at the dress. It really is awful, but her mother is so proud of it. For the first time in all her years of sewing, a dress has come out looking exactly as it does in the picture on the pattern package.

'And that ridiculous name. Bernadette is bad enough. Babe is just vulgar.'

That's unfair. She never asked to be called Babe. Somewhere along the way, the boys pinned it on her, perhaps because of her throwing arm, perhaps out of wishful thinking. If she comes from below Sixth Street, she must be fast. She is not fast. She is curious. And alive, for heaven's sake. She does not understand other girls, the ones who don't balk at the rules. She suspects they are made differently. That's another reason she is grateful to Claude. If she had not fallen in love with him, there is no telling the trouble she might have got up to.

'Of course, he's no catch either. Not an ounce of ambition. And there's something wrong with a boy who doesn't like sports,' Mrs Painter goes on. 'Besides, she must be as tall as he is in her stocking feet. Imagine spending your entire life never being able to wear high heels. Not that he'll marry her. It would break his parents' hearts if he did, but he doesn't have the backbone.'

Poor Claude, Babe thinks. He's damned if he does, damned if he doesn't.

She recognizes what others see as Claude's short-comings. He is exactly her height, though she does not see why that means she cannot wear high heels. His sharp-featured face would be handsome were it not for his nose. The kindly call it snub, the unkindly whisper the word *snout*. He has the pale, quick-to-ruddy complexion so winning in English schoolboys, but he is not a schoolboy, he is a grown man, and he tends to appear inebriated or embarrassed when he is neither. His wiry compact body makes him look like an athlete, but, as Mrs Painter pointed out, he is not good at sports. His best feature is a pair of heavily fringed black-velvet eyes that have, when he takes off his horn-rimmed glasses, the wondrous gleam of myopia. But he rarely takes off his glasses. And as Mrs Painter also pointed out, he has no desire to set the world on fire, at least in any way that would singe her. He is perfectly happy teaching history in the town's one high school. Maybe someday he will rise to the principal's office, though no one is putting any bets on it, especially since he got mixed up with Babe Dion. The principal's wife does not have to have gone to college, though it would be nice if she had, but she ought not to have worked behind the ribbon counter at Diamond's.

However, none of Claude's flaws, if they are flaws, matter to Babe. Being with him unhinges her. No one has ever had that effect on her, not even Jimmy Doyle, whose death she is sorry for, no matter what her initial reaction when she saw the telegram. Claude's arm around her shoulders in the movies makes the hair on the back of her

21

neck stand on end. His tongue in her mouth makes her back arch and her pelvis strain against him. Around him, she feels like an exposed nerve. After she has been with him, she is sore with sensation.

Claude has one more trait she cannot resist. He is kind. Some girls do not like kindness in a man. They say they do, but then they fall for men who chase other women, or drink too much, or make fun of them. Isn't that just like a woman. Woman driver. It's lucky she's pretty, because she sure ain't smart. Claude never makes fun of her.

She has known Claude, like everyone else in her life, forever, but she did not find out about the kindness until an afternoon six years earlier in the South Downs Public Library. She was fifteen, and he was eighteen, and if that difference was not enough, he was home from his first year of college, which as far as she was concerned might as well have been the moon. The town that afternoon sweltered under a brassy July sky, but inside the big stone library, compliments of Mr Andrew Carnegie, the air was cool and hushed. The only sound was the whisper of the fan on the librarian's desk.

Claude was sitting at a table near the window, reading a book of poetry. She knew because, when she went by, she saw the uneven lines on the right-hand margin of the page. He did not notice her – why would he notice her – until she went up to the desk to check out her books, and she did not find out he noticed her then until later.

The librarian frowned down at the three volumes Babe slid across the desk to be checked out. *The Good Earth* and two mysteries. If Louella Hammond had her way, her books would never leave the building. It was bad enough she had to let them go to nice homes, where she could only hope they would rest on polished tables and have their pages turned by scrubbed hands with clean fingernails, but it broke her heart to send them to the shabby houses below Sixth Street, where they were likely to get their pages dog-eared, and smudged with heaven only knew what, and – she had seen it with her own eyes – insulted in the margins with dirty words. Bernadette Dion had a passel of younger brothers and sisters who were likely to do all that and more.

'These are one-week books,' she said.

Babe did not argue. She knew better than to argue with the librarian.

'You cannot possibly read all three of them in a single week.'

'One is for my mother,' she lied.

'I'll let you check out one,' the librarian said, and made a mental note to put the other two on hold before Bernadette Dion returned.

Babe took *The Good Earth* and started out of the library. She was halfway down the block when Claude Huggins caught up with her. He held two books out to her. She stood looking down at them. They were the two mysteries she had wanted.

'I took them out for you.'

'In your name?'

He shrugged.

'What if I don't return them?'

He grinned. 'You'll return them.'

'Thanks.' Her voice was wary. She was not accustomed to being trusted. Once, when Grace brought Babe home after school, Mrs Painter picked up a quarter she had left lying on the counter and put it in the pocket of her apron. Larceny was not one of Babe's vices. When other kids pinched candy and gum and barrettes from the five-and-dime, she was not even tempted. But watching Mrs Painter slip that quarter into her pocket made Babe want to swipe it.

He shrugged again. 'I just hate bullies.'

Three years later, they began going together. By then he was teaching at the high school, and she was selling ribbons at Diamond's. His mother, sensing a rebellious nature as well as an inferior bloodline, was brokenhearted; his father merely disapproved. The town was full of nice girls from good families. Why did their son have to get mixed up with one whose father worked in the hat factory and who had to work herself?

Then the war came, the weddings began piling up like crashed cars on an icy highway, and Babe caught Millie Swallow's bouquet. She was careful not to look at Claude. When she finally did, he was looking at his spit-polished government-issue shoes.

They have been over it again and again. She

24

never brings it up, but he cannot let it go, a terrier with a bone.

'It's crazy,' he says.

They have been to the movies, a double feature, which was at least one movie and probably two too long for them. They do not want to be here, drinking coffee and eating pie in the last booth at Swallow's either, but there are rules about this sort of thing. Sometimes she wonders what would happen if she broke the rules, if she said, let's skip the movie and the drugstore and go straight to that spot on the road out beyond the pond.

'What's going to happen if they don't come home?' he asks. 'What're the girls going to do?'

He is turned sideways to the table, and as he speaks, his leg goes back and forth, steady as a metronome. He could hypnotize her with that leg.

'And what about the babies? There are bound to be babies.'

'Thanks for the biology lesson.'

'It's not fair to the girls, or the children,' he goes on.

She takes her eyes from his mesmerizing leg and faces him across the table. Their cups sit between them, hers with a slick of black at the bottom, his with a pale-brown foam. Claude likes his cream.

'The girls know what they're getting into,' she says.

He shakes his head. 'It's irresponsible.'

She is in love with a high-minded man. Or is that merely an excuse? Whatever the reason, the outcome is the same. He is a careful driver. He will not crash their vehicle into that marital pileup on the icy road to war.

And yet. And yet. They cannot leave things as they are.

She makes up her mind the following night, on the front seat of his secondhand Ford, parked way out of town, beyond the pond, on a road no one is likely to risk in the snow. Sometimes Claude can be fearless. That makes two of them, because even as she decides to hell with being a nice girl, to hell with hypocrisy, she knows she is joining a long line of reckless women who have flirted with heartbreak and disgrace since the idea of disgrace was hatched. She knows heartbreak has always been around.

Her decision is not based on altruism, a motive most of the girls, at least those who get caught, will later claim. He was shipping out the next day, they will plead. It is pure selfishness. She wants Claude any way she can have him. She wants this experience with him, not with some other boy down the road after he's gone back to camp, after . . . But, no, she will not think of that.

He has taken off her blouse and then her bra, and she has opened his shirt, and this time when he reaches under her skirt, she does not push away his hand but hikes the fabric up for him. He slides his fingers beneath her girdle and under her panties. She holds her breath for what comes next. A few weeks before Grace's wedding, Mrs Painter

26

gave Grace a book. Grace and Babe and Millie spent nights poring over it, trying to keep their giggles from seeping under the closed bedroom door, but unfortunately it was not very specific.

His fingers creep inside her. She gasps. The stealth entry becomes more confident. The book said nothing about this. Jimmy Doyle never tried this. But then, Jimmy was not as smart as Claude. She buries her face in his shoulder to keep from crying out, though no one is around to hear her.

With his free hand, he reaches for his wallet. He took it out of the buttoned pocket of his army jacket and put it on the dashboard before he even slipped off his glasses. Now he picks it up and begins fumbling with it. His breathing saws the darkness.

'Damn,' he says.

'What?'

He takes his hand away, sits up, and begins going through the wallet with both hands.

'What?' she asks again.

He reaches up and switches on the dim overhead light. It casts a sickly yellow pall over the front seat. She sits up and crosses her hands over her breasts.

'It's gone,' he says.

'What do you mean, it's gone?'

'I mean it was in my wallet, and now it's gone.'

She is shivering. She reaches into the backseat to retrieve her coat.

'It didn't just disappear.' She tries to keep the

edge from her voice. He has been with her every night. He could not have used it with someone else. But things do not just disappear.

He sits turned away from the steering wheel, sifting through the money and license and scraps of paper spread between them on the front seat. Suddenly he stops.

His fist strikes the steering wheel. He leans on the horn. Rage screeches through the darkness. 'I'll kill the little bastard.'

'Who?'

'Marty.'

'Your brother?'

'I wondered what he was doing at my dresser when I came out of the shower.'

He sounds the horn again, a shriek of protest against the injustice of it, then jams the money and papers back in the wallet and sits with his arms crossed on the steering wheel and his head resting on them.

She puts an arm around him and leans close to his ear. 'We could risk it. I think it would be okay. I mean as far as timing.' Grace's book has taught her that much.

He turns to look at her. She has seen him without his glasses before, but he has never looked so naked. The corner of his mouth twitches. A moment goes by.

'I'm too much of a coward.'

Later, she will come to think it is the bravest statement she has ever heard. But that will be later. She digs her bra out from the upholstery and puts it on.

The following night, he is better prepared. So is she. There will be blood. The thought came to her the night before as she lay in bed, her nerves jangling, her skin raw from his touch, her stomach hollow with disappointment. There will be blood on the worn gray upholstery of the front seat. Does he not care, or does he think she is more experienced than she is? What Jimmy Doyle had to tell was damaging but not devastating, but he would not be the first boy to embellish the facts. Claude would not, but Jimmy Doyle had not been Claude, not by a long shot.

Before he comes to pick her up, she takes an old towel and stuffs it in her handbag. It sits at her feet all through the movie, giving off a glow in the darkened theater. She glances around at the audience. Their faces, lit by the reflected light from the screen, hang in the blackness like a galaxy of pale moons. Their mouths open into small holes of laughter. Their eyes, as they follow the action, careen like the steel globes in a pinball machine. They are watching the movie as if nothing is about to happen. Their obliviousness shocks her. How can they be going about their lives as if this is an ordinary night, when she is about to take such a momentous step? Don't they know? Can't they see it on her face and Claude's? Don't the two of them give off some animal sound or scent?

The first thing she does after Claude comes to a stop at the end of the road, but leaves on the engine for the heater, is take the towel from her handbag and spread it on the front seat.

He looks surprised.

'Didn't you think we'd need it?' She tries to keep the edge out of her voice.

'I was pretty sure we'd need it, but that wasn't the precaution I was thinking about.' His grin sparks, then dies, extinguished by nervousness.

In the past, the articles of clothing came off in a slow, tentative ritual. Is this okay? Do I try this? Should I say no? Now they are lightning quick but awkward, unsure whether to undress each other or themselves. He unbuttons her blouse. She pulls out the tie that is tucked into his khaki shirt, military style, and undoes the knot. He unhooks her bra. When he takes off his pants, the metal belt buckle strikes the dashboard like a gong. They stop in guilty surprise as the sound echoes into the darkness. Finally naked, they are almost too shy to look at each other but too enthralled to look away. They pilfer glimpses from under lowered lashes. His dog tags gleam in the dim moonlight.

The front seat is narrow and not very long. They lie with their legs entwined, face-to-face on their sides, so close she can see nothing but those naked eyes, getting closer still. His mouth is tentative at first, but she feels the insistence behind it. His erection is hard against her stomach. She is fascinated, though she has a feeling no nice girl should be. But she cannot help herself. She reaches down to touch it. She sees the surprise in those velvet eyes. She moves her hand. His groan comes from some cave deep within him.

His hand begins to move down her body. She thinks she will howl with the sensation of his fingers inside her, and then she does howl, and the sound tolls through the darkness, religious as a church bell.

After that, it goes exactly as Grace's book says it should. He opens the packet that he checked before he left the house, and she watches him put it on. She has never seen anything so intriguing. She feels no pain when he enters her, and when he roars his pleasure into the snow-muffled night, she hangs on to him to steal a little more for herself.

Afterward, as they lie stunned and stupid with the wonder of it, she thinks how relieved she is, how glad, how strutting proud that she did not waste this wonder on Jimmy Doyle.

She untangles her arms and legs and props herself up on her elbow. The car is freezing, despite the heater he has kept running, and the upholstery is scratchy against her skin, but his body gives off warmth, and she toasts herself against it as she looks down at him. He is lying on his back, staring at the roof of the car.

She leans down to kiss him. That is when she feels it. His face is wet.

Years later, one of Grace's granddaughters, to whom Babe is close, will fall in love with a young man who, as the girl will explain to Babe, is so in touch with his feelings – that's the way she talks; that's the way they all talk by then – that he can cry. Babe could tell her there is nothing new about that. Fifty years earlier, she was in love with a man who cried because they had just made love for the first time and now he was leaving her to go off to war. But she will not tell the girl. It is nobody's damn business.

CHAPTER 2

January 1942

As soon as Babe walks in to Grace's house that night, she smells the fear. It overpowers the aroma of roasting meat, and the women's perfume, and the Christmas tree that lingers like a broken promise, peace on earth, goodwill to men, and ten days of leave. Grace greets them with the announcement that Charlie wanted to take the tree down before he left, but she made him leave it up for tonight. She makes it sound as if they are having a party, not staving off panic.

The fear is not of what will happen to the men – though there is that too, there is always that these days – but that left alone on this last night, two by two, Babe and Claude, Grace and Charlie, Millie and Pete, they will behave badly. That is why Grace, the only one with a house of her own, offers to make the dinner. There will be no scenes if they are all together. She does not add that it will keep her busy, too busy even to glance at the clock.

★　★　★

Grace saw it as soon as she opened her eyes that morning. The two hands of the alarm clock formed a straight line, six o'clock. Twenty-four hours, she thought, all that was left, and resolved not to look at it again.

She manages not to, all day, until Charlie comes up behind her as she is standing at the sink scrubbing potatoes and puts his arms around her waist. He is still wearing his overcoat and smells from the cold and the drink he had with the boys in the newsroom. As he kisses the back of her neck, she bends her head forward. That's when she sees the watch on his wrist. The brown leather band nestles in among the forest of fine black hairs. The gold-rimmed face screams up at her. Four-twenty.

'I didn't expect you this early,' she says. 'I thought they'd want to send you off with a bang.'

He lets go of her, takes a step back, and shrugs. He is working hard to pretend nothing is happening. That makes two of them.

'They tried, but I said I wasn't about to spend my last evening on leave with a bunch of newsroom drunks, not when I have two gorgeous women waiting at home for me. She still napping?'

'She went down late.'

He glances at the brown-butcher-paper-wrapped object on the counter. 'What did you decide to make?'

'A rib roast.'

'Rib roast,' he sighs. 'Who knows when I'll get that again?'

34

Whose fault is that? she wants to scream. 'The management aims to please,' she says sweetly.

'I think I'll put some more salt on the front walk. Just to be safe.'

Safe. Surely he is joking. 'Good idea.'

She stands at the kitchen window, watching him go down the steps and into the snowy yard. The winter sun sits low in the sky, just above the garage, red as the slab of beef she has bought for dinner. As he stands for a moment, staring into the middle distance, the long slanting rays glint off his black hair, iridescent as a crow's. He glances over at the hedges separating their property from the Gordons', then begins to turn his head slowly, like a camera panning a shot, from one end of the yard to the other and back, as if he is memorizing it.

Talk to me, she wants to throw open the window and shout. Tell me. Are you afraid? Are you secretly thrilled, a little boy with a stick playing at being a soldier, a man going off on a great adventure, leaving us behind, breaking my heart? No, that isn't fair. He is not enjoying this either.

She watches him cross the yard and disappear into the garage. A moment later, he comes out dragging a sack of salt and the shovel. It is the Christmas tree all over again. He will not leave her with a tree to take down or an icy sidewalk. He will leave her, but he will do it neatly.

By the time he comes in, she has brought the baby down from her nap, put her in the high chair,

35

and is standing at the counter, mashing carrots. He comes up behind her again, and puts his arms around her again, and she looks down at his wrist again. Five-fifteen. They have wasted fifty-five minutes salting and shoveling the sidewalk, and preparing dinner, and going through the motions of ordinary life. But what should they be doing? Savoring every minute. That's the catchphrase of the day, like some silly jingle on the radio. How can you savor every minute when the only twenty-four hours you have left for God knows how long – forever maybe – are running through you like sand through the egg timer on the kitchen counter?

'You smell good,' she says, though in the past the odor of cold air, the sweat he worked up shoveling because he found some patches that needed more than salt, and the whiskey he had with the men from the newsroom who wanted to send him off with a bang would not have made her ache with premature longing.

'I smell, period. Do I have time for a quick shower?'

'All the time in the world.' Oh, God, why did she say that? 'They're not coming until seven.'

His feet pound up the stairs, then begin moving around overhead. She hears the squeak of the metal top to the hamper followed by the faint whoosh of clothes going down the chute, which is behind the kitchen wall.

'All the amenities,' his father said when he bought

them the house just a few blocks from the solid Tudor where Charlie grew up. They both felt uneasy about the wedding gift. None of their friends had anything half so grand. It was certainly more than a reporter on a local paper could afford. But she and Charlie got used to it pretty quickly, though she is careful to play it down. She does not want Babe or Millie or her other friends to think marrying into the Goodings has gone to her head.

She hears the shower go on upstairs. He starts to sing. She grips the rim of the sink and closes her eyes. He can sing. He is going off and leaving her and the baby, and he can sing his silly Fats Waller imitation.

You're not the only oyster in the stew,
Not the only tea leaf in the tea,
However, I'm convinced, completely, fully, firmly
*   convinced,*
You're the only one for me!

Overhead, feet are moving around the bedroom. How long has she been standing here, hanging on to the sink, while the minutes slip away? She will not do this. She will not ruin his last night home.

She carries the small silver bowl with Amy's initials engraved on the side to the high chair, sits beside it, and begins spooning food into the baby's mouth. It will be better once the others are here. The company of misery.

She wipes Amy's face with the bib and gives her

37

a zwieback to keep her quiet while she sets the table. The good dishes are on the top shelf. She has to go up on her toes to reach them. She carefully takes down six plates, carries them into the dining room, and puts them on the sideboard. Then she goes back into the kitchen to get the silverware. She pulls open the drawer where she keeps the sterling. It goes past the stops, comes all the way out, and hits her shin. Forks, knives, and spoons clatter to the floor.

The baby looks up from the zwieback she has been chewing, her sunflower black eyes startled at the noise.

'Damn it to hell!'

The crumb-crusted mouth opens. The howl comes rolling out.

'I didn't mean you, sweetie.' But she goes on standing where she is, torn between picking up the baby and picking up the silverware, unable to do either.

'What happened?' Charlie appears in the doorway, his khaki trousers ironed to a razor-sharp crease, his khaki shirt immaculate, his jaw smooth. He has shaved.

'Nothing. I pulled the drawer out too far. It's okay. Everything's under control.'

He has already lifted the high-chair tray and is picking up the baby. She clings to him, leaving zwieback handprints on his freshly shaved face and pristine shirt. He bounces her gently.

'Hey, Amy pie,' he croons, and the wails descend by fits and starts to hiccups, then whimpers.

'Women are putty in your hands.' Her voice is beginning to sound the way saccharine tastes.

'I've got Gable quaking in his boots. You want to take her, and I'll pick up that stuff?'

'No, I dropped it. I'll pick it up. You take care of her.'

He turns and starts toward the living room, holding the baby against his chest like a dancing partner, snaking his way through the hall.

There's seven million people in New York,
Fifty million Frenchmen in Paree,
Not to mention such as English, Irish, Italians,
*   and Dutch,*
But you're the only one for me!

She gets down on her hands and knees and begins picking up the silverware. At least she didn't drop plates or glasses. Nothing is broken. Except her life.

Stop it!

She goes on working, reaching up to put the handfuls of silverware on the counter. Finally, she straightens and stands, holding the last batch in her hands. She looks at the pile on the counter. How long will it take to wash and dry each piece? Twenty minutes? Half an hour? Damn it!

When did she start cursing so much? I'll tell you when. When the damn government mobilized the damn National Guard.

'You won't have to worry in the Guard,' King

Gooding said. Her father-in-law is Charles Gooding, Sr., but everyone calls him King. 'We learned our lesson last time. Even that man in the White House isn't crazy enough to get us into another European war. You heard his campaign speeches. He swore he wouldn't send American boys to fight in a foreign war.'

She waited for Charlie to say something. During the campaign, he had heard from one of the reporters covering it, who had heard from someone on the inside, that the catch was, according to Roosevelt, once we were in the war, it would not be a foreign war. Charlie remained silent.

You'd think a man smart enough to run a bank would not succumb to wishful thinking. You'd think Charlie, who hung on every dispatch and broadcast from Europe, would have seen what was coming. But most of the young men in town, the boys Charlie grew up with, were joining the National Guard. If all your friends jumped off a cliff, her mother used to argue, would you follow? The friend her mother had in mind was Babe, a.k.a. the bad influence, the girl from below Sixth Street she never asked to stay to dinner when she invited the other girls, but that was another story. Charlie had followed his friends off the cliff. He said he would not feel right malingering. King agreed. Once you lose the respect of your neighbors, there is no getting it back. You can run away to a big city like Boston, but you cannot mend fences at home. Then the draft went into effect, and Charlie said wasn't it smart of him to have joined the National Guard. When the government mobilized the National Guard, he did not say anything at all. Neither did his father. She, however, had barely been able to keep from screaming at them that had Charlie not joined the National Guard he would not have been drafted. He had Amy and her.

She stands looking down at the counter and thinks to hell with washing the silverware. They can all get sick and die.

She has to stop this. She is a grown woman, a wife, a mother, the first of her friends to be either, the mature one. She has to pull herself together. None of what is happening is his fault. Then whose fault is it? She wasn't the one who went off a cliff because her friends were jumping. Stop it, the voice shrieks as she carries the silverware into the dining room.

When she finishes setting the table, she steps back to survey her handiwork. The crystal and silver and china gleam on the white damask cloth. All her wedding presents, not on display but being used, because they are married and have a home and a child and a shared life. At least for another twelve hours.

She crosses the front hall and stands in the archway to the living room. Charlie is lying on the Turkish rug with the baby on his chest. She's gripping him with her fat legs, and he's talking nonsense to her. Grace stands watching them and wonders, how can I be angry at this man?

Amy looks up and sees her standing there. Her round face opens into a baby-toothed grin. Mommy, Daddy, baby. Bliss.

Charlie tips his head back to follow the baby's gaze. His upside-down smile that looks like a frown turns into an upside-down frown that looks like a smile.

'Sweetheart, don't, please . . .'

Until then she did not know she was crying.

'Gracie, please . . .'

That makes it worse. She never let anyone call her Gracie until him. Now she loves it. If anything happens to him, no one will ever call her Gracie again. The silent tears explode in a sob.

He starts to get up.

She lifts her hand with her palm toward him and begins backing away. 'No. Don't.' Her shoes clatter up the stairs. She reaches the bathroom and closes the door behind her, careful not to slam it. She does not want him to think she is angry.

The image in the mirror shocks her. The silky red hair hangs lank around her face. The blotches on her pale translucent skin make her look as if she is breaking out in hives. Her sharp features have become haglike. He came downstairs fresh as a bandbox, an image she can hold on to. She's sending him off with a picture of an ugly unkempt harridan.

She slips on a headband to hold back her hair and turns on the water. By the time she emerges from the bathroom, scrubbed, combed, and lipsticked, he is coming out of the baby's room.

'She went out like the proverbial light,' he says.

He puts his arm around her shoulders, and she puts hers around his waist, and they start down the stairs in lockstep. Only they aren't, because he is leaving and she is being left. He already has one foot out the door.

For the rest of her life, Babe will be able to run the evening through her mind like one of the movies she and Millie and Grace used to see again and again when they were kids, until the usher found them lingering between shows and threw them out. And even when she is an old woman, her muscles will tense at the memory, like Claude's biceps as she takes his arm to navigate the icy steps to the house.

Grace opens the door to them, her face as fragile as her good bone china, ready to crack at the drop of a word. Charlie stands behind her with a martini pitcher in one hand and a half empty glass in the other.

Millie and Pete arrive a moment later. Millie is all starry blue eyes and flushed pink cheeks, as if this really is a party. Pete helps her out of her coat, shrugs out of his own, slaps Charlie on the back, gives Claude an affectionate punch in the arm, kisses Grace and Babe, feels in his pockets for his cigarettes, pats himself down for a match. He is a rangy, rawboned perpetual-motion machine.

They move into the living room. Charlie pours drinks. Pete tells him not to be so stingy, though the glass is full to the brim. Claude knocks back half of his in one swallow. They pretend to settle in, but Babe can feel the tension vibrating like a tuning fork.

Charlie circles the room, supposedly keeping an eye on empty glasses and full ashtrays but really taking it all in, holding himself outside. Grace's eyes cling to him like a shadow.

Pete springs out of his chair, does a lap around the room, flops back into it, lights another cigarette, stubs it out, grabs a paper cocktail napkin, starts one of his sketches, crumples it.

Babe's voice is brittle in her own ears. Beside her on the sofa, Claude sits, shoulder-to-shoulder, hip-to-hip. She can feel the anticipation beating in him like a pulse. The men do not want to go, but if everyone else is going . . . Oh, hell, let's just get it over with.

Only Millie is calm, the eye at the center of this hurricane of dread and desperation. She perches on the side of Pete's chair, her arm draped around his shoulders when he's in it, her Christmas-red fingertips splayed over his heart as if she is shielding it. Her blatant blond blue-eyed prettiness has deepened to a Madonna's grave beauty. Babe cannot understand her serenity in the face of their panic. Then it comes to her.

When Millie was six, her father took her on his lap and explained that her mother was never coming home from the hospital. Eight months later, her aunt came upstairs, sat on the side of the bed, and told her that her father was not coming back either. A car skidding on ice, a tree, driven by grief. Years later she will hear a slightly different version of the story with the word *drink* substituted for *grief*. They are not mutually exclusive.

Millie went to live with the aunt and her husband. Childless, wanting a child, they were good to her. She likes to say she could not love them more if they were her real parents. Millie always knew how to get what she wanted. Her parents' deaths taught her to want what she could get.

Babe, wanting, wanting, but never sure what, envies her that. But now Babe sees another legacy of the loss. Millie sits smiling into the terrifying future that is barreling down on the rest of them, because she thinks she has immunity. She has paid her dues. God, or fate, or simply the law of averages cannot smite her again.

Babe wants to shake her. She wants to tell her that, around the world, cities are going up in flames, and men and women and children are dying, and God does not have time to worry about Millie Swallow. She wants to shout that fate has no logic and, in war, the law of averages does not obtain.

Somehow they make it through dinner and more drinks without a mishap, though the men clutch their highball glasses so tightly they will surely break and the thin-stemmed crystal trembles in the women's hands. Just as they are getting ready to leave, Charlie's father and mother show up. All the parents will be at the bus depot tomorrow morning, but that dawn goodbye is not enough for King Gooding. He wants a piece of the last night too.

Dorothy Gooding, a small woman whose pinched but once-lovely face always seems to be apologizing for something, steps into the hall hesitantly, as if she knows they are intruding on the young people, but King strides into the house like a man who has paid for it. Just stopped by for a minute, he says, and a minute is all it takes to ratchet up the pressure. Sir, sir, sir, the men, suddenly boys, say. They cannot wait for him to go. Charlie is the most impatient. But King is in no hurry to leave. The minute swells to half an hour. Even as the rest of them are putting on their coats, he lingers. Only Charlie's comment about getting up before dawn persuades his father to leave.

Grace and Charlie stand in their front doorway, his arm around her shoulders, hers around his waist, waving, as they watch the others make their way down the path, their galoshes crunching on the freshly scattered salt, the frost of their good nights hanging in the air like speech balloons above the heads of cartoon characters. Good night, good night, thank you, thank you, see you in the morning, morning, morning. The words echo in the darkness. Mourning, mourning, mourning.

Charlie locks the door, Grace moves around the living room, turning off lights, and they go upstairs. She is sitting on the side of the bed with her back to him, but she feels the mattress shift as he lowers himself onto it.

'Better set the alarm.'

She has managed not to look at the time all night. Now she takes the clock off the night table, moves the alarm hand to five o'clock, and begins winding. She will not need an alarm in the morning. She cannot believe he will either. But if he wants to keep up the pretense, she will match his game.

He reaches out and turns off the lamp on his side of the bed. They lie side by side in the darkness, stiff and bleak as twin sarcophagi, queen and king, wife and husband. *Husband.* She has always loved the sound of the word. At least, she has since she married him. The rustling intimacy of the first syllable, the proud boast of the second. In the early months of marriage, she used it every chance she got. My husband does not like starch in his shirts. My husband takes his coffee black. I'll ask my husband. Now she has a new sentence. My husband has gone to war.

She feels the mattress shift again as he turns on his side. She wills herself to face him, but she cannot move. He reaches out and slides his hand inside her nightgown. Surely now her body will

47

respond. It remains unyielding as stone. He must know something is wrong, but he will not admit it. Her husband can be stubborn. His hand goes on moving, slowly, maddeningly she would say at any other time, but it is not maddening, at least not in that sense.

'Take off your nightgown,' he murmurs.

He has never had to tell her to do that, not even on their wedding night. She worried then that her eagerness was unladylike, but he did not seem to mind. She wriggles out of her nightgown, a good wife following directions, but she still cannot bring herself to turn to him.

He rolls on top of her, and she puts her arms around him dutifully and goes through the motions, but only the motions. Her body is dead, and her mind will not give up the fight, and the worst part of it is, she knows that in a few hours he will be gone, and for weeks and months she will not forgive herself for her stubbornness.

Millie lies in the narrow bed in Pete's old bedroom, spooned around him. When they first came back to his parents' house from their weekend honeymoon, he joked about all the times he lay in this bed, staring at the pennants and trophies and team pictures, thinking of her, imagining the then forbidden and now permitted. Hubba, hubba, he'd whisper as he got into bed beside her, and she'd giggle, and they'd hush each other because his parents were just down the hall.

They tried to be quiet, but the bed creaked and the headboard pounded against the wall, until Pete put a pillow behind it to muffle the sound.

The bed is silent now, though they set up quite a racket a little while ago. He sleeps. She cannot. She does not mind. She will have plenty of time to sleep after he's gone. She closes her eyes against the thought, but the tears seep out. She tightens her grip around him. He goes on sleeping. She wishes she could fall asleep. No, she doesn't. She does not want to waste the minutes she has left with him.

The thought goes through her like a sob. The tears come faster. They run down her cheeks and onto his shoulder. Her body convulses with them. She will not do this. She will not wake him up with her crying. She will not spoil their last night together.

She looks at the clock. It is four-thirty. She gets out of bed and goes down the hall to the bathroom. By the time she comes back, he is awake. And she is bathed and dressed and wearing a big perfectly lipsticked smile. Nobody likes a gloomy Gertie.

'Hiya, beautiful,' he says. His voice is a pitch-perfect imitation of all the normal times he has said it.

It is almost dawn by the time Claude turns on the ignition and they start back to town. It would be different if they were married. They would not have to stay up half the night in a car. But now that the black sky is curling along its edge like a charred scrap of paper, and a thin ribbon of gray lies beneath it, marriage is beside the point. All that matters is that he is leaving. Marriage is no insurance against that.

CHAPTER 3

March 1942

After the men go back to camp, the women close ranks. Babe is working at Diamond's, but on Tuesdays and Sundays, her days off, she and Millie and Grace go window-shopping, or to Swallow's for a soda or hot chocolate, or sit in Grace's kitchen and talk about the war. Not about the fall of the Philippines, or the fighting in North Africa, or even the German U-boats off the East Coast that are sinking ships in view of civilians on shore, but about the exhaustion, boredom, and inanity of army life that fill the letters they get from camp. The men, who in the past rarely wrote more than a mother-forced thank-you note – except for Charlie, who made a living at the impersonal who, what, when, where, why, and how – are suddenly gushing words, even words of love.

The women try to shore one another up. They are not always successful. Grace is short-tempered, even with the baby. Millie is so fiercely bright she sets their teeth on edge. Babe is more cynical than ever, or so the other two say.

51

The weather does not help. It seems to be in cahoots with the times. While the men were home on leave, they lived in a tropical climate. Though the thermometer outside registered below freezing, in the living rooms and kitchens and bedrooms, the air was sultry, the breezes were soft, and a hectic moon burned down on them round the clock. But once the men left, the heavens opened, and the snow, sleet, and freezing rain came down. The women awaken to battleship-gray mornings and turn on the lights at four in the afternoon. Outdoors, the wind stings their faces; indoors, the clanking heat from the radiators turns their skin to parchment. Grace bundles the baby in layer upon layer until she looks like a small fat mummy, tucks her under blankets in the carriage, and pushes her along the snow-narrowed sidewalks, down one side of the street and up the other, because the books say that no matter what the weather, babies need fresh air. Babe listens to the sucking sounds galoshes make on the marble first floor of Diamond's and thinks they sound like sobs. Millie sits in her childhood room – after Pete left, she moved from his parents' house on the west side to her aunt and uncle's smaller place five blocks away – and makes lists on long yellow legal pads. On the left, she writes the reasons in favor; on the right, the arguments against. As the weeks pass and she gets her period, the column on the left grows longer and the one on the right shrinks. She wants a baby, and if that means following Pete to camp, she will follow him, no matter what the government, or her aunt and uncle, or Pete's parents, or even Pete say.

The three women debate the issue endlessly.

'It's unpatriotic,' Grace says as she puts Amy in the high chair and draws it close to the kitchen table.

'She's not exactly hoarding,' Babe points out.

'The government says wives shouldn't follow their husbands to the camps,' Grace insists.

Babe does not answer. If wives should not follow the men to the camps, girlfriends cannot, not if they want to remain nice girls, as she is still supposed to be. Wives use the words *camp follower* as a badge of daring and devotion. Girlfriends steer clear of the expression.

They sit in silence for a moment, until Babe notices the hum of a vacuum cleaner overhead.

'Who's upstairs?'

'Naomi Hart.'

'Naomi Hart works for you?'

'She really works for Charlie's mother, but King thought I could use some help. With this big house and the baby and all. Just a morning or two a week.'

'Doesn't it make you uncomfortable?' Millie asks.

Doesn't it make Naomi uncomfortable, Babe thinks. If she had not got the job at Diamond's, it would have been the five-and-dime, and if the five-and-dime had not come through – until the war started in Europe, no one was hiring – she would have been cleaning other women's houses, if she was lucky. She wonders if that's why Grace cannot meet her eyes.

'I told King I didn't feel right having a girl I'd sat next to in home-room cleaning my house, but he said he was going to send someone and wouldn't I rather have Naomi get the money than some stranger. Heaven knows she needs it. And this way she can bring her little boy with her when her mother can't take him.' Grace scrapes the oatmeal from around Amy's mouth and spoons it in. 'Her husband is stationed somewhere in Mississippi. She says it's rough on colored soldiers—'

'Negro soldiers,' Babe interrupts.

'. . . rough on Negro soldiers down there. She told me some terrible stories, but King says not to believe everything I hear.' Grace turns to Millie. 'Naomi says Frank forbid her to go down there to be with him.'

'Well, Pete's in North Carolina, and I'm not colored. Negro. Not that there's anything wrong with it.'

Sometimes, Babe thinks, Millie's willful sunniness is like a nail going down the blackboard of experience.

'Do you have any idea what you'll be letting yourself in for?' Grace asks. 'The trains and buses are mobbed. Charlie says the town is a hellhole. You'll never find a room. Even if you do, you'll only get to see Pete a couple of hours a night.'

'That's a couple of hours more than I have now,' Millie says. 'It's enough to make a baby.'

'It's too dangerous,' Grace insists.

'Dangerous?' Babe asks.

'The trains are full of soldiers,' Grace explains. 'And you'll be alone.'

'As if all those perfectly nice boys are going to turn into ruffians the minute they leave home. Besides, I'm an army wife.'

'What does that have to do with it?' Babe asks.

'Pete says the men will go up to strange girls on the street and say the most awful things, but if the girls are wives of other servicemen, it's hands off. They know you're another man's property.'

'That's sweet.' Grace's voice softens.

Babe does not think it's sweet, but she doesn't know why. It can't be only that she is not a wife.

'Pete's brother thinks I should go,' Millie says.

'I don't believe it,' Grace answers. 'Mac is too sensible.'

'That proves it's a good idea. He even offered to give me money for the trip, if I needed it.'

Babe shakes her head. 'Just because he said he'd stake you doesn't mean he thinks it's a good idea.'

'Why else would he offer?'

'Because he still has a few months before he finishes medical school. After that, he'll end up in a hospital, maybe here, maybe in England or Hawaii, at worst behind the lines. Meanwhile, his kid brother, and his best friend Charlie, and lots of other boys he grew up with will be fighting the war. Mac's loan is guilt money.'

'I don't care what you call it,' Millie insists. 'He wouldn't offer if he didn't think I should go.'

Four days later, Babe gets the telegram. It is the first cable she has ever received. Maybe that's why later, after Claude ships out, she applies for the job in the Western Union office. Maybe she is trying to hold on to some of the innocence of that wire.

DEAREST BABE STOP I MADE A BIG MISTAKE STOP HAVE WEDDING RING STOP HOW SOON CAN YOU GET HERE TO SLIP INTO IT STOP ALL MY LOVE CLAUDE

She gives notice at Diamond's that afternoon. Then she studies the timetables, though she knows she cannot count on them. Trains are shunted off to sidings to let soldiers and priority materials through. Departures are delayed. Arrival times mean nothing. She wires Claude to tell him when she is leaving, and says she'll cable again when she gets to Virginia or North Carolina.

Later, in one of the rooming houses Babe will pass through that year – perhaps the fourth or the fifth, she never can remember – the landlady, a sour woman who collected injustices the way others did scrap metal, will tell her that army wives are good-for-nothings, and no present-company-excluded either.

'All they want to do is smoke cigarettes and sleep with their husbands.'

'I don't smoke,' Babe says.

But the landlady is not entirely wrong. Those raw recruits and the wives who follow them live an abnormal hothouse existence in the run-down small towns that were never meant for an influx of desperate young men and women carrying mortality around with them like their battered suitcases, tired babies, and threadbare hope. If you're lucky, you get to see your husband for a few hours each night and maybe an overnight on the weekend. When you're unlucky, you bathe as best you can in the communal bathroom, then dress and sit alone in your room, waiting, because at the last minute he pulled KP or guard duty and has no way in heaven to let you know he is not coming. Life on the base is hard and boring, and life in town is unpleasant and boring, but the difficulty and the boredom take different forms. The husbands speak the language of drills, marches, and officers who don't know which end is up; the wives speak the dialect of carping landladies, dirty bathrooms with no hot water to wash their hair, and endless spirit-killing games of bridge. Since there is no common tongue between them, they communicate in sex. It is all the men, who are exhausted from training, brutalized by anonymity, and starving for a woman's touch that will remind them who they are, want after a lousy day on the base. It is all the girls, who are lonely and homesick and longing to be held, can give them, besides doing their laundry.

The trip from Massachusetts to North Carolina takes her seventy-seven hours. If you count the other layover, it takes longer than that. Often, she cannot find a seat on the trains. Passengers perch on suitcases in the aisles and stand in vestibules. Two hours is a short wait for the dining car. The men selling sandwiches and coffee run out halfway through the train. But the boys, and the other girls who are going to see them, make up for the hardship, or maybe they simply endure it together.

Soldiers and sailors give her their seats, and make standing room for her in the vestibule, and offer her drinks. Most of them have bottles stashed somewhere in their duffels or on their persons, and who can blame them? They urge her to have a pick-me-up in the morning, produce nips in the afternoon, and say, come on, have a few drinks, at night. When there are other wives – that is the way she thinks of herself now – in the group, she accepts. They also offer her encouragement. They tell her it's swell of her to go south to be with Claude. They say he'll be in seventh heaven to see her. And when she walks the aisles to the ladies' room or the dining car or just for exercise, they say, some gams, and look at those pins, and hubba hubba. She bought a new suit for the trip, and the narrow short skirt and austere jacket mandated by the war restrictions flatter her. She has left the pink tulle for her sister Brigit. Brigit has narrow slope shoulders and a tiny waist.

Mostly the boys want to talk and to show her pictures of their wives and sweethearts and families. They tell her where they come from; and ask where she's going; and say the army is hell, and the army isn't so bad, and the trouble with the army is. She knows she will never see any of them again, not the boys, not the wives, but sitting side by side in those worn seats, waiting shoulder-to-shoulder in lines for the dining car and the washroom, careening against one another as they try to navigate the crowded aisles, she feels part of something. And all the time she is saving up stories to tell Claude.

The wives want to talk and show her pictures too. When they do, she takes out her photo of Claude. It is not a particularly good likeness, but it is the only one of him in uniform, and though neither of them has said as much, they both know it's the one she has to carry. The garrison cap sits so low on his forehead it gives him a disreputable air, and the army haircut makes his ears stick out. But none of that matters, because he is smiling into the camera, not the wide mindless grin that makes so many of the men look goofy in those military pictures but a thin sardonic slice of smile that takes in the world's, and his own, failings with a self-deprecating wryness.

Most of the wives are novices like her, but a few have been following their husbands for a while and are eager to pass on tips. Travelers Aid is supposed to be the official housing agency for army wives, and sometimes they even manage to find you a room. If you're hoping to get a job, don't admit you're an army wife, because then the employer will know you'll be moving on and won't hire you. When you get to whatever town you're headed for, near whatever camp – and whichever one is mentioned, it's always the most godforsaken in the whole country – beware of taxi drivers.

'If they tell you they know where you can find a room and say, just hop in, run for the hills. White slavery, hon.'

'In North Carolina?' Babe asks.

'North Carolina, South, Florida, Missouri, California. It's all-American.'

But Babe has been taking care of herself all her life. She has no intention of getting into a car with a strange man, even a taxi driver.

Every now and then, the crowding and the shortages and the fear of what is ahead take a toll. In Philadelphia, a soldier and a sailor get into an ugly exchange about which of them is going to carry a girl's suitcase. After they get off the train, everyone blames the girl for leading them on.

At the same stop, a boy carrying a Bible boards the train and takes the empty seat next to her. He tells her about his big Christian family and the revival meeting he went to while he was home on leave and says he hopes she is going to be a good Christian wife. She thinks of the nights in Claude's

60

car but says she will try to be, and he rewards her with a smile as wide as a bath towel.

'That's what we're fighting for,' he says.

While she and one of the wives are waiting in line for the ladies' room, a soldier, who looks as if he is sleeping on his feet, opens his eyes, produces a bottle from one pocket and three small glasses with the railroad crest that he has swiped from the pantry from the other, and insists they have a drink with him. The whiskey is warm from being carried against his body and raw, but Babe is not sorry. If Claude has a bottle going somewhere on a train, she does not want him to drink alone.

In Washington, she checks her bag, as one of the wives has warned her to, so she will not have to worry about it being stolen out from under her while she sleeps. Using a sweater as a pillow and her coat for a blanket, she spends a restless night curled up at the end of one of the wooden benches in the waiting room. At six, she goes into the ladies' room to wash her face, brush her teeth, and repair as much of the damage as she can. The reflection that faces her in the mirror is not encouraging. Her hat is covered with lint. Her hair hangs limp. Her eyes are sunk in smudgy black sockets. The collar and cuffs of her white blouse are sooty, but she will not change now. She wants to save the clean one in her suitcase for Claude. She combs her hair, puts on lipstick, replaces her hat, and makes her way to the baggage check to reclaim her suitcase.

On the way to the platform, she runs into the boy with the Bible. He asks if she needs help. She says she is fine. He insists on taking her bag from her nonetheless. He is only a boy. Where has he picked up a man's habit of not listening to what she says?

Though the sign at the entrance to the platform reads SERVICEMEN WILL BOARD ALL TRAINS BEFORE CIVILIANS, nobody is paying attention to it. She hesitates, but the boy keeps going, and he has her bag. She lengthens her stride to keep up with him.

He makes his way past the first car. From what she can see through the windows, it's not crowded.

'What about that one?' she says.

If he hears her above the din on the platform, he does not stop.

She spots more empty seats in the next car, but he still keeps going. When they reach the last door to the second car, she tries to take her suitcase from him.

'There are seats in there.' She points to the windows.

'That's the nigger car,' he says, and keeps moving down the platform with her suitcase.

'That's what we're fighting for too,' she says, but he is ahead of her again and does not hear.

He finally turns in to the fourth car and heaves her suitcase onto the overhead rack above the first empty seat. She does not want to thank him, but he has carried her suitcase, and he is going off to war, so she does, and dislikes herself for it.

After she settles into her seat with her coat and magazines and handbag and a copy of *The Grapes of Wrath* on her lap, she steals a glance at the passenger beside her. He wears a lieutenant's bars on his collar, and though the train has not even pulled out of the station, his eyes are closed, his head is thrown back against the headrest, and his mouth is creased in a faint smile.

It happens the first time about ten minutes after the train leaves the station. She is reading, but out of the corner of her eye she notices the lieutenant's head begin to nod forward and his body list toward her. He pulls himself up short without opening his eyes and goes on sleeping. The next time, the train is rounding a curve. This time he falls against her before he straightens. The third time, his head drops onto her shoulder. She wriggles gently. He does not move. She shakes her shoulders. He snaps upright, opens his eyes, and looks around.

'Jeez, I'm sorry.'

'No harm done.'

'No, I'm a real knucklehead. You should have slapped me.'

'For nodding off. That would be downright unpatriotic.'

He grins. His teeth, straight and white as a picket fence, scream of fresh vegetables, homogenized milk, and regular checkups. According to the newspapers, a shocking number of draftees turn up for their physicals suffering from rotting teeth, malnourished bodies, and stunted growth, the result of the Depression. But this boy, like Claude and the others who grew up above Sixth Street, has had a sunnier time of it.

He takes a roll of mints from his pocket, offers her one, pops two in his mouth, smooths his hair back from his forehead, and begins to talk. He says his name is Norm and asks hers, tells her he's from Bristol and wants to know where she's from, and when she tells him, he says they're practically neighbors. 'The Bay State and the Ocean State. Kind of like Sears and Roebuck.' He flashes the teeth again.

He extracts a photo from his wallet and hands it to her. Officers and enlisted men, they're all alike. She wonders if Claude drew the photo of her from his wallet and showed it to some girl going to meet her husband.

She takes the picture from the boy called Norm. An older couple stands in the center, with Norm on one side, a boy with the same toothy grin on the other, and two girls, one about thirteen, the other a few years younger, sitting cross-legged on the grass. A respectable red-brick house looms behind them. It's the usual family snapshot. She must have seen a dozen of them in the past two days, though usually the house is smaller and more rickety, if there is a house in the picture at all. But something about this photo strikes her as odd. It takes her a moment to figure out what. His left arm and part of his left shoulder are missing. So is the white border on that side of the photograph.

He must notice her staring at it. 'I cut off the end,' he explains.

'To fit in your wallet?'

'To get rid of my girl. After she got rid of me.'

Perhaps he has not had such a sunny time of it after all.

'I'm sorry.'

He shrugs. '*C'est la guerre*. It means, that's war.'

Even in the new suit, she still looks like a girl who does not understand a French phrase.

'I know what it means,' she says, then regrets the words. He is only trying to set himself apart. Even officers are interchangeable once they put on a uniform.

'You going to see your husband or your boyfriend?' he asks.

'We're going to be married as soon as I get there.'

'He's a lucky guy.'

It's the kind of thing soldiers on trains say, but she wishes he hadn't. She does not like meaningless compliments. She is almost as suspicious of the ones that might be sincere. It's the other side of the who-do-you-think-you-are coin. No one special.

He turns to the window then and is quiet, and after a while he asks if she'll excuse him, and she stands and steps into the aisle to let him out. He unwinds himself from the seat. She had not realized how big he is.

'You might as well take the window seat,' he tells her. 'You'll be doing me a favor. More leg room on the aisle.' He heads down to the end of the car.

A while later, she sees him coming back up the aisle. He is holding a stack of sandwiches against his chest and balancing two cups of coffee in his other hand.

'By the time I got to the head of the line, I figured I might as well get some for you too.'

She thanks him.

He sits, puts the two coffees on the floor, and holds the four sandwiches out to her. 'Take your choice. Ham, ham, ham, or ham.'

'I'll take ham.'

'Good girl. One or two?'

'One.'

'Swell. That leaves more for me.' He flashes the grin again. She wonders why the girl ditched him.

She puts the sandwich down, opens her handbag, and takes out her change purse.

'Forget it,' he says.

'No, I insist.' She opens the purse. A single nickel lies inside. She unzips the inner pocket of her handbag, takes out a billfold, and extracts a dollar. She holds it out to him.

'Sorry. Coffee and sandwich cost two bits, and I don't have change.'

'I can't just take it.'

'Consider it a wedding present.'

'You don't even know me.' Even as she says it, she knows she is making too much of a fuss.

He shakes his head and holds out his hand, palm up. 'Okay, give me the nickel. You can owe me the rest.'

She hands him the nickel. He tosses it in the air as if he is doing heads-or-tails, slaps it down on the back of the other hand, and puts it in his pocket.

'Is your guy meeting you at the station?' he asks.

'I didn't know when I'd be getting in, with all the delays. I said I'd wire him when I change trains.'

'Smart cookie.'

Sometime after they cross from Virginia into North Carolina, he falls asleep again. His head slips to her shoulder. She shifts position. He goes on sleeping. She lifts and drops her shoulder several times. His head remains heavily on it. She shakes him. He sits up and apologizes again. This time she does not say it's nothing. Something about the accident, if it was an accident, bothers her. Or maybe she is just feeling uncomfortable about the coffee and sandwich.

Four hours later, two of which they spend on sidings, a conductor comes through, shouting, 'Raleigh,' and the train begins to slow. Norm stands and takes his duffel and her suitcase down from the rack.

'I can carry it,' she says.

'Wouldn't think of it.' He hefts the duffel onto his shoulder and balances it there with one hand, picks up her suitcase with the other, and steps back for her to go ahead of him down the aisle.

She stands. She does not want him to carry her bag. She should insist. She should yank it out of his hand. If he refuses to give it up, she should ask for help from one of the other men. She can just picture that. He bothering you, ma'am? Yes, he's trying to carry my suitcase. She will not make a scene on a train full of men going off to war. She steps into the aisle. He takes his place behind her. Anyone looking at them would think they are a couple.

The car comes to a halt with a hissing of steam and a grinding of brakes, and he begins nudging her forward with the elbow of the arm that's holding his duffel in place. She makes her way along the aisle and down the steps. He is right behind her. She knows without turning, because he keeps bumping into her.

The platform is packed with servicemen and girls and civilians getting off the train and others waiting to board. He is striding toward the waiting room. There is nothing she can do but try to keep up with him. As soon as she steps inside, she sees the chalk letters on the board. DELAYED.

'Damn,' he says. 'We'll never get there in time now.'

'In time for what?'

'Curfew. No point in wiring your guy. By the time the train gets in, he'll be back at the base.' He puts a hand on her shoulder. 'Tough luck, kid.'

She shrugs it off. Why does he keep touching her?

If he notices her annoyance, he does not let on. 'Look, you stay here with the stuff, and I'll see if I can find out when we're going to get out of here. Maybe it won't be that late after all.'

It takes him a while to make his way through the crowd. When he comes back, he is frowning. 'Earliest it will be is two hours. We'll never get there before midnight. He has to be back on the base by then. But it's okay. I had a brainstorm. It comes under the heading of everything turns out for the best.'

She hates the phrase. From what she has seen, very little in life turns out for the best. Millie's parents' deaths did not turn out for the best. Her father's visits to O'Hanlon's after he gets paid on Saturday rarely turn out for the best. This war will not turn out for the best, no matter what happens.

'My girl's mother runs a boardinghouse.'

'I thought you said your girl left you.' She did not mean to blurt that out. 'I'm sorry.'

'Don't be. I told you, everything works out for the best. The old one ditched me, so I got myself a new one. Right there in Fayetteville. I'll take you to her mother's place. That way you can get some shut-eye and a hot bath and be fresh as a daisy for the big day.'

He grins down at her with those huge piano-key teeth. He is not a taxi driver, he is a soldier, an officer, but she is not going anywhere with him.

She tells him the waiting room is too hot. She will wait on the platform. He grabs her suitcase and goes outside with her. It is not much cooler on the platform. When she left home, it was winter. Here the air is swampy with spring. Under her heavy coat, she feels the perspiration running down her sides like insects. She starts to slip out of the coat. He helps her off with it. Mosquitoes buzz around them. She says she thinks she'll wait inside after all. He picks up her suitcase and follows her.

People mill around. Soldiers grouse. Girls sigh. Babies cry. Perhaps she can find one of the wives she talked to on the train and hang on to her, but he will not let her out of his sight. She sits on her suitcase and leans forward with her arms crossed over her knees and her head resting on them.

He puts a hand on her back. 'You okay, kid?'

She shakes off his hand and sits up. She has got to get away from him, but she is afraid of a scene like the one on the train when the sailor and soldier got into a fight about carrying the girl's suitcase. Everyone blamed the girl.

The waiting room is boiling. Mosquitoes whir in her ears. The floor is littered with candy wrappers, empty cigarette packs, and torn newspapers. The smoke of a couple of hundred cigarettes burns her eyes. Through the blue haze she makes out three doors on the far wall. LADIES. MEN. COLORED. The ploy is drastic, but she has no choice. As soon as the train is announced, she will say she has to go to the ladies' room and hide there until it pulls out. It will mean another night sleeping on a station bench, but she will probably have to do that anyway, given what time the train will get in.

A voice booms through the crowded waiting room and out onto the platform. People begin standing, picking up their luggage, and heading outside.

She gets up and starts to lift her suitcase. He grabs the handle.

'I have to go in there.' She points to the door labeled LADIES.

He frowns down at her. 'I'll hold your bag. It'll be faster.'

She lowers her eyelashes, as she has seen Millie do, in an attempt to suggest an array of feminine mysteries. 'I need it,' she whispers.

'Okay, but step on it. We don't want to miss that train. You got a guy waiting.'

She crosses to the door, pushes it open, and closes it behind her. Then, just to be safe, she goes into one of the stalls and locks it. She knows she is being ridiculous, hiding out in a stall of the ladies' room from some poor boy who is just trying to be helpful. So he showed off his silly French. So he told bad jokes. That does not make him a criminal. But the new girlfriend with the convenient mother makes him suspect.

Through an open window high up in the wall, she hears the train approaching. As she stands leaning against the locked door, it hisses to a halt. The sound of feet shuffling and conductors calling all aboard floats through the window.

'Hey, Babe.' His words are muffled. No window

71

opens onto the waiting room. And why is he calling her Babe, anyway? Shouldn't she be Miss Dion to him? She wishes that when he asked her name, she said Bernadette, but she almost never uses Bernadette anymore.

'Babe! We're going to miss the train.'

She has not thought of this. She assumed he would run to catch the train without her. He really does want to be helpful.

A hand is knocking on the outside door. 'Come on, Babe.'

She feels foolish. He has not done anything except buy her a sandwich and accidentally fall asleep on her shoulder. And now he'll be late getting back to camp. For all she knows, he'll end up in the guardhouse. And it's her fault.

She picks up her suitcase. It is not too late. She starts to lift the rusty hook. She drops her hand to her side. She knows she is silly, but something is holding her back.

A second all aboard comes through the open window. She waits. The train begins wheezing and clanking into motion. The sound builds to a deafening racket, then grows more and more distant until finally the world goes quiet. All she hears is her own breathing in the empty bathroom. Now that he is gone, she is ashamed of herself.

She unlocks the stall, carries her suitcase out, and stands at the sink staring into the streaked mirror above it. Has she been sensible or foolish? She will never know.

'Bitch!' The door bangs open, and the word comes hurtling at her. 'Cunt!' Then he is behind the words. He pulls her around, pushes her against the sink, and begins hitching up her skirt. She starts to scream. His hand over her mouth is slippery with sweat.

'Scream all you want, bitch. There's no one out there.'

She tries to bite his hand. He slaps her with his other one, then goes back to fumbling between her legs.

She does not know how long it lasts. It is over in minutes. It goes on for a lifetime. The sweaty face with its bared teeth gasping into hers. The eyes squinched shut in ferocious ecstasy. The brutal thrusts hammering her against the sink. The words he shouts as he pounds. Cunt, bitch, whore, cunt, bitch, whore. Then, in an earthquake of shuddering, he is finished. He pulls out, buttons his pants, and starts to turn away. Suddenly he twists back and lifts his hand. She shrinks from the blow. He lays his palm against her cheek almost tenderly, then pinches it between thumb and forefinger, the way grown-ups do to children.

'That's what you get for being a tease, Babe.'

He is gone.

She sits on the dirt-streaked floor with the words beating in her head. She tries to silence them. She even puts her hands over her ears. But the filth is inside her. Bitch, cunt, whore. And one more, the mildest but the worst. Tease. She has brought this on herself.

She goes over it again and again. When he apologized for his head slipping onto her shoulder, she should have given him a chilly nod and turned away. The line about it being downright unpatriotic was flirtatious, something Millie would say. But men do not do this to Millie. Men want to protect Millie. In Babe, they sense something else, something easy, loose, dirty.

She puts her hands on the sink and pulls herself up. The sight of her face in the mirror disgusts her. Tease.

She turns away from the sight, hikes up her skirt, takes off her torn panties, and throws them in the trash can. Then she unhooks her garters, peels down her girdle, and begins washing herself. By the time she finishes, the sliver of acrid-smelling yellow soap is gone. She still feels filthy.

A single soiled towel hangs on a hook. She opens her suitcase, takes out a cotton nightgown, and dries herself. She finds a pair of clean panties. Only after she is completely dressed does she dare to look at her face in the mirror again. She had not noticed the smudge of dried blood on her chin. She bit him, and he left his mark. She bends over the sink and begins washing her face, though there is no soap left. When she straightens to the mirror again, the blood is gone.

She finds her hat under the sink, picks up her coat and suitcase and handbag, and goes out into the waiting room. No trains are due until tomorrow, and her heels echo like gunshots through the empty space. No one was there to hear her scream, but then, no one is there to witness her shame.

Tease.

She sits on one of the wooden benches and arranges her coat and handbag beside her and her suitcase at her feet. She crosses her ankles, folds her hands, and waits for morning. She knows what she has to do.

The doctor is short and round, with soft puppy eyes behind rimless glasses, a faintly absurd toothbrush mustache, and three chins. He looks kind. It's small comfort, but she will take any comfort she can get. This is not going to be easy. But she has no choice. She remembers Claude's letters about the training films and lectures. *If you can't say no, take a pro. Put it on before you put it in.*

The doctor closes the door to the inner office behind them, gestures to a chair on one side of the desk, and takes a high-backed swivel one on the other. A framed photograph of a woman and two children stands on the desk, turned out to face her. The woman is as short and round as the doctor. But she is no tease. Babe bets she never made love with the doctor in a car before they were married, or stood naked in front of a mirror, or touched herself under the bedclothes. She looks from the picture to the doctor.

He picks up a pen and pad and asks what the problem is.

Looking at him is no easier than looking at his wife. She lifts her eyes to the framed diplomas on the wall above his head.

'I need some tests.'

'What sort of tests?'

'For venereal disease.'

He cups his hand behind his ear. 'You'll have to speak up.'

'For venereal disease,' she repeats.

His eyes snap up from the pad. The puppy softness is gone. They are hard pebbles in his fat face.

'What makes you think you might be infected?'

'I'm on my way to see my fiancé.' The word is not familiar below Sixth Street, and she is careful to pronounce it in three syllables rather than two, but she has to use it. She does not want him to think she's a tramp. 'We're going to be married.' She stops.

'Yes?'

'On the train, or not on the train, but on the way . . .' She stops again.

This time he does not encourage her with a word. He sits staring at her with those hard little eyes.

'. . . something happened.'

'You had sexual intercourse?'

She stares at the diplomas and nods.

'Did you have sexual intercourse?' The syllables hit her like hammer blows.

76

'Yes.'

Out of the corner of her eye, she sees him shake his head. 'You army wives take the cake. You say you're on the road to see your husbands, but from where I sit, you're just out for a good time. If it was up to me, I'd lock the whole bunch of you up and throw away the key. For endangering your husbands. For endangering every good American boy in uniform. Tramps. Every one of you.'

She is no longer looking at the diplomas. Her head is down, her eyes are on her lap, and she is digging her nails into her palms. She does not try to explain. There is no explanation. She was not out for a good time. But she had been on those nights in the car with Claude. And the officer on the train sensed it.

She hears the swivel chair squeak. She looks up. The doctor is standing. She did not think of this. She steeled herself for the humiliation of asking for the tests but not the possibility that he might refuse to give them to her. She has to have those tests. Without them, she cannot marry Claude. Without them, she cannot even see him. That's what the training films say. If you get one of those diseases, you can never go near a nice girl again. They don't bother to say what happens if a nice girl gets a disease, because nice girls don't.

He crosses the office, opens the door to the examining room, and tells her to go in, take off all her clothes from the waist down, and put on the gown.

The examination is painful. That might be the result of the night before, or perhaps the doctor wants to punish her. That's all right. She deserves to be punished. The more he hurts her, the better she feels.

'There's one more thing,' she says to the ceiling, and tries not to gasp at the pain. 'How can I tell if I'm pregnant?'

He does not answer.

'Is there any way to tell if I'm pregnant?' she repeats.

'I see the intercourse was recent.' The voice comes from between her legs.

She nods.

'Was it recent or not?' he shouts.

'Last night,' she mumbles.

'I can't hear you.'

'Last night.'

'In that case, there's no point in giving you a pregnancy test. All you'd get would be a false negative. When was your last period?'

She calculates. 'A week ago. I was finished on Tuesday, just before I left home.'

He stands and peels off his rubber gloves with a nasty snap.

'Then you're safe in that department. Probably.'

She stays in town for four days. That's how long it takes to get the results of the tests. The hotel is grim. She is too overwrought to read, but she would sell her soul for a radio. She sits in her room, stares at the walls, and thinks that no one in the world knows where she is. She used to dream of escaping from South Downs, but not like this.

She longs to talk to someone. An arm around her shoulders. Words of solace. Not your fault. She would not believe them, but she still wants to hear them. There is no one she can tell. Grace would be horrified. Millie would listen and somehow manage not to hear. Only Claude would understand. He is the one she confides in and explains to and pleads with as she paces the hotel room. But Claude is the one person she can never tell.

Marie Bours was the girl's name. Babe has not thought of her in years. She was a hardworking girl with pasty skin that tended to break out but a sweet smile and pale-blue eyes, and Babe's cousin Louis was crazy about her. They had posted the banns. That's how close the wedding was. Maybe that was what gave the son of the family Marie kept house for the idea. *Droit du seigneur.* One morning when the rest of the family was out, he cornered her in the kitchen. Marie refused to go back to work. Louis naturally wanted to know why. When she told him, he broke the engagement. Slut. Whore. Temptress. Claude is not her cousin Louis, but she cannot take the chance.

She thinks of going to confession, though she cannot remember the last time she went. Stranded in that bare hotel room, she longs for the painted Madonnas with their gilded crowns and forgiving

79

smiles, and the flickering candles, and the sweet sickly smell of sin expiated and innocence redeemed. She remembers a Saturday when she was about eight or nine. She went into the confessional, terrified. She had so much on her conscience. The ice she and Grace and Millie had put in Mrs Dawson's milk bottles. The lies to her father. The way she shook the carriage in the hope that the baby sister she had to mind would tumble out. But she got one of the young fathers with a kind voice, and her penance was just heavy enough to make her feel clean, and when she finished, she ran down the aisle and banged out the front door with – she could not help it – her best Indian war whoop. But this time a clear conscience will not suffice. She needs a clean bill of health.

On the fourth day, she goes back to the doctor's office. The receptionist looks up from her desk. On her first visit, the woman could not have been more friendly. She asked where Babe was from, and where Claude was stationed, and whether she was going for a visit or to live there until he was assigned elsewhere. Now she hands Babe an envelope without a word.

'Doesn't the doctor want to see me?'

'The results of your tests are in there.' She nods at the envelope without looking at Babe.

There is nothing Babe can do but take it. She starts to leave the office, then decides to open it there. She cannot risk misunderstanding the results.

She crosses the room to a chair in a corner, away from the two women who are waiting. As she slides her finger under the flap, she feels the paper slice her skin. A red spot spreads on the back of the envelope.

Holding the finger with the cut away from it, she draws out the sheet of paper and unfolds it. The words wriggle across the page. She cannot understand most of them. But one word, repeated twice, she does know.

NEGATIVE.

NEGATIVE.

She carries the paper back to the receptionist.

'This says negative.'

'Yes.' Her voice is curt.

'That means I don't have . . . anything.'

'I don't know about anything. It means you do not have syphilis and you do not have gonorrhea.'

She feels the other two women's eyes snap up to stare at her. She does not care. She is saved. She goes to the Western Union office and wires Claude that she was delayed several times, but she will arrive tonight.

The train is packed again, but she manages to find a seat next to a girl who is holding a baby on her lap and clearly pregnant with another. The girl is sitting on the aisle, and Babe has to climb over her to get to the empty seat. When she is settled, she turns to face the window, though there is little to see at this hour. Here and there, a light from a farmhouse burns a hole in the darkness. For a short stretch, the beams of twin lights keep company with the train. Then the window goes dark again, and her face stares back at her from the black glass.

The smudges under her eyes are gone. Beneath her freshly brushed hat, her hair hangs clean and carefully curled under. Her lipstick is impeccable. Her face gives away nothing. And neither will she. She will never tell anyone. If she tells no one, it never happened.

After a while, the lights in the window begin to crowd closer together, the beams of the cars grow more numerous, and she feels the train beginning to slow. People are standing, taking their luggage down from the overhead racks, and lining up in the aisle. The soldiers' faces turn flat. Their eyes go out like snuffed flames. The smiles slip from their mouths. They are back. The wives take compacts from their handbags, smooth their hair, and reapply lipstick, though most of them have been powdering their noses and putting on lipstick for the past twenty minutes. Then they put their compacts away and, leaning on the backs of the seats, bend to look out the windows.

Babe snaps her own compact closed, puts it in her pocketbook, and bends. Through the window, she sees crowds of men in uniform, but no sign of Claude.

The train lurches to a stop. She hears the scraping sound of the metal doors being opened. The line begins to inch forward. When they reach the steps, she holds the pregnant girl's baby, while a soldier helps the girl maneuver her suitcases down. The baby's breath is warm and faintly sour against her neck. She hands the baby to his mother, picks up her suitcase, and goes down the steps.

The platform is mobbed but strangely hushed. The girls take a few steps away from the train, then stand on tiptoe, searching the crowd. Here and there, a soldier breaks away from the group of men waiting along the platform, and a name detonates in the night air. Then two bodies go crashing through the crowd like wild animals through underbrush, and the other soldiers and wives avert their eyes to give them privacy.

Babe's name explodes in the darkness, and Claude is coming toward her, not the Claude she said goodbye to last New Year's but Claude all the same. He is lean and taut as an iron rail, and even in the dim light of the station platform, his skin is burnished to a reddish brown. The angles of his cheekbones and the hollows beneath them lengthen his nose. His face is sharp as an ax. She drops her suitcase, and he grabs her, and all around them eyes turn away in decency.

He has managed to get a room. It's only temporary, he warns her, as they make their way through the center of town. He is sure with a little footwork she can find something better.

The rooming house needs a coat of paint. The

entire building seems to list to one side. As they climb to the third floor, the stairs protest under their feet. He opens the door and switches on a light. She blinks against the glare of the uncovered bulb hanging from a wire. One wall has a stain as big and brown as a gorilla. Three rusty hooks jut out from another wall. There is no dresser, closet, or mirror, but the two windows have shades, and there is a straight-backed chair and, in the middle of the room, a bed.

'I'll start looking for another place tomorrow,' she says.

He grins. 'I missed you like nobody's business,' he tells her, then adds that he has only forty minutes before the last bus back to camp.

They get out of their clothes quickly and into the bed. The sheets are damp, and the mattress is lumpy, but they have never been in a bed before. An image of the stinking bathroom flashes in her mind like a cheap neon sign. She opens her eyes. He is watching her. She swims up into his gaze and molds herself against the length of him.

He lets out a sweet velvet moan.

The neon sign blinks once more, then goes out.

CHAPTER 4

July 1942

S he is a fraud. She lies in the hospital bed, with Claude sitting beside her, holding her hand, and Millie tiptoeing in and out in her billowing maternity blouse, and pretends to feel what she does not feel, to feel the opposite of what she feels. Relief. Her relief is so huge it takes up half the hospital room. She is amazed no one else sees it.

The doctor with the hard pebble eyes was wrong. Or was he? She will never know. But the fear dogged her. It hovered over her like the Confederate flag the justice of the peace had hung in the study where he married Claude and her, took up residence in the creaky bed in the new room she found, and kept her awake at night and on edge during the day. As soon as the other doctor, the one here in Rockfish, told her the news, she knew she would never stop looking for markers. She would rejoice in crooked teeth that needed braces. She would monitor the marks on the wall measuring growth, praying the child would not tower over Claude. She would hope for a bookish bent and despair over a major-league arm, though both could come from her. That was the point. She would never know. It was her life sentence.

She and Millie went to the doctor in Rockfish together. After Babe left South Downs, Millie made up her mind to follow Pete to camp. Her trip was difficult too. She stepped off the train talking of long waits on sidings, and endless lines for the dining car, and no seats. 'But everyone was so nice,' she told them. 'The boys couldn't have been sweeter.'

Pete reached an arm around her shoulders and gave her a squeeze. 'How could they resist?'

'Don't be silly. They knew I was married.' She held up her left hand and wiggled her ring finger.

Just as he knew I wasn't, Babe thought, and felt a flash of anger at Millie, at all the good girls who played by the rules.

Three months later, she and Millie went to the doctor. Millie could not wait to find out. Babe had been putting it off. A few days later they got the news.

'Thank heavens,' Millie said. 'It would have been awful if one of us was pregnant and the other wasn't. I would have been so jealous.'

The real surprise was Claude. What about the children? he had demanded when they – no, not they, *he* – had argued the issue endlessly in Swallow's Drugstore. There are bound to be children. But now he was all for children. A piece of himself for posterity. He never said that, but she knew.

He started making plans. Chances were he would not be here for the delivery, but she could go back to South Downs and stay with his parents. They wrote they would love to have her. Funny how imminent mortality and the birth of a baby obliterate the Sixth Street divide. Perhaps she should go north now. He would miss her, but a camp town is no place for an expectant mother. He ticked off the food shortages, the inadequate cooking arrangements, the walk up the steep hill to the club where the wives gathered each day.

The last gave her an idea. She began walking up the hill several times a day. Sometimes she ran. It did no good, nor did the scalding hot baths. She would not try anything more dire. The fathers' and nuns' hold on her was tenuous but not broken.

Millie bloomed. Her Dresden-doll prettiness grew more vivid, her blue eyes brighter, her cheeks more flushed. She started wearing loose smock blouses long before she needed them. Babe looked awful. That was what she told herself as she faced her image in the cracked mirror of the boarding-house bathroom. She was into her fourth month and still throwing up. She knelt over the toilet bowl, spewing food, dry-heaving her rage at the man, at all men except Claude. He was one of them, but he wasn't. Try to make sense of that.

Then all of a sudden it is over. In the middle of the night blood gushes. The pain makes her cry out. Millie, who has the room next to hers, comes running. Another wife clatters down the stairs to the telephone. The landlady stands in the doorway, arms folded across her withered chest, watching her sheets being ruined. To her credit, she waits until Babe comes home from the hospital to demand payment for them.

The doctor puts his black bag on the bed and leans over her. A striped pajama top shows beneath his suit coat. His breath is sour, but his hands are gentle. His voice is too.

These things happen, he says. Nobody's fault. Nature's way. You'll have more babies down the road.

Nonetheless, he puts her in the hospital and keeps her there for a week. During the day, when the men are in camp, Millie sits in the single chair beside the bed, her hands crossed over her belly as if she is trying to hide her good fortune. Other wives come with bunches of wildflowers and plants from the nursery, a word no one will speak in front of Babe, and murmured condolences.

Babe lies on the white hospital sheets, listening to the cries up and down the hall. She is in the maternity ward. The baby from Brooklyn – the infants are identified by the places their mothers left to follow their fathers to camp – is colicky. The baby from Indiana suffers from jaundice. The baby from Louisiana will not nurse. Her own baby made no protest. He, she – Babe does not want to know – went silently.

You cannot kill a baby by will. If you could, her cousin Corinne would not have married at fifteen. But she will never get over the feeling that she has.

The doctor discharges her on a Sunday so Claude can take her back to the boardinghouse. The doctor comes in to sign the papers while Claude is packing her things and goes through the litany again.

These things happen. Nobody's fault. Nature's way.

Claude stops him. 'Nature's way. Are you saying there was something wrong with the baby?' He is not challenging the doctor. He is looking for a lifeline.

Sitting on the side of the high hospital bed, Babe reaches out and takes his hand.

'There'll be other babies,' she says, picking up where the doctor has left off.

Claude turns to her. The miscarriage has knocked him back, like one of the obstacles on the training course. But she has come up swinging. He has never admired her so much.

There will be other babies, they reassure each other. But not before he ships out. Her body needs a rest, the doctor says. They must be careful. And they are.

CHAPTER 5

NOVEMBER 16, 1942

Dearest Babe,

Get ready for a good laugh. Despite all evidence to the contrary for the past eleven months, somewhere in the back of my head I couldn't quite rid myself of the idea that I was going 'abroad.' A military version of Henry James, don't you know. Boy, has the army disabused me of that misconception. I'm on what the ads used to call a luxury liner, but the government has managed to siphon off any vestige of luxury.

Instead of a stateroom, I have a narrow bunk with a bunch of sweaty guys above me and below me, to the right of me and to the left of me, and all up and down the deck. Most of them are probably all right, but not cheek by jowl. Instead of shuffleboard, we practice abandon-ship drills. In place of horse racing on the afterdeck, the men while away their time whittling their names and various profane, oops, I mean profound words into railings, like my students carving up their desks. Are these kids old enough to fight a war?

Forget the caviar and foie gras in the dining saloon. We eat standing up. Only officers get to sit down for meals, and they do it in shifts. As for what we're eating, it's anybody's guess. Sometimes it's gray, sometimes beige, sometimes brown, but always the same taste, or lack thereof.

Seasickness is endemic. (You can imagine how that adds to the charm of the cramped quarters.) Craps games are ubiquitous. My longing for you is unceasing. The ship is speedy, but not fast enough for me. The sooner I get over there, the sooner I can get home to you.

> All my love,
> Claude

DECEMBER 3, 1942

Dearest Babe,

What a country. Incessant rain. Bone-chilling cold. Inedible food. And the most cockamamie monetary system anyone ever dreamed up. But is it beautiful! I never dreamed green came in so many different shades. The entire country is a patchwork quilt of it. And those rolling hills. Remember the images of Tom Buchanan's lawn in *Gatsby*, running and jumping over sundials and brick walls and burning gardens? England is acres and acres of running, jumping green. On the rare day the sun comes out, you can almost forget you've just marched thirty miles and have another twenty ahead of you.

The only thing that can rival the scenery is the intensely present past. The history I've read is alive here. Sometimes when I'm dog tired, and that's most of the time, it seems I could be marching with Henry V and his band of brothers.

After the long drought – in letters, not weather – yesterday I hit the jackpot. Six from you at one mail call. I was, and still am, a happy man.

The job with Western Union sounds interesting, and don't worry about not measuring up. You can do it with both hands tied behind you. Do you realize, sweetheart, you're the only one of your crowd who has a war job? That's what I love about you, one of the things I love about you. You've got the gumption I haven't. I suppose it's the old opposites-attract story. You throw like a boy; I throw like a girl. (If I had your arm, my entire life would have been a different story.) But whatever the attraction is, it gets stronger every day. Believe that, Babe, and hold on to it until I get home to tell you in person.

> All my love,
> Claude

DECEMBER 10, 1942

Hi, Millie Mine, my heart, my soul, my blood, my cheeseburger with fried onions, my chocolate chip cookie the way only you can make them.

I can't believe the big day is almost here. I'd give anything to be there. Unfortunately, Uncle Sam has other plans for me. But my dad promises he'll pace the hospital waiting room in my place, and with my mom and your aunt and uncle, I figure the kid will have a good welcoming committee, even if his dad isn't on hand.

Listen, toots, I hope you don't mind, but I really wish you wouldn't call him, if he's a him, Peter. The poor kid will spend the first couple of decades of his life being known as little Pete. I wouldn't wish that on my worst enemy, let alone my firstborn son and heir. If he's a she, I like all the names you listed, but my favorite is Elizabeth. She can be Liz or Betsy or Libby or Bess or any number of variations on the theme. As long as she looks like her knockout mom, I'm a happy man.

93

I was going to send you a sketch of the old heap of brick we're billeted in, but the rains came and destroyed it. The sketch, not the barracks. I take that back. The rains didn't come. They're always here. No loss though. It wasn't one of my better efforts. Remember that 'Sex Hygiene and VD' brochure the war department so considerately gave me? It said sex wasn't necessary for a healthy mind and body. Maybe not, but it sure does improve the mood and keep the creative juices flowing. I miss you like an old Kentucky colonel misses his rye. I'd put it better, and stronger, but it's none of the censor's damn business.

The craps game a few feet away is heating up, so I better get cracking and relieve those guys of their dough. Did I tell you I won fifty-five bucks last week? The military is deadening to the mind and hell on the body, but not bad for the wallet.

Honestly, toots, I'm thinking of you every minute and waiting for that telegram. Whoever thought I'd be over the moon (that's a limey expression) about having a kid? Consider yourself smooched and hugged and all the other good stuff, no matter how you say you look. This is one pfc who doesn't believe it.

Lots o' love,
Pete

SEPTEMBER 23, 1943

Dearest Babe,

We've just come off a 150-mile march to our new camp. Miraculously, the rain held off for most of it, and now I'm even crazier about 'this sceptred isle, this other Eden.' Someday you and I are going to come back here, not just for some Cook's tour, but for a real stay. (One of the advantages of being a teacher, or being married to one, sweetheart, is two months off every summer.) We'll get a cottage near the sea, and go up to London for culture with a capital C, and make up for entirely too much lost time. That's a promise.

In the meantime, things here are heating up. Yesterday I ran a hundred yards in army boots and uniform in twelve seconds, did thirty-five push-ups and ten chin-ups, crossed an obstacle course on the double, and proved my marksmanship with a variety of firearms. I still can't throw, but I can shoot. The only thing that amazes me more than that is the fact that I'm proud of it. I hate this war, but I'd hate even more to be bad at it. Of course, I have not yet fired a shot in anger, as the expression goes.

We're training seven days a week now with one two-day leave a month. The funny part is, the worse it gets, the harder we all work. Boredom and inactivity are what undermine.

The men are developing what I call foot-soldier swagger. (Swagger is not a trait I thought myself capable of, but I'm as bad as the next man.) It's the only compensation for being in the infantry. We work harder, and have it tougher, and don't we rub everyone else's nose in the fact?

The two-day pass is coming up this weekend. That means next Monday there'll be some powerful hangovers and a rush on the prophylactics stations. I make no promises about the former. Pubs are something else I love about this country. Every time I walk in to one, I feel as if I'm stepping into a Dickens novel. But you don't have to worry about the latter. Brothel-crawling with a bunch of drunken soldiers is not my idea of a good time. War does funny things to a man. Okay, we're not at war yet, only training for it, but you get the idea. Some guys just want a warm body, any warm body, as many warm bodies as possible. I'm not judging them. If that makes them happy, they're lucky, because there's plenty of that around. But the prospect of war has the opposite effect on me. I want the real thing. And that's you, Babe. As the ads say, I will accept no substitutes. So barring your turning up in Piccadilly this weekend, I'll settle for an afternoon wandering those antiquarian bookshops in Cecil Court I wrote you about, a show in the West End, and a couple of pubs. But wouldn't it be something to do that together? And after the war, we will. I promise you that.

All my love,
Claude

P.S. I'm growing a mustache.

JANUARY 24, 1944

Gracie darling,

I will tell you a secret about military life. The best part of the day isn't chow, even at the rare meals where it's edible. It isn't dropping into the sack after a day of endless marching and drilling. It isn't even getting into town for some warm stout at the pub. It's mail call. There isn't a guy in the outfit who doesn't live for getting letters. And I've got every one of those Joes beat by miles. At first they couldn't believe it. Come on, Gooding, they'd say, what are you, some kind of Mormon? Nobody's wife writes that many letters. But my wife does. And what letters they are, darling. Each one brings me closer to you and Amy. I read them over and over. Some of them are falling apart at the folds, but that's okay, because I know them by heart. I can read them in my sleep.

And speaking of sleep, I had the strangest experience the other night. A couple of us went into the village to that little pub I wrote you about. I was beat from a day of practicing something I'm probably not supposed to tell you about, again, and again, and again, and I must have dozed off sitting straight up on that hard wooden bench. When I came to, the first thing I saw was an old Queen Anne wingback chair in the corner in front of the fireplace, just like the one in our living room. Okay, more beat-up than ours, but you get the idea. And I don't know if you can understand this, but for a minute or two, I was back there. I don't mean I was daydreaming. I was really there. I could see the Sunday paper on the floor, smell the coffee perking and bacon and eggs frying, and hear you singing along with the radio in the kitchen. It was all real, as real as the ache when I snapped out of it.

But that experience, darling, is emblematic of something I've learned over here. I used to have big dreams and make big plans. I was going to break some hot story, or get posted to the Washington bureau of some big-city newspaper, or win a Pulitzer. I still think all that would be nice, but now I know none of it is essential. What is essential is coming home to you and Amy and spending the rest of my life with the two of you. I can see that so clearly that, like the business in the pub, it hurts. I see the little things, like walking arm in arm from the garage to the house on a summer evening when you hear the car and come out to meet me, going to the movies on a Saturday night, waking up together on Sunday morning the way we used to before Amy was born and will again. Come to think of it, that last is not little. It's earth-shattering.

I see the big moments too, like bringing another baby into the world, and watching Amy walk down the aisle someday, and growing older and older and finally old with you. So just try to hold on to that, darling. Someday we'll tell our grandchildren about how much we longed for each other, and they won't believe those two old fogies were capable of such love. But we are, my darling, and then some.

Love,
Charlie

MARCH 12, 1944

Dearest Babe,

As they say in those boy-meets-girl movies, you're cute when you're angry. But don't let those black-market boys with their scotch and steaks and nylons get to you. Though judging from the last batch of photos you sent, I don't blame them for trying to get to you. The only good thing that's come out of this war is women wearing pants. Let me rephrase that. The only good thing is you wearing pants. As for the black market operators, I don't suppose there ever was a war without profiteers of one sort or another.

We've been training like crazy for the past few weeks. As a result, foot-soldier swagger has been ratcheted up a couple of decibels. You can sense it in the barracks, see it in the men's faces, and hear it in their language. The last was never what would pass muster at a church supper, but now it's beyond the pale. The men have a word, a single all-purpose word, that both describes and embodies army life. It has four letters, and you know it, but if I wrote it, the censor would only take it out. Nonetheless, most of the men cannot get through a sentence without it. They use it as a noun, a verb, an adjective, an adverb, and just about everything but a conjunction. If a creature came here from another planet and heard them talking, he would assume that was what we're fighting for. And maybe we are. I suppose it's as good a cause as any, though I wish they would find more ways of phrasing it. You can take the man out of the classroom, but you can't take the classroom out of the man.

And while we're on the subject of what we're

fighting for, did I ever thank you for following me to those godforsaken bases all over the country? I know how hard it was on you. The awful rooming houses. The boredom. Those landladies. Remember Mrs Lacey, who said all army wives were good-for-nothings who just wanted to smoke cigarettes and sleep with their husbands? And you told her in your best Katharine Hepburn voice that you didn't smoke. What I'm trying to tell you, sweetheart, is how grateful I am. Those months were hell, but they were also the best time of my life, despite what happened to the baby. I always knew I loved you, but until that time with you, I didn't have an inkling what love was. Now, thanks to you, I do. So whatever happens, sweetheart, just remember for the rest of your life how grateful I am.

All my love,
Claude

APRIL 19, 1944

Dear Gracie,

From everything I read, the invasion is the big topic of interest at home. I know you worry about it, but don't, please. I'm all right, really. And I intend to continue that way. For one thing, I'm not after heroism, and I don't plan on courting disaster. For another, I have a secret weapon, twin-barreled. You and Amy. The two of you are on my mind and in my heart every moment, both waking and sleeping. I carry the picture of the two of you all the time, of course, but I don't need it. I see you everywhere I look. The funny thing is, most of the guys keep showing pictures of their wives and kids around. I did a few times in the beginning, but not anymore. Now I hoard you. I never knew what a miser I was until I started missing you and Amy.

I don't know what to tell you to do about the car. You can take my father's advice or you don't have to. I'm glad he's looking after you, but don't let him steamroll over you.

Something occurred to me the other day during mail call, when I was the envy of all the guys again. Remember how you used to complain that I never wrote you love letters? You can't beef now, darling. Maybe that's the only good thing about this war. I get to tell you the things I never did face-to-face. But I'm a changed man. Expect to hear how much you are loved at least once a day for the rest of your life.

> With more love
> than I ever knew,
> Charlie

Dear Millie o' mine,

Forgive me for starting out on a sour note, but please remind my mother that Peter John Swallow is known as Jack – that was the deal – not little Pete. I'd write her myself, but I'm too steamed. Besides, I'd rather spend the time writing to you.

The pictures of the little guy are swell. I'm glad you took them in front of that big old sugar maple in my folks' yard. I know exactly how it looks as I write this, and it makes me even more homesick. Is bouncing baby boy's hair as blond as it looks? As for his being a good baby, what did you expect from our son? He's going to be sharp as a tack, a four-letter man in sports, and from the way he's gripping that rattle in the picture, a demon with a paintbrush.

Which reminds me. I've been sketching every free minute I get. It keeps me from going nuts, or as far from nuts as anyone can be over here. I've tried doing some of the town and even a couple of landscapes, but what I like doing most are the other guys and the local kids. Their arms and legs are like twigs, and their faces pinched – the war and the shortages have been going on here for a long time – but, boy, do they have moxie. That's what I want to get down on paper.

Wouldn't it be something if I turned out to have just a little talent? One thing I know for sure. When I get home, I'm going back to school to learn how to do this stuff right. Don't worry. I don't have delusions of becoming a great artist. But lots of guys make perfectly good livings as illustrators. I'm sorry if that disappoints my dad, but I've seen more of the world now than he has. I know what I want, and it isn't taking over the pharmacy. Besides, he still has one respectable son. Dr MacKinley Swallow will carry on the family medicinal tradition.

I'll send the two sketch pads I've already filled home to you first chance I get, but one of them will be missing a page. I did a sketch of you in the altogether from memory, and I'll be damned if I let the censor get a gander at that. Just looking at it makes me break out in a sweat. How did I ever get so lucky?

And on that subject, toots, I have to tell you something. You don't have to worry about me. I know I pulled some crazy stunts in my callow youth, but I'm a different man now, thanks to you and Jack. I plan to keep my head down and never volunteer for anything except that ship headed home. But if anything does happen to me, and let's face it, it could happen while I was driving to church, if I went to church – no one knows that better than you, you poor kid – I want

104

you to remember how much I love you. No matter what happens, I will always have had you and Jack, which is more than any guy deserves and more than this particular guy ever thought he'd get. One more thing, honey, in the unlikely event anything does happen, I don't want you sitting around pining. What I'm trying to say, and it feels funny as heck to write, is if anything should happen to me, I want you to marry again. You're too wonderful a wife, you're too swell a girl, to go to waste.

Okay, enough of this gloom 'n' doom. A year from now you'll be nagging me to take out the garbage, I'll be grousing about the bills, and Jack will be shouting Daddy, Daddy, Daddy, every time I walk in the door. And, oh, yes, one more thing, we'll be making love round the clock. We've got a lot of lost time to make up for.

> With more love
> than is probably legal,
> Pete

MAY 18, 1944

Dearest Babe,

It can't be long now. Nobody knows when it's coming or where we're going, but everyone knows the invasion is on. As far as I'm concerned, the sooner we get over there, the sooner I get home. In the meantime, sweetheart, I have to warn you that you may not hear from me for a while. There's talk about mail not getting out of here for some time. But just remember, even if you can't read it in writing, you know it's in my head and heart and soul. I love you, Babe. No matter what happens, I want you to remember that. Thank you so much, my darling, for so much.

All my love,
Claude

JUNE 9, 1944

Dear Claude,

The town has not stopped talking about the invasion. For the first twenty-four hours, everyone was glued to the radio. All the regular programs were canceled, and only news bulletins were broadcast. When the programs came back on, even Bob Hope skipped the gags and turned serious. And all I could think of was whether you were in it.

I dreaded coming in to work the next day, but the good news is that we did not have a single cable from the war department. When I told your father that, he said he guessed you and the others who went over in the local Guard probably weren't in the invasion after all. I can't tell you what a relief that is. I'm also glad you warned me that mail might not be getting out for a while, or I'd be worried sick, because I haven't heard from you in ten days. Grace had two letters from Charlie postmarked after the invasion, but I guess some mail getting through and some not is what you call a SNAFU.

Who am I kidding? I'm still worried sick. I wish I could believe your father, but from everything you wrote about training, I can't help thinking you were in it. I'm so scared I even tried going to church the other day, but it didn't help. I haven't been much good at that sort of thing since I was seven years old and had visions of becoming a nun. Okay, stop laughing. But I couldn't pray. No, that's not true. I prayed you. I don't mean I prayed for you or to you (blasphemy). I just got down on my knees, and bowed my head, and thought about how much I love you. Maybe that's not as good as the prayers I grew up with, but at least it's honest.

Please take care of yourself, darling. There's a failed nun counting the days until you come home.

> All my love,
> Babe

Dear Pete,

I haven't had a letter from you since the one dated May 2, but I refuse to worry. I just keep reading the old ones over and over and waiting for the next. The way I figure it, all I can do is try to be one-one-hundredth as brave as you are and get on with things until I hear from you again.

Now for the good news. Are you ready? Yesterday, Master Peter John Swallow drew a circle. I wrote you that he's been scribbling for a couple of months now – he's a chip off the old block, all right – but yesterday he was on the floor doing what we call sketching, which I've told him is what Daddy does, and he drew a circle. I didn't tell him to. I didn't show him. He just did it! Move over, Picasso. Here comes Swallow, Jr.

I hope this cheers you up, darling, and that you're not too wet and muddy and miserable wherever you are. In case you don't remember from my last letter, I love you more than is legal in the state of Massachusetts or anywhere else on this planet.

> Love and hugs and
> kisses from Jack and
> his mommy

JUNE 24, 1944

My darling Charlie,

I haven't heard from you for almost two weeks, and the letters I did get were postmarked after the invasion but written before. I'm trying not to worry, but I can't tell you how hard it is. I'm not asking for a love letter. Just to see your handwriting on an envelope would be enough. More than enough. It would be heaven.

I try not to show how terrified I am around Amy, but our daughter takes after her daddy. She's a smart cookie. What's wrong, Mommy? she keeps asking. What's wrong? Of course, I don't tell her.

Oh, darling, if only I had a word from you. I keep thinking this is some kind of divine retribution for that one night I didn't write last month. I know that's crazy, but being away from you makes me crazy.

I'll stop now, darling, because I'm ashamed of myself for all this whining, especially when I think of what you're going through. The next letter will be more cheerful, I promise.

All my love,
Your Gracie

CHAPTER 6

July 17, 1944

At first Grace does not see Sam Shaker sitting in his truck at the side of the road. The sun is in her eyes, and she is standing waist high in the water, supporting Amy, who is splashing to beat the band. For the space of a heartbeat she has pushed the aching worry from the front of her consciousness. Then she looks past Claude Huggins's mother, who is sitting at the edge of the water, knitting, and sees Mr Shaker push open the door, unfold his long body, and step down from the truck. She wonders what he's doing at the pond in the middle of the afternoon. Shouldn't he be minding the store?

'Kick, Amy, kick,' she shouts. The spray cascades over them, and she feels the water-lightened weight of her daughter's body on her outspread hands. Beyond Mrs Huggins, Sam Shaker starts toward the pond. He is wearing heavy shoes that remind her of combat boots. Combat boots. The fear obscures her view again, but she goes on holding Amy afloat, while Mr Shaker keeps coming, moving from the hard yellow light into the green shadows and back again.

Mrs Huggins looks up from her knitting. The other matrons stop talking. What is the proprietor of the hardware store doing at the pond in the middle of the afternoon? He hasn't come for a swim. He's dressed in a suit coat and straw hat.

He stops beside Millie. She is sitting on a blanket with her legs crossed and Jack caught in their embrace. As she lifts her face to Mr Shaker, her straw hat falls off. She shades her eyes with her hand, though she is wearing sunglasses. Mr Shaker takes off his own hat. His mouth moves. Grace strains for the words, but though the afternoon is still enough to hear a hummingbird's wings, Amy is sending up a racket.

Mr Shaker holds out his hand to help Millie up. She puts Jack on the blanket, takes Mr Shaker's hand, and pulls herself to a standing position, then reaches down and tugs the leg of her bathing suit into place. Grace will always remember that instinctive gesture of modesty.

Mr Shaker's hand moves to the pocket of his wrinkled seersucker jacket. He feels around for something and draws it out. The sun glints off the cellophane insert of the Western Union envelope. Grace takes one hand from under Amy to shade her eyes. She cannot be seeing what she thinks she is seeing.

Mrs Swallow's hand flutters to her chest.

Mr Shaker holds the envelope out to Millie. She

rubs her hand on the side of her thigh as if to clean it but does not reach for the telegram. She goes on staring at it in his hand.

Mrs Swallow tries to stand, but she cannot struggle up from the low canvas chair.

Grace lifts her daughter out of the water and holds her against her chest.

Mr Shaker moves the envelope an inch closer to Millie.

Don't take it, Grace wants to shout.

Millie's thumb and forefinger close on it.

Grace stands holding Amy to her, transfixed by the pale yellow envelope.

Millie turns it over and runs her finger under the flap. She takes out the piece of paper.

Grace is struck by how small it is, a few inches long, a few more wide. How can something that small upend the world?

Millie stands staring down at the telegram. Jack lets go of his pail, winds his arms around his mother's leg, and pulls himself to a standing position. Unsteady as a pint-size drunk, he lifts his arms to his mother.

Millie slides the piece of paper back into the envelope, and bends. She is still clutching it when her arms go around the boy. She lifts him and folds his body to hers. His small head, under the sun-whitened hair, settles into the safe haven between her neck and shoulder.

Grace starts out of the water to her, then stops when she sees Millie has already turned away.

She is heading toward the stand of willows. Her mouth is moving, but Grace cannot make out the words. They are a secret between Millie and her son.

Grace goes on standing in the water, holding Amy to her, waiting for Mr Shaker to head back to his truck. It is not his fault, but she wants him away from here. And she wants Pete back. A moment ago he existed. Now, in the ripping open of an envelope, he is gone.

Mr Shaker turns toward the pond. He is moving with the slow-motion ponderousness of someone in a dream. Grace shifts Amy to her hip. At the edge of the pond, Mrs Huggins puts down her knitting. Beside her, Grace's mother-in-law tries to set her glass of lemonade on the ground and spills it.

Mr Shaker is still coming toward them, his long morose face going on and off like a lightbulb as he moves from the shade of the trees into the open and back again.

He is abreast of the women sitting in a line. The telegrams will not be handed to them. They gave birth to the boys. They raised them to be men. But the men belong to other women now. The mothers will get the news secondhand. Unless there are two for Mrs Swallow. But that cannot be. Not two sons in one day. Even in wartime, life cannot be that cruel.

He takes a step past the women.

Go back, Grace wants to shout. Go away from here. He takes a second step, then a third. When he reaches the edge of the water, he stops.

Grace sees his hand move to his pocket. It disappears into the fabric. She does not wait for him to draw it out. She turns and begins to swim.

She is clutching Amy with one arm and thrashing the water with the other. Her legs churn. Water surges up her nose and down her throat. The sunlight splintering off the surface of the pond blinds her. Amy begins to cry. Grace beats the water with her hand and kicks it with her feet. Her daughter's nails dig into her shoulder. The cries turn to howls. She keeps going. She will outswim him.

She is almost at the other side of the pond. Her knee sinks into mud. She tries to stand, stumbles, tries again, falls again. She crawls toward the shore, dragging Amy through the mud, feeling it oozing into her bathing suit. She catches a branch with her free hand and pulls herself up. She is standing. She has made it to the other side of the pond.

She pushes the hair back from her eyes and looks up the incline of the bank. Mr Shaker is standing above, holding the Western Union envelope out to her.

A few weeks later, the letters begin coming back. Grace gets thirty-eight; Millie, thirty-two. The word stamped on each envelope is so bold and black it might have been put there with a branding iron.

DECEASED.

After that, Babe never again thinks about playing God and withholding telegrams. And she never writes another letter to Claude without wondering whether she is already too late.

BOOK II

1945

CHAPTER 7

BABE

June 1945

The boys are coming home. The town simmers with the news. In the big Tudor and Victorian and colonial houses behind the money-green lawns on the west side of town, in the respectable frame houses perched on handkerchief squares of grass on the east, and in the run-down flats south of Sixth Street, wives and girlfriends and mothers and fathers sit over cocktails in living rooms before dinner, around kitchen tables after supper, on porches and stoops any time of day, and study the points system – so many points for months or years in service, so many for combat duty, so many for having a wife and child – trying to calculate when their particular boy will return.

They get letters from Camp Lucky Strike and Camp Philip Morris, staging areas in France; cables from England; and long-distance calls from Fort Dix in New Jersey. I'll be there as soon as I can wrangle a berth on a ship, hitch a ride on a plane, get on that bus or train.

Babe sits in the Western Union office and cuts and pastes the cables from the boys. They're a relief next to the wires that continue to arrive from the war department. The fighting is still going on in the Pacific. Those islands with strange names thousands of miles away are not so distant when local boys storm them. Pete's brother, Mac, is a battalion doctor. When Babe goes next door to the pharmacy for her Cokes, Mr Swallow reads her parts of fiercely cheerful letters about performing surgery in a cave and endless attempts to outsmart the pesky local fauna, which is even more challenging. Mac says not to worry about malaria, because he takes his Atabrine religiously. Mr Swallow nods approvingly as he reads the words. He knows about Atabrine. The knowledge makes him feel connected, almost useful.

Rumor says some of the local boys who survived the war in Europe will be sent to invade the Japanese homeland. Rumor also says it will be a slaughter. Later Babe will read that the government made half a million Purple Heart medals for the invasion. But she does not have to worry about Claude. He has four years of service, eleven months of combat, and a wife. He is a sure thing. Only a child could make him a safer bet. She has heard stories of men who fought in Europe and turned around and signed up for the Pacific, but Claude will not do that. He has changed, she knows that from his letters, but he is not crazy.

The changes are subtle. She has to read between

120

the lines for them. He no longer makes plans for the future. He lives in the present. He writes about having his fingers freeze in winter, and crawling through mud in spring, and being parched in summer; about dirt-encrusted, lice-infested uniforms, and lousy K rations, and the sheer pleasure of a shave, even with cold water in a helmet with a piece of tin for a mirror. After D-Day, he wrote about Pete never making it to shore and Charlie being blown up by a German shell. He also wrote to Millie and Grace saying they both died instantly. Neither suffered. But as he moved on through France and into Germany, he never mentioned casualties again. Only after several weeks did she notice that his buddy Herb, and Joe Ritter – as opposed to the other Joe, Dumbrowsky – and the new kid from Cleveland, who was recently attached to their outfit, disappeared from his letters. She would not call him secretive, but he has become more closed.

Then, after all the anticipation, the boys suddenly begin showing up. Some call or wire to say they're on the way; others simply walk in the front door or the back. Why didn't you warn me? the girls cry as they run to them. I just managed to grab a transport, train, bus, and didn't have time, the men answer as they catch them. All over town, men and women, stunned by their good luck, embrace and cling together for dear life, then take a step back and stand staring at each other like the strangers they are.

Babe keeps herself ready. Her hair is always clean and neatly curled under. Each morning she dresses for work as if he might walk in the door at any moment. When she wears skirts rather than the slacks he wrote he liked, the crayon seams down the backs of her legs are straight.

She hovers over the teletypewriter. Before, she hung over it with dread. Now she hears Fred Astaire tapping again. One of the Wohl boys, the older brother of the one who died, is on his way home; and Grace's brother; and two of Babe's cousins; and Millie's uncle, not the one who raised her but a younger one, though not so young that he could not have kept out of it if he had wanted. But no cable comes from Claude saying he is on the way. She does, however, get a telegram.

She is about to go next door to get a Coke to go with her sandwich when the teletype machine begins spewing tape. She leans over to look at the check. It is from the Western Union business office. The second line reads MRS CLAUDE HUGGINS.

YOUR SERVICES NO LONGER REQUIRED AS OF
LAST DAY OF JULY STOP

Millie comes into the office while Babe is reading the tape, a bandbox of a girl in a straw hat with a striped ribbon and short white gloves. She has taken a job in the cosmetics department at

Diamond's and often brings her lunch to the Western Union office so they can eat together.

'I can't say I didn't know it was coming,' Babe says.

Millie puts the brown paper bag down on the counter. 'Didn't know what was coming?'

Babe hands her the tape.

Millie glances down at it, then back up at Babe. 'Perfect timing. Claude will be home any day now. You'll be pregnant before the summer is over.' Her smile is wide, bogus, and tragic as a clown's. Babe has to stifle the impulse to say she's sorry.

After they finish their sandwiches, Millie re-applies her lipstick, pulls on her white cotton gloves, and stands, but when she reaches the door, she turns back.

'Babe?'

She looks up from the pile of forms she is straightening and waits.

'Have you ever heard the word *shiksa*?'

Babe remembers a family she worked for on Saturday afternoons when she was a kid. 'It rings a bell.'

'Do you know what it means?'

'I think it's what Jewish people call a Christian girl. Why?'

Millie shrugs. 'I was just wondering.'

After Millie leaves, Babe picks up the scissors. She could throw the ticker tape away. She has got the message. But her sense of responsibility – to the company, to the people who send telegrams

123

and those who receive them, to her own pride of job – is too ingrained. Besides, she wants to keep the cable, as a reminder of the way things were.

Babe goes up the back steps and opens the door to Grace's kitchen. Naomi is standing at the sink, her dark arms disappearing into the white suds. At least she is not wearing a uniform. At Grace's in-laws' house, she wears a uniform. Now she is dressed in a flower-print housedress and flat shoes. She is tall, even taller than Babe, and rail thin. Her hair is wiry as a Brillo pad, but her cheekbones are high and sharp, and her skin is smooth and dark as a ripe eggplant. Once Claude said she was beautiful, but everyone laughed at him, and he never said it again.

Amy is sitting at the table, her elbows resting on the Formica surface, her chin on her hand, staring at a glass of milk as if it is the enemy. Babe is struck again by how old she seems. She has always been one of those strangely grown-up children, not the precocious cloying kind who make arch statements of the out-of-the-mouths-of-babes variety but the little girls – it seems to Babe they are mostly girls – who wear the fully formed faces of grown-ups and do not so much mimic adult gestures as are born with them. In the past year, she has become a miniature matron.

Babe kisses the top of her head. Amy does not shake her off, but she does not look up either.

'What's cooking?'

'Nothing.'

'Nothing! How can you say nothing with Naomi's super-duper brownies sitting in front of you? They're cooking, or they just were, right?'

Amy looks up, finally. Her long almond eyes narrow, but her smile is indulgent, as if Babe is the child who must be humored.

'What's the word from Frank?' Babe asks Naomi. 'Any news about when he's coming home?'

Naomi shakes her head. Her hair trembles like a dark halo.

'He must have plenty of points.'

Naomi shrugs. Her last letter from Frank said the points system, like everything else in the world, meant one thing for whites and something else for coloreds. He has seventy points, and he is still getting shuffled around from unit to unit, but he knows white soldiers with sixty points, even fifty-five, who are on their way home. She is not going to try to explain that to a white woman. And she is not going to complain. As long as they don't send him to the Pacific, she's happy. He did not see action in Europe, but they need fighting men in the Pacific. They need them so badly they will even let Negroes fight. She is not sure that is something to cheer about.

It's all very well for Mr A. Philip Randolph, and Mr Walter White, and all the rest of those fine gentlemen to go around kicking up a ruckus to get more colored boys into combat. According to them, having colored boys fighting and dying will show white folks that Negroes are the same as them and deserve the same treatment after the war is over. She isn't so sure it will, but that's not what bothers her. Mr A. Philip Randolph, and Mr Walter White, and the rest of those fine gentlemen are not the ones who will have to fight, and they are not the ones who will come home without an arm or leg or face you can look at or not come home at all. She is glad the government will not let colored boys fight. She doesn't care that they say Negroes are not smart enough or brave enough or reliable enough. They can call Frank dumb or cowardly or shiftless or any name they want, as long as they keep him safe. Sometimes she wonders if Frank feels the same way, but she never asks. She knows her husband. All she has to do is let on that she is relieved, and he'll start moving heaven and earth to get into a combat unit headed for the war in the Pacific.

'Where's Grace?' Babe asks.

'Mrs Gooding's not home yet. She went out to have some more pictures framed.'

'More pictures?'

Naomi shrugs and keeps her eyes on the dishes. Babe is the only one of them she still calls Babe. Babe insists on it. But Babe is one of them, and Naomi knows better than to talk about one of them to another. Even about this picture business. Grace – she's Grace in Naomi's head, even if she's Mrs Gooding to her face – says she's doing it for the baby. That's another thing. That child is not a baby. But it's none of her business. She does not have to go looking for trouble. It knows where to find her.

'She's having some old pictures of Mr Gooding framed.' Her voice gives away nothing.

July 1945

Claude comes out of South Station onto Atlantic Avenue and stands with his back to the wall – he is accustomed to keeping his back to walls – getting his bearings. He recognizes the buildings. The façades stand just as they did when he left. The Ballantine Ale and Beer billboard still tells him they're brewed for flavor. The red and green traffic lights blink off and on. No jagged concrete or broken bricks litter the landscape. No torn rooms expose their intimacies to passersby, kitchen pots and easy chairs and teddy bears. No dead bodies with twisted limbs, staring eyes, and oozing intestines lie in the gutter. The light changes to green and the traffic starts moving again. Are gas rationing and tire shortages myths circulated at the front? People hurry past him on their way to the dentist and the office and shopping. Men in business suits stride with purpose. Boys in caps loiter, studying the passing girls in their summer hats and thin cotton dresses. When a particularly pretty one with painted toenails winking from her open-toed shoes goes by, she sets off a cacophony of whistles. The innocence of it all stuns him. Worse than that, it frightens him.

He remembers the pamphlets they passed out at Camp Lucky Strike in France. 'Coming Home.' 'Since You Went Away.' 'Readjustment Tips.' He had laughed. The tips were for the kids and the flyboys. Once, on leave in London, he saw a kid flyboy in a pub. He could not have been older than some of the seniors Claude had taught, but this one was wearing the uniform of an air force lieutenant. He was with a girl, and not the pickup kind either. At least not the kind this raw kid with his brash slang and mangled syntax could have picked up before the war. Her accent sounded as if she were delivering Noël Coward lines from a West End stage; her tweed skirt and twin sweaters were made for a brisk walk in the country; her single strand of pearls encased her creamy neck like a chastity belt. But damned if the boy didn't have his hand up that tweed skirt. Now, there was a kid who was going to have a hard time re-adjusting. But not Claude Huggins. All he needs is to get out of uniform and home to Babe, and readjustment will take care of itself, no matter how much home has changed since he went away.

Only it hasn't. It is going on, safe, carefree, oblivious to bombed-out cities, ten-year-old girls offering their bodies for a tin of K rations, and dead buddies – oh, dear God, don't let me think of Herb's brains spilling. . . . He shuts his eyes, clenches his fists, and waits for the image to pass.

He opens his eyes. The buildings, the traffic, and the Ballantine sign are still there. He cannot believe it. They are as alien and unreal to him now as those other sights were to him when he first landed in France. A sudden longing for that world runs through his body like a spasm. He misses it. He is shocked, but he cannot help himself. He misses the clarity, the purpose, the men he trusts with his life.

He shoulders his duffel. He had planned to go straight to the hotel and check in, but now the thought of that muffled lobby of thick carpets, soft upholstery, and smug strangers makes his bowels churn, just as they did when he first went under fire.

He turns around, goes back into the station, and checks his duffel. When he comes out again, he sets off down Summer Street. He does not remember a bar, but he will find one.

During the past few years, he has walked into dozens of pubs and cafés and beer gardens in dozens of towns and villages, and his father has never followed him into any of them, but now that he's home, he can hear the rasping Yankee voice in his ear. Dutch courage. He glances at his watch. Four-twenty. Babe wired that if the bus is on time, she will get to the hotel by six-thirty. You're damn right it's Dutch courage. He'll take any kind of courage he can get.

He stands in the doorway, trying to adjust his eyes to the gloom after the glare of the July afternoon. At least it's cooler inside. Two men sit at one end of the bar. He walks to the other end and slides onto a stool. The girl behind the bar looks up from filing her nails, studies him for a moment, then takes her time getting off the stool and making her way down to where he's sitting. He orders a scotch, straight.

'No ice?'

Another nicety he has forgotten.

'Sure, ice, why not?'

She brings the drink and puts it down on the bar in front of him. He reaches for it with his right hand, resting his left on the bar. Her eyes go to his left hand. He has forgotten. Where he has come from, no one ever looked at the two middle stumps. They were not avoiding it. They didn't see it, any more than they saw the filth on their skin, or the blood on their uniforms, or the lice in their hair. They had seen too much else.

She turns away, embarrassed, and makes her way to the other end of the bar. He puts his left hand in his pocket.

He really did forget about it, just as he kept forgetting to write Babe about it. He isn't hiding it. You can't hide something like that. But every time he remembered to tell her, the letter was already in the envelope, and the envelope was sealed, and he didn't see the point of tearing it open and addressing another one.

The girl has gone back to filing her nails, but she must be watching him out of the corner of her eye, because when he takes the last swallow of his drink, she shuffles down the bar again and asks if he wants another. He says he does.

He has one more after that. By the time he slides off the stool and puts his right hand in his pocket for his money, he is feeling fine. Babe is not the kind of girl to go weak in the knees over a couple of missing fingers. He takes a wad of bills from his pocket with his right hand, peels off a dollar, and drops it on the bar.

Outside, the sun has disappeared behind the buildings, and the street lies in a blue haze. He starts back toward the station. He'll pick up his duffel and get to the hotel in plenty of time for a shower and a shave.

At the baggage check, he hands over his ticket. The boy takes it, disappears into the back, and returns with his duffel. Claude reaches for it with both hands. The boy glances at the finger stumps, then away. You can't blame the kid. But Claude does.

He comes out of the station into the deepening dusk. The air feels sticky against his skin. His shirt sticks to his back. He wonders if he smells. He has got so used to stinking he can no longer tell. He shoulders his duffel again and starts for the taxi stand.

It happens as he reaches the head of the line. A taxi pulls up. He leans over to open the door. He is using his right hand, so it has nothing to do with the missing fingers. He straightens and steps back to let the woman behind him take the cab.

The fear engulfs Babe like the summer heat. It muffles her senses. The faces of the other people on the bus blur. The driver's voice comes from a distance. As she makes her way down the aisle, she feels as if she is swimming. She has been waiting for this day for too long. She cannot believe it's here.

I took a room for Mr and Mrs Claude Huggins at the Copley Plaza, he wrote. *I have two years' pay burning a hole in my pocket, and we deserve a honeymoon.*

The wind coming in the open window of the bus is hot on her face. Or does the heat come from within? She is not even sure she remembers what he looks like.

She takes the small leather case with the photograph he sent her from France out of her handbag and stares at it. No wonder she cannot remember what he looks like. This is not the Claude she saw off, and not only because of the mustache. His face is leaner, his jaw more prominent. His cheeks look as if they have been hollowed out, though that might be the angle of the light. Even his stance is different. His feet are planted far apart, and he has one hand in his pocket. She wishes she could see his eyes. She is sure she would recognize him if she could see that myopic velvet gaze. But he is wearing dark glasses. She puts the photograph back in her bag.

She tries to recall his voice. She can remember the words he spoke as they walked the strange streets of Southern camp towns and hid from the world and the war in the darkness of seedy boardinghouse bedrooms, but she cannot hear him speaking them. You can write your heart out in letters. You can send photographs. But there is no V-mail for transmitting a voice. For two and a half years the silence pained her. Now it terrifies her.

She does not know what to expect. She does not know what he expects. She thinks of a joke making the rounds. What's the first thing you're going to do when you get home? the reporter asks the soldier. Throw my wife down on the bed and make love to her. What's the second thing? Take off these damn boots. The joke is a sign of their fear. The joke is a long low wolf whistle in the dark.

Someday you'll laugh at this, people always say, but Babe knows she will never live long enough to laugh at this night. By ten o'clock, alone in the hotel room that is as unreal as a movie set, as unreal as everything else about this day, she knows something has happened. If he missed a connection, he would call or wire. But something has kept him from letting her know. An army plane has crashed. A speeding car has careened out of control. He has made it through the war to be done in by civilian life.

She stands at the open window, watching the traffic. There isn't much at this hour. A taxi pulls up in front of the hotel. The doorman crosses the sidewalk and opens the door. A man in a uniform emerges. She leans out to get a better look. The doorman reaches back into the taxi. A girl in a white suit, wearing a corsage that screams wedding so loud Babe can hear it eight floors up, emerges from the taxi. The telephone rings.

She runs for it, her heart thumping like the tire on Grace's car when she got the blowout and kept driving for a block. She picks up the receiver and says hello.

Silence comes down the wire.

'Claude?'

More silence, then finally a voice, tentative but unmistakable.

'Babe.'

She grips the receiver.

'Where are you?'

He does not answer.

'Are you all right?'

'Yeah . . . sure.'

He does not sound all right.

'Where are you?' she asks again.

'Here.'

'Where's here?' She tries to keep the impatience out of her voice.

'Boston.'

'Where in Boston?'

He does not answer. She waits. The silence drags on.

'Claude, please, tell me where you are.'

'In a phone booth.'

'I know that. A phone booth where?'

Another silence.

'Claude,' she begs, 'where are you?'

'In a recruiting office.'

'What?' She has not shouted. She is sure of it.

'I'm in a recruiting office.'

Her hand is wound around the receiver so tightly that her nails, freshly manicured for this day, dig into her palm.

'You didn't. Tell me you didn't.'

'I didn't do anything.' An undercurrent of a sob runs beneath his voice. 'I can't seem to do anything. I'm just sitting here.'

She beats back the panic she feels rising. 'Claude,' she says quietly, 'listen to me. Hang up the telephone and get out of there. Now,' she adds softly. 'Please.'

'I can't.'

'Do you want me to come get you? Tell me where the office is.'

'I can't.' His voice cracks.

'Then you come here. I'm at the Copley Plaza Hotel. You reserved a room, remember? I'm waiting here.'

He says nothing.

'Claude.'

She hears his breathing. At least he has not hung up.

'Get out of there, please. Get out of there and come here.'

She waits through another silence.

'Everything is going to be all right. I promise. As soon as you get here, it will be all right.'

She hears the click at the other end of the line, sits listening to the silence, then hangs up the receiver and begins pulling out the drawers of the night table. The phone book is in the bottom one. Is it under *U* for U.S. Army Recruiting Office or *A* for Army Recruiting? Her fingers fly through the pages, but her mind races ahead. She cannot go looking for him. What if he listens to her and comes to the hotel? He'll think she has abandoned him. She cannot even use the telephone in case he tries to call back. And what if he doesn't call back or show up? How will she pay for the room? An insane thought at the moment, but Claude is not the only one who has gone crazy tonight. She thinks of a quick call to the police. What's the problem, ma'am? My husband is reenlisting. She can do nothing but wait. She has been waiting for thirty-two months. Another twenty minutes or half hour or hour will not make a difference. Only she does not think she can stand it.

She hears the elevator open down the hall, goes to the door, and leans out. An elderly couple in evening dress make their way toward her. She closes the door, goes back to the open window, and sits on the ledge. Below, a handful of people go about their business. A man walks a Scottish terrier. A couple, the woman's arm through the man's, turns in to the hotel. A driver leans against his taxi. She remembers – crazy to remember it now – that night in the movie before she and Claude made love for the first time. She could not understand how all those people were behaving as if the world was spinning as usual when her life was stopped.

A man in uniform comes striding up Huntington Avenue. She braces herself against the window frame and leans out an inch more. His head is down, and she cannot see his face, but she knows the walk is not Claude's.

The knock on the door startles her. She has been busy concentrating on the scene below. She is across the room in a second. It has to be Claude. It cannot be a bellboy with a telegram.

She pulls open the door. A stranger stands in the hall. She recognizes the features, but she does not know the man. Behind wire-rimmed glasses, his eyes are hard as walnut shells. His mouth is a thin zipper in his face. His cheeks are hollow.

She wants to hurl herself at him. She stands rooted to the thick carpet of what was supposed to be their honeymoon suite.

'Sweetheart,' she manages. The sibilant word hisses in the quiet.

He goes on standing there, staring at her with those dead eyes.

She reaches for his arm. As she starts to pull him toward her, his hand comes out of his pocket. She sees the two stubs where his middle fingers used to be and knows this is a test. If she stares, she is in trouble. If she looks away, she is doomed.

She takes his hand in hers and holds it against her cheek.

Claude's hand. Two missing fingers. Not much to lose, not these days. But that maimed hand cups their first hours together as if the time is water. How easily she could spill it and lose everything.

She clings to that poor damaged hand, and it clings to her. In the dim lights from the night-table lamps – they do not turn them off; they have to see each other to make sure they are real – she watches the hand, browned by the sun, against her skin, and feels it on her body, and by morning, she is sure they are going to be all right.

August 1945

Babe puts the book on the night table, turns out the light, and lies in the dark, waiting. She wants him to reach for her – she no longer reaches for him; it is too dangerous – but she is afraid of what it will be like if he does. It is not only that they make love less often. During the months when she followed him from camp to camp, they could not get enough of each other, but marriage was new then, and the war was a looming fear rather

138

than a poisonous memory. It is the way they make love. He is not inconsiderate. He is careful to pleasure her. But once he has, he is gone. Eyes closed, face averted, he is alone, and angry. Her flesh knows that, even if her mind tries to deny it. Her body feels the fury in his thrusts. Sometimes she watches him – she refuses to close her eyes – and sees the brutality in his face and is back in the railroad-station bathroom. Sometimes when that happens, she cries silently. He does not notice. He is in his own world. She could be anyone. And she knows now there were anyones.

She found the evidence by accident, or perhaps her discovery was not unintended on his part. He is a deliberate man. Perhaps he left it there as a confession, or a taunt.

The proof was tucked among the army-issue shirts and trousers and underwear. It was army issue too. She got up and closed the door to their room. They were still living with his parents and looking for an apartment of their own, no easy quest given the housing shortage triggered by all those war-minted husbands and wives and babies who needed a place to live. Millie seemed to have rented the last vacant space in South Downs. It was not much, one room above the Millers' garage on the east side of town, with a kitchen and a sleeping alcove, but it is the story of Millie getting a job that no vet can fill all over again. No one would call Millie lucky, but she does have a knack for survival.

Babe locked the door – she did not want her mother-in-law walking in and finding her with this – and sat cross-legged on the floor among the contents of the duffel. She picked up the brown paper package.

PRO KIT CONTENTS
1. Tube containing 5 grams ointment
2. Directions sheet
3. Soap-impregnated cloth
4. Cleansing tissue

COMFORT MANUFACTURING COMPANY
CHICAGO, ILLINOIS, U.S.A.

The kit meant nothing. He had not even opened it. But he had opened the other box. There was a list of contents on the outside of that too.

Three prophylactics

She opened the lid. One foil packet lay inside. She could not say she had not been prepared. *Your man has been through a difficult time,* the magazines warned. *Do not ask if he has been faithful,* the pamphlets cautioned. Her favorite was an article by a psychiatrist. *Often the man who loves his wife most dearly is the most likely to stray. He is the man most responsive to a woman's love, most in need of a woman's support.* When it came to absolution, the church had nothing on that psychiatrist.

She sat on the floor, trying to figure out what she felt. He had not exactly lied in his letters. *The prospect of war has the opposite effect on me. I want the real thing. And that's you, Babe. As the ads say, I will accept no substitutes.* For all she knew, he meant it at the time. But that was before he watched them die, one after another, Charlie, Pete, his buddy Herb, others she never met, more she never heard of. She cannot begrudge him a moment of escape from that any more than she can resent the water he drank when he was thirsty, or the rations he ate when he was hungry, or the sleep he snatched when he was exhausted. It was sex and death all over again.

There is another reason she does not blame him. She remembers her own loneliness. Maybe she was just lucky that the strange men who came into the Western Union office tended to be on-the-make traveling salesmen and slick black-market Johnnies dangling nylons and good times.

She does not begrudge him those moments of respite during the war, but she does resent being nothing more than that to him now. Open your eyes, she wants to scream. Look at me. I'm your wife, not some girl you picked up for a moment's release. She does not scream, at least not at him. The battle she wages goes on in her head, a place where no one wins.

That morning she was about to put the packets

back in the duffel to be stored in his parents' attic with the other things they would never need. Then her mind skidded ahead. Mommy, Mommy, what's this? the small boy playing soldier in his father's uniform asks. She wrapped the packages in an old issue of *Newsweek* that was on the night table, carried them down to the kitchen, and put them in the trash, way at the bottom, under the coffee grounds and eggshells.

August 14, 1945

One of the soda jerks has turned up the volume on the radio behind the counter at Swallow's, and the announcement comes rolling out the open door and stops Babe on the pavement.

'President Truman has announced that the Japanese have accepted our terms unconditionally. Ladies and gentlemen, this is the end of the Second World War.'

People are spilling out of buildings, shouting, cheering, waving flags. On the street, drivers lean on their horns or honk them to a staccato beat. The kids at the counter abandon their sodas, sundaes, and malteds to form a conga line that comes snaking out the door. One of the older boys tries to grab Babe, but she steps out of the way. Men are throwing their hats in the air. It is a common expression, but Babe has never seen anyone do it, except in newsreels of Annapolis graduations. People are embracing. Not just the

142

kids in the conga line, but couples and friends and people who barely know one another. Mr Creighton, the undertaker, grabs Miss Hammond, the librarian, and plants a kiss on her mouth. For the rest of her life, Babe will not be able to look at the famous picture of a sailor kissing a nurse in Times Square without remembering Mr Creighton in his somber black suit and hat and Miss Hammond in her dowdy print dress, locked in an embrace. The librarian even has one lisle-stocking-and-oxford-clad foot raised in girlish exuberance. Then the fire department sirens begin going off, and church bells are tolling. The boy who plays the tuba in the high school band is marching down the street beside the stopped cars, playing 'God Bless America' to the same martial beat as Kate Smith, America's patriotic songbird, sings it.

Mr Swallow comes out of the drugstore and stands beside Babe, his starched white pharma-cist's coat glowing in the slanting rays of the setting sun, his scalp rosy inside his tonsure of white hair.

'Mac will be coming home,' she says.

'Mac will be coming home,' he agrees. Then he takes off his glasses and rubs his eyes with his thumb and forefinger. Everyone, even Mrs Swallow, thinks Mac, the diligent son, the dutiful son, the doctor, is his favorite, and he is in a way, but even when Mr Swallow had to spank Pete as a little boy, or discipline him as a teenager, or have a serious talk when he was in college, he had been in secret thrall to his younger son's spirit. Perhaps Babe Huggins guesses his secret, because she puts her hand on his arm for a moment. His daughter-in-law Millie, for all her sweetness, never does that.

Babe takes her hand from Mr Swallow's arm – it rested there of its own sudden will – and moves off down Broad Street, through the soft August evening that trembles with the vibrations of half a dozen church bells. She has to get home. She has to get home to Claude. She starts to run and remembers the last time she hurried down Broad Street, careful not to run then, because she did not want to start a panic. There is no fear of that now.

As she turns the corner onto Elm, she notices King Gooding's big gray Cadillac parked halfway down the block. She cannot imagine what it is doing there. He always parks directly in front of the bank, not around the corner from it.

Someone is sitting behind the wheel. As she gets closer, she recognizes the wide shoulders beneath the tan linen suit jacket and the big head under the straw hat. She stops. She does not want to see him. She will have to speak. At this moment in time, you cannot pass someone you know, you cannot pass even a stranger, without speaking. But she is too angry at King Gooding to speak to him.

A week earlier, she and Claude were walking down the street, and Claude was in a good mood, because they had finally found an apartment. They were laughing and kidding around, and she ducked her head at something he said, and when she looked up, she saw King Gooding coming toward them. He saw them at the same moment. Without missing a beat, he crossed the street and continued down the sidewalk on the other side. He has known Claude since he was a boy. Claude and Charlie grew up together. And now he crosses the street to avoid having to say hello to Claude, having to look at Claude, because Claude is alive and Charlie is dead. She feels sorry for Mr Gooding. But it isn't Claude's fault. Except Claude saw King cross the street and remembered that it was.

The sirens are still screaming, and the horns honking, and the bells pealing, and as she stands watching King Gooding, he crosses his arms over the steering wheel and puts his head on his hands. His big shoulders heave.

Babe closes the apartment door behind her. The streets are pandemonium. Across the way, someone has brought a Victrola out on the porch, and people are jitterbugging up and down the block. A small boy marches along the sidewalk, banging two pot tops together. A dog yelps after him deliriously. As she stands just inside the door to the apartment, she hears the noise outside but feels the hush in the dusk-gray room.

She does not switch on a light, though she does not yet know her way around the furniture-stuffed apartment by instinct. They moved in only last week.

'Claude,' she says quietly.

The hush deepens.

He had a meeting at school. Classes start the day after Labor Day. But he should be home by now. She tries to remember if she passed the car parked in front of the house. She was too busy waving back at her neighbors.

'Claude.'

She switches on the light. The worn sofa with the shiny arms, the standing lamp with the fringed shade, and the small table they use for meals spring out of the gloom. No one else is there.

She goes to the window and looks out at the street. His car, their car, is parked in front.

'Claude,' she calls again.

She hears a rustling sound in the bedroom and starts toward it. The door is open a crack. She pushes it wide and steps into the room.

It faces the tree-shaded back of the house and is darker than the living room. She turns on the light. A movement catches her eye. She looks down at the carpet. One combat boot is sticking out from under the bed. Some mornings he forgets and puts on his boots. Usually, she notices and reminds him to change to his brogues or loafers, but she was preoccupied this morning. She got her period, damn it.

She gets down on her hands and knees and peers

under the bed. He is lying on his stomach with his arms crossed over his head.

'Claude.'

He does not answer. He does not even take his arms from over his head.

She lies flat on her stomach. The carpet smells faintly of dog. The bristles scratch through her thin summer blouse. She shimmies a little way under the bed until she can reach him and puts her hand on his back. He shakes it off. She puts it there again, gently, as gently as she knows how.

'Claude, sweetheart, it's all right.'

He does not move.

'It's not gunfire. It's a celebration. The war is over.'

CHAPTER 8

GRACE

June 1945

'Help,' Grace says as she stands outside the screen door of her kitchen, her hands full of packages.

Babe pushes open the door and takes two of them from her. Naomi takes the rest.

'You've been on a spree,' Babe says.

'Just getting some more pictures framed.'

Grace crosses the kitchen to where Amy is sitting with her milk and brownies and leans down to kiss her. 'Wait till you see what I got. More pictures for our wall. You can help me after you finish your milk.'

At first she was afraid to let Amy near the wall. She does not want the photographs damaged. But the wall is for Amy as much as for her. She wants her daughter to remember her father. As they put up each photograph, Grace tells Amy stories about Charlie. Amy probably knows more about her dead father than most children do about their living parents.

'Did Amy show you our wall?' she asks Babe.

'What wall?'

'Come on.' She leads Babe through the dining room, front hall, and living room, out to the sunporch, and stands for a moment facing the windows. She likes to sneak up on the wall, to surprise herself with it. She turns to face it and shivers, though the room faces west and is warm at this time of day, even with the windows open. But that's the effect it has on her.

Framed photographs cover the top two-thirds of the wall. The last row, about three feet from the floor, stops halfway across. She is working from top to bottom, left to right. The pictures are in chronological order. At the top left, an infant Charlie peers out from a baby carriage. In the last frame she has hung so far, he is wearing a cap and gown and holding a diploma. At first she could not decide whether he was graduating from high school or college, but she showed it to his mother, and they agreed it was from college.

'I was thinking I'd frame some of his newspaper pieces too, but I'll probably have to do that somewhere else in the house. I don't have space in here. The windows take up too much room.'

'The windows don't take up too much room. It's a sunporch,' Babe says, because she does not know what else to say.

Grace does not hear her. She is too busy staring at the pictures.

'I think I'm going to have to move them one

place over though. These are all of Charlie alone, but some of the ones I just brought home are of Charlie and me and Charlie and Amy. That's what made me realize I hadn't put up any pictures of Charlie with his parents. I don't want them to be hurt when they come over to see it.'

Babe has stopped looking at the wall. She is staring at Grace, whose eyes are fastened on the photographs. 'Grace,' she says gently.

Grace's head whips from the wall to her. 'What?'

'Nothing.'

August 1945

Grace is in the yard with Babe, struggling to untangle the hose, when she feels the emotion welling up, as overpowering as nausea. She drops the hose, pounds up the back steps, and reaches the powder room under the stairs just in time. The sobs explode from her like vomit from Amy when she has a sick stomach, but there is no one to hold Grace's head to keep her body from thrusting forward. She stands hunched over the sink, her shoulders heaving, her misery spewing out like a foul-smelling bodily fluid.

She has stopped trying to make sense of her misery. At the memorial service, she did not shed a tear. She pressed her back against the pew until it hurt, and dug her nails into her thighs, and managed to restrain herself. But the sight of the snarled hose blindsided her.

If you just wind it up, it won't get tangled. She can still hear the exasperation in Charlie's voice.

But you do it so much better, she teased him.

She stands over the sink, holding on to the sides while she rocks back and forth, waiting for the sobs to subside. She knows by now she cannot force them back. When they finally die, she takes off her dark glasses and runs water over them to get rid of the tear stains, then washes her face, dries it and the glasses, puts them back on, and goes out to the yard.

Babe has managed to untangle the hose and drag it across the yard. She is sitting in one of the low canvas chairs, holding the nozzle so the water arcs over the lawn. Amy and Jack, whom Babe has taken for the day because Millie is still working at Diamond's, dance through the spray, squealing with delight. The water winks and glistens on their brown bodies, and the soles of their feet glint pale and, it seems to Grace, terrifyingly vulnerable in the afternoon sun.

She sits in the other canvas chair, then raises her bottom to tug down her shorts. With her free hand, Babe is taking the cubes from her glass of iced tea and holding them to her forehead and neck. The afternoon festers around them like a piece of rotting fruit. It would be cooler at the pond, but Grace cannot bring herself to go to the pond, and Babe does not insist. Grace has to give her credit for that.

She thinks of going in and getting more tea and

some cookies, but she does not move. She has seen the way Babe sometimes looks at her when she's eating. Let her look. Babe has someone to watch her figure for. Babe doesn't know what emptiness is. But she, Grace, knows the breadth and depth and yawning horror of it. After the telegram came, she could not bear the sight of food. Her stomach lurched, her throat closed, and when Millie or Babe or one of the others urged her to eat something, her insides howled in protest. But after a few months, the hollowness set in. Now she eats and eats and eats and still cannot fill it. She has put on twelve pounds, and all her clothes are too tight, and she doesn't give a damn. She stands, goes into the house, comes back carrying a tray with a pitcher of iced tea and a plate of cookies, and puts it on the grass. Then she says the words that have been on her mind for days now.

'Someone has to speak to Millie.'

'About what?' Babe asks.

Isn't that Babe all over? She knows perfectly well about what.

'That Al Baum.'

'*That* Al Baum? You mean the one with horns?'

'I didn't mean it that way. You can't say I haven't been perfectly nice to him every time I've seen him. But Millie can't marry a Jew. She never would have dreamed of it before the war.'

At least Babe has the sense not to argue with that.

'Besides, she's only known him a few months.'

Babe lifts the hose and makes figure eights in the air. The children chase the spray, trying to grab it with their hands. 'During the war, lots of people got married faster than that.'

'And all you have to do is look around you to see how well some of those marriages are working out. But it's not just how long she's known him; it's how long Pete's been gone. How can she even think of getting married again so soon?'

'It's more than a year,' Babe says, and Grace wants to shout at her: You think a year is any time at all? You think a year is long enough to stop reaching out in half sleep and finding that the sheets beside you are cold and empty? You think a year can make you feel whole? Instead, she says, 'Just because she put away Pete's things doesn't mean she's over him. Mac agrees with me. And he had a psychiatry course in medical school.'

'How do you know what Mac thinks?'

'He wrote to me after he heard about Charlie, and we've corresponded a little since. I told him about Millie – after all, he's Pete's brother – and he agrees with me. It's too soon. That's why you have to talk to her.'

'How did we get from someone has to talk to her to *I* have to talk to her?'

'Because she'll think I have an ax to grind.'

The sound of a car honking up the driveway almost drowns out Grace's words. The children forget the spray and run shrieking across the yard.

153

Uncle Claude, Uncle Claude, Uncle Claude, they scream.

He scoops them up, one in each arm. Grace notices the way his left hand cups Jack's small bathing-suit-clad bottom and thinks, two fingers, only two fingers, such a puny loss.

Jack clings to Claude for a moment, then wriggles down, but Amy winds her skinny arms around his neck and hangs on for dear life.

Grace squints at the sight, and in her narrowed vision, Claude becomes Charlie. The sun bounces off his hair, iridescent as a crow's, and his face breaks into a grin, and she sees herself rising from the chair, crossing the yard, and walking into his arms. The three of them stand there, she and Charlie and Amy, holding one another under the rainbow of water from the hose, which later she will wind up and carefully put away.

Someone has to talk to Grace. King knows that as soon as he hears the rumors about Millie Swallow. Poor Pete is barely in his grave, and his widow is running around with somebody new. A Yid no less. King saw them coming out of a movie one night, holding hands. It made him sick to his stomach. Grace is a sensible girl, no Millie Swallow, but he is not taking any chances.

The first thing Grace sees as she comes down the back steps is the hose. She did not put it away after Babe left yesterday. It coils across the yard, menacing as a snake. She takes Amy's hand and gives it a wide berth on her way to the garage.

In the car, Amy sits at the other end of the front seat, her small face set in a long-suffering mask, her thin body squirmingly hot in her pink dress with the smocked top and puffed sleeves. Grace should have put her in a pinafore, but King and Dorothy take Sunday dinner seriously.

'Don't lean against the door.' She does not mean to snap. She is not looking forward to this any more than Amy is. But pleasure is beside the point. They are Charlie's parents. Charlie is alive in that house as much as he is in theirs. In a way, he is more alive. She is so inured to the photographs of Charlie in her house that sometimes she cannot see them. The thought shocks her. But the pictures in King and Dorothy's house are less familiar. Charlie ambushes her from end tables, and hutches, and the big portrait in the entrance hall. King commissioned it when Charlie was six. It is the one possession of her mother-in-law's she covets. Dorothy has told her more than once that she will get the pearls, the diamond clip, and her other jewelry, the silver and the linens and the crystal, all of it in safekeeping for Amy, but what she cannot wait for is the portrait of a six-year-old Charlie, sitting with one leg tucked under him, his level – even then – brown eyes staring out at the world.

They stand under the portrait now. It hangs over them, golden as the sun, hallowed as a cross. He is with them. Grace can feel his presence. Then Amy darts away to find Naomi in the kitchen, King says he wants to talk to her, and Charlie slips away. He is always doing that to her.

She has never seen King uneasy, but he is uneasy now in his den with the heavy leather sofa and the massive desk and the dark Turkish carpet. She knows because he starts to sit behind the desk, then thinks better of it, takes the other end of the sofa, and turns halfway to face her. He asks her if she minds if he smokes. King never asks anyone if he can smoke. When she says she doesn't – though she does – he picks up a cigar, then puts it down again without lighting it. They are both ill at ease.

'I hear Millie Swallow is getting married.'

He does not have to say another word. She understands.

'You don't have to worry about me. I have no intention of remarrying. Ever.' The photograph on King's desk swims into focus. Charlie is standing on a dock, grinning into the sunlight, holding a big fish. 'Not after Charlie.'

He opens his mouth to say, you're a young woman, of course you will. 'You may change your mind' comes out.

'I won't.'

She starts to stand. He clears his throat. There is more. She cannot imagine what. He is not interested in Amy, though he thinks he is. He never talks to her about finances. He sends her checks and pays her bills, but he never discusses those matters. Her mother-in-law says he is the same with her.

'Let's assume,' he says, 'just for argument's sake. Let's assume that some man comes along – after a respectable period of time, of course, not like Millie Swallow – and wants to court you.'

'I have no interest in being courted.'

'For argument's sake,' he repeats, then hesitates. 'Forgive me if this is embarrassing . . . Grace . . . dear. But you've led a sheltered life, thank heavens. You went from your parents to Charlie.'

He stops again. Charlie. Sometimes he thinks he will choke on it. Charlie. Sometimes he rolls it around in his mouth and can barely keep from shuddering with the ecstasy of the sound. Charlie. Charlie. Charlie. He gulps down the word and goes on.

'You don't know about men. But I do. I'm not saying they're all bad or all after one thing. But you have to be careful.'

As he reaches up to rub his chin, his shirt cuff pulls back. She sees the fine dark hairs on his wrist, and her stomach curls over on itself. She is looking at Charlie's wrist.

'The men you meet won't be boys. They'll be grown, experienced, war veterans probably.' He stops again. War veterans. They're all over the place, with their cocky smiles, and long loping strides, and greedy hunger to make up for lost time. They're noisy and brash and arrogant, and not one of them can hold a candle to Charlie. Why have they come home when he has not? He closes his eyes and sees Charlie. He opens them. He has to get on with this.

'I don't want to be indelicate, but once a man has known, well, carnal passion, he will have difficulty controlling himself.'

She looks past him to the photograph of Charlie with the big fish. She does not understand what King is trying to tell her. Charlie knew what King calls carnal passion before her, he told her that, and he never had any trouble controlling himself until they were married. But Charlie was not like other men. Still, it gives her a shudder of pleasure to think she knows something about Charlie his father doesn't. She owns more of Charlie than King or Dorothy do.

'And when it comes to experience, they may make assumptions about you. After all, you're a widow.'

Charlie's widow, he thinks, and the rage rises in him again at the thought that she goes on living without Charlie.

'What I'm trying to tell you is that any decent man, any man who truly cares for you, will not try to take liberties. He will treat you with respect.'

She thinks of Millie and Al. He cannot keep his hands off her. The two of them make her uncomfortable. The other evening she could not wait for them to leave. Then she ended up dreaming about them.

'So I want you to be careful . . . dear. You and Amy are all we have of Charlie.'

This girl is not Charlie. Not even Amy is Charlie.

He pushes himself up from the leather sofa. 'And now I won't mention the subject again.'

He never does, but later, after he has his heart attack, she will blame him and this talk for the way things turn out.

August 14, 1945

Grace goes through the house, closing the windows against the noise. When she turns, she sees Amy watching her, her long almond eyes widened with fear.

'I'm afraid it's going to rain,' she says. 'A thunderstorm.'

Amy looks from her mother to the window. A ray of sun beats against the glass. 'It's hot.'

'I'll turn on a fan.'

'I want to go out. I want to go out and play.'

'Not now,' Grace says.

Horns blow, and church bells toll, and fire sirens slice the early evening air. She closes another window. The sounds still rattle the house.

'I want to go out,' Amy says, and begins to cry.

Grace sits in the big Queen Anne chair that was Charlie's chair, pulls her daughter onto her lap, and holds her.

Years later, that will be Amy's memory of V-J Day. When a boy she never should have got mixed

159

up with tells her about setting off firecrackers on the day the war ended, she will remember sitting on Grace's lap, crushed by her embrace, as her mother sobbed into her hair.

King has parked on a side street, around the corner from the bank. He does not want anyone to find him sitting in his car, his arms on the steering wheel, his head on his hands, while the rest of the town celebrates. He sits up, takes off his glasses, and wipes his eyes with the heels of his hands. He has to go home. It is cowardly of him to leave Dorothy alone now. Charlie is – was – her son too. But not the way he is his.

He knows what people think. That he was son proud, the same way he was bank proud, and power proud, and even house proud. They think he was vain of Charlie. Son and heir. Chip off the old block. Following in my footsteps, even if he didn't go into the bank. But Charlie was not a chip off the old block. That was why King never tried to make him go into the bank. Charlie was better than he was. Charlie was the best thing about him. And Charlie made him better, because Charlie filled him with love. Charlie was the only selflessness he ever knew.

He ought to go home to comfort Dorothy. Thirty-four years of marriage. She is entitled to an arm around her shoulder, a few words of consolation, as if either of them can be consoled for this. But he cannot touch her. He cannot even look at her. He is too ashamed. Their young bodies made Charlie together, and now Charlie is gone, and he cannot understand how he let that happen.

He thinks of what is in the trunk. He will not do that to her. He will not leave her alone. But the idea that he can is the closest thing he knows to solace.

CHAPTER 9

MILLIE

June 1945

The men are coming home. Even standing behind the cosmetics counter of Diamond's, Millie is not immune to the fever of excitement. She is in the thick of it. She watches the women slick lipsticks over their mouths, and blot with tissues, and pucker up into the mirror. Millie smiles at them until she thinks her face will crack, tells them the pink is lovely but with their coloring the coral is warmer, and assures them their husbands and boyfriends and even sons will love it.

The store has not yet opened this morning, and she is arranging a display of compacts when the manager comes over and tells her Mr Diamond wants to see her in his office.

'Now?'

'He said as soon as you got in.'

She is glad she came in early this morning. Then she realizes. The time she arrived does not matter. Mr Diamond can have only one reason for wanting to see her. The firings are beginning. She did not think he would do them himself, but then what does she know about getting and losing jobs. She never thought she would even have a job. She does not need the money. Pete's death benefit – she hates the term – is ten thousand dollars. Ten thousand dollars will last a long time, at least until she marries again. And she does not like the idea of leaving Jack with her aunt. But she hates staying home with her aunt even more. The house reeks of grief. The smell and the taste and the gloom remind her of the way it felt when she went there to live after her mother and father died. It is worse now. Then they made allowances for her child-ishness. Now she is not let off so easily. She is expected to grieve. She is grieving, but that does not mean she does not go on living. She is desperate to go on living. She has spent too much of her life in bereavement. That is why she has to get out of that house of mourning. She will pick up Jack from her aunt's at the end of the day and the two of them will go to their own home, where they can raise their voices, and laugh, and breathe. She does not care how cramped the apartment is, as long as she can chase Jack around the place, let him ride her like a pony as a father would, and tickle him until he shrieks. He is missing so much. She can at least give him that.

She took the job at Diamond's to get money for a small apartment or even a room. Her uncle would have lectured her darkly if she tried to use Pete's death benefit for such a frivolous purpose when she had a perfectly good home with them. The money must rest in a bank, as in rest in peace, where it will accrue three-and-a-quarter percent interest for Jack to go to college, or a rainy day, whichever comes first.

She planned to start looking for a place as soon as her aunt and uncle, and Pete's parents, and the rest of the town got used to her working, but now she will not be able to. And she cannot even get angry about it, because she believes she ought to be fired. All those returning vets are entitled to jobs. True, they cannot have a man selling cosmetics, but when they give the vets back their jobs in the men's departments, the women who have been working there will return to their old jobs in cosmetics and hats and foundations.

She steps into the elevator and faces herself in the mirror. Her makeup is still fresh, but she takes out her compact and powders her nose, then removes the top from her lipstick and runs it over her mouth. She does not know why she wants to look her best to be fired, but she does. Later she will say she's glad she did, because Al never would have given her a second glance if her nose was shiny or her lips pale. Baloney, Al always answers.

She has never been in Mr Diamond's office. It's small and dusty and crowded with too much furniture, too many papers and ledgers, and odd articles of clothing hanging from the backs of chairs and the ends of shelves. The one plant on the windowsill is dead.

Mr Diamond does not stand, or ask her to sit, or close the door. This will not take long.

'Around the bush I don't believe in beating, Mrs Swallow,' he says, and rubs his chin. It is not even ten o'clock in the morning, and his jaw is sooty with five-o'clock shadow. 'You're a widow, right?'

She hates the word. The *o* opens like a howling mouth. 'My husband died in the war.'

He leans back in his chair and looks at her. 'I'm sorry. My heart breaks to bring up such a painful situation. But I got to make sure. Married women I don't hire. Not now the war's over. Almost over.'

'I don't understand.'

'What's not to understand? A girl got a husband, she should be home taking care of him. A girl got a husband to take care of her, she shouldn't take a job away from a man.'

'I agree.'

'Good. But a horse of a different color we got here. You like pretty clothes? Sure you do. What girl looks like you don't? Well, now that the war's over, Diamond's is going to have plenty of pretty clothes. Now we don't have to worry about those crazy regulations: No pleats. No ruffles. One measly patch pocket per blouse. No skirt more than seventy-two inches around. No hems more than two inches. Merchandise like that I was ashamed to sell. But from now on it's going to be different. Already I'm seeing some of the samples. Couple of months from now, weeks even, Diamond's is going to be full of dresses and suits and gowns with pleats and pockets and real hems. Quality goods. And all you got to do is walk around the store wearing the merchandise. Hats too. No raise. We got to watch out for inflation. But it's a nice job. You smile. You look pretty. You make people happy. You sell clothes. What do you say?'

She says fine.

He rubs his hands together. 'Good, we got a deal.' He glances past her through the open door. 'Now you got to excuse me. You got a counter to cover, and I see my brother-in-law, you know, Baum from men's shoes, out there with his son. A regular war hero I don't keep waiting.'

Mr Baum from men's shoes is already coming in the door as she starts to go out, but the younger man in navy dress whites steps back to let her leave. He is dark, with a lean face and a long jaw that, like his uncle's, wears a midnight-blue shadow, though it is clear from the nick on his chin that he has recently shaved. As she goes through the door, the memory of Pete's cheeks after he shaved, smooth as a baby's, makes her rub her fingertips against her skirt.

'Come on in, Al,' she hears Mr Diamond say as she heads for the elevator. 'What're you standing there looking at? A shiksa in the family we don't need.'

Millie makes up her mind on the way home from the store that evening. It has nothing to do with the man in dress whites. Grace is the one who drives her to it. Grace and her wall.

She sits in her room, waiting until she hears the big console radio in the living room go silent and her aunt's and uncle's tread on the steps, then for another ten minutes while feet go back and forth to the bathroom at the end of the hall, and water runs, and doors open and close. Finally, when the house is silent, she makes her way down one flight of stairs, then the second, to the basement, where her uncle keeps the empty boxes for storing old magazines. The attic is full of cartons of *Life*s and *Saturday Evening Post*s and *Reader's Digest*s. She takes an empty box and carries it up to her room, careful to avoid the step next to the top, the one that creaks badly.

She closes the door to her bedroom quietly, sits on the floor with the empty box, and pulls open the bottom drawer of the dresser. A wedding picture of her and Pete stares up at her.

Everyone said he would never marry her. Her uncle warned of the folly of waiting for a boy to sow his wild oats. Her aunt used the word *wild* and let it go at that. Every time Pete took up with a new girl, Grace and Babe insisted he wasn't half good enough for her. But goodness had nothing to do with it. She could not explain the attraction. Who can explain love? He's handsome, girls say. He's a snappy dresser, or a swell dancer, or the life of the party. He comes from a good family, mothers pronounce. He has fine prospects, fathers predict. And none of it matters. At least it didn't for her.

She was supposed to fall for Mac, the older brother, the good brother, the one who would take care of her, because heaven knows she'd had enough hardship in her life. Grace kept throwing them together. But the more Millie saw of Mac, the harder it was to take her eyes off Pete. Maybe it was the smile. Maybe it did come down to something as simple as that. Both Swallow boys had smiles that could light up a moonless midnight sky, but there the similarity ended. Mac's smile – easy, warm, true – seduced mothers. Pete's grin made them want to lock up their daughters. People said he would never settle down. People had not counted on the war.

She puts the photograph in the box, takes out a handful of letters, taps the edges to align them, puts them on top of the picture, and reaches into the drawer for a second batch. One slips out onto her lap. She places the second batch in the box, then picks up the stray that has fallen in her lap and slides it out of the envelope.

Hi, Millie Mine, my heart, my soul, my blood, my cheeseburger with fried onions, my chocolate chip cookie the way only you can make them.

The words rustle through the room as if he is whispering them. He used to do that, lie in bed murmuring strings of absurd endearments in her ear, and she would giggle and tell him to be serious, because she wanted him to tell her he loved her the way they did in the movies. What a dope she'd been, begging for lies when she had the real thing.

She folds the letter along its creases and puts it back in the envelope. She will not do this. If she starts reading the letters and looking at the pictures, she will never finish.

She places the envelope in the box and turns back to the drawer. It's a jumble of papers and pictures and sketches. She is usually neat, but after the telegram, she began shoving things in any which way. As long as she got them out of sight. She will sort them now, and that will be the end of it.

She spreads several pictures on the floor and sits staring down at them, though she just swore she would not. How did she miss the change? The first photograph was taken right after he was called up. In it, the Pete she fell in love with stares out from candid eyes, set far apart in a square face. He is smiling at a world that he knows cannot help but smile back at him. The next picture was taken in North Carolina. He is still grinning, but now his mouth is lopsided, as if the joke is on him. In the next two photos, the grin has shrunk to a bemused grimace. The last picture was taken in England. He is squinting into the camera, and his smile bears as much resemblance to the real thing as powdered eggs do to fresh. He used to

169

write how much he hated powdered eggs and dreamed of a couple of eggs over easy, the way she served them up. The photos make a progression. If she holds them together on one side and riffles through them on the other, they will be like one of those penny books that simulate moving pictures. The Last Days of Peter Swallow.

She cannot do this. She scoops up the pictures and puts them in the box.

The sketches are easier. Most of them are of strangers, British children she will never know, other men she has not met. She wonders how many of them are still alive. She will not do this. She will not turn into Grace, hoarding her pain.

She kneels over the open drawer and begins working quickly, scooping the letters and photos and sketches up out of the drawer, stacking them in the box. She wishes she could do it with her eyes closed.

She reaches the bottom of the drawer. Only a handful of envelopes remain, all addressed in her handwriting. The big black letters stamped across them stare up at her. DECEASED. DECEASED. DECEASED. The flaps are still sealed. She could not read what she had written to him after he was dead. The words would jeer at her.

She starts at the noise and turns to the door, but it is still closed. The sound came from her, an escaped moan.

She takes the envelopes with the cruel brands in both her hands and dumps them in the box. To hell with neatness.

As she starts to close the drawer, she notices a single letter stuck in the back. It will not hurt to read one.

She takes out the envelope and extracts the letter. The words crawl across the page. She can hear them in his voice, though this is not something he whispered in bed. This is not something he thought of, until he went to war.

> *One more thing, honey, in the unlikely event anything does happen, I don't want you sitting around pining. What I'm trying to say, and it feels funny as heck to write, is if anything should happen to me, I want you to marry again. You're too wonderful a wife, you're too swell a girl, to go to waste.*

She folds the letter, puts it back in the envelope, and puts the envelope in the box. Then she closes the carton and seals it with the roll of tape she brought up from the basement. She does not label it. The contents are nobody's business.

By the time she comes down from the attic, a ribbon of pink, hot as a fever, lies on the horizon. But she has finished the job.

August 1945

She is sitting on the steps that lead up to the apartment over the garage, shelling peas into a bowl on her lap. Al is behind her, one step up, leaning back on his elbows with his long legs stretched out beside her. Every now and then, he sits up and massages her neck and shoulders. Saturdays are the worst days of the week at the store. Mr Diamond makes her change outfits every hour. And she has to keep moving through the crowds, practically singing what she's wearing. Tab-buttoned gray wool wrap dress, $19.95. Little-waisted deep-yoke coat, $29.95. Checkmate cardigan jacket, wool and rayon, $15.95. She cannot wait to quit. Al doesn't make much, sitting in his uncle's back office, toting up figures, but he says it's enough to take care of the three of them. No wife of his is going to work. Besides, he isn't planning to spend the rest of his life in that back office. His uncle sometimes speaks of bringing him along, but Al is impatient. He has his own plans, or at least ideas, though Millie is not sure what they are.

He sits up and begins to massage her shoulders again. She is wearing a sundress, and she likes the feel of his hands on her skin. It has been so long since a man touched her. That's another reason to marry quickly. Sometimes she feels herself getting carried away, and she cannot afford to. Just because she is no longer a virgin, that is not a license. If anything, it is a reason to be more careful.

As Claude's car turns in to the driveway, she shrugs her shoulders, and Al takes his hands from them, but not before he runs one finger along the back of her sundress just inside the fabric. She shivers.

Babe climbs out of the car and takes Jack's hands so he can jump down from the running board. He dashes toward the steps, and Babe and Claude follow.

'There's a wonderful invention,' Babe says. 'It's called canned vegetables.'

Millie steadies the bowl with one hand while she hugs Jack with the other.

'This man spent three years aboard ship eating canned vegetables and canned fruit and canned meat,' she says. 'It's about time he got the real thing.'

'And now I have it,' Al says. His finger traces the line inside her sundress again.

She thanks Babe for taking care of Jack, and Babe says it's her pleasure. Millie hears the wistfulness in Babe's tone and wants to tell her not to be impatient. Claude has been home for only a month. But Babe never brings up the subject, any more than she mentions the baby she lost. Millie does not understand her. She can get hot under the collar about things that have nothing to do with her, public things, political things, but she is cool as a cucumber about the things that count.

After Babe and Claude leave, Millie bathes Jack and puts him to bed. Then Al mixes two gin fizzes, and they carry them out to the steps. She sits one below him, leans her shoulders against his legs, and tilts her head back on his knees. Thin clouds skulk across the sky, and in the intervals between them, a full moon gloats down. She does not know if she is happy. She is not stupid enough to think she is safe. But she no longer feels as if she is in free fall. I can do this. Pete wanted me to.

The sound of Jack's whimper, faint as a distant siren, floats through the open window. She lifts her head from Al's knee and listens. Sometimes he falls back to sleep. Sometimes who knows what monsters and bogeymen will not let him.

The whimper builds to a full-fledged cry. She starts to stand, but Al puts his hand on her shoulder.

'I'll go.'

The stairs creak as he climbs them, and she thinks, yes, this is right. This is not Pete, but it's right.

Al steps into the darkened room. His foot hits the wastebasket and knocks it over. He switches on the lamp, crosses to the narrow bed, and sits on the side. Jack stares up at him, his dark-blue eyes inky with half-remembered fear.

'Bad dream, buddy?' He scoops up the small body. It is rigid in his arms.

'Want to tell me about it?'

Jack shakes his head no. The silky hair grazes Al's chin. The small tight muscles begin to ease. He did not even know he liked kids. He knew he would have them. Everybody does. It would kill his parents if he didn't. But that is not what he means.

They sit that way for a few minutes, until Jack's breathing becomes regular and his head drops from Al's shoulder and bobs against his chest. He lays the boy on the bed, stands, and notices the over-turned wastebasket. As he stoops to right it, a sheet of paper that has fallen out catches his eye.

He does not mean to read it. He is not the kind of man who reads other people's mail, except aboard ship when he had the censorship duty. But the lines jump out at him. He recognizes them from a letter one of the men on the ship sent to his girl. As a joke, the kid said when Al not only blacked them out but called him on them. Can't you take a joke, Lieutenant? He straightens and stands looking down at them now. He censored them, but he cannot stamp them out. The joke is still going around, though now it's in an anonymous letter. He takes the envelope out of the wastebasket. It's to Mrs Peter Swallow, but there is no return address.

First man to sink an enemy battleship – Colin Kelly
First man to set foot on enemy territory – Robert O'Hara
First woman to lose five sons – Mrs Sullivan
First son of a bitch to get four new tires – Hymie Goldstein

He has not thought of this side of it. He has been too busy fighting the other side.

His mother threatened to sit shivah for him.

'Mom,' he pleaded, 'for three years you were worried sick something was going to happen to me. Now I'm home safe and sound, and you want to pretend I'm dead?'

His father said after all the Jews they killed in Europe, it was up to him to bring new ones into the world.

'That's why I'm getting married, Pop.'

'A Jewish mother you need, for Jewish children.'

'Since when did you get so religious?'

It's the war, his parents lamented. This time he did not argue with them.

He had spent half the war fighting Krauts and half fighting his shipmates – not all of them, only the ones off the farm, who never saw a Jew before but knew they hated them; and the ones from the city, who worked alongside them and fought them for neighborhood turf and knew they hated them; and the country-club boys, after they discovered the name Baum was not German but Jewish. Better to be a German, even in this war, than a Jew anytime.

But there was another side to it, and that had to do not with what they did to him but with what he did to himself. The first week in training at the base in Florida, he had no trouble eating ham for Uncle Sam, as the saying went. Some of the other Jewish guys couldn't stomach it. They could handle the bacon, but they froze at the sight of ham. Pork chops, a Sunday special, were the worst. One guy he knew stepped out of the chow line when the man doling out the food put a pat of butter on his pork chop. Al liked the Sunday pork chops. The ham for breakfast was even better.

Not all of it was that easy, though he did not have to wrestle with the dog-tag issue. He had heard of Jewish guys in the army who took them off before they went into battle. If they were taken prisoner, they did not want the Germans to find that telltale *H* on the tag. He stood a better chance of getting blown up or drowning than of ending up in a German POW camp. But even if he had been at risk of a camp, he would not have taken off the tags. He would not give up the identity, the amalgam of himself, he had just begun to forge. For the first time in his life, he was not a Jew first and everything else an afterthought. In training, he was either a good seaman or not. When the call to battle stations sounded, they either could count on him or they couldn't. On leave, he was just another Yank – not the best thing to be, but not as suspect as a Jew. He was still different, but not as different as before.

The world has not changed as much as he has. His parents have not changed at all. But they are right when they blame Millie on the war. Before the war, he never would have gone after her. He would not have had the crust. The war did not make a man of him – he likes to think he was already that – but it did make an American.

He takes the sheet of paper and goes back outside. She is still sitting on the steps.

'Thanks,' she says.

He sits on the stair above her.

'I wasn't being lazy. I want him to get used to his new daddy.'

When he does not answer, she twists around to see his face and notices the paper in his hand. Even in the dim light from the overcast moon, he can see the blood rise in her cheeks.

'I threw it out.'

'There are more where it came from.'

'What do you mean?'

'I mean it's an ugly Jew-hating world out there.'

'I don't care.'

Tell her the truth. She's going to have to care, for herself, for Jack, for the children still to come. But he can't. He wants to protect her, but not from him.

'It isn't as if you're religious,' she goes on. 'You don't even seem Jewish. You don't talk like your uncle.'

'I was born here. He wasn't.'

'See what I mean. You don't even look Jewish. Not with those eyes.' The first time she saw him, she noticed the five-o'clock shadow at ten in the morning. When he took her out to dinner a week later, she noticed the eyes. 'Jews don't have African violet eyes.'

The phrases should have warned him. You don't sound Jewish. You don't look Jewish. Some of my best friends are Jews. But he is too besotted to hear them.

August 14, 1945

She has not been able to stop worrying the problem since Al found the letter in the waste-basket, the one about all the Irish war heroes and the Jew who got four new tires. I can do this, she thought that night. It's right. But maybe it isn't and she can't. The issue is not the timing. Grace says it's been only a year, but it feels much longer than that. The days and weeks of widowhood drag more slowly than those of marriage. The problem is the letter, or what it warned of. Maybe that's why she didn't tear it up before she threw it away. She wanted Al to find it. She wanted him to make up her mind for her.

The uneasiness stalks her as she struts the floors of Diamond's in the dresses and suits and coats she cannot afford to wear outside the store. Now, on her day off, as she sits on the steps, mending Jack's shorts and sewing missing buttons on his overalls and her blouses, while he plays in the sandbox Al has built for him, the problem throbs like a headache. She would be a fool not to marry him. She would be a fool to.

Her aunt and uncle are opposed to the idea. Mixed marriages never work, they tell her. Think

179

of Jack, they warn. She does not explain to them that she is thinking of Jack. At least partly.

Al's family is against it too. Their opposition surprised her. She thought they would be happy he was marrying a Christian girl. She isn't saying Christians are better or anything like that, but his children will be Christian or at least part Christian, and as he says, in this world being a Christian is easier than being a Jew. He laughed when he heard her reasoning and explained that his parents did not see it that way.

Her fingers are sweaty. She puts down the needle and thread and wipes her hand on her shorts. As she picks it up again, a siren slices through the thick August air. Then people are bursting out of doors, radios are blaring out of windows, and a car comes cruising down the street honking its horn. Mr Miller, the man who rents her the garage apartment, bangs out of his house, the screen door slamming behind him.

'It's over, Mrs Swallow,' he calls across the small yard. 'The war is over!' he shouts, then looks as if he would like to clamp his hand over his mouth. He has remembered she is a war widow. He has remembered that for her it will never be over.

He goes back into the house, but the crowd in the street is growing thicker. Men and women and children are screaming and laughing and dancing and embracing. Everyone is embracing.

She goes down the steps, sits on the side of

the sandbox, and takes Jack on her lap. He tries to squirm away. He does not want to be held on her lap while other boys are running up and down the street and grown-ups are shouting, dancing, and carrying on as he has never seen them do.

Mr Miller comes out again with his grandson riding on his shoulders. Jack stops fighting her and looks up at them. Envy is smeared on his face like the dirt from his play.

'Jackie want to ride,' he says, as Mr Miller goes by at a clip and joins the crowd in the street.

'Jackie want to ride,' he calls after them.

She tries to pull him onto her lap again, but he splays his hands on her shoulders and pushes away from her.

'Jackie want to ride,' he shouts.

'Okay, okay. Jackie ride on Mommy's shoulders.'

She picks him up and tries to lift him over her head, but he is too heavy. His hands box her ears; his knees dig into her shoulders.

She carries him to the stairs and puts him on the fourth one up. He stamps his bare feet.

'Jackie ride,' he shrieks.

'Jackie's going to ride,' she says, and her voice is harsher than she intended.

She sits on the second step with her back to him, reaches around, puts one leg over her shoulder, and starts to position the other. He slips backward and grabs her hair.

'Ouch!'

He begins to cry.

'It's okay, Jackie. Mommy didn't mean to yell.'

She tries to pull him onto her lap again. He pummels her chest.

He is crying, and she is cajoling, and the entire neighborhood is in such an uproar of celebration that she does not hear the car pull up behind her and the door slam. Al is standing over them.

'The whole town is celebrating, and I find you two sitting here as if it's the end of the world.'

She looks up at him. With the sun behind him, he is only a silhouette. She cannot see his face, but she can make out the suit he wears to the back office at Diamond's. He must have been working late and left as soon as he heard.

Jack has stopped crying, but his face is twisted in a mean scowl that says he is poised to begin again.

'I was trying to get him on my shoulders. Mr Miller came out of the house carrying his grandson on his shoulders, and Jack wanted to ride that way too.'

He bends to Jack's level. 'Hey, buddy, that's nothing to cry about.' He slips out of his jacket, folds it inside out, and puts it on the step. Then he reaches out his long arms, scoops Jack up over his head, and positions him on his shoulders. Jack's chubby legs hang around his neck like a scarf; his hands grip Al's ears like handles.

'Giddyup,' he screams, and the three of them start down the driveway toward the celebration.

She looks up at Al towering above her and sees

Jack floating above him like a willful dirt-streaked cherub with his head in the clouds.

'You're the tallest boy in the parade,' she calls up to him.

BOOK III

1946–1951

CHAPTER 10

BABE

September 1946

Millie bends over and puts the baby in Babe's arms. She is always doing that to her, as if fertility is contagious. Babe looks down at the child cradled in the crook of her elbow, and Betsy squints up, a miniature red-faced Winston Churchill.

Al leans over Babe's chair and chucks his daughter under the chin. 'Is she something or is she something?'

'She's something,' Babe agrees.

He reaches down to take the baby from Babe. He cannot keep his hands off her. He is the same way with Millie. Babe wonders how it feels to be married to a demonstrative man.

She glances around the yard, placing Claude in the group. He is sitting in a canvas chair, a beer in one hand, a cigarette in the other. The pose is supposed to be relaxed, but she can sense the tension halfway across the yard. His knee bounces like the valve on an engine trying to let off steam so it won't explode.

187

Millie takes the baby from her husband and tells him Grace wants him to start the grill. He does not argue. Grace is the widow among them. Al and Claude must take care of her.

Claude puts down his beer, grinds out his cigarette, and starts to get up to help, but before he can, Millie gives him the baby. Babe wishes they would stop passing her around like a bowl of fruit. It can't be good for her. She glances at the back steps, where Amy and Jack are huddled. All the fuss over the baby can't be good for them either.

She looks back at Claude. His face glows hot red. A film of sweat swelters on his upper lip where his wartime mustache used to be. He holds the baby in one arm. The other, with the missing fingers, hangs limp beside him, as if he does not want to touch her with his wounded hand. He looks up. Babe cannot read his eyes behind the dark glasses, but she recognizes the nervous tic at the side of his mouth. His knee is going faster. She gets up and takes the baby from him, and as she does, she remembers his grief in the hospital room in the camp town. He'll be fine when the baby he's holding is his own.

He starts to get up again, but before he can, Amy comes over, stands behind his chair, and puts her hands over his eyes.

'Guess who,' she says.

'Mickey Mouse?'

'Nope.'

'Donald Duck?'

'Nope.'

'Eleanor Roosevelt!' He reaches his arm behind him, brings her forward, and pulls her onto his lap. She rests her head against his shoulder. His knee slows.

He'll be just fine when he has a baby of his own.

Babe knows he is lying to her. People do not make decisions like this because of the atomic bomb, or the iron curtain, or the threat of another war. They do not run their lives according to what politicians and diplomats do thousands of miles away. Whatever his reason, it dwells closer to home.

They lie side by side in the double bed with the windows open to the September night and a faint breeze walking over the thin sheet that covers them. A slippery slice of moon swings outside the window. He has waited until they are in bed to spring it. He needs the cover of darkness.

At first she cannot imagine what he's driving at. She knows he worries about the bomb, and another war, and the end of civilization, they both do, but not in bed. At the small table in the living room, he looks up from the morning paper while they sit having coffee, says can you beat this, and reads her a paragraph, and they agree that it's unconscionable, but for all their indignation, they know it has nothing to do with them. His demons lurk in the past, not the future.

But now he is saying atomic bomb, and iron curtain, and – there it is, the needle in the haystack, the nugget of gold among the dross – not fair to bring a baby into this world.

She turns her head on the pillow to look at him. His profile carves a pale mask from the dark sky beyond the window. His eyes are fixed on the pattern of leaves cast on the ceiling by the street-light below. He cannot look at her as he says those words.

She could argue with him. She could tell him that if an unsettled world were reason not to have a baby, people would have stopped reproducing during the Thirty Years' War and the Plague and every other moment in the human past. He knows that; he's a history teacher. She could say, tell me the real reason. But she knows he will not tell her. Sometimes she looks up from the book she's reading or the dishes she's washing and catches him, sitting, his own book forgotten in his lap or papers ungraded on the table in front of him, his face hard and closed, his eyes staring. At what? She knows from experience not to ask.

Grace would tell her she must make him see the error of his ways. Millie would say tell him it's an accident; he'll never know. But she will not argue with a bleeding man, and she will not trick him. She will give him time.

He is a liar. It is the one condition they did not warn him about. They gave him physical therapy for his hand. They passed out pamphlets about readjusting to civilian life. But they never told him he would have to become a liar to survive. He would have to deny everything he has seen and learned and done. No, he never watched a baby-faced kid from Ohio cut the balls off a dead German because he just lost his buddy. No, he never saw swarms of rats feasting on human corpses. No, he never sat with Herb's head, oh, God, please, not that again. And no, no, no, I did not feel my hands crushing Millie's baby, hear the limbs cracking like chicken bones when you're trying to get at the moist meat, see the skull splitting and the brains oozing out onto my lap, as Herb's did. He starts to sweat at the memory of the tiny body in his arms and the damage he could do to it. No, I never saw or thought any of that. I simply think no sane person would bring a child into a world divided by an iron curtain, shadowed by an atomic bomb, stalked by another war.

Three days later she goes to a woman doctor in Boston. On the bus ride home, she sits cradling the diaphragm, wrapped in plain brown paper like a dirty book, in her lap. She always knew she got off too easily for that night in the station bathroom and for wishing the baby away.

April 1948

The sun should not be out. The light is too buttery, the buds on the trees too tender. The daffodils, just like the ones a ten-year-old Charlie ran down a line decapitating with a stick, break Babe's heart. She would prefer rain.

Grace has dressed Amy in a black spring coat, with a black hat that trails a mournful black grosgrain ribbon down her back, and black patent-leather Mary Janes. Only her short socks are white. She stands, an eight-year-old widow, barelegged in the spring wind, pregnant with loss.

Grace is all in black too. The veil of her hat hides her eyes. Once during the ceremony, she reaches for Amy's hand. Amy pulls it away and jams it in her pocket. A moment later, she takes it out and clasps her mother's hand. She is such a good girl. Babe wishes she was not such a good girl.

They are all in mourning clothes: Babe and Millie in black coats, Claude and Al and Mac Swallow, home for the first time since he moved to Boston, in dark suits, holding dark hats against dark serge thighs. Al feels uncomfortable being here. He does not hold a grudge, he insists, but after what happened at the bank, he does not think King Gooding wants him at his son's grave.

'He doesn't want any of us,' Claude says on the way to the cemetery.

Naomi has come. After all, she works for the family. Frank has stayed away. He always liked Charlie Gooding, but he cannot forgive King's treatment of him when he comes to the house to pick up Naomi. Like a goddamn field hand, Frank says, but Naomi insists it has nothing to do with Frank's color, only with King's misery. If any other white

192

man in town treated you that way, she tells Frank, it would be because you're a Negro. But these days King Gooding is color-blind. He hates everyone who came home from the war, black or white.

King's dark suit hangs on him as if on a scarecrow. His neck rises scrawny as a chicken's from his shirt collar.

'May his soul, and the souls of all the departed, through the mercy of God, rest in peace. Amen.'

The minister steps back from the grave, and the four workmen come forward. They slip two heavy belts under the coffin, then each of them grips an end. The coffin begins to descend. The belts groan under the weight as it inches lower and lower, until only the top half is visible, then only the cover, then it is gone from view. Babe wonders how a thud so quiet can shake the earth.

She sees Grace drop Amy's hand and take a step forward. Oh, God, no, she's going to throw herself in after him. But she doesn't. She stands there, so close that the toes of her black pumps jut out over the open grave, teetering. The sight makes Babe dizzy. She reaches for Claude's hand.

He is silent in the car on the way home. This is his second funeral in as many weeks. Ten days earlier, he drove to Haverhill to bury Joe Dumbrowsky, who fought his way through France and Germany only to go into the garage in his own backyard, close the door, and turn on the car engine. Babe did not go with Claude to the funeral. You never knew him, Claude said. I know you, she wanted to shout. I could keep you company on the drive. I could stand beside you at the grave. I could comfort you, or try to. But she does not argue with him. Men he trusted with his life, he says. And what about me, she wants to scream, don't you trust me with your life? But she did not cover him while he ran across a field under fire; or walk through enemy territory by his side, relying on each other's eyes and ears and reflexes; or crouch together in a foxhole, sharing cold and mud and lice and fear. He does not trust her with his life. He shuts her out of it.

She knew better than to ask him about the funeral when he came home that night. But he surprised her. He told her about a letter Dumbrowsky's widow showed him. Forgive me, his old buddy had written, but I just can't do it anymore, to myself, or to you and the kids. You'll be better off without me.

The poor guy, Claude said.

The poor wife and children, Babe thought, to have to live with that for the rest of their lives. She did not blame the man. Only a tortured soul takes his own life. But they would not be better off without him. With the exception of someone throwing himself on a grenade or stepping in front of a bullet, suicide is never altruistic.

Summer 1950

Through the open window of the upstairs bedroom, Babe hears the newspaper hit the front

194

His parents, however, know their own minds – mind, because they are in perfect accord about this. They have never in their lives bought anything they have not saved for patiently and paid for in full. A penny saved is a penny earned, they insist. Neither a borrower nor a lender be. Rather go to bed without dinner than rise in debt.

'You were raised by a couple of Yankee samplers,' she says on the way home from a Sunday dinner.

Claude takes his hand from the wheel and puts it on her knee. She has charmed a smile out of him. It is no easy feat, but every now and then she carries it off. She will get her house. That's the way he thinks of it – her house.

She reads everything about the G.I. Bill she can get her hands on. It is not just for buying houses. All over the country, veterans are going to college and starting businesses on it. The government pays tuition and backs half the loans, and the banks administer them, and everything comes up roses. All over the country, but not in South Downs.

King Gooding has never said he will not make loans on the G.I. Bill. He merely murmurs, in his silkiest tones, phrases like discretion of the lender, and responsibility to the bank's investors, and rates of small-business failure. For your protection as well as ours, he tells Al Baum, when Al applies for a loan to open an appliance store to outfit all those houses that all those vets are buying on the G.I. Bill. The sinister word *bankruptcy* hangs in the air between them.

But a house is its own collateral, and King cannot stop the loans to Babe and Claude and the scores of other veterans who are snapping up the Cape Cods and ranches and moderns in the development called Riverview, which is springing up in what used to be hay and cranberry and cornfields north of town.

On weekends she and Claude drive out to see their house. They cannot believe how quickly it grows. One Sunday, they stand in a chill drizzle looking down at the concrete foundation. This is no slapdash job going up on a slab. By the next Sunday, the frame is up. As spring softens the earth, windows and plumbing and electrical wiring sprout like tender shoots. Claude gets caught up. He climbs through the unfinished rooms and makes lists; he drives out after school to talk to the foreman. At night, he still thrashes and shouts and rages, but in the light of day he takes an interest. Babe is hopeful.

They move in the last week of May. Millie and Grace come to help Babe unpack, though she and Claude have little in the way of furniture and household effects. Millie, who is still living in half of a two-family house, which is more cramped than ever with three children, wanders the rooms, running her fingers lovingly over the smooth Formica counters, shiny bathroom fixtures, and an avocado-green washing machine and dryer that come with the house.

That was more than a year ago. The Formica is still pristine, the bathroom fixtures continue to gleam, and the washing machine and dryer whir regularly. Babe is a good housekeeper. Claude does his part. He cuts the grass, cleans the gutters, and fixes a drip in the shower. She watches him doing all that and could swear he is happy. Sometimes he even hums. But one Saturday, after they have been living there for several months, she comes home from doing the marketing to find the floor of the bathroom covered with shards of glass and bloody footprints. The door to the medicine cabinet is a piece of splintered plywood. The wooden bowl of shaving soap sits on the sink; a razor lies in it. On her way through the bedroom to get a broom and mop, she sees a letter from Dumbrowsky's widow on his dresser.

She does not ask him what happened. Her imagination is as vivid as his memory. She sees him facing off with himself in the mirror. He lifts the razor to his cheek. His hand trembles so badly he cannot draw it down his skin. She has seen that happen. He drops the razor and stands gripping the sink, staring into his eyes. The bloodshot mirrors of the horrors he has witnessed, and perpetrated, reproach him. His fist comes up and punches the face in the mirror.

She opens her eyes and looks at the clock again. The hands read six-ten. He went down for the paper twenty-five minutes ago.

She kicks off the covers, gets into her robe and slippers, and goes downstairs. He is not in the kitchen, or the living room, or what the architectural plans call the family room and she calls the den. She looks out the sliding glass doors. He is not in the yard. She goes back up to the living room and notices that the front door is still open. She goes to it. Claude is sitting on the top step, reading the paper. There is nothing wrong with that, though Mrs Wright would probably disagree, but she is surprised. He always brings the paper back to bed.

She goes out on the stoop and stands behind him, her knees touching his shoulders. The headline jumps up at her.

NORTH KOREA DECLARES WAR
COMMUNISTS ATTACK SOUTH

This has nothing to do with you, she wants to say. Instead, she sits beside him on the stoop and leans over to read the article, which is not exactly news. Guerrilla raids have been going on for the past year. Claude has been following them religiously.

Her eyes comb the columns of words. They speak of mortar and artillery bombardment, small-craft landings, and all-out warfare. The words are sickeningly familiar. She puts a hand on his arm.

'Let's go back to bed.'

She says it without a trace of seduction. War is back, but for him, at this moment, Thanatos and Eros do not go hand in hand.

She begins going down to get the paper each

morning, though she hates bringing the headlines into their bed.

33 COUNTRIES BACK U.N.
ACTION ON KOREA

ARMY SECRETARY SAYS
FULL-SCALE LAND WAR

PRESIDENT SIGNS BILL
EXTENDING THE DRAFT

They will not draft him. He is too old. He has her. But who knows what is going on in his mind as he sits at the table, drinking his coffee and studying the news.

'What gets me,' he says one morning, 'is that no one gives a damn. It's not like the war. They don't even call it a war. It's a police action. Guys are over there fighting and dying, and the rest of us go about business as usual.'

She wants to ask what they are supposed to do but doesn't. She thinks of his telephone call from the recruiting office in Boston.

She watches for signs, but he gives away nothing, until one night he turns on her and warns her to stop spying on him.

'I'm not spying,' she says, though she knows better than to try to reason with him when he is like this.

'Maybe you need a hobby,' he sneers, 'other than me, I mean.'

201

An hour later, he goes through the house looking for her and finds her in the yard. He comes up behind her, puts his arms around her, and says he's sorry. But it is too late. She is rigid in his embrace. He feels her anger, drops his arms, heads back into the house. Now they are both angry. It is a cycle – worse than that, a downward spiral.

She goes on standing in the yard, staring at the lights in her neighbors' windows. Strange how happy other people's lives look, even if you know the glow is a lie. Her mind knows it, but her heart is swollen with envy and sore with self-pity.

The night has turned cool. She should have grabbed a sweater, but she did not know she was coming out to the yard until she was here. As she stands hugging herself in the light from a stingy sliver of moon and her neighbors' windows, she wonders what life would be like without him. The thought is terrifying. It is also heady. She turns and goes back into the house, stealthy as a felon trying to hide the crime she has committed in her mind.

For her birthday, Millie and Grace chip in and give her *The Cordon Bleu Cook Book*. He says she needs a hobby. She'll show him. Vindictiveness spices the meals she begins to labor over with seeming love.

She starts simply, but before long she is spending her afternoons poaching chicken breasts in butter with wine and cream sauce, sautéing veal scallops with chicken livers and ham and mushrooms, and roasting duck. Even an all-American steak is not permitted to arrive at the table without a béarnaise sauce. Claude says the last reminds him of something he ate in France. He never talks about France. The vindictiveness begins to burn off, like the alcohol in a sauce. She redoubles her efforts.

She starts her preparations at three or four in the afternoon, as early as two for the really elaborate dishes. She moves around the kitchen, chopping, dicing, boiling, reducing. As the afternoon progresses, she sometimes lurches. The wine is not only for cooking. She reads the recipe. One cup, two tablespoons, a pinch. She forgets, crosses the kitchen to the cookbook, reads it again. She is distracted. She is distracted by herself. How did she get here? She can picture Millie in her place, or Grace, but she cannot put herself in focus. And where is Claude in this setup? He compliments her on the sole and poulet and boeuf bourguignon, but she knows it's just fish and chicken and stew to him, despite the comment about the béarnaise sauce and France.

One afternoon, just before he walks in the door, the knife slips. He finds her standing over the sink, trying to stanch the flow of blood with a kitchen towel. The white cotton is already soaked red. His face blanches. The sweat beads on his forehead. For a moment he looks as if he is going to bolt. He shakes himself, a wet dog let in by mistake, then steps to the sink and unwraps the towel. He takes her hand in his. His touch is gentle. It does not go with the crazed eyes and wet dog of a moment ago. He peers down at her finger. The tip hangs by the skin. Her knees go weak as she looks at it, but he examines it closely. He wraps the finger with a clean towel, hustles her into the car, and drives to Dr Flanner's office, which was, briefly, Mac's office. The doctor stitches. Good as new, he says as he wraps the gauze around her finger. On the way home, neither of them mentions that she has sliced the second finger of her left hand, which is one of the two he is missing.

At first she thinks the noise is Claude shouting. He is having another nightmare. Then she realizes it's the telephone. It is on her side of the bed, and he is already reaching over her to pick up the receiver. The clock on the night table says three-twenty.

Her head feels as if someone has put a steel band around it and kept winching tighter. Her mouth is dry. The night before, Claude came home and decided to make old-fashioneds.

'Who is it?' she whispers.

He goes on listening.

She puts her head close to his. A man's voice on the other end is saying something about neighbors complaining. He made old-fashioneds, but they did not make any noise. She is sure of it.

'I understand,' Claude says.

The voice on the other end goes on.

'I bet it was Mrs Wright, the old killjoy,' she whispers.

Claude shakes his head no. 'I'll be right there,' he says into the phone, then reaches over her and puts the receiver back in the cradle.

'What is it?'

'Grace.'

'What about Grace?'

He is already pulling on his trousers.

'She was out on her front lawn. In her night-gown. Screaming. Cursing, actually. From the way the cop told it, words I didn't think Grace knew. The neighbors called the police.'

She throws her legs over the side of the bed and stands. A knife slices through her scalp. 'I'll go with you.'

She goes into the bathroom, swallows two aspirins, and brushes her teeth. The toothpaste helps. The aspirins will take longer.

She comes out of the bathroom, finds the slacks and shirt she threw on the chair the night before, pulls them on.

'Where is she, home or the police station?'

'Home. The cop said they'll stay with her until we get there.'

'What about Amy?'

He smiled for the first time. 'One of the policemen is looking after her. I'd like to think it's sheer altruism, but I doubt the fact that she's King Gooding's granddaughter is lost on any of them.'

The first thing Babe notices is that Grace is wearing a trench coat over her nightgown. The second is that the nightgown is sheer and the coat is buttoned wrong. Her hair is a furious tangle. Her face is puffy and pallid as uncooked dough. Her eyes look pink and raw.

Babe sits on the sofa and reaches an arm around her. Grace begins to cry. Claude walks the policeman to the door. The other one is already there, waiting.

'The kid's asleep,' he says.

'Thanks.' Claude wonders if he is supposed to give them money. He is sure King would. But he is not King, and he doesn't want them to think he's trying to hush up the incident or obstruct justice, whatever that means under the circumstances.

'There are no charges,' the first cop says, as if reading his mind. 'Neighbors reported an intruder on the grounds. We investigated and didn't find anything.'

'Thank you,' Claude says again, but keeps his hand out of his pocket.

After he closes the door behind them, he climbs the stairs to check on Amy. She is sleeping on her stomach with her arms and legs spread out, like the photographs of men parachuting out of planes. He stands looking down at her. Strange that he has never feared hurting her as he did Millie's baby. He is good with Amy. Sometimes she strikes him as another of the walking wounded.

He goes down the stairs and back to the sunporch. Grace is still sitting on the couch in her misbuttoned coat with Babe's arm around her shoulders, but she has stopped crying. On the phone, the policeman said she was screaming obscenities. He insisted on quoting a few. The man has probably never read Kipling, but he's a cop. He knows about *the Colonel's Lady* – or in this case the King's daughter-in-law – *an' Judy O'Grady*. He also said that she was screaming the obscenities at Charlie. Claude looks at the wall covered with pictures of Charlie.

'Let's go into the kitchen.'

'Do you want coffee?' Babe asks when they're seated around the table.

Grace shakes her head no.

'Hot milk?'

'Are you trying to make me sick?' Her voice is ragged as a serrated knife. Her anger embraces the world, then collapses in on itself. 'Did the police tell you what happened?'

'A little,' Claude says.

'How can you be angry at someone you love?'

'Who else is worth getting angry at?' Babe asks, and does not look at Claude.

'But it's different. Charlie's not here.' Grace starts to cry again. 'How could I have yelled those things at Charlie?'

How could you not, Babe wants to ask.

October 1950

Babe stands at the stove, scrambling eggs. She makes enough for the three of them, though she knows Amy, who is staying with them while

207

Grace is in the sanitarium, will eat only a bite or two. She refuses to worry about that. What ten-year-old girl eats a hearty breakfast?

She hears Claude's step on the stairs but does not turn. She is afraid to look at him this morning. No, she is afraid to have him see her watching him. Don't look at me that way, he shouted once after he'd had the third old-fashioned. I'm not some wounded mutt you're debating whether to put out of his misery.

He comes up behind her at the stove and puts his hand on her shoulder. Some mornings he cups her bottom. This is a shoulder day. It has been a shoulder month, if not longer. He still keeps his eyes closed when they make love, but she doesn't. His face is brutal. Sex as assault.

She puts down the spatula and covers his hand with hers.

He takes his away. 'I'm sorry about last night.'

'No need to be. I went back to sleep,' she lies.

She picks up the spatula and starts scrambling again, but she is waiting to see if he is going to say more. Last night was worse than it has been in a long time. The sweat was so heavy he drenched the sheets. She was sure the shouting would wake Amy. Screams in nightmares are supposed to come out as whimpers in the real world. Hers do. She thinks she's shouting help, only to wake to find she's mewling. But Claude yells and howls and sobs. His are not nightmares. They are his real world.

'What time are you and Millie leaving?' he asks,

as if he cares, as if he is not simply trying to change the subject.

'Around nine. I don't want to be late and have Grace think we're not coming.'

He pulls out a chair and sits at the table. 'Maybe I'm the one you ought to be visiting in the funny farm.'

He says it before she can, though he knows she would never say it. Still, he has to head her off, just in case.

'You have your nightmares in bed, not on the front lawn,' she says as she spoons eggs onto his plate. 'In this cockamamie world, that qualifies as sane.'

His smile comes out as a grimace.

As Claude steps out of Bill Simpson's Chevy and thanks him for the lift, he notices that the garage door is open and the car is not there. Babe knew she would be late, so she arranged for Amy to go to a friend's after school. No one will be home. He is relieved.

He walks through the garage, lets himself in the side door, and climbs from the den to the kitchen. The only sound is the hum of the refrigerator. Sometimes he finds the noise homey, like the purring of a cat. Now it is only the whirring of an engine. Magnify it, and it could be a tank or a ship or a plane.

He goes to a cabinet, takes out the bottle of scotch, and begins to pour. He drinks too much. They both drink too much. Just about everyone he knows who came home from the war drinks too much. But he needs it now. The bottle clinks against the glass. His hands are still shaking.

Nothing happened. He recovered in time. He is sure none of the kids in the class caught on. He pretended he was picking up a piece of chalk. But if Babe walks in now, she will see, with those eyes that are always tracking him, that something is wrong. And she will add it to her list, her loving long-suffering list. The thrashing and shouting and sweats in the night. The silences during the day. The quick temper and the withering sarcasm. The child they do not have.

He has a logical explanation for it, half a dozen logical explanations. The episode last night. The kid who came into class this morning wearing a Soviet jacket his older brother took off some dead North Korean. What kind of a man takes a jacket off a dead soldier and sends it to his kid brother? No wonder it goes on and on. The fact that his back was to the class when the fire alarm went off. But you cannot write on the blackboard without turning your back to the class.

He started to hit the ground. Only started. That's the important thing to remember. He recovered in time and jumped up, waving the piece of chalk in his hand to show his agility. Lucky he still had the piece of chalk in his hand.

'Got it,' he announced to the class in triumph, and began herding them out of the room for the fire drill.

Horsing around, flirting, and looking for trouble, they burst out of the building into a lush autumn afternoon as dazzling as a stained-glass window. By the time he marched them back inside, they had forgotten what some old geezer who taught history did. But he hadn't forgotten.

Five and a half years after the goddamn war, and it's still going on. He was sure it would get easier with time.

He carries his drink upstairs and goes into their room. The sight of the bed sends a wave of nausea through him. She left it unmade with the top sheet and blanket pulled back, because she had to take Amy and him to school, then drive to the sanitarium. A wavy salt line runs down the middle of the bottom sheet, dividing his sweat-drenched side from hers, her normal world from his madness. She usually strips the bed and puts on clean sheets before he gets home. She's a stickler for hiding the evidence. Sparing his feelings. Why does it make him angry? Would he prefer to come home to the proof, as he has now?

He takes a swallow of his drink, puts it on the night table, and begins stripping the bed. A model husband, if you don't count the rest, the only part that counts.

CHAPTER 11

GRACE

September 1946

Amy sits on the swing in the corner of the yard and watches the grown-ups. You'd think they never saw a baby before.

She hates the baby. She hates the frilly pink dress, and the pink sunbonnet, and the tiny pink Mary Janes. Why does she need Mary Janes? She can't even walk. Everyone carries her around. You'd think she's some prize they're fighting over, like the ones in the Cracker Jacks boxes. Her mommy can't get enough of the thing.

Now Uncle Al is holding the stupid baby to his chest, walking around the yard singing 'Ain't She Sweet.' Her mommy says her daddy used to sing to her the same way. A song called 'You're Not the Only Oyster in the Stew.' She even knows the words but she doesn't remember her daddy singing them to her. She's not even sure she remembers her daddy. She knows what he looks like, but that's just the pictures on the wall.

She walks her sandals around in a circle on the grass until the chains of the swing are twisted, then closes her eyes, picks up her feet, and lets the swing twirl her around. It makes her dizzy. She opens her eyes.

Her mommy is holding the baby again. Drop it, she shouts in her head. Drop the stupid baby on her stupid head. Babies are supposed to have a place in their head that isn't finished, and if you touch them there you can kill them.

Now Aunt Millie has the baby. She puts it in Uncle Claude's lap. He holds it with one arm – drop it, drop it, drop it – and lets the other, the one without the fingers, hang down at the side of his chair. She used to be afraid of Uncle Claude's hand, until he told her he got tired of trying to keep all those fingernails clean so he decided to get rid of some of them. She knew he was teasing her, but now she isn't afraid anymore.

Aunt Babe takes the baby from Uncle Claude, and Amy jumps off the swing and goes over to where he is sitting. She puts her hands over his eyes. Guess who, she says, and after he makes silly guesses, he reaches around and pulls her onto his lap. She rests her head against him in the space under his chin. She loves the way he smells. It's from the soap he puts on his face to shave. Once when she went to stay overnight with him and Aunt Babe, he let her watch him shave in the morning. He took a wooden bowl with white soap from the cabinet, mixed it up with water and a brush, and spread it on his cheeks and chin. Then he took the brush and spread some on her cheeks and chin and even a dab on her nose. He held her up to the mirror. I always thought we looked alike, he said. And for the rest of the day, even after he wiped off the soap, she smelled like him.

Naomi's husband, Frank, smells the same way. She knows because, sometimes when he's waiting for Naomi, he lets her sit on his lap. Once when she was sitting on his lap in Grandma's kitchen while Naomi was making dinner, Grandpa came in, yelled at her to get off, and told Frank he could wait for Naomi in the yard. Frank lifted her off his lap and walked out of the kitchen without a word. She started to cry, but Naomi told her to hush.

'Your grandpa can't help being mean.'

She stopped crying, not because Naomi told her to but because she was surprised. She knew her grandfather was mean, but she never heard anyone come out and say it.

'Because of your daddy,' Naomi added, in that funny tone people use when they mention her daddy.

The grown-ups are still carrying the stinking baby around, but she doesn't care. She's the one Uncle Claude is holding. She leans back against him, and the two of them sit very still in the middle of all the fuss.

After a while Uncle Claude has to lift her off his lap, because the grill is hot and he has to help Uncle Al make the hamburgers and hot dogs. When they're ready, he calls her over and asks what she wants, and she says a hot dog with mustard please. He puts one in a bun, takes the mustard in his good hand, and writes *Amy* with it on the hot dog. She says thank you and carries it to the back steps, where Jack is eating. They have to lean apart to let Aunt Millie go up the steps to the kitchen. She comes back carrying the stinking baby's stinking bottle. 'I'll give it to her,' her mommy says to Aunt Millie.

All of a sudden her hot dog tastes funny. The mustard *Amy* is just *ny*. She puts her paper plate on the steps, stands, and looks around to see if anyone is watching her. They're all too busy with the baby, except Uncle Claude, who's sitting with a bottle of beer in one hand, resting it on the arm of the chair. His eyes are closed. He's tired of looking at the baby too.

She's careful not to let the screen door bang behind her. The bottles are standing in a row on the counter beside the stove. Her mommy boiled them when everyone came, because Aunt Millie said she didn't have time to at home. It's called sterilizing. So the baby won't get sick. She takes a bottle and one of the tops with a nipple off the counter and carries them upstairs.

A week later, Naomi finds the bottle when she is cleaning out the cabinet under the bathroom sink. At first she thinks it's shampoo, because of the color. But why would anyone put shampoo in a baby's bottle? When she picks it up, the liquid looks too thin for shampoo. She unscrews the top.

The smell of urine stings her nose. The idea of someone peeing into a baby bottle is even less understandable than the idea of someone storing shampoo in a baby bottle. She opens the toilet and empties the bottle into it, then puts the bottle in the wastebasket to be taken out with the rest of the trash. She will not mention it to Grace. That child of hers has enough problems.

She won't tell Frank either. He'll say she's protecting the Goodings again, the same way he did when King threw him out of the kitchen. She isn't protecting the Goodings, she's using them. King Gooding is mean-spirited, but he's not stingy. He pays better than anyone in town. He pays almost as much as Frank makes at the factory. She'll put up with more than Frank's having to wait in the yard if it means their boys can go to college someday.

April 1948

'It was nice of you to come,' Grace says to Mac Swallow, and wishes he would leave.

She wants to be alone. She wants to go into the sunporch, and sit with Amy tucked under her arm, and think about Charlie. Sometimes she reads Charlie's letters aloud to Amy. Not the whole letters, of course, but the parts about Amy's growing up and getting married and Charlie and her growing old together. That's what she wants to do this evening. It's fitting after the funeral.

But Amy has disappeared into her room, and Mac is standing here, leaning against the kitchen counter, his hands in his pockets, watching her make coffee. He was Charlie's best friend and Pete's brother, and she has known him for as long as she can remember, a gangly boy with a body that always seemed to be growing too fast and a radiant smile that inspired trust in every mother's heart. He has lost the radiant smile somewhere along the way, and now he makes her nervous. It has nothing to do with that business after he came home from the war. She is not afraid of Mac, no matter how peculiar people say he has grown. She just does not want him in her kitchen, leaning against the counter the way Charlie used to, watching her the way Charlie used to.

Mac's eyes follow her around the kitchen. How many times had he stood here with Charlie, or sat at the kitchen table with coffee or a beer or a drink with Charlie, teasing Grace, making Grace blush, watching Grace pretend to get angry at them? Stop ganging up on me, she'd say. But she didn't mean it. She loved Charlie. God knows she loved him. Look at that crazy wall in the sunporch. But she loved having Mac around too. The husband's good buddy; the hanger-on just enough in love with her to keep her color high, her shoulders back, and her stomach tucked in as she moved around the kitchen. She knew they were both watching her, and she reveled in it.

She does not revel in it now. He wonders if she is self-conscious about her weight. Or is that the point? She has put on the pounds like armor, to keep him and every other man away. But it isn't working. She still looks good to him.

She carries the coffeepot and a plate of cookies to the table. He starts to pull out the chair at right angles to hers, sees the way her face begins to collapse, like Amy's when she's going to cry, and sits across from her. The other chair was Charlie's. The other chair is Charlie's.

She rearranges her face, pours him a cup of coffee, inches the plate of cookies nearer to him, and begins to talk. She will keep him at arm's length with conversation. Nice service . . . perfect weather . . . Charlie would have liked it.

Stop it! he wants to shout. The service was just like any other burial, only worse. The sun was too citrusy, the air too soft with spring, and Charlie would not give a damn how he was buried. All he cared about was living.

'I wish Millie wouldn't be so stubborn.'

He has missed something, too busy arguing with her in his head.

'About what?'

'What I just said. About bringing Pete home.'

Pete's body, he wants to say.

'I know it's breaking your parents' hearts.'

His parents' hearts are already broken. He knows that from the way his mother watches him when he comes home. Is that another reason he moved away? No, it has nothing to do with his mother, only with him. He is the reason he walked out of his brand-new office full of shiny new equipment, leaving a waiting room full of patients and another half naked on the examining table. Six months later he took a job in research at a hospital in Boston. Microscopes and slides and test tubes, but no sick bodies or maimed flesh or festering wounds. He has seen enough of all that to last several lifetimes.

The Jap barrage was a galaxy of shrieking red stars in the steaming air. Bodies lay on the jungle floor, mangled, moaning, reproachfully silent. The stretcher bearers could not keep up. A single machine-gun burst sliced through three of them. He did not stop to debate. He did not think about which of the men was single and which married and which a father. Tomkins, he shouted at the nearest man. Forrester. Rizzo. Go! They went. Two did not come back. Forrester was dragged in. He can still see the flies swarming over his wounds as he worked on him. He got him to the evac hospital, where they could do real surgery. Forrester died on the table.

'Couldn't they do it themselves?' Grace is saying. 'I bet they could. Millie is his wife, but they're his parents. You ought to look into it for them.'

She stands, goes to a drawer in the corner, and begins rifling through papers.

'I know I have it here. The name and address of the organization you write to. You ought to do it, Mac. You really should.'

The papers rustle in the silence. He takes a swallow of coffee. He has let it get cold.

'Here it is.' She comes back to the table with a piece of paper and hands it to him. He takes it from her, though he knows he is not going to do anything about it.

He stands, thanks her for the coffee, tries not to read the relief in her face. She walks him to the door and thanks him for coming. They are both so grateful.

'Charlie would have liked it,' she says again.

'Stop saying that.'

She rears back as if he has slapped her.

'I'm sorry. I didn't mean that.'

He stands with his hand on the doorknob, looking down at her. She pushes her hair out of her eyes and stands up straight, the old Grace, conscious of herself, conscious of his looking at her. Is that what makes him do it?

He takes her hand. 'Gracie.'

She pulls her hand away.

He is halfway down the front walk when the light comes on behind him. It illuminates a narrow strip of the yard. She has put on the front light for him. The gesture makes his heart swell, though he knows he should not let it, not in his condition. If he cannot put his hands on an ailing body, he has no right to touch her. But he cannot help himself. He turns to wave. That's when he sees it. The light is not from the vestibule but from an upstairs window, the bathroom. She has not had time to pull down the shade. As he stands looking up, her head appears in the window, lurches forward out of sight, appears again. She is throwing up.

She brushes her teeth and gargles with mouthwash, but the bitter black taste lingers. It is still there when she gets into bed. The book does not put her to sleep. She keeps looking from the page to the clock on the night table, waiting for a reasonable time to turn out the light, though she knows darkness will not bring sleep any more than the book does. Finally, at eleven, a respectable hour, a normal hour, she closes the book, clicks off the lamp, and turns on her side.

Gracie.

The word comes back to her, almost as if someone is whispering it in the darkness. Charlie is whispering. Before she can stop it, her hand slides across the sheets. This time he will be there.

Summer 1950

She does not know how she got here. She does not remember getting out of bed. She has no recollection of going downstairs. She must have unlocked the front door. She never goes to sleep without making sure it's bolted, not with her and Amy alone in the house. But suddenly here she is, standing on the front lawn, screaming, howling the foulest words she knows, words she never uses when she's awake, not even in her head. And here, a moment later, is a police car. No sirens, thank heavens, no flashing lights, just one policeman behind the wheel and another getting out of the car and coming up the walk.

She is suddenly aware of her nightgown. It is white, and she knows from the days when she wore it with Charlie that her nipples and pubic hair are visible through the thin fabric. She turns and runs back into the house. The policeman's footsteps sound on the path behind her. She grabs a coat from the front closet, pulls it on, and tries to button it, but her hands are shaking. At least she is covered by the time he reaches the door.

'Mrs Gooding?' he asks.

'Yes.'

'Are you all right?'

'I'm fine.' A sound escapes. She does not know if it's a laugh or a sob.

He is still standing in the doorway. 'Can I come in?'

'I'm fine,' she insists.

'Well, if you don't mind my saying so, ma'am, you don't look fine. And you didn't sound fine out in the yard a minute ago. How 'bout if I call Mr Gooding?'

'Mr Gooding is dead.' It comes out as a shriek. Now he'll never let her alone.

'I meant Mr King Gooding.'

'He's out of town,' she almost shrieks again. Thank God he and Dorothy have gone to Maine. She is shamed enough without King's knowing.

'Is there someone else I can call, someone to stay with you for a while?'

'I'm fine,' she insists.

'With all due respect, ma'am, I can't leave you like this. Let me call a friend to come stay with you.'

She does not want anyone to know, but she has to get rid of him. She thinks of Millie. You'd never find Millie standing on the front lawn screaming obscenities. You wouldn't find Babe either, but you might find Claude. She gives him Babe's number.

'Do you mind if I use your phone?' he asks, but he has already moved to the small telephone table and picked up the receiver. The other policeman is standing in the doorway.

'Mommy.' The voice comes from the top of the stairs.

Grace looks up. Amy stands in her pink-and-white nightgown, her fist kneading her eye.

'Go back to bed, sweetheart. Everything is all right.'

'Is this Mr Huggins?' the policeman says into the phone.

'Mommy!' Amy's voice is more insistent.

'Go back to bed.' So is Grace's. She can feel the hysteria mounting again.

The policeman on the phone turns to the one standing in the doorway and tilts his head toward the top of the stairs. The other policeman steps into the hall and looks up at Amy. 'Hi,' he says.

She stands staring down at him.

'What's your name?'

She goes on staring.

He moves to the foot of the stairs. 'Want me to guess?'

She still does not answer, but she comes down a step. He isn't as nice as Uncle Claude, but she likes the way he smiles at her. And she likes his voice. His talk sounds like singing.

'I have a little girl just about your age.'

She takes a step back up. Who cares about his little girl?

'That's how I know little girls like to be read to. Would you like me to read you a story?'

'I'm too old to be read to.'

'Then would you like me to sing you back to sleep? Everyone says I have a fine voice. "Danny boy . . ." ' He sings the last two words.

'Do you know "You're not the only oyster in the stew"?'

'If you sing it for me, I bet I can learn it.' He starts up the stairs. Amy stands at the top, waiting for him.

'I'm calling from Mrs Gooding's house,' the other policeman says into the phone. 'She's fine, but I think somebody ought to be with her.'

Grace goes into the sunporch. She does not want to hear the rest.

As soon as she sees Babe, she starts to cry.

'Did the policeman tell you what happened?'

'Some of it,' Claude says, and Grace knows from the way he says it that the policeman has told them everything, including the dirty words and the fact that she was screaming them at Charlie.

It takes until dawn, but she finally agrees to let them call Mac.

'He'll understand,' Babe insists. 'He's a doctor. And there was that business of walking out of his office.'

Claude goes into the hall to place the long-distance call, though there is a phone in the kitchen. A few minutes later, he comes back. 'He wants to talk to you,' he says, as he picks up the extension and hands it to her.

'You need a rest,' Mac says. 'There's a sanitarium outside Boston.'

'You mean a crazy house?'

'I mean a sanitarium.'

'What will people say?' She is ashamed for herself, but she is also worried about Amy. She does not want her to become known as the daughter of a crazy woman.

'No one will know. We'll say you're on a long cruise or visiting friends in California.'

'Are you sure they won't know?'

'You didn't know I was there, did you? After I walked out of my office and couldn't go back.'

October 1950

Grace sits in her room on the third floor of the sanitarium, waiting. They are her oldest and dearest friends. But that was before.

Dr Gold says there is nothing to be ashamed of, but there is plenty to be ashamed of, and she is not thinking only of standing on the front lawn screaming obscenities at Charlie. She is ashamed of her existence. She is ashamed of being a woman alone in the world without a man, unclaimed, unvalued, a reproach to the laws of society and nature. When she found Charlie, she thought she had taken care of all that for life.

The nurse comes to the door and tells her that her visitors are here. She goes to the mirror over the dresser, smooths her hair, which is pulled back in a French twist, then straightens the jacket of the new suit her mother brought her, because most of her clothes hang on her as if they're still on hangers. At least she can say that for the sanitarium. She doesn't know if she's better, but she is thinner.

Going downstairs, she holds on to the banister. A carpet runs down the center of the stairs, but the wood on both sides of it is slippery, and she is afraid of falling. She is afraid of so much these days.

As she comes around the second-floor landing and starts down to the first, she hears their voices in the parlor. Millie's is shrill. Even Babe's sounds higher than usual. They are nervous. They are as nervous as she is.

Babe is sitting on the horsehair love seat. Millie is pacing among the Victorian chairs and tables and lamps. Grace stops in the entrance and strikes a pose with one hand on her hip and the other suspended in air. 'Ta da.'

Millie comes running. Babe follows. Millie hugs her first, then Babe. They tell her how wonderful she looks. The silence that follows ticks like a clock. They all start talking at once. They stop and look at one another. No one can be normal around her. Her mother and mother-in-law came together, just as Millie and Babe have, as if they need moral support. King and her father have not come at all. They claim the demands of work, but she knows her father is afraid and King is disgusted. Only Mac, when he came to visit, behaved normally.

'Listen,' Grace begins, and her voice is quieter than theirs, 'it's really nice of you to come see me.' She hesitates, debating whether to go on. 'And you don't have to be afraid. I'm not crazy or anything. They wouldn't let me go out with you if I was crazy.'

Babe and Millie shout her down with denials, but she notices they do not look at each other.

They drive to the restaurant where Mac took her for dinner on her first outing from the sanitarium, and by the time they finish lunch, they are easy with one another again. Then Babe and Millie insist on paying for her, and she remembers this is not an ordinary lunch.

'It's not my birthday,' she says.

'And don't think we won't remind you of that when we don't take you out for your birthday.' Babe picks up the check before Grace can get it.

'Oh, shoot,' Millie says, as she opens her handbag and takes out her wallet.

'What's wrong?' Grace asks.

'I just remembered I paid the diaper service yesterday and forgot to ask Al for money this morning.'

'Then let me pay. Please.'

'Absolutely not,' Babe says. 'I'll pay, and Millie can pay me back.'

On the return to the sanitarium, the ease evaporates in half-finished sentences and broken conversations. Grace stares out at the trees burning like fire in the sun-shot afternoon. She does not want to go back, but she does not know what she does want.

They drive past the sign saying THE WILLOWS – as if it is a country inn – through the big wrought-iron gates, and on toward the sprawling Victorian heap of wraparound porch, fretwork, and turrets nestled in the raucously colored trees. To Grace it does not feel as if they are driving toward it. It feels as if it is bearing down on them.

Babe pulls the car up in front of the wide steps. Before she can turn off the engine, Grace tells them not to bother coming in with her. They do not argue. Grace climbs out of the car, and Millie gets out of the backseat and into the front.

'You'll be home in no time,' Millie says.

'Hug Amy for me.' Grace takes a handkerchief out of her pocket and blows her nose.

'More than once,' Babe promises.

Grace stands at the bottom of the steps, watching the car grow smaller as it moves down

228

the drive, turns onto the road, and disappears. She knows this feeling of being left behind. It has become the story of her life.

She climbs the steps and goes into the eerily still building. At this hour, patients are lying down, taking their prescribed walks, or having sessions with their doctors. And she is adrift, floating in the vastness of the silence, like the helium balloon Amy let go of at a fair a few years ago. They stood watching it soar, higher and higher, until it disappeared into the emptiness. She wishes she could forget the sight of that balloon.

She climbs the wide hall staircase to the second floor, then the narrower one to the third. Her room, halfway down the corridor, faces west. Honeyed light floods in the windows, illuminating the flowered chintz upholstery and draperies, the rose-patterned carpet, and the Victorian furniture with its curves and bevels and rounded edges. There are no sharp surfaces in this room, no dark corners. In this room, there is nothing to be afraid of. So why is she filled with dread?

Dr Gold says she needs something to hold on to. An anchor to ground her so she will not float off like that helium balloon. To put it simply, Mrs Gooding, a husband. That is the cure for her illness.

January 1951

Amy is quiet going down the stairs. She does not want to wake her mother. She likes being alone

229

in the house. Not really alone, she wants her mother there, but doing something else, something that has nothing to do with her. The trouble is, her mother doesn't do much that doesn't have to do with her. Her mother even admits it. You're my whole life, she says. It's just the two of us. What would I do without you? It makes Amy feel bad, because there's plenty she likes to do without her mother. Now she wants to go downstairs and watch television in the sunporch. Her mother doesn't let her do that in the morning, even on Saturday mornings like this, but if she keeps the sound real low, her mother won't know.

She switches on the television and stands waiting for it to warm up. When it does, she moves the knob until Uncle Jim of *Acrobat Ranch* is whispering, then turns to go to the couch. That's when she sees it. The pictures are gone. There is nothing but row after row of hooks.

She cannot believe it. The pictures were there last night. Her mother could not have taken them down. Her mother loves that wall. It's her favorite thing in the whole house. As Amy goes on staring at it, she suddenly understands. Her mother is going crazy again. She will have to go back to the hospital.

Her mother does not go back to the hospital. Instead, a man arrives at the house, spreads big color-spattered cloths over the furniture and the floor, and paints the wall. When it's dry, Aunt Millie comes to help her mother hang a new picture.

'Just one photograph,' her mother says. 'One photograph can't hurt.'

'One photograph on the end table,' Aunt Millie says. 'We agreed a still life would look perfect on this wall.'

And a picture of a big bowl of flowers goes up.

The call surprises Grace. At first she does not recognize the name.

'Morris Banks,' he says a second time. 'Mac Swallow introduced us. When we ran into you at lunch with your friends a few months ago.'

Now she remembers. He was wide-shouldered and thick-necked, with a big square face under brown hair that stood up like a recently mown lawn. But there was nothing brutal about him. He reminded her of one of those gentle giants in children's stories. The only disconcerting thing about him was that he kept staring at her. That was how she knew he was a psychiatrist. He had spotted her as crazy right off. But why is he calling her now?

He is saying something about wanting to see South Downs, about living in Boston all his life and being tired of it, about looking for a small town where he can set up a practice.

'A psychiatrist here?'

'Pardon me?'

'I don't think you'd have many patients. People here don't go to psychiatrists.' Except me.

He laughs. 'Where did you get the idea that I'm

a psychiatrist? I'm a GP. What I'd like to be is a small-town GP. I was thinking you could show me around the area, and then we could have dinner.'

'I have a daughter.' She does not think of the statement as a non sequitur.

'I know. Amy. Mac told me all about her. I'd love to meet her. The three of us can have dinner. What do you say?'

She starts to say no. Even with Amy along, it is not a good idea. But she feels Dr Gold standing behind her, his hands on her shoulders, pushing her forward. She says yes.

'Now, this is just a ride around town and dinner,' her mother says. She is standing in front of the mirror over her dresser, screwing on an earring. 'We don't need some man coming in here, trying to take your daddy's place.'

Yes, we do, Amy thinks, but keeps her mouth shut.

Then her mother says something really strange. 'In the car, I want you to sit in the front seat, between us.'

'I'll be all squooshed.'

'You'll be fine.'

'Why can't I sit in back, like I do when you're with Aunt Babe or Aunt Millie?'

'Because I asked you to sit in the front between us.'

Amy lets it go. She does not want to do anything to ruin this.

When the bell rings, her mother tells her to go

down and open the door. She doesn't argue about that either, though her mother is ready too. She goes down the stairs fast, stops at the bottom to smooth her dress, then crosses to the door and peers through one of the long windows on either side of it. He's big, much taller than Uncle Claude, taller even than Uncle Al, and more solid. She can't see what color his hair is, because he has his hat on. He wears glasses – all men wear glasses – and his mouth is pursed as if he's whistling, but he must be doing it under his breath, because no sound is coming out.

She opens the door, and right away he says, 'You must be Amy,' then steps into the hall. He holds out his hand. 'I'm Dr Banks.'

She takes it the way her mother has taught her to. 'My mother will be right down.' Her mother hasn't told her to say that, but it sounds grown-up.

Then, as if her mother has been standing at the top of the stairs listening, she is coming down them.

Dr Banks helps her mother on with her coat. Then, as Amy is getting into hers, he takes it and helps her too. She likes the way he pays attention to her. He is definitely dad material.

In the car, she is squooshed as she knew she would be, but she wants to keep her mother happy. She wants her mother to do this again. And again and again. Not just for her. A man in the house will cheer up her mother too.

At the restaurant, he asks her mother what she'd like to drink, then repeats the question to her. She doesn't know what to say. She always has a glass of milk with supper, her mother makes her, but they're not eating supper yet. They haven't even looked at the menus.

'Would you like a Shirley Temple?'

'What's that?'

'You don't know what a Shirley Temple is? We'll have to remedy that.'

The next thing she knows, sitting in front of her is a fancy glass full of something red with a slice of orange and a big fat cherry on top. Dr Banks's glass is the same shape, but whatever is in his is clear. Her mother's glass is shaped differently. He lifts his glass and clinks it against her mother's, then hers. 'Happy days,' he says.

She tastes the drink, though she really wants to get to the cherry.

'How do you like it?' he asks.

'It's good.' She takes another sip. 'Why's it called a Shirley Temple?'

He takes a sip of his own drink and leans across the table toward her. 'I thought you'd never ask. The drink was invented at the Royal Hawaiian Hotel in Honolulu. When Shirley Temple was a little girl making all those movies, she used to stay at the hotel.'

'I never stayed at a hotel.'

He presses his lips together and raises his eyebrows until they make two points in his forehead. 'I never made a movie. We obviously have a lot in common.'

'Did you ever stay at that hotel?'

'I never stayed there, but I was in Honolulu once during the war, and I had a drink in the bar where they invented what you're drinking, or so they say.' He turns to her mother and says, 'Imagine someone like me going to Hawaii, let alone drinking at the Royal Hawaiian Hotel.' Then he tells her mother a long story about being poor, working his way through school, and helping his younger brothers and sisters. She picks up the cherry by its stem, puts it in her mouth, and pretends not to listen, but she doesn't miss a word.

The three of them stand in the front hall. Grace can tell from the way Amy leans against her that she is sleepy from the hour, the big meal, the excitement. She puts an arm around her shoulders. Hang on a little, the gesture says. She does not want her to go up to bed, not until he leaves.

Amy pulls out from her grasp, not the sullen withdrawal Grace knows too well. She is, in fact, all smiles and good manners. She is the child other people see. Grace would be proud of her, if she weren't so frightened of him.

'Thank you, Dr Banks,' Amy says. 'I had a very nice time.'

He takes her hand. 'So did I.' He hesitates a moment, then goes on. 'Do you think we know each other well enough?' He leans down and offers his cheek for a kiss. Amy blushes, but she plants one. Then she is gone.

This is what Grace has been dreading. This is what King warned her about. His words have been in the back of her head all night. Any decent man, any man who truly cares for you, will not try to take liberties. He will not try to take liberties with Amy rattling around over their heads, she is fairly sure of that, but she cannot even imagine kissing him. She cannot imagine kissing any man except Charlie, and she can barely remember kissing him.

She takes a step back from him and thanks him for the evening. 'Amy really did have a wonderful time.'

'So did I.' A moment passes. 'I guess that means you're the one we have to worry about.'

'I enjoyed it. Thank you.'

'Enough to repeat the experience?'

'Amy would love it.'

'I was thinking next time it could be grown-ups only.'

Liberties. The word rolls around in her head, fat and fleshy and shameful.

'What will I do with Amy?'

'I believe there are such things as babysitters. Dinner next week, just you and me, then the following Sunday I'll drive out and the three of us can do something. Maybe I can dig out my old ice skates. What do you say?'

She means to say no, but again Dr Gold nudges her, and it comes out as yes.

He moves a step toward her. She never should

have said yes. He takes her hand between his big ones and says thanks, then lets go and turns toward the door. He opens it, hesitates, and turns back to her.

'Look, I hope this doesn't scare you off, but I have to say something. You and Amy are quite a team. You're the family I've always dreamed of.' His big face flushes. 'Me and my big mouth,' he says, and is out the door in seconds.

Babe is the first person Mac sees as he walks into the drugstore. He did not want to come down to the store, he never wants to when he returns home for the weekend, but he does it for his father. His father likes to show him off, or at least let people see that he is not crazy, merely someone who prefers doing medical research in a big city to practicing medicine in a small town.

Babe is standing at the prescription counter. Mac hangs back to give her privacy, but when the assistant pharmacist says in a voice loud enough for him to hear, 'The directions for Mr Huggins are right on it; one at hour of sleep as needed,' he knows she is picking up sedatives for Claude.

She puts them in her handbag, turns away from the counter, and sees him. Her faces opens into a smile. She is genuinely happy to see him. The expression makes him realize how few people in town are. No matter how good a face his father tries to put on his flight, they still know there is something wrong with him.

'Come on, I'll buy you a cup of coffee.' He takes her arm and steers her to a booth.

They slip out of their heavy coats and scarves and gloves. When the coffee comes, she rubs her hands together in the cloud of steam rising from it and asks how things are in Boston, and he inquires what's going on in town, and all the time he is circling the real question.

'How's Grace?' he asks finally.

'Fine, as far as I can tell. Did you know your friend Dr Banks called her?'

Mac tries to keep his face impassive. 'How do you think he got her number? He even asked me if I minded.'

'And you said you didn't?'

He shrugs.

'But you do.'

He stubs out his cigarette in the ashtray, finds he has nothing to do with his hands, taps another out of the pack, and lights it. When he looks up, she is still watching him.

'You do mind,' she insists.

He goes on looking at her for a moment, wondering how far he can go. 'You and Claude married before the war,' he says finally.

'What does that have to do with anything?'

He inhales, then exhales. 'Promise you won't get angry?'

'As Grace has explained to me since her stay at the sanitarium, I can't control what I feel, Doctor,

238

only how I express it. I promise not to make a scene in Swallow's Drugstore.'

'Would you marry Claude the way he is now? No, that's not fair. Let me put it another way. Would he ask you to marry him the way he is now?'

'How did you know?'

'Remember the old playground taunt? Takes one to know one. How's he doing?'

'A little too interested in the news from Korea, if you ask me.'

'I understand how he feels.'

'You understand!' The word comes out as a hiss. 'Then you damn well better explain it to me. Because I'm just a woman, and I do not understand this morbid fascination. You all say you hate the war. But you can't stay away from it.' She stops suddenly, looks around, then back at him. 'And I wasn't going to make a scene.'

He reaches out and takes her hand. As he does, the cuff of his flannel shirt pulls back. Her eyes go to a thin welt of white flesh on the inside of his wrist, like a pale puffy worm crawling across the veins. She wonders if he has shown it to her intentionally. I know what you're going through, he is trying to tell her. And I will not inflict it on Grace.

CHAPTER 12

MILLIE

April 1948

From where Jack sits in the backseat of the car, he can see the grown-ups standing under the trees. Amy is the only kid. She's allowed to be there because they're burying her daddy, but he has to wait in the car. Aunt Grace wanted his mommy to bury his daddy too, but his mommy said he's already buried in France. Then she tipped her head toward him and said *PLEASE* to Aunt Grace.

He kneels on the backseat and rests his arms on the open window. The men are still shoveling dirt into the big hole, but his mommy and daddy and the rest of them are walking around like they don't know what to do. They look like the kids on the street when they can't decide what to play. Only this game is over. He knows because Amy's grandpa, Mr Gooding, is coming along the path toward the car. His head is down, like a football player running a field. He takes out a big white handkerchief, blows his nose, and jams the handkerchief back in his pocket.

240

Jack starts to get off his knees. He is afraid of Mr Gooding. Even Amy says he's mean. His daddy – this daddy, not the one buried in France – doesn't like him. Jack is not sure why. But before he can slide down to where Mr Gooding can't see him, Mr Gooding is standing next to the car looking down at him. His face has a lot of loose skin, like Tommy Janeway's basset hound, but his neck is skinny.

'You're Pete Swallow's boy.' The way he pronounces *boy* makes Jack think of corks popping up in water. He doesn't sound so mean. 'Young Pete Swallow, aren't you?'

He does not know what to answer. His mommy says his name is Baum, like hers and Daddy's and his sisters', and everyone calls him Jack, but when he started kindergarten last fall, and the teacher read out the names, she read Peter John Swallow Baum, then looked up and said, your mother says you're called Jack. Sometimes Grandma and Grandpa Swallow call him little Pete, but not when his mommy is around.

'I guess so,' Jack says.

'You guess so,' Mr Gooding repeats. 'Are you young Pete Swallow or aren't you?'

Jack rocks back and forth on his knees. Swallow sounds like a nice name, like he could fly, like Superman. And it would be fun to pretend. 'I am.'

Mr Gooding goes on staring down at him. 'You look like him.' His voice is so soft Jack almost doesn't hear what he says.

Mr Gooding reaches into his pocket, then draws out his hand. A dollar bill flutters in the breeze. 'This is for you, Pete.' He gives him the bill, then turns and walks away.

Jack looks down at the money. He cannot believe it. He gets ten cents a week allowance for making his bed and bringing in the milk bottles in the morning. Mr Gooding gave him a whole dollar just for being Pete Swallow.

He can't wait to tell his mommy. She is coming down the path toward the car now. He opens his mouth to say, look what Mr Gooding gave me. Just for being Pete Swallow. He closes his mouth. He likes having a secret. All the way home he keeps saying it in his head. Pete Swallow. Pete Swallow. Pete Swallow.

Summer 1950

'Keep your eye on the ball,' Al calls as Jack swings the bat and misses.

Jack retrieves the ball and throws it back, and Al pitches again. This time the thwack of bat hitting ball resounds through the small yard.

'A-okay,' Al calls.

He pitches again. Jack swings furiously. The ball goes past him.

'You don't have to hit a homer every time, champ. Think about connecting with the ball, not knocking it out of the stands.'

Al pitches again, and Jack hits it, and Al says

they might as well call it a day. He likes to end on a triumphant note.

As he collects the bat and ball and glove, and they start up the back steps to the house, he cannot help thinking about it, though he would never mention it. He is glad he and Millie had girls. If they'd had a son, he would not have been unhappy – who could be unhappy about having a son? – but he would have been on guard against himself. He would have worried about playing favorites. He would have weighed his love for Jack and his love for the other boy, who was not born, on his own scale of justice. This is easier. You love girls differently from the way you love boys.

Jack is chattering about the movie he saw the previous Saturday. You talk to boys differently from the way you talk to girls. And they talk to you differently. Betsy and Susan are too young for the movies, but they will not come home nattering about guns and battles and imitating the way men die. Why do little boys always clutch their chests or stomachs as they pretend to fall, as if the rest of the body is invulnerable? The girls will recount stories of love and romance and happily-ever-after last scenes.

'Nuts!' Jack says. 'That's what the guy tells the Kraut when he says surrender or die. Nuts!' he shouts to the sky, and Al reaches over and tousles his head. It releases the strangely moving scent children carry in from play, a blend of grass and fresh air and sweat too young to go sour.

'And then Rodriguez gets it, but they can't carry

243

him out because of the snow, so they hide him under a jeep and promise to come back for him. Only when they do, he's dead.' He stops at the top of the steps and looks up at Al.

'Dad,' he says, and Al knows what is coming. 'Did you ever kill anyone? In the war, I mean.'

'It's different on a ship. You're pretty far away.'

It is different on a ship. You do not see death close up, unless your ship is the one that takes the fish or the bomb, but you see death. A ship is not a free ride.

'Did you see guys die?' Jack's voice still throbs with an undercurrent of excitement. He'll take second best to killing. Nuts! the Americans shout in the face of slaughter.

Al stops on the small wooden back porch, searching for an answer, and suddenly he is a thousand miles to the east, standing on a deck in another world. The convoy is zigzagging through a calm summer night, with a moon thin as gauze rising on his right and a blush of pink hugging the horizon on his left, and he feels the strange peace that sometimes came over him at a crystalline sunset or silvery sunrise on a clement ocean, despite the knowledge of submarines beneath and bombers overhead. Then something in his peripheral vision makes him turn his head. He is just in time to see it. The next ship over cracks in half, the two parts slip into the sea, and hundreds of men go with them. It does not happen in the blink of an eye. He knows, because he keeps blinking in disbelief. But it happens in minutes. It is not the same as having a buddy die in your arms. It is not the same as the ghoulish sight of the men in lifeboats waving for help, who, when they came alongside, turned out not to be men waving for help but bodies frozen upright and rocked by the sea. But the speed of it, and the closeness, and the thought that maybe tomorrow or in three months or in two minutes still stalk him. He is not like Claude, who starts at the sound of a car back-firing, or Mac, whose eyes are as dead as those of all the men he has failed to keep alive, but as long as he lives, he will never forget the sight of that ship cracking open like an egg and spilling its men into the sea. They rescued some. Not enough.

'Yes,' he says to Jack.

'What's it like?'

'Something I hope you never experience,' Al says, but he knows Jack does not agree. He is almost eight years old; he has just seen the fog lift, and the American bombers fly over, and the men of the 101st Airborne Division march out of the woods, filthy, decimated, wounded, but singing, sound off, one, two, sound off, three, four; and nothing is going to persuade him that all that isn't more fun than a barrel of monkeys.

October 1950

There is no reason to make a fuss about it, Millie insists. She forgot to ask him for money before they went to visit Grace, so Babe paid for lunch, and now she has to pay her back. It's not exactly a crime. 'The three of us are always borrowing and paying one another back.'

'That's different,' he says.

'Why?'

He does not want to explain it to her. He loves her innocence. He is tired of his own paranoia, and his parents' paranoia, and his grandparents', and that of generations before them. For all he knows, that's another reason he married her. Because she does not know what people say about Jews and money. Because in the playground of her childhood, no one tossed a penny on the cement and yelled Jew at the first one to bend for it. Because no one ever accused her of Jewing someone down. Why doesn't anyone ever accuse his good Yankee neighbors of Protestanting someone down? I'll tell you why. Because Yankees are frugal. Jews are money-grubbing. But if she hasn't heard the rumor, he is not going to tell her. His silence is one of the secrets of their happy marriage, and it is happy. The dissension his parents and his uncle and Millie's friends – he suspects, though she has never said – predicted has never surfaced.

He takes money from his pocket, comes up behind her at the sink, and tucks the bills into the top of her blouse. Her skin inside her bra is warm, and he lets his hand linger.

'Forget it,' he says.

But he cannot. He is still thinking about it the

next morning in the shower. Months later, he continues to think about it. The idea is not original. Others are trying it. But nobody, as far as he knows, in Massachusetts. He can get in on the ground floor.

January 1951

'It was touch-and-go,' Millie tells Al that night. 'At the last minute, Grace wanted to put one photograph back up.'

'Would that be so terrible?' he asks.

'Paintings go on walls. Photographs belong on tables.'

He is standing beside her drying dishes, and he snaps to attention and salutes. 'Aye, aye, sir.'

Jack looks up from the kitchen table where he is doing his homework. He likes to see his dad salute. His dad says most people don't do it right. They just put their hands next to their foreheads, all floppy, and think they're saluting. But he taught Jack to do it properly.

'You know,' his dad says quietly, not quite a whisper, but almost, and Jack knows what that means. He pretends to go back to his spelling list, but he is listening. 'It wouldn't hurt to have one picture around. For . . .' Out of the corner of his eye, Jack sees his dad tip his head toward him.

'We've been through this,' his mom says, and Jack knows from the tone of her voice that that's the end of that.

Only it isn't, because as he's getting into bed, he hears them talking again. Their voices float up through the big iron grate where the heat comes into the room. He lies down on his stomach to hear better.

'We ought to have some trace of him around,' his dad says. 'It's not right. If it makes me uncomfortable, I can imagine how Jack feels about it.'

'Jack doesn't feel anything about it,' his mom says. 'You're the only father he knows.'

'Sure, and he's my son, but still. The way things are now, it's almost as if he's more a presence in the house than if we had a picture of him around. Jack sees pictures at his grandparents'. He must wonder.'

'Oh, shoot.'

'I don't want to argue about it.'

'No, all I meant was oh, shoot, I forgot to iron your new dress shirt.'

Jack hears her feet crossing the kitchen, then the squeak of the ironing board opening.

'You're going to iron it at this hour?'

'I'm not about to let you walk into that bank in Boston tomorrow in one of your old shirts when you have a brand-new one with French cuffs.'

Al refuses to see it as a bad-luck omen. He does not believe in luck, at least the kind that has to do with jinxes and curses and primitive mumbo jumbo. He just doesn't want to lose his confidence. He wants to walk into that bank in Boston with all flags flying. But as he pulls up at a traffic light on the road out of South Downs and recognizes King's big gray Cadillac in front of him, the humiliation returns.

'You asked me, I would have told you not to go to King Gooding,' his uncle said afterward. 'An anti-Semite of the first water.'

'You think the bankers in Boston aren't anti-Semites?'

'In Boston, they're not afraid you're going to make a bundle on this meshugeneh idea and move in next door. Plus, you came home. His son didn't. For the man, I got no sympathy. For his loss, my heart breaks. You got any idea what my sister would be like, you didn't come home? Ach, I don't like to think about it.'

His uncle was right. He never should have gone to King Gooding. He'd already had one go-round with him when he wanted to open the appliance store. But this is different. This will make money for the bank too. And the government says he has a right to the loan.

The G.I. Bill is a great idea. He's in love with the goddamn G.I. Bill. It's the people who administer it who screw things up. Look at the raw deal they gave Frank Hart. Naomi's husband got himself accepted at a college, but the veterans' counselor refused to sign off on it. He told Frank he would be better off going to trade school. No jobs for college-educated colored men, he told him. The guy takes night courses for two years to

249

get into college – and how many guys, let alone colored guys, will do that? – then the VA counselor tells him, no deal, buddy, you belong in trade school. Just as King said, no deal, Baum, the government's money is not for the likes of you.

King glances in the rearview mirror and recognizes Al Baum in the car behind him. He can't get away from the man. Last time he stopped at Grace's to make sure Frank Hart was shoveling her snow and not just taking his money and saying he was shoveling her snow, Baum and his wife and that brood of theirs were there. Poor young Pete Swallow, to get mixed up with that. Then a couple of weeks later, Baum comes in with some cockamamie idea for a new business. Business! It sounded more like a Ponzi scheme, though no one, especially not Baum, is going to get rich on it. The idea makes the appliance store look like a sure thing. How many times does he have to say no before the man understands?

It has nothing to do with the fact that he's a Yid. Hell, that's one thing you can say for Yids: They know how to make money. But this is the most harebrained scheme he's ever heard. Baum's wife forgets to ask him for money one morning – and why isn't she on an allowance, anyway? – and he comes up with some pie-in-the-sky plan to do away with cash.

A cardboard card, he explained, like the ones his uncle issues to get people to shop at

Diamond's. Only this card will be good at all the stores in town. All you have to do is have an account at First Farmers Bank, and you can go into any store in town – not just stores but restaurants and maybe even the movies – and hand them the card. Then the bank reimburses the merchant and collects payment from the customer, and everyone comes out ahead. The customer has convenience, the stores and restaurants do more business, and the bank gets a percentage of the transactions.

'Why not pool halls?' he asked.

'What?' Baum said.

'Why stop at stores and restaurants? Why not pool halls?'

But Baum just went on talking. He didn't even get the joke.

King did not tell him how crazy the idea was. He just said it wasn't right for First Farmers. Maybe a bigger bank, he suggested. Maybe one with a couple of branches in the state. That way people could use the cardboard card in the next town over. Before you know it, they'll be using it all over the state. He could not resist having a little fun with him. But the Yid still didn't get the joke. He really thought that people were going to stop using money and start running up bills for every little thing they bought.

BOOK IV

1952

CHAPTER 13

BABE

January 1952

Babe stands in the window of the darkened living room, staring out into the winter evening. The snow has stopped, and the plows have come through, but the front yard is a ghostly expanse of white. No footprint or animal track or fallen branch mars the icy loneliness. Overhead, light that started out thousands, millions, of years ago burns holes in the cloudless black sky. The inhuman beauty of it assaults her with her own insignificance. When the phone rings, she dashes for it.

'I hate to bother you,' Grace says, 'especially on a night like this, but the babysitter just called. She has a cold, and her mother won't let her go out. Could you stay with Amy for a few hours? I wouldn't ask, but we're supposed to have dinner with the Johnsons.' She drops her voice conspiratorially. 'Morris is thinking of opening a practice here, and he has to sound out the other doctors. I'd say I'd drop Amy there, but it will be less disruptive if she sleeps in her own bed and can walk to school in the morning.'

Babe thinks it will also be less disruptive if Amy is not awakened by shouting in the night. She says she'll be happy to drive over and stay with Amy for the evening.

'I won't be late,' Grace promises. 'Morris has to get back to Boston.'

Babe leaves a covered plate for Claude on the stove and makes another dinner for Amy and her in Grace's kitchen.

'Do you think my mother is going to marry him?' Amy asks as soon as they sit down in the small breakfast nook.

Babe stares across the table into the dark slanting eyes and full lips, and for a moment she is looking at Charlie.

'Do you? I've only met him occasionally. You're with them all the time.'

Amy stops with a fork full of pork chop in midair. 'I think he's going to ask her, but maybe that's just because I want him to.'

'You like him?'

She nods.

'Well, for what it's worth, I don't think he'd be talking about leaving Boston and opening a practice here if he wasn't planning to marry her.'

'He says he's always wanted to live and work in a small town.'

'What do you want to bet he has never lived and worked in a small town?'

Amy looks up from her plate. Her black eyebrows are set in a quizzical frown.

'That's a joke,' Babe says.

'How come your jokes aren't like everyone else's?'

'Oh, sweetie, how I wish I knew the answer to that.'

Amy stabs a string bean but does not lift it to her mouth.

'Do you think she'll say yes?'

'I don't think she'd be seeing this much of him if she wasn't thinking of marrying him.' The word comes hurtling out of nowhere. Tease.

She is on her way upstairs to kiss Amy good night when the phone rings. She picks up the receiver.

'How are things on the babysitting front?' Claude asks.

'I should be home soon.'

'It's okay. I'm a grown-up. I can be left alone.'

'I didn't mean that,' she says, though she did. 'Is something wrong?' Other than our whole lives.

'I just wanted to hear your voice.'

How long has it been since he said something like that? Since he called from Fort Dix right before he shipped out.

'No, more than that. I wanted to tell you something. I know things have been rough on you—'

'Not as rough as on you,' she interrupts, but he ignores her and keeps going.

'I know I've been rough on you. But not anymore.'

She cannot imagine where this is coming from. She does not dare ask.

'I've been sitting here thinking about it.'

Don't, she wants to shout. Stop thinking about it. Forget about it.

'What I'm trying to say is I know I haven't been exactly easy to live with. I also know you deserve better.'

'I'm not complaining.' The hell I'm not. You think because you don't say anything, he doesn't know how you feel?

'Maybe not, but I wanted to tell you that from now on things will be different. From now on you won't have anything to complain about. That's a promise.'

'In that case, I'd better hurry home.'

'Take your time. No rush. And drive carefully,' he adds. 'The roads are icy.'

She hangs up the phone and starts up the stairs again. She will not get her hopes up. He has promised new starts in the past, though he has never telephoned her at someone else's house with the news. But she cannot help herself. She is her mother all over again, believing her father's promises of abstinence and hard work and putting a little by for the children.

But something about this call is different. From now on you won't have anything to complain about. She stands on the landing, remembering his buddy Dumbrowsky's letter to his wife. You'll be better off without me. Then he went into the garage, closed the door behind him, and turned on the car engine. And he wasn't the only one. She sees the welt of puckered white flesh across Mac's wrist. And she pictures the bottle on the right side of the top shelf of their medicine cabinet. Take one at hour of sleep as needed. Occasionally she checks the contents, though she hates herself for snooping. A few days ago, she was pleased to see that the bottle was almost full. She thought he wasn't taking the pills because he didn't need them. It never occurred to her that he was hoarding them.

She is down the hall in a couple of steps and swoops into Amy's room. 'Up, Amy, up!'

The light is still on, but she has fallen asleep waiting for Babe. She rubs her eyes.

Babe grabs a sweater and a pair of dungarees. 'Come on, sweetie. On the double.' She pulls back the covers and begins tugging the sweater over Amy's head.

'I have to take off my pajamas.'

'No time.'

'Where are we going?'

Babe does not answer. This is not something you can explain to an eleven-year-old. She hustles her down the stairs, bundles her into her coat, pulls on her own, and races for the car, Amy in tow.

She tries not to speed. Then hears him again. Take your time. No rush. Pills are slow, but a razor to the wrist is speedy. A gunshot is instant. Her foot inches down on the accelerator. A car comes around the bend, its brights blinding her so she does not see the patch of black ice. She feels the car begin to skid and manages to resist the urge to slam on the brakes. They slide along the shoulder for what seems like a lifetime, then they're back on the road.

She swerves into the driveway. From here, she can see no lights. She pulls the car into the garage and starts to turn off the ignition, then changes her mind. She cannot take Amy in with her. She does not know what she is going to find. She leaves the engine running – the garage door is open – and switches on the heater. She forgot to on the drive over.

'You wait here, sweetie.'

'Alone?'

'I'll only be a minute.'

'It's dark.'

'Wait!' She sounds like Claude. 'I'll turn the light on in the garage,' she calls back as she sprints to the switch beside the door, then into the house.

He is not in the den. She pounds up the four steps and races through the kitchen, on to the dining room, and around through the living room. He is not there either.

She starts up the stairs to the second floor. The house is quiet except for her own breathing. It sounds like a buzz saw in her ears.

The door to the bedroom is closed. He rarely closes it when he is alone in the house. A dim light seeps out from under it. She has never taken so long to cross that small hall. She opens the door. He is stretched out in bed with a book propped up on his chest.

She stands staring at him.

He looks up. 'What's wrong?'

She shakes her head. She cannot speak.

He gets out of bed, comes over, and puts his arm around her. That's when she realizes how much she is sweating. She is sweating the way he does in his nightmares.

'You feel as if you ran all the way. What's wrong?' he repeats.

'Nothing.' She coughs up the word, a bone in her throat. 'Just give me a minute to catch my breath.' She remembers Amy. 'Oh, my God, I'll be right back.'

'Where are you going?'

'I left Amy in the car. I have to drive her home.'

'You brought Amy with you and left her in the car?'

She sees the understanding sink into his face and is on her way down the stairs before he can say anything.

He is sitting at the kitchen table, his good hand curled around a drink, when she gets home.

'I got back before Grace.'

'So our little secret is safe. Unless Amy talks about a strange ride in the night.' His voice curdles with cruelty, but he cannot help himself.

He watches her as she goes to the counter where

he has left the bottle, takes a glass down from the cabinet, half fills it with scotch, and drops in a few ice cubes. She is still wearing her coat, and the bulk makes her movements awkward. Her face is gray; her cheeks sag. She is – he never believed he would think this – ugly.

She carries the drink to the table, sits across from him, and shrugs out of her coat. There is a stain on the front of her sweater. It is not the sort of thing he would normally notice. Now it disgusts him.

'What did you think I was going to do?'

She does not answer.

'Or were you overcome by a sudden need to see me?' Why is he doing this? She was worried about him. She loves him. That's why he's doing it. He does not deserve love. 'You thought I was going to pull a Dumbrowsky, right?'

She still does not answer.

'Go into the garage and turn on the engine?'

'It was the line about my not having anything to complain about from now on.'

'Sorry to disappoint you' – why is he doing this? – 'but I'm not that much of a hero. I have no intention of turning on the engine or even downing that bottle of pills in the medicine cabinet so you can live happily ever after with someone else.'

'Stop it.'

'Stop what? Talking about killing myself so you can find someone else?' He smirks. He never thought he was capable of gratuitous cruelty. Then again, he never thought he could kill.

He takes a swallow of his drink. 'But I won't put up a fight if you want to divorce me.' Grandstander.

He has spoken the forbidden word, the one she would wash her own mouth out with soap for uttering.

'Please stop it,' she says.

'But that's as far as I'll go. Divorce, yes. Suicide, no.' Prick.

'Stop it!' This time she shouts.

Is that what he wanted, to get her as angry as he is? Because suddenly he is calm.

He stands. 'Come on, it's late.'

As he follows her up the stairs, he waits for the desire that is often the aftermath of spent anger to rise. He is limp as a towel.

Even as she does it, she knows she is making a mistake. Marie Bours, the girl her cousin Louis left at the altar, whispers a warning in the darkness, but she does not listen. At least wait until morning. The light will burn away this rush to self-destruction. But perhaps she is not rushing toward self-destruction. Perhaps she is grasping at freedom. He has said the word. Divorce. But she cannot leave him, so she will force him to leave her. She would rather be a slut, whore, temptress, tease, than a woman who walks out on her husband when he is down.

He is lying with his back to her. She puts a hand on his shoulder. 'Are you awake?'

The dark shadow that is his head nods.

'I want to talk to you.'

He groans. Talk to me, she used to say. Tell me what's wrong. Tell me what you see in those dreams.

He turns on his back. 'I meant it about the divorce,' he says to the ceiling. 'If that's what you want.'

'This is about me. It has nothing to do with you.' Is that true?

He turns his head on the pillow to look at her. 'Go on.'

'Remember that letter about how grateful you were to me for following you to all those camps?'

'I was. I am.'

'Something happened to me then.'

'You mean losing the baby?'

'Something else. Before that.' There it is, the timing. He is a smart man. He will put it together.

His hand moves toward the lamp on the night table.

'No! Don't turn on the light. I won't be able to say this if you turn on the light.'

He rolls on his side to face her. She wishes he hadn't. It would be easier to tell this to his back.

She has difficulty starting, but once she does, the words flood out, a rush of guilt, rage, and relief so intense it runs through her body in spasms. The stench of the station bathroom. The door bursting open. The sweaty palm stifling her screams. The doctor who wanted to lock up all army wives for endangering good American boys. Tease. The last word comes out like a sob. Then the room goes silent.

They lie facing each other in the darkness. She can see the outline of his features, but she cannot read his expression. As she heard the story, her cousin Louis gave Marie a couple of slaps in the bargain. If he hits her, he will make it easy. She will not live with a man who beats her. She is not that much her mother. But she knows Claude will not hit her.

He puts his arms around her and draws her to him. At first she cannot interpret the movement of his body. Then she realizes. For the second time in their life together, he is crying. The thought that she might have lost him, the idea that she tried to drive him away, terrifies her.

He lies on his back with her head on his shoulder, his hand cradling her skull. He is remembering their running toward each other on the platform that night; and the rooming house with the lumpy bed, their first bed; and the hospital room, the memory of which still, after all these years, brings back the sickly sweet reek of flowers and loss. Through all of it, and the months and years after, she has not said a word. She has kept it from him, a lie of sorts, he supposes. If the baby had lived, she never would have told him. But she has told him. Something went off in her tonight, his imagined suicide, and the story spilled out, just as Herb's brains did. He cradles her head on his shoulder with his good hand, just as he held Herb's head, and cries for all the casualties.

August 1952

Babe and Amy lie side by side on the blanket, each propped up over a book. They often come to the pond together. Grace refuses to join them. After she came home from the hospital, she began coming to the pond again, and before she and Morris married, they took Amy skating here all the time, but she has not been back since she and Morris returned from their wedding trip to Bermuda last May. Babe does not mind. She feels a companionable glow spending time alone with Amy like this, more companionable perhaps than mother and daughter. She has many of the pleasures and few of the responsibilities. The thought is not new, but it is heresy, so she keeps it to herself.

Amy looks up from her book, and, sensing the movement, Babe does too.

'Can I stay at your house tonight?' Her braces flash in the sunlight as she speaks. Then she must remember they're there, because she presses her lips together.

Babe puts her finger between the pages of *The Caine Mutiny* to hold her place.

'We don't call it the Amy Gooding Bedroom for nothing.'

Amy grins, her braces momentarily forgotten, then returns to *Anne of Avonlea*. A curtain of dark hair falls forward to hide her face. As a baby, her hair was curly, but now it is as straight as Charlie's was and iridescent in the beating sunlight.

'Providing your mother says it's okay.'

She looks up again. 'Can't we just tell her?'

'You know your mother better than that.' Forget heresy. This is treachery.

Amy crosses her hands over the book and rests her face on them. 'But I really want to stay with you.'

Babe looks out over the child-churned water, debating. 'Look, kiddo,' she says finally, 'I don't want to pry, but are you angry at your mother about something?'

She shakes her head no.

'Because you can tell me if you are.' Heresy, treachery, and child larceny.

She mumbles something into the book.

'What?'

She turns her face away from Babe so she can speak but not be seen. 'I can't tell you. I'm not supposed to tell anyone. I promised.'

Babe's senses prick up as surely as if beneath all the noise of the women and children she hears a snake slithering through the grass. She knows this instinctively. She knows this from experience. Not her father. That was one vice he did not succumb

267

to. But she and her sisters and female cousins learned early never to let Uncle Jerome get them alone. Just as the boys knew to steer clear of Father Sebastian. But Morris is such a sweet man – the gentle giant in children's stories is the way Grace describes him – and a doctor. And Father Sebastian was a priest. And this does not happen only below Sixth Street, though that is what people above Sixth Street would have you believe.

'Who made you promise?'

'My mother.'

'Not your dad?' The last word doesn't taste right. She used to think it was the newness, but now she wonders if she hasn't sensed something all along.

'My mother,' Amy repeats.

Babe is still uneasy. She cannot imagine Grace sacrificing her daughter to protect Morris, but neither can she shake the feeling that she has put her finger on something.

She reaches over and puts her hand on Amy's head. Her hair is hot as metal. 'Okay, kiddo, then don't tell me. But if you change your mind, remember, your secret will be safe with me.'

When Babe and Amy pull into the driveway of Grace's house the next morning, Naomi's older son, Frankie, is pushing the heavy lawn mower across the backyard. The sun-baked air undulates in waves around him. Sweat covers his face and makes dark half-moons under his arms. When he turns to push the mower back the other way, she sees that the back of his shirt is soaked through. He's a kid, only a couple of years older than Amy. He ought to be at the pond.

Amy reaches in back for her canvas satchel, and they get out of the car. As they start toward the house, they wave to Frankie. He takes one hand off the mower to wave back and keeps going.

Grace is standing at the sink, peeling peaches. A Pyrex pie plate lined with a flour-dusted circle of dough sits on the counter. The scene is picture perfect, a spread in one of the women's magazines she and Millie subscribe to. Except it can't be, because in the world of those glossy pictures, mothers do not ask their daughters to keep secrets.

'Thanks for the overnight,' Amy says as she starts up the stairs.

'The pleasure is entirely mine,' Babe answers. 'I'm going to the pond tomorrow, if the weather's good. Let me know if you want to come along.'

'Karen telephoned,' Grace calls after her daughter. 'She said something about the pond tomorrow.'

'Sorry,' Babe says.

'Nothing to be sorry for.' Grace smiles, sweeter than the pie she's making, which she likes tart. 'Iced coffee or tea? We can take it out on the porch.'

Babe says either, and Grace pours two glasses of iced coffee, puts in two long hollow silver spoons that double as straws, and they carry them out to the screened-in porch Morris has added to the house. He bought the house from King and, as far as Babe can tell, is doing his best to erase all traces of the older man. The effort is mutual. King stopped coming by as soon as Morris began turning up. And King had one more trick up his sleeve. The day before Grace married Morris in a small ceremony in the living room, King had a heart attack. Mild, the doctor said, but enough to cast a pall.

They settle at opposite ends of the wicker sofa. The lawn mower is still growling through the hot morning, and they have to raise their voices to talk over it.

'Amy asked if she could stay over,' Babe says. 'It wasn't my idea.'

Grace stares into her iced coffee and says nothing.

'I was a little surprised, to tell you the truth.'

Still nothing.

'Is she all right?'

Grace's head snaps up. 'Why shouldn't she be?'

'I don't know. She seemed kind of moody yesterday. I asked her if anything was bothering her, and she said she promised not to tell.'

The lawn mower comes to a stop, and the sound of silver spoon hitting crystal glass as Grace stirs her coffee pings into the sudden silence. To Babe it is the sound of polite society, and skeletons in closets, and crimes and misdemeanors swept under the rug.

'This has to do with Morris, doesn't it? He's bothering her.'

Grace sits staring at her but does not answer. 'Well, is he?'

Grace goes on staring at her. Suddenly her mouth opens, and the laughter comes rolling out. There is no joy in the sound. It turns Grace's face, with its pale skin stretched over the beautiful thin bones, haggard and mean. The laughter stops as abruptly as the sound of the lawn mower did.

'Bothering? Since when did you become so polite? You mean sex. You mean is Morris making advances, touching, sleeping with – oh, damn, that's a euphemism too. I wish I could use four-letter words when I'm not standing in the yard in my nightgown. No, that is not the problem, thank heavens. Amy and Morris are just fine.'

'Are you sure?' Now that Babe has latched on to the idea, she cannot let it go.

'Amy and Morris are the best thing about this marriage.'

'Then what?'

'Nothing. Everything is fine. We're the perfect family. The family Morris says he's always dreamed of. And he didn't have to do a thing. Instant family. Like instant coffee. Just add hot water and stir.' She starts to cry.

Babe watches the tears run down Grace's cheeks and thinks, exults, I am not the only one. Her relief is shameful, but so was her envy of what she thought was Grace's normality at being married to a man who does not thrash in the night, or take swings at himself in the bathroom mirror,

271

or make love as if he is wreaking vengeance. She slides down the wicker sofa and puts her hand on Grace's shoulder. She can be magnanimous now.

'I never should have married again,' Grace says. 'I should have left well enough alone. I had Amy. I had my memories of Charlie. Why did I go and spoil it?'

'You didn't spoil it. But you have to give Morris a chance. It's not his fault he isn't Charlie. No one is ever going to be Charlie. But he's a good man. He's crazy about you and Amy.'

Grace sits staring at her, then shakes her head. 'Oh, Babe, I know you're the smart one. The one who reads all the books. But about some things you really are a babe in the woods.'

Babe clatters down the porch steps. No one likes to be called naïve, especially by someone she considers more naïve. The charge brings out her seditious side. Maybe that's why she makes the offer to Frankie, though later she will swear to Claude she did it out of kindness, or maybe only thoughtlessness.

He is walking down the driveway as she backs out, and she asks if she can give him a lift.

He stands staring at her for a moment. He is a good-looking boy, tall and reedy like his mother, with sharp cheekbones and tight close-cropped hair. He is wearing sunglasses, so she cannot see his eyes.

'If it's no trouble, Mrs Huggins,' he says. Naomi has raised him carefully.

'None at all.' She reaches over to push open the door on the passenger side. He climbs in but keeps his distance, hugging the door.

She asks how his mother is, and he says fine, and they make halting small talk. The idea comes to her at the intersection. She can turn south toward her old neighborhood, though the Negro corner of it is even more disreputable, or north toward the pond, which is only a short detour on the way to Riverview and her own house. He looks as if he could use a cooling off.

'If you like, I can drop you at the pond. It isn't much out of the way.'

His head swivels to her. She still cannot see his eyes, but she does not have to. The alarm is written all over his face. It comes to her suddenly. She has never seen a Negro at the pond. She is horrified at her blunder. Then she is disgusted that she never noticed the absence.

September 1952

The news is all over town before the grills are fired up for the Labor Day barbecues. Babe only wishes she was there to see it, but she has been in the kitchen all morning, dicing potatoes for the potato salad and shredding cabbage for the coleslaw. The barbecue is at Millie's. Now that Millie and Al have bought a house in Riverview, they have a real yard for it. But all three women pitch in to do the cooking.

Babe hears the news from Grace, who hears it from Morris, who has come back from a house call. Some doctors are beginning to refuse to make house calls, but Morris picks up his black doctor's bag at the ring of a telephone. That's another reason his patients adore him.

'Naomi's son Frankie and two other boys.' Grace's voice on the other end of the telephone line pulses with excitement.

'I assume all three were Negro,' Babe says.

'Of course. That's the point. They were trying to make trouble.'

'Not trouble, a stand.'

'I feel sorry for Naomi.'

'Why would you feel sorry for her? She ought to be proud.'

'A lot of people don't like what he did.'

'Then let them get out of the pond.'

'They did.'

Babe does not know why she is surprised. She remembers a wife she knew in one of the southern camp towns during the war. She was from New Jersey and explained smugly that the town she hailed from was nothing like this bigoted backwater where they'd washed up. The pool in her hometown was integrated. Negroes were permitted to swim there one day a week, then it was drained, cleaned, and refilled for whites.

'Look, Babe,' Grace goes on, 'I feel sorry for colored people – Negroes – too. All that stuff that goes on in the South.'

'Apparently not only in the South.'

'But when you have children, it's different.'

'Exactly. You have to set an example. If I were Frankie's mother, I'd be proud.'

'If you were anybody's mother, you'd be terrified. I'm sorry, that may sound unkind, but it's true. There isn't a mother in this town who isn't scared to death of polio.'

'What does polio have to do with it?'

'You know.'

'No, I don't know,' though she is beginning to think she does.

'Letting Negroes swim in the pond.'

'What are you saying? That Negroes spread polio?'

Grace does not answer.

'You're a doctor's wife. You know better than that.'

'All I know is you can't be too careful. If you were a mother,' she repeats, 'you'd understand. I'm sorry if that hurts your feelings, but it's true.'

'It doesn't hurt my feelings,' she says, 'but it does make me wonder where you draw the line. I hear there's a rumor that people born below Sixth Street spread polio. And what about letting Al swim in the pond? Someone told me Jews spread polio.'

'You always do that.'

'Do what?'

'Make me sound like a fool for saying what other people are thinking. You're not the only one with a conscience. But sometimes when you have children you can't afford one.'

'Do you think anything will happen to Frankie and the other two boys?' Babe asks Claude in the car on the way to Millie's. Though Millie and Al live only two blocks away, they drive. There are no sidewalks in Riverview. There is no river view either.

'There are always ways to retaliate. Especially against Frankie. They'll see him as the ringleader. The star of the track team. On the honor roll. The coach won't kick him off the team. He's too good. But they'll find something. He used to be a credit to his race. Now he's uppity.'

'I never should have said anything.'

'To Grace about people born below Sixth Street? Forget it. If she doesn't know you by now, she never will.'

'To Frankie about the pond.'

He takes his eyes from the road and glances at her. 'Where do you come into it?'

She tells him about offering Frankie a lift. 'I wasn't thinking.'

He looks over at her again, and this time he is grinning. 'I bet you're the one who persuaded Truman to integrate the armed forces too.' He puts his hand on her thigh, right below where her shorts stop. 'I hate to burst your bubble, sweetheart, but I think the fact that his father and several hundred thousand other Negroes went off

276

to war and came back from it mad as hell at how they were treated during and after has more to do with it than your offering Frankie a ride.'

He is still grinning. And he has his hand on her thigh. They are talking about the war, and he has not gone sullen or silent or angry. She will not tempt fate. She will not stop holding her breath. But perhaps he is beginning to mend.

Three days later, on the first day of track practice, Frankie falls and sprains his ankle. The rumor spreads through school, and beyond, that one of his teammates tripped him. Frankie isn't saying.

Two days after that, a cold front comes through, and the temperature drops to an unseasonable forty-eight degrees. The chill weather lasts for the better part of a week, and by the time it begins to turn warm again, fall is in the air, football practice has started, and no one feels like swimming.

That's the end of that, people tell one another.

I hope not, Babe says, and swears she will not let the issue die, though she hasn't an inkling what she can do about it.

November 1952

Babe sits at one of the two bridge tables set up in Grace's glass-enclosed sunporch, watching Millie deal the cards. Her Kiss-Me-Pink nails spark in the dull autumn light. The conversation has moved from recipes to clothes. As the cigarettes pile up in the ashtrays, the feeling of closeness – just-us-eight-girls-together – will grow thick as the smoke-filled air, and they will move on to children and, finally, husbands. There will be no unexpected revelations, but no good can come of an afternoon spent this way, Babe thinks.

Millie hums beneath her breath as she arranges her cards.

'Please,' Grace snaps from the next table.

The humming stops.

'I'm sorry.' Grace's fingers toy nervously with the top button of her shirtwaist dress, which is tight. She is putting on weight again.

'No, *I'm* sorry,' Millie says, and Babe wonders if she ever gets angry. She tries to imagine Millie howling at Al the way she does at Claude, but other people's marital brawls are like other people's lovemaking. You can't imagine the real thing.

They have been her best friends since the first day of kindergarten. In those days, there was only one primary school in town. Grace cried that she wanted her mother; and Millie held her hand and said, my mother left too and I'm not crying; and Babe told her there was nothing to cry about, because the mothers would be back to get them in a few hours. And here they are all these years later. They love one another with an atavistic ferocity, though, it occurs to Babe sitting in the sunporch, these days perhaps they do not much like one another. But she is asking too much of them. Friendship, like marriage, is not all of a piece. Sometimes she thinks she would kill for them. Sometimes she wants to kill them. Perhaps parental love is the only exception to the fluctuating law of the social jungle, or maybe she thinks that only because she is not a parent. She has seen mothers smack their children, not for discipline but in blind savage fury. She knows grown children and parents who do not speak to one another. She speaks to her parents, but no warmth flows between them. Her father always resented her, and now her mother does too. She sees Babe's life as an indictment of her own. Babe thinks of Claude. It always comes back to Claude. Love may endure a lifetime, but it is less reliable on a day-to-day basis.

She glances around the table, realizes they are waiting for her, and makes a bid. Sharon Dobson glares at her. Why does she come? She is no good at bridge.

She puts her cards on the table, a relieved dummy, and stands. From the other end of the house, she can hear the sound of cabinets opening and closing. Naomi is taking out the cups and saucers and cake plates. She feels an overwhelming desire for a drink and looks at her watch. It is only a little after three. She cannot start drinking in the middle of the afternoon. Nonetheless, she heads for the kitchen. She will not ask Naomi for a drink. She just wants to get away from the bridge party.

'Need help?' she asks.

Naomi looks up from the tray and shakes her head with a polite smile. No, not polite, forced. She does not want me here in the kitchen with her. Naomi is as uncomfortable with me as she is with them. The injustice of it stings. I am not like them. I will not let her call me Mrs Huggins. I cheered when Frankie went to the pond. I'm on her side.

'I think it's wonderful what Frankie did.'

Naomi does not answer.

'You must be so proud of him.'

She takes a cake plate down from the cabinet and puts a doily on it.

'It took a lot of courage.'

She slides the layer cake onto the doily.

'Think of it. He's making history.'

She looks up from the cake. Her face is impassive, but her eyes are hard as granite. 'Mrs Huggins—'

'Babe.'

'Mrs Huggins, I don't want Frankie to make history. I want him to graduate high school. I want those boys on the track team to leave him alone so he can graduate high school in one piece. Then I want him to go to college. I want him to go to college like his daddy never could, even though that G.I. Bill said he was entitled. So, do me a favor, please. Say what you want to me. But don't tell him how brave he is, and don't tell him he's making history, and, please, don't offer him any more rides to anywhere.'

Shame dogs Babe's steps as she lets herself into her house. She is as bad as the rest of them. She insists Naomi call her Babe. Isn't that broad-minded of her? She goads Frankie to take risks. Isn't that brave of her? She is a silly futile woman, who wastes her afternoons playing bridge and feeling superior to the women she is playing bridge with.

She looks around the den and feels even worse. Claude is alive and well, almost. They own a house. They have two cars in the garage, both used but still an astonishing number. If anyone had told her before the war that she would have all these possessions, she would not have believed it. Now she takes prosperity for granted. They all do. They are awash in houses, and cars, and washing machines, and television sets, and air conditioners, and dishwashers, and deep freezes, and pressure cookers, and extension telephones, and Polaroid cameras, and stereos, and long-playing records, and power tools, and every other convenience they never knew they needed. So why is she dissatisfied? What is wrong with her? Why, now that Claude is getting better, is she falling apart? She hates the thought. She does not want to believe that his illness held her together.

She hangs her coat in the closet, goes into the

kitchen, and stands staring at the shelf of cook-books. The sight of them makes her feel exhausted. How can she be tired? She has not done anything all day except play bridge. Lately she is always worn out. Claude wants her to go for a checkup, but she keeps putting it off, partly because she believes she is not sick, merely ungrateful, and partly because she will not go to Morris but feels disloyal to Grace going back to Dr Flanner. A few weeks ago she tried to explain the problem to Grace. She cannot imagine taking off her clothes with Morris.

'He won't even notice,' Grace said.

'Thanks a lot.'

Grace flushed. 'I mean he's a doctor.'

Babe looks at her watch. It is a little after four. A respectable hour for a drink, almost. She pries the ice out of the ice tray, puts it in a glass, and pours enough scotch to cover the cubes. Then she takes *The Cordon Bleu Cook Book* from the shelf and gets to work.

From where he is sitting in the dining room, Claude hears the oven door squeak open and closed.

'Damn.'

She is speaking to herself, but he calls inside to ask what's wrong.

She comes in carrying a baking dish. 'It's a mess.'

'What's a mess?'

'Poulet Creole One.' She puts the baking dish

on a trivet. A spongy beige blob lies under several slices of chicken. 'I should have made the Poulet Creole Two. In that one, you don't have to form the stuff that goes under the chicken into the shape of a chicken.'

'You're supposed to make the non-chicken part look like a chicken?'

'It's called presentation.'

He takes the serving spoon, puts some on her plate, then his, and lifts a forkful to his mouth. 'It's good.'

She goes back into the kitchen to get the broccoli and her drink.

'I'm trying to think of what it tastes like,' he says when she returns.

She sits at right angles to him, her back to the low sideboard with his mother's silver candlesticks, which she gave them for their last anniversary, his to the bay window that looks out over the backyard. She picks up her own fork and tastes it.

'It's not awful. It just looks that way.'

He takes another bite and sits chewing for a moment. 'I know. It reminds me of that chicken hash you used to make when they'd let you cook in the boardinghouses.'

'Poulet Creole tastes like chicken hash?'

'Poulet Creole is chicken hash.'

She puts down her fork, picks up her drink, and polishes off what's left of it. 'That chicken hash took twenty minutes. The landladies were always rushing us out of the kitchen. I spent two and a half hours whipping up this mess.'

'It's good,' he says again.

'Not two and a half hours good.' She reaches for the wine he has poured her, takes a sip, and sits staring at her plate.

She cannot imagine how she did not see it before. It's Dior's New Look all over again. She still remembers the day Millie dragged her into a fitting room at Diamond's to try on a New Look dress, Paris original $450, Diamond's knockoff $19.99, with Al's discount. Babe stood staring at her reflection in the mirror. The dress was as unflattering as the frilly pink homemade number that had turned her into a wad of cotton candy. It was also wildly, willfully impractical. The tight bodice constrained her arms like a straitjacket. The cinched waist over a boned undergarment made it difficult to bend. She could barely walk in the yards and yards of full skirt that reached almost to her ankles. The wartime trousers and short skirts encouraged striding and reaching. Dior's New Look was designed for standing in place.

'The two and a half hours is the point, isn't it?'

He looks up from the chicken, which he seems to be enjoying. 'What do you mean?'

'The official line is that, after the war, women couldn't wait to leave the offices and assembly lines and government agencies. But the real story was that the economy couldn't have men coming home without women going home, not unless it wanted a lot of unemployed vets. So the problem became unemployed women. "How you gonna keep us down on the farm after we've seen the world," ' she ad-libs to the old World War I tune. 'Enter the women's magazines, and cookbook publishers, and all those advertising agencies carrying on about the scourge of germs in the toilet bowl, and scuffs on the kitchen floor, and, my favorite, house B.O. Enter chicken hash that takes two and a half hours to prepare. I can just hear them sitting around the conference tables. "That'll keep the gals out of trouble." '

She waits for him to tell her she's paranoid. What he usually means is she has had too much to drink.

He takes another bite of his chicken hash and says nothing.

A week later, she quits the bridge club. No one argues with her. Even Grace and Millie do not urge her to reconsider. She spends the bridge afternoon reading *East of Eden* and feels vaguely guilty about it. Shouldn't she be doing something useful? Bridge is not useful, but it is sociable and therefore acceptable. To make matters worse, she finds herself looking up at the clock periodically, measuring the time until she can have a drink.

At five o'clock, she closes the book, goes into the kitchen, pours herself a scotch, and takes down the cookbook. It falls open to the marker she has left at Poulet Creole I.

The first swallow of scotch sizzles through her. She closes the book, goes to the refrigerator, takes out the chicken, and puts it in a roasting pan. Salt, pepper, paprika. Her hand halts halfway to the spice rack. To hell with paprika. She slides the chicken into the oven. She is thumbing her nose at someone, though she is not sure at whom.

CHAPTER 14

GRACE

August 1952

Give Morris a chance, Babe said. It's not his fault he isn't Charlie. He's a good man. He's crazy about you and Amy.

If only she knew. But Grace has promised herself she will tell no one. It is her failure, and she will live with it. She only wishes she had not let on to Amy that anything was wrong. She never would have if Amy hadn't come dancing into the bedroom the night she and Morris came home from their wedding trip. He was still downstairs getting the luggage out of the car.

'You must be so happy,' Amy almost sang to the room that was now a normal parents' bedroom, with two people living in it, like the parental bedrooms in all her friends' houses, a bedroom where the door will be closed against her rather than left open to lure her in, a bedroom that she can close her own door against.

Grace did not even know the sob was there until it escaped from her. The sound was as contagious as the flu. They stood in the middle of the bedroom, hugging each other and crying, though Amy did not know what she was crying about. She knew only that her mother was unhappy, again. And that it was her job to cheer her up, again.

They let go of each other when they heard Morris on the stairs.

'It's nothing,' Grace said. 'Forget about it. Whatever you do, don't tell anyone I came home from my honeymoon and cried.'

The words did not reassure. Amy's eyes were still wide with fear, and something else – reproach. She wanted no part of her mother's misery. She was fed up with it.

Grace felt a flash of anger at the realization. Get used to it, she almost snapped, because you're going to grow up to be a woman too. Her fury frightened her. She did not mean that. She is not a bad mother. She did not confess. She broke down, but she did not come clean.

She did not tell Amy about how she felt that first night in her new nightgown, her pulse thumping like a drumbeat, her body prickly with fear. She had been frightened with Charlie, but that was because she did not know what to expect. She is scared now, because she can think of too many permutations of what to expect. She knows more about sex, but she knows nothing about this man, her sudden husband.

He comes out of the bathroom wearing a pair of pale blue cotton pajamas. The sharp creases are a giveaway. He bought something new to sleep in on their honeymoon too. The sweetness of the gesture undoes her fear.

He gets into bed next to her. She turns on her side toward him. He leans over, puts a hand on her shoulder, and kisses her. The kiss is chaste, a replica of the one he gave her in front of the handful of guests at the ceremony in her living room that afternoon. She wore a beige suit, carried a Bible with a single orchid, and managed not to cry. It was lucky her hat had a veil so no one could see her face.

'Good night, Mrs Banks,' he says, and turns over with his back to her.

She turns and lies staring into the darkness. Perhaps he is tired. Perhaps he thinks she is. She knows little about him, but she does know he is considerate. The ceremony. The long drive. And they have to get up early the next morning to catch the boat to Bermuda. He is waiting until they're on the ship. It will be more romantic. Charlie would not have waited. But she has to stop thinking about Charlie. Everyone has told her so – Babe, Millie, Dr Gold, everyone except King. You'll always be Charlie's wife to me, he said when she told him she was getting married. She had wondered if she was supposed to postpone the ceremony because of his heart attack. She considered it, but even her mother-in-law told her not to. The doctor said it was mild. Later she would come to think of it as an omen.

The next night, she is glad he waited. Moonlight puddles on the sea outside their porthole. The sound of the hull whooshing through the waves lulls her. The night is clement. She has no fear of seasickness.

She takes her nightgown into the bathroom. While she unpacked, she kept stubbing her toe on the raised ledge of the watertight door, but now she remembers to step over it. After she takes off her clothes, she slips on the nightgown, brushes her teeth, and gives her hair several strokes. She comes out of the small bathroom less nervous than the night before. They have begun their life together. She feels herself settling into the rhythm, his rhythm.

He has turned out the lamps, but she can make him out in the light from the waxy moon that hangs outside the porthole. He is lying on his back with his hands crossed over his chest. She lifts the covers and slips into bed. The mattress shifts as he turns on his side and leans toward her. He kisses her.

'Good night, Mrs Banks,' he says, and turns on his other side with his back to her.

She is up before him in the morning, but then, she did not sleep much during the night. How can she sleep with a stranger beside her in bed? She is quiet going into the bathroom. She positions herself on the toilet so the stream will hit the side of the bowl rather than the water. She does not want to make noise. She brushes her teeth. He will not want to kiss her if she has morning mouth, though Charlie never minded. She combs her hair. She considers putting on lipstick, but she does not want to get it all over the sheets or him. She has figured it out. Her new husband is not a nocturnal man. Before Amy was born, Charlie used to love Sunday mornings, and Saturday afternoons as well. But she will not think of Charlie.

She gets back in bed. He is still asleep. She thinks of reading. She has brought several books, though Millie teased her about it. On your honeymoon? she said, and arched her eyebrows devilishly. She does not take a book from the night table. It seems somehow unromantic.

He sleeps until nine-thirty. 'Holy cow,' he says when he opens his eyes and sees the clock. 'We'll miss breakfast. We'd better step on it.'

Charlie would have gone hungry. She does not even fight the thought of him.

That night, she gets up her nerve. The whiskey sour he orders for her before dinner helps.

They are sitting across the table from each other in the dining saloon. He has just finished ordering. She likes the way he does that. My wife will have it medium. I'll have it rare. He hands his menu to the waiter and smiles through the candlelight at her, and she takes the last swallow of her whiskey sour and does it. She asks him if there is anything wrong with her.

'I'm sure I'll find something. That you burn the

toast or forget to tell the laundry not to put starch in my shirts. I already know you don't leave the cap off the toothpaste. So far I have no complaints, Mrs Banks.'

'Then why don't . . .' Her voice trails off.

He smiles. 'Oh, Gracie.'

She swore she would never let anyone call her Gracie again, but suddenly she does not mind. The name is a balm.

'You know I do,' he goes on, 'but I feel like such a kid saying it.' He takes another sip of his drink. 'Okay, here goes. I love you.' He shakes his head in wonderment. 'As far as I'm concerned, you and Amy are the best thing that ever happened to me.'

That night the same thing happens. 'Good night, Mrs Banks,' he says, and turns his back to her.

The next evening, when he starts to order her a whiskey sour, she says she wants a martini. She has never had one.

'My wife will have a martini too,' he tells the waiter. 'Dry.'

She is halfway through it before she gets the courage to bring up the subject again.

'You know what I asked you last night, about something being wrong with me?'

He grins. He has a nice smile, wide as the open air. He is a kind man. He is a good man. He spends his life healing people. Not like Mac. She does not blame Mac, but she admires Morris.

'Still haven't found anything. Though I have to admit I'm not looking too hard.'

'Then why . . .' She takes another swallow of her drink. 'At night, when we go to bed . . .' Her voice trails off again.

He is still smiling, but he is not helping her.

'Is there something wrong with me that you don't want to . . .'

The smile has slid from his face, but he still doesn't say anything.

She takes a big swallow of the drink. 'Make love.' The second word escapes as a lament. The candle on the table between them flickers in its force.

He leans back in his chair, an indulgent look on his face, the patient expression of an adult for a bewildered child. And he loves children.

'Gracie. I'm forty-one. You're thirty-two. I thought we agreed we were beyond that kind of kid stuff.'

Agreed? She never agreed.

It's the martini, she tells him. She has never had one before. It has gone to her head. She'll be fine. She just has to lie down. No. You stay here. The words come faster. Fine. I'm fine.

She starts to stand. A steward is pulling back her chair. She stumbles through the maze of tables. The room is spinning. It is the drink. It must be the drink. The steward holds the door for her. Her heel catches on the low ledge. He puts a hand on her elbow. His touch humiliates. She twists away.

She is running down the passageway, holding on to the railing, ricocheting off the walls. The door of the cabin is locked. Morris has the key. He has locked her out. He has locked her up. Their stewardess is coming down the hall. Sick, Grace hisses. The stewardess unlocks the door. She starts to ask if there's anything – but Grace stumbles into the room and slams the door behind her. She hurls herself onto the blue satin spread. She does not care if she is sick all over it.

She is not sick, not that way. She is shamed. Humiliated. Furious. At Dr Gold for telling her what she needs is a husband to keep her from floating off into the stratosphere. At Morris for making her beg. At King for warning her about men. At herself for being so gullible. Any man who truly cares for you will not try to take liberties, King said. She took the absence of an arm around her shoulders for respect, the ascetic kiss at the end of the evening for self-control, the want of sweet touch for patience. Morris is not wrong. She did agree. And the terrible joke, the joke on her, is that if he had been demonstrative and ardent and insistent, she would have run for her life.

She wraps her arms around herself. She wants to be held. She wants Charlie to hold her.

September 1952

I was a nice girl once, Grace will tell herself when she cringes at the memory of her ridicule of Morris at the barbecue. She almost said it to Babe. I was

294

a nice girl once, wasn't I? But if you have to ask someone else, you know the answer.

All day, as the sun sears its way up the sky, and the coals grow hot in the grill, and the children chase one another around the yard, they keep coming back to it. Can't we change the subject? Millie pleads. What do you think of those Red Sox? Al says. But they cannot get away from it. Babe says good for Frankie and the other two boys. She sounds as if she is the one who caused the fuss. Al says it's disgraceful.

'That the boys went swimming?' Babe's voice is spoiling for a fight.

'That other people got out of the pond,' Al answers.

Grace looks at Millie, who stares back at her unhappily. They are against bigotry. They are for justice. But they are mothers.

Then Babe makes it worse. She and Grace are putting the paper plates, plastic utensils, mustard, ketchup, and relish on the picnic table when Morris comes over carrying a gin and tonic in each hand.

'Just what the doctor ordered,' he says, holding the water-beaded glasses out to them.

Babe takes hers. 'And while you're passing out medical advice, I wish you'd explain to your wife that Negroes do not spread polio.'

Grace is furious. If Babe is going to make fun of anyone, it ought to be Morris.

'That's right,' she says as she takes the other

drink from him. 'Explain it to me, Morris.' She turns to Babe. 'Morris is an expert on the human body. At least in theory.'

That night she lies in bed listening to the even breathing of her husband. Husband. She used to roll the word around in her mouth to savor the taste. Now it turns sour on her tongue. The breathing comes from a little distance. They have bought twin beds. Like a married couple in a movie. She lives with her own Motion Picture Production Code.

When did she become a cynic? She used to be a nice girl, she keeps reminding herself. Now she's a wife, though she doesn't feel like one to Morris, making tasteless marital jokes in front of other people. Spiteful. Malicious. A bitch. Her daughter thinks so too.

'Why can't I call him Dad?' Amy asks. 'I thought you wanted me to.'

'That was before.'

'Before what?' Amy taunts.

Watch yourself, or I'll tell you. She is dying to unburden herself.

'You can call him Uncle Morris,' she says.

'I have plenty of uncles. Uncle Claude. Uncle Al. Uncle Mac. I don't need any more.'

'Fine. Have it your way. Call him Dad.'

She does, though Grace can tell she doesn't mean it. Amy senses something is not right in the house. She intuits something is off about this man she counted on to turn them into a normal family.

But she calls him Dad anyway. She knows it riles her mother.

November 1952

Two or three times a week he brings her flowers. He comes walking in the door, his black doctor's bag in one hand, a bouquet of roses or peonies or whatever is at the local florist in the other, and holds them out to her.

The first time he did it, she was suspicious. It wasn't her birthday or an anniversary or any special occasion. 'What are these for?'

'Do I need an excuse to bring my wife flowers?' he asked, and leaned over to kiss her cheek on the way to the front hall closet.

But she knew what they were for. He was making a guilt offering.

At first, after she got over the shock of their honeymoon, she began to wonder if he was . . . well, one of those men she has heard about, though never met. But he can't be. He doesn't look effeminate, or speak in a high voice, or walk funny. Besides, if he was that way, why would he have pursued her, and he did pursue.

As the weeks and months pass, and she throws out one bouquet after another, and washes the bowls and vases, and fills them with the fresh flowers he brings, she realizes the bouquets are not guilt offerings. He does not think he has anything to feel guilty about. He thinks they are happy. He thinks they are normal. It makes her crazy. But he is oblivious. He is like a cartoon character who walks through life leaving fallen trees and collapsed buildings and maimed bodies in his wake, emerging not only unscathed but unaware of all the mayhem and disaster behind him. That is the way she thinks of him sometimes, her cartoon husband.

Tonight he has brought her red velvet tulips. They glow in the bright light of the kitchen as he comes up behind her at the counter, where she is making a salad. Charlie would have put his arms around her, cupped her breasts, and pressed himself against her. Morris reaches around and holds the flowers in front of her.

'They're lovely.' Her voice is flat. Can't he hear how flat her voice is?

'Think of them as a peace offering.'

This is a new twist. 'For what?'

'I should have phoned to ask if it was all right, but it would have been awkward to call him back after we hung up. And I knew you wouldn't mind. I spoke to Mac Swallow today. Some medical business. He said he was coming home this weekend, and I asked him to dinner Friday night.'

Mac stands watching Grace move around the kitchen. The last time he stood this way, tracking her with his eyes, remembering old times, was after Charlie's reburial. Now he is here because another friend, another husband, has asked him to dinner.

298

She is putting on weight again. It does not bother him, but he notices. This time, he reminds himself, the gain is the result of contentment, not grief.

'He called half an hour ago,' she says, 'and swore he wouldn't be too late, but the Willis boy has pains in his lower-right abdomen, and Mrs Willis is sure it's appendicitis, so naturally Morris agreed to stop in on his way home.'

'Your husband is the last doctor standing who makes house calls.'

'He loves taking care of people,' she says, and he wonders if that is a dig at him.

He asks if he can do anything to help, and she tells him he can pour himself a drink, which he does. Then he stands leaning against the counter, watching her lift the lids off pots, peer into the oven, take things from the refrigerator, and put other things back. She pushes a recalcitrant piece of butter from knife to pan with her index finger, then raises the finger to her mouth and licks it. She might as well have driven the knife into his heart.

'You sure I can't do anything to help?' he says again.

'Do you know how to set a table?'

'I do it every night. Just because I live alone doesn't mean I'm a barbarian. Like the Englishman in the jungle, I dress for dinner, or at least use a knife and fork.'

She takes out the place mats and silverware and hands them to him, and he carries them into the dining room. By the time she follows with the plates and glasses, he has set four places. She stands looking at the table.

'Well done. Morris can never remember which side things go on.'

'Maybe you married the wrong man.'

'Maybe I did,' she says without looking up at him, and something in her voice plunges the knife into his heart again.

CHAPTER 15

MILLIE

August 1952

The children pile out of the car and swoop over the grass still glistening with early-morning dew, but Millie stops and stands at the bottom of the path. She has never seen anything so gorgeous. The big bay window offers a glimpse into the still-empty living room, and the freshly painted green shutters glint in the slanting shafts of sunlight. Off to the right, the wide garage stands waiting for cars, bikes, lawn mowers, and gardening tools.

Al had been reluctant. Wait another year or two, he said, until the business is really up and running. She had tried, but everywhere she went, FOR SALE signs and model-house lures kept popping up. It was as if she were trying to diet or go on the wagon and people kept plying her with chocolate or offering her drinks. Then Babe mentioned that a new area of Riverview was opening, and Millie knew the time was right, no matter what Al said. She did not even give him a chance to take off his hat and coat when he got home that night.

'Okay.' He laughed and held up his hands with his palms toward her. 'I give up.'

He comes around the car now and stands beside her with his arm around her waist.

'Not bad,' he says, 'for a house built of cards – those cardboard credit cards that King Gooding, my uncle, and everyone else said would never catch on. Plastic now. A quarter of the state' – he gives her waist a squeeze – 'and growing.'

Then the moving truck pulls up, Al says he has to get to the office and climbs back into the car, and Millie walks up the path to her house.

Babe and Grace come over to help her unpack. Naomi arrives to clean the new bathrooms and scrub the new kitchen. Millie follows the movers around, telling them where to put things, warning them not to chip the paint, and reminding them to watch the chandelier and be careful with that chest because it has been in her family for generations. There is so much to unpack and so many things to do that she does not notice that one of the boxes she had stored in her aunt's house is missing. Why would she notice a single box unless it held the toaster or alarm clock or something they needed immediately?

Jack follows the movers upstairs. His mom told him to go out to the backyard, where Amy is taking care of his sisters, but he likes it better in here with the two big burly movers and the skinny one, who is even stronger. 'Watch the paint job,' one

302

of the burly ones says as they maneuver the big mattress for his parents' bed into the bedroom. He knows they're making fun of his mom, but they don't sound mean about it. They sound as if they like her. His dad says his mom could charm the birds out of the trees.

The skinny mover is bringing a stack of boxes up the stairs. As he bends to put them down, the top one slides off, and the flaps burst open. The man says a word Jack gets punished for, but that's nothing compared to what spills out of the box. Letters and drawings and pictures slide across the floor. Jack stands looking down at the photographs. The man in them looks back up at him. In the light coming through the window and glinting off the shiny surface of the photographs, the man seems to be winking at him. You know who I am. You see my picture at Grandma and Grandpa Swallow's. I'm the guy Mr Gooding gave you a dollar just for looking like. I'm Pete Swallow.

He hears his mom calling upstairs to ask if the men want lemonade. He shoves the photographs and drawings and letters back in the box, drags the box into his room, and closes the door behind him.

September 1952

'There's nothing to be scared of,' his mom says, as she puts the sandwich, banana, and cookies in his lunch box. She said it last night after everyone

303

went home from the barbecue, and she keeps saying it this morning. He wishes she'd stop.

'He's not scared,' his dad says. 'What's to be scared of?'

Jack knows it's not a real question, so he doesn't tell him.

'You already know Billy Craig down the block,' his mom says.

Billy Craig is a bully. He's also dumb. The two even out. Billy can beat up Jack, but Jack can outsmart him. Sometimes if Billy is winning at a game, Jack changes the rules halfway through, and Billy doesn't even get it.

'I bet by the end of the week you'll have a whole bunch of new friends,' his mom says.

He wishes she'd stop it.

'Are you sure you don't want to walk to school with the girls and me?'

'That's the last thing he wants,' his dad says, and winks at him over his coffee cup.

His dad's okay. He can't help it if he's not like the guy in the pictures, his real dad, Pete Swallow. Pete Swallow played football in high school. When Jack saw the picture of him in his uniform, he asked this dad if he played football in high school. This dad said he was too busy working to make money for college.

There's the business of the other uniforms too, the ones from the war. This dad wore a fancy white suit, the kind you couldn't do anything in, the kind his mom would keep telling him not to get dirty. His real dad, Pete Swallow, wore the kind of uniform they wear in the movies. Nobody worries about keeping those clean. His mom says this dad was wearing his dress whites the first time she laid eyes on him, and didn't he look handsome. Jack doesn't care about looking handsome. He wants to look tough, like the guy in the pictures, like Pete Swallow.

There's one more thing his real dad has over this dad. His real dad would never yell at him for fighting with his sisters, or take his bike away for a whole weekend just because he rode it out to the big road where he isn't allowed, or make him go back into the magazine-and-candy store and apologize to Mr Gray for swiping the pack of chewing gum. His real dad would understand him, and approve of him, and never ever punish him.

His mom hands him his lunch box, then does that thing he hates, licking her finger and smoothing down the cowlick at the back of his head. He doesn't want to go to this new school, but he can't wait to get out of the house.

He hangs around the side until he sees Billy Craig come down his driveway, then gives him half a block head start before he sets out. This dad is right. What's there to be afraid of? So it's a new school. So he doesn't know anyone except dumb Billy Craig. What's the big deal? The big deal is it's a new school and he doesn't know anyone except dumb Billy Craig.

He puts his hand in the pocket of his new

corduroy pants and feels the picture. Pete Swallow wouldn't be scared. He knows that from the football pictures and all the others. The letters too. He didn't read the whole letters – he had to skip the mushy parts – but he read enough to know Pete Swallow wouldn't be scared of starting some dumb new school. *The craps game is heating up, so I better get cracking and relieve those guys of their dough. I know I pulled some crazy stunts in my youth.* Jack has never pulled any crazy stunts. Except maybe hiding the box with the pictures and letters in his closet. Every night after his mom tells him to turn out his light, he goes into the closet, takes the flashlight from its hiding place, and looks at the pictures and letters. It's his secret. It's his secret society, just him and his dad Pete Swallow. Just Pete Swallow and Pete Swallow. That gives him an idea.

He hangs around on the edge of the playground until the teachers begin telling them to line up by class. Fifth grade over here, one of the teachers says, and dumb Billy Craig tries to trip him as he gets in line. Some of the other boys look at him as if he comes from outer space. Others don't look at him at all. He's the invisible boy. A girl says hello, but she's a girl, and that's worse than no one talking to him. He turns away from her.

The lines start moving, kindergarten, first, second. The fifth grade is next to the last. First the girls march in, then the boys. They line up along the sides of the room. The teacher says her name is Miss Tobias, and when she calls their names, they should take the next empty desk so they'll be in alphabetical order. Fred Adams takes the first seat, then Judy Atkins, then Belle Berkow.

'Peter John Swallow Baum,' Miss Tobias calls, and snickers from the back of the room tell him how silly the long name is.

'Pete Swallow,' his voice rings out. It doesn't even sound scared.

'Pardon me?' Miss Tobias says.

'My name is Pete Swallow.'

'Are you sure?'

'He ought to know his own name,' Billy says. He doesn't know what Jack is up to, but he can't resist a chance to make trouble.

'That will be enough out of you, William Craig.' She turns to Jack. 'If your name is Peter Swallow, I don't understand where the Baum came from.'

'That was someone else at my old school. He was Peter John too, and they were always getting us mixed up.' He can hardly keep from grinning. It's the kind of thing Pete Swallow would pull. It's relieving guys of their dough. It's a crazy stunt from his youth.

'All right, then, Peter Swallow. You just hang on until we get to the S's. William Craig, you take that desk, and zip your mouth.' She makes believe she is zippering her mouth, just like the teacher at his old school used to. 'I don't want to hear another word out of you until you're called on.'

Pete Swallow stands with his back against the

wall, fingering the picture in his pocket, and waits for his name to be called.

October 1952

The phone is ringing as Millie opens the door. Betsy runs for it. Susan dashes after her. Millie has picked them up, but Jack prefers to come home on his own, and Al insists she let him. It's lucky I came along, he tells her. You would have turned him into a real mama's boy.

'Baum residence.' Betsy's voice bristles with self-importance. She has just won permission to answer the phone. Susan stands watching her, half adoration, half raging envy.

A moment passes.

'I'm sorry, you have the wrong number,' she says, and replaces the receiver.

A moment later, the phone rings again.

'I'll get it,' Millie says, and takes the receiver from Betsy's hand.

'Is this Mrs Swallow?' a woman's voice on the other end of the line asks.

Millie's first thought is that someone is playing a cruel joke.

'This is Mrs Baum.'

The woman on the other end gives the phone number she is trying to reach. Millie says she has the right number. 'I was Mrs Swallow,' she admits.

'Are you Pete Swallow's mother?' the voice asks.

'I was married to Pete Swallow.'

The voice laughs. 'No, I mean young Pete Swallow. Pete Swallow, Jr., I would imagine. Your son.'

'My son's name is Jack,' Millie says. 'Jack Baum.'

There is a brief silence. 'I'm afraid there's been some confusion. Or else Pete – Jack has played a trick. On me. I'm Miss Tobias. His teacher. When I called out the names the first day of school, he told me Baum was another boy at his old school, and he was Peter Swallow. That's what we've been calling him.'

'His name is Jack Baum,' Millie says again. She feels stupid. She is having trouble understanding what this is about.

'I'm afraid that makes it worse. I knew he was a troublemaker, but—'

'Jack isn't a troublemaker.'

'He starts fights, Mrs Swallow.'

'Mrs Baum.'

'Your son starts fights. And apparently he lies as well.'

'You must have misunderstood him about his name.'

'I'm not the one who misunderstood. That's why I sent you the note.'

'What note?'

'I sent a note home with Pete – Jack last week asking you to come in to see me.'

'I never got any note.'

Miss Tobias does not answer, but Millie can feel the smug satisfaction seeping down the line.

'Little boys fight,' Millie says.

'And our job is to teach them not to. I haven't had much luck with your son. I think it's time for his parents to step in.'

'My husband and I will take care of it,' Millie says.

As soon as she gets off the phone with the teacher, she dials Al's office.

'I'm less upset about the fighting,' he says, 'than I am about the note he didn't bring home. I don't want him to . . . Tell him I'll be right with him,' he goes on, and Millie knows he is not speaking to her. 'Listen, Mil, I can't talk about this now. We'll discuss it when I get home.'

After supper, they send Betsy and Susan to the family room to watch television. The girls drag their feet, looking back into the kitchen as they go. They worship Jack, but every now and then they like to see him catch it.

Millie puts the last of the dessert bowls in the sink, then sits. The three of them form a triangle at the long oval table.

Al asks about the fights. Jack insists he did not start them. He was only defending himself. Millie tells him next time to walk away. Al is silent, listening to the phrases ringing in his head. Dirty Jew. Sheenie. Kike.

'Sometimes,' he says carefully, 'it's all right to fight back. You just have to know when.'

Jack is intrigued. 'When is it all right?'

Al ponders the question. He does not want

to visit his past, his heritage, on Jack any more than he does on Millie. He loves their innocence.

'When someone is trying to bully you. Or bully someone else.' He can tell from the way Jack looks at him that he wants more specifics, but Al moves on. 'It's the business of the note you didn't bring home that bothers me.'

Jack knows if he looks down he is done for. He holds Al's gaze. 'I lost it.'

Al taps his fingers on the Formica tabletop. The explanation is not implausible. A boy's world is full of lost mittens, balls, magazines, trading cards, and parts for model airplanes, boats, and cars. And the eye contact is reassuring. 'You should have told us you lost it.'

Now Jack drops his eyes, a charade of remorse. 'I know,' he says, in the sullen mumble that passes for contrition in a ten-year-old boy.

Al starts to say no bike for three days and no movies this Saturday, then softens and settles for only the bike.

'If you ask me,' he says later in the bedroom, as he unknots his tie and pulls it out from under his collar, 'the teacher is making a mountain out of a molehill. Boys fight.'

'That's what I told her,' Millie answers on her way to the bathroom. 'She said it's our job to teach them not to.'

She closes the door behind her, slips a hair band on, and begins creaming her face. Boys fight, and Jack lost the note, and the business about his name

311

was only a joke. That's why she didn't mention it to Al.

But later, after he has fallen asleep, she lies in bed thinking about the incident. The house is silent. Beneath the windows, open a crack to the night, rain strums the garage roof. She usually loves lying beside Al in the freshly laundered fragrance of their king-sized bed, thinking of the children dreaming in their rooms. The fleeting sizzle of car tires on wet pavement, like bacon in a skillet, heightens the stillness and sharpens her pleasure. They are warm and dry and safe. But tonight the beat of the rain makes her edgy. At the sound of a car, she holds her breath until it passes.

The business about his name must have been a joke. Jack is too young to understand the implications of Baum. But she has learned. The first time it happened, she was taking Al's blue pinstripe suit to a new dry cleaner. As she pushed the suit across the counter, the man behind it asked her name. Baum, she said. He looked up from the trousers he was inspecting and asked if the name was German. He was too old to have been in the war, but you never knew. Maybe he had lost a son. She said it was not, though to tell the truth, she is not sure where Al's people come from. Oh, was all he said. She did not like the way he said it and resolved to go to a different dry cleaner next time, but when she picked up the suit, he had done such a good job that she could not bring herself to change.

She turns on her side and winds herself around Al. He reaches back and pats her bottom. The gesture is instinctive. He is asleep.

She never mentioned the occurrence, or a few others like it, to Al. And when he frets about similar incidents, she pretends not to understand. Like that time he got annoyed because she forgot to ask him for money and Babe had to pay for lunch. She knew perfectly well why he was upset, but there was no point in dwelling on it. People say mixed marriages don't work, but if you do not make a fuss about the little things, they work just fine. She and Al are proof. That's why she did not mention Jack's joke about his name. It has nothing to do with Baum sounding Jewish, but Al might not see it that way, and she has no intention of upsetting him for no reason.

November 1952

'The best part,' Jack says, 'is when you see the tank in the sights. Then all of a sudden – pow! – and the whole thing goes up in flames.'

'Nah, the best was the commando raid,' Bobby Summers says, and begins dodging in and out among the boys, rat-tat-tatting with his arm. 'All those Krauts they killed. Rat-tat-tat.'

'My dad killed lots of Krauts,' Jack says. 'Just like the heroes who broke the back of Rommel's vaunted Afrika Korps.' He quotes the line on the movie poster, then decides not to stray too far from the truth. 'Only he killed them in France. He was in D-Day, and he killed lots and lots and lots of Krauts. He died killing Krauts.'

'Whadya mean?' Billy Craig says. 'Your dad didn't die. My dad says your dad probably wasn't even in the war. He probably had a cushy desk job. He says Jews always find ways to stay out of the fighting. He knows because he had a Jew guy in his outfit.'

'I mean my real dad,' Jack says.

'Whadya mean your real dad? You only got one dad, and that's the Jew who wasn't even in the war. This guy who killed Krauts is just some make-believe guy.'

'Is not.'

'Is so.'

'I got pictures of him.'

'Show me.'

'I don't carry them around. Even if I did, I wouldn't show you. You'd get your cooties all over them.'

'Look who's talking about cooties, Jewboy.'

'I'm not a Jewboy. My real dad was as good as yours.'

'Jewboy.'

'Take that back!'

'Jewboy, Jewboy, Jewboy.'

Billy is still bigger than he is, though not as much as he used to be, but Jack doesn't care. He lunges and pushes as hard as he can. Billy stumbles into the street, regains his balance, and comes back at

Jack. Suddenly Jack is on his back in the dirt, and Billy is straddling him with his big meaty legs and pummeling him with his fists. Jack tastes the blood and swings back, but Billy fends him off. He tries to push Billy, but it's like having an elephant sitting on him. He manages to get his right hand free and swings again. It hits Billy in the nose.

'Fucking Jewboy,' Billy howls, and lands another punch to Jack's eye.

The other guys pull Billy off him.

Jack does not want to get up. He wants to turn over on his stomach, lie there in the dirt, and cry, but he knows he has to stand. He manages to prop himself up on his hands and knees, then gets to his feet. He has a mouthful of blood from his nose, and his eye hurts, but Billy's nose is bleeding too. He wishes his dad, his real dad, Pete Swallow, could see that.

Millie almost drops the laundry basket when she sees Jack standing in the doorway. His face is encrusted with dirt and blood, and his hair is standing up like a madman's, and his dungarees are torn. Her body cringes in referred pain, like the men she has read about who have physical symptoms when their wives go into labor. The years they spent alone together, waiting for Pete, grieving for Pete, have left her too exquisitely attuned to Jack.

He is trying not to cry, but when he sees Millie, his face collapses and his chest begins to heave.

She does not ask what happened. She knows. She puts down the basket of laundry, takes his hand, and leads him up the two short flights from the family room to the children's bathroom. The girls, who spotted him across the yard and came running, start to follow, but she tells them to stay where they are.

She takes him into the bathroom, sits him on the closed toilet, and turns him toward the light. The sight makes her bite her lip. She tells him to open his mouth. His teeth are all there.

She takes a washcloth, soaks it in warm water, and begins working on his face. The area below his nose is like a carapace. She goes to the linen closet and gets a fresh washcloth. His crying has turned to a series of shudders.

She unbuttons his shirt and helps him out of it, then his dungarees. Sitting there in his cotton Jockey shorts, he is a skinny little boy again. He shivers, and she puts a towel around his shoulders while she washes the scraped and skinned areas of his arms and legs.

When she finishes cleaning the abrasions, she takes out the bottle of Merthiolate. He does not cry as she applies it. With each dab, they wince in unison.

As she goes to his bedroom to get a clean pair of pajamas, she hears Al's car in the driveway, then Betsy and Susan shouting Daddy, Daddy, Daddy, and Jack, and all bloody, and upstairs with Mommy.

He does not pound up the stairs, but he takes them quickly and appears in the bathroom door.

'Are you okay?' he asks Jack.

Jack nods and sniffles.

Al looks at Millie.

'All teeth are present and accounted for. His nose has stopped bleeding. But I wish you'd take a look at that eye.'

Al steps into the bathroom, bends, and examines Jack's eye. Again, she and Jack wince in unison when Al touches the lid.

He straightens. 'You're going to have a real shiner tomorrow. Know what your line is?'

Jack looks up at him and sniffles.

'You should see the other guy.'

Jack goes on looking up at him.

'It's a joke.'

Millie puts him to bed. He says he is not hungry, but she brings him a bowl of soup on a tray. She sits on the side of the bed and feeds it to him. She is amazed he lets her.

Al comes into the room while she is spooning the soup into his mouth and stands at the foot of the bed.

'You want to tell us what happened?' His voice is as gentle as his hands when he examined the bruised eye.

Jack shakes his head no.

'Okay, it can wait till tomorrow,' he says, and goes out again.

When Jack finishes the soup, Millie asks him if

he wants anything else, and he shakes his head no again. She puts the tray on the floor, leans over him, and brushes the hair back from his forehead. He usually pushes her hand away, but not now. Awful as this is, she likes having her little boy back. Maybe that's why she goes on.

'We don't have to talk about it now, but just tell me who you were fighting with.'

He does not answer.

'Billy Craig?'

His nod is almost imperceptible.

'Oh, Jackie, I told you to ignore him. Everyone on the street knows he's a bully.'

'I tried to, but he kept doing it.'

'Doing what?'

'Calling me names.'

'You're too old to get angry at that. You know about sticks and stones.'

He does not answer.

'Next time he calls you a name, just walk away.'

'But it wasn't true.'

'Of course it wasn't true. No nasty name he calls you could be true.'

'He called me Jewboy.'

She stiffens.

'I'm not, am I?'

She is not sure how to answer. Al adopted him when they married. Does that make him Jewish? They celebrate Christmas and Chanukah. More presents for the kids, Al says. She and the girls color Easter eggs, and they go to Al's parents for a seder, but the way his father conducts it makes it feel like a big family dinner with presents for the kids when they find the piece of matzo he has hidden. Betsy and Susan were not christened. Al says there is no such thing as a Jewish christening, at least for girls. It's one of the reasons she's glad they had girls. Less to worry about with his parents, and, she suspects, with him. Jack was christened, but that was in another life. And one other thing, a fortuitous accident: Thanks to his uncle Mac's medical advice, Jack was circumcised. Father and son look alike. But that does not make him Jewish.

'Well, am I?'

'No.'

'But Dad is?'

'It's a long story, and you have to get some sleep.' She stands. 'We'll discuss it some other time.'

'You're sure I'm not?'

She bends over to hug him. 'You're as Christian as I am. And don't let Billy Craig or anyone else tell you differently.'

She arranges the pillows behind his head. Only when she turns to leave does she see Al standing in the doorway again.

He turns, goes back down to the kitchen, and pours himself a drink. Why is he surprised? His parents, his uncle, everyone warned him. One day a word will slip, and you'll know how she really feels. If he is going to be reasonable about it – and he is trying to be reasonable; he came downstairs and poured a drink to be reasonable – who would choose to be a Jew, or a Negro, when it's so much easier not to be? Since the war, it's not as hard as it used to be, but it is still not a piece of cake. For him to deny being Jewish would be shameful. For her to be relieved she is not Jewish is only human nature. Only she was not talking about its being difficult or easy; she was talking about its being not as good as and better than. You're as Christian as I am.

What does that make me? he wants to storm back upstairs and ask her. What does that make Betsy and Susan, your own daughters?

He does not go back upstairs to confront her. He pours more scotch into his glass and carries it down to the family room, where the girls are watching television.

'Make room for Daddy,' he says, and they spring apart on the sofa, then move in beneath the shelter of his spread arms.

After a moment, Betsy wriggles. 'Not so tight, Daddy.'

Neither of them mentions the incident during dinner. There is nothing unusual about that. Both girls are chatterboxes. A chip off their mother, Al sometimes teases her, though he does not tease her tonight. Nor does he sit at the kitchen table with the evening paper to keep her company while she does the dishes. He takes it down to the family room.

She clears the table and begins putting the leftover meat loaf and potatoes and string beans into plastic containers.

The children are where they hurt you. She does not mind the tradesmen who look funny at the mention of her name, or the invitation to join the ladies' historical society that never came, or even the way her aunt and uncle watch their words around her. Well they might, she thinks, when she remembers a joke – it was supposed to be a joke – her uncle used to tell before America got into the war. I pray to heaven the English will stop Hitler, he used to say, but not too soon. She can take the slurs and slights and innuendos, but she will not let them be visited on Jack.

She puts the plates in the sink, pulls on her rubber gloves, and begins rinsing and stacking them in the dishwasher. She wonders if Al is waiting for an apology. What can she apologize for – telling Jack he is Christian? She just wishes she hadn't said, as Christian as I am. Somehow that makes it worse, though she is not sure why.

She puts the last plate in the dishwasher, closes it, and straightens. This is ridiculous. She is doing what she has sworn she will not, making mountains out of molehills. For all she knows, Al did not even hear what she said. He was silent during dinner because something happened at the office. It would not be the first time he brought his business worries home.

She wrings out the sponge and begins wiping

the counters. Someone has left the top off the Aunt Jemima cookie jar. She looks inside. It's empty. She carries it to the sink and begins washing. It was, she remembers as she soaps, the first gift Al's mother gave her. Fancy china it's not, she said, but cookies like you make, Al and the children should know where to find. It was more than a compliment, it was a concession. Perhaps Al had not made such a big mistake after all. She puts the top in the drain board and picks up the bottom. It's bulbous and unwieldy. She reaches inside to sponge it, runs the water in, turns it over to let the water out. She feels the jar slipping and tries to catch it, but the gloves make her clumsy. It hits the sink and shatters. She stands looking down at the pieces. It is an inexpensive cookie jar, nothing to cry over. But she does.

A few days later, Al comes home from the office and says he'd like to have his parents over for dinner that Friday night, and his uncle, and the cousin his uncle brought over after the war, the one who was in a concentration camp. He says it as if he is expecting an argument, though he must know she will not give him one.

'I think the kids ought to get to know him,' he adds.

She does not disagree with that either.

The week after Al's family comes to dinner, she goes downtown to Diamond's and buys another cookie jar. This one is a Dutch girl with a cap. By the time the children get home from school, it is filled with chocolate chip cookies. Jack doesn't notice the jar is new. Betsy likes it. Susan grieves for the old one. Even inanimate objects make a claim on her soft heart. Millie knows how she feels. Every time she looks at the jar, it reproaches her.

Al does not reproach her. He has never mentioned the incident. His silence is worse than a quarrel. It eats away at them. That's why she makes the offer. She lost one husband. She is not going to forfeit another.

If she had not already made up her mind, the item on the late news would have persuaded her. They are sitting side by side on the sofa in the family room when the announcer launches into it.

A military transport plane has crashed in Washington state, the ninth crash in three weeks. Thirty-six people are dead, three women and eight children among them. Whole families were wiped out, the announcer intones. She feels as if someone has laid an icy hand on the back of her neck.

Half an hour later, the story follows them upstairs. It is like a shadow lurking in the corners of the bedroom. When she goes into the bathroom to cream her face, she thinks a light over the mirror has burned out, the room strikes her as that dim.

'Al,' she says as she comes back into the bedroom.

He is setting the radio alarm and does not look up.

'How would you like it if I converted?'

Now he looks up.

'To Judaism, I mean.'

'I know what you mean.'

'Would you like me to? It doesn't make that much difference to me one way or the other, and if it would make you happy . . .'

He sits staring at her. It doesn't make that much difference to her one way or the other. Imagine the luxury. Imagine religion being a choice, not a brand. The thought of it makes him dizzy. But the rest of the sentence anchors him. If it would make you happy.

His face cracks open and a grin spills out. 'Thanks,' he says, 'but let's not get carried away.'

BOOK V

1954–1957

CHAPTER 16

BABE

June 1954

Babe stands in front of the Western Union office. She has no idea how she got here. Yes, she does. Claude's reunion propelled her.

The night before, he drove to Springfield to see some of his old army buddies. The men he trusted with his life. She did not use the phrase, though she still cannot get it out of her head. She merely told him to have a good time. But she was apprehensive. She remembers the aftermath of the funeral he went to in Haverhill. He was silent for weeks. Then he took a swing at himself in the bathroom mirror. But that time he went to a burial. This is a reunion. And that was years ago, before he started to mend.

When she heard him coming up the stairs, she pretended to be asleep. She did not want him to think she was waiting up for him. She did not want him to know she was still holding her breath.

When she wakes the next morning, he is asleep. She is quiet going into the shower. He comes into the bathroom a few minutes later. She braces herself, though she has no idea for what. He calls good morning over the sound of running water.

By the time she turns off the shower and reaches for a towel, he is at the sink, shaving. She wraps the towel around herself and stands watching him. His hand is steady as he draws the razor down his cheek, carving a smooth path through the white lather. The otherness of the act sends an erotic charge. It is the sexual divide that binds – not the otherness of the war that slams down like a wall between them.

She asks if he had a good time. He says he was glad to see the men again. The ones he trusts with his life. She has got to stop this. He is better. She is happy for him. She is relieved for herself. And she could not be more jealous if he had been with another woman.

After she puts the breakfast dishes in the dishwasher, makes the bed, and starts a load of laundry in the washing machine, she drives downtown. She will return her books to the library, take out new ones, and go to the post office for stamps. She is sure she can think of a few other errands as well.

She parks the car in a lot a block from the Western Union office. These days nobody even thinks of looking for a spot on the street. It seems as if every family in town has two cars, and that doesn't include the kids with their jalopies.

As she is getting out of the car, she spots Mac

Swallow going into the drugstore. He comes home more often than he used to when he first moved to Boston. He even turns up at Grace and Morris's for dinner every now and then, just as he used to when it was Grace and Charlie.

She goes to the library, stops at the post office, and spends half an hour in Diamond's, examining sheets she is not going to buy. Then, without knowing why or how, she finds herself standing in front of the Western Union office, staring through the plate-glass window. She will not go in. She has no business there. She just wants to see it again.

Sid Taylor sits behind the desk reading a magazine. The bench where B.J. used to wait is empty. She has heard that the office is not as busy as it used to be. These days people tend to pick up the telephone, especially now that they don't have to use an operator and can dial long distance direct.

She is glad the office is not busy. She does not want it to go on without her. She wants it to be as arrested as she has been.

She has no desire to go back to those days. Only a crazy woman would want to go back to a life of constant fear, aching longing, and unbearable loneliness. Only a fool would want to go back to that office reeking of death and grief. But it was her own front line in the war, and for three years she womaned it with a singleness of purpose. That is what she misses. Being useful. Having a cause.

It occurs to her as she stands staring through

the window at Sid Taylor, who sits at the desk where she used to cut the ticker tape, paste it on the forms, and put the forms in the envelopes to be delivered, that she is as bad as the men. She has become a war lover.

Autumn 1955

Babe does not stop to open her umbrella. She is too eager to get out of the house. She puts her head down like a charging bull and makes a dash for the car.

Sometimes she wonders why she still bothers to visit them. Her father barely says hello to her. Her mother wears her resentment like the old sweaters she sits huddled in at the oilcloth-covered kitchen table. She wonders where the new sweaters she gives her every Christmas go. Perhaps she passes them on to her sisters. Babe would not mind that. Or maybe when her mother sees her drive up in front of the house, she runs into the bedroom to take off one of the Christmas sweaters and put on an old ratty one. Just to show Miss Too-Big-For-Her-Britches, as her father calls her. Her mother is more devious. Babe used to think her mother sewed her that awful pink cotton-candy dress because it was the kind of thing her mother would have looked good in when she was young and had no idea all those flounces would be a disaster on a girl with wide shoulders and a rangy body. Now she is not so sure the sabotage was unintentional.

'When did you start using that color lipstick?' her mother asks.

'Don't you like it?'

Silence.

'You changed your hair.'

'It's exactly the same.'

'That must be it. I was you, I'd get a new 'do.'

This time Babe does not take the bait.

'You better not let yourself go,' her mother warns. 'I bet there are plenty of pretty young teachers at that school of Claude's.'

'I bet there are,' she says as she stands, puts on her raincoat, and gets ready to make the dash to the car.

Inside it, she brushes the drops off her coat, but she cannot shake off the lingering ache of their meanness. She fears becoming like them. She never used to. When she went to work at Diamond's, when she married Claude, when she ran the Western Union office, she knew she was escaping them. But these days, as she listens to them going at each other – not the way they used to, with shouts and threats and, from her father, slaps, but with verbal penknives – she hears her own voice nicking away at Claude. She hates herself for it, but the more ashamed of herself she is, the harder she runs at him.

She sits in the car, staring through the rain-sluiced windshield at the house she has just escaped. It is even shabbier now than when she was growing up in it. The street looks almost as forlorn as the pictures in *Life* of bombed-out cities after the war. Cardboard-patched windows gape like missing teeth in the run-down buildings. Front stoops lack a stair here, a railing there. The rain has turned the bald front yards into mud holes. The block is a wasteland of neglect and despair. The responsible neighbors, the ones who used to repair and paint and weed, have fled to the respectable frame houses on the east side of town or even to the new developments, thanks to prudent saving of their windfall wartime wages. Only the spendthrift, the slapdash, and the willfully shortsighted remain.

She starts the engine, pulls away from the curb, and heads north toward Sixth Street. The wipers beat back and forth against the windshield. The reflection of the traffic light is a red smear on the wet glass. She stops and sits waiting for it to change. When the wipers swipe past again, she sees a figure standing at the bus stop. The wipers have to go across a third time before she recognizes Frankie Hart. He does not even have an umbrella. She rolls down the window and shouts at him to get in. He sprints around the car to the passenger side, pulls open the door, and sticks his head in.

'You sure? I'm pretty soaked.'

'That's why I'm offering you a ride. Get in.'

He climbs in. Water puddles around his feet. A damp stain begins to spread on the upholstery.

'You headed for the factory?'

Claude said Frankie has an after-school job

cleaning up scraps at the hat factory. He is saving money for Howard, where he is sure to be accepted.

'The bus depot,' he says.

She glances over at him, then back at the road. It is none of her business, but she cannot help being curious.

'Running away from home?'

'Just going to a meeting. Over in Amherst.'

He says no more, but as she turns onto Sixth Street and pulls up in front of the bus depot, he puts his hand on the door handle, then hesitates and turns back to her.

'Could I ask you another favor, Mrs Huggins?'

'Sure.'

'Don't tell my mother you gave me a lift. And especially don't tell her I was going to a meeting in Amherst. I never should have mentioned it to you, but . . .' He shrugs.

'Your secret is safe with me.'

She is getting out of the car in her own garage when she notices the magazine on the front seat. It must have fallen out of Frankie's pocket. *JET* is written in bold letters at the top. Beneath the name, a pretty young woman is showing plenty of leg. The magazine looks like a dozen others displayed on newsstands. The only difference is the girl on this cover is Negro. Babe does not know why she is surprised. She should have known that there are magazines published by Negroes about Negroes for Negroes. Only she didn't. She carries the magazine inside and puts it with a stack of others.

A few days later, as she is making a pile of papers to take out to the trash, she comes across the magazine again. The caption beside the leggy girl on the cover asks, *How Many Negroes in College?* She sits on the ottoman next to the low magazine rack and begins leafing through it. The experience is at once eerily familiar and strangely disorienting. She turns page after page of pictures of actresses and bathing beauties and sports stars and society figures she has never heard of. Even the news roundup and book reviews have different slants. The ads promise her whiter skin and straighter hair.

She turns a page. The photograph hits her like a fist. Her eyes veer away from it. She forces them back. The face is a mass of bloated pulp. Her glance flees the horror to the photo beside it. A teenage boy in a white shirt and a black tie smiles out at the world. She reads the caption that runs beneath the two pictures. *Fished from the river, Emmett Till, 14, was a bloodcurdling sight. His alleged crime: whistling at a Delta white woman.*

She sits staring down at the two photographs and knows why Frankie asked her not to tell his mother he was going to a meeting in Amherst. She also knows – and the fact that she did not know it before shames her – why Naomi did not want her driving Frankie anywhere anytime.

★　　★　　★

She becomes obsessed with the case. Though she is dying to ask Frankie about the meeting in Amherst, she fears Naomi will think she is aiding and abetting. Instead, she reads every newspaper and magazine account she can get her hands on. Claude walks in each night to find her poring over them.

'Wait till you hear this,' she greets him one night before he has taken off his hat and coat. 'A white grand jury in Mississippi – Mississippi! – indicted two white men for the murder of a Negro.'

'Listen to this,' she tells him as he walks in the door two weeks later. 'Emmett Till's great-uncle – a Negro, obviously – stood up in court and pointed a finger to identify the two white men who kidnapped the boy. Talk about guts.'

Things are changing, she insists. Perhaps all those Negro soldiers who fought in the war really have made a difference.

Life magazine runs an editorial in memory of the boy that cites his G.I. father, who was killed in France fighting for the American proposition that *all men are equal.*

'Sic,' Claude says as she reads the line to him.

' . . . *created* equal,' she finishes for him.

The moment clicks between them like a snapshot, and she knows it is one of those unremarkable instants that for some inexplicable reason sear the memory. She will remember it always.

She feels close to Claude. She feels caught up

in something bigger than herself, though her only contribution is writing letters to the editor, most of which don't even get printed. But then, her only contribution to the war was cutting and pasting and delivering usually bad news.

'Personally, I liked it better when she was just drinking too much,' Millie confesses to Grace one evening in the kitchen before Babe and Claude arrive for their monthly potluck dinner. 'At least she was fun then.

'For once,' she goes on when Babe comes in carrying a casserole of scalloped potatoes, 'can we not talk about Emmett Till?'

Babe puts the casserole on the counter and glares at Millie, but Millie's back is turned as she peers into the oven.

'Don't you even care?'

'Of course she cares,' Grace says as she goes on tearing lettuce. 'We all care. But we're not obsessed with it.'

Millie closes the oven door and turns back to them. 'I make it a rule never to worry over things I can't do anything about. Now, if someone would tell me what goes on in the mind of a twelve-year-old boy, I'd be extremely interested. Boys,' she sighs. 'The girls are so much easier.'

'Wait until they're teenagers,' Grace says.

Claude comes into the kitchen carrying a martini in each hand and gives one to Babe.

'Just the man I want to see,' Grace says. 'What do you know about a boy named Eddie Montrose?'

'Nice enough kid,' Claude says. 'Editor of the school paper. Why?'

'Amy is at the movies with him as we speak.'

'Are his intentions honorable?' Morris asks from the kitchen doorway.

'I doubt it.'

'I'm serious.'

'Do you know any seventeen-year-old boy whose intentions are honorable?'

'Mine were,' Morris says.

'They still are.' Grace's voice hits a sour note, and they all turn to look at her. The color rises in her cheeks. 'All I meant is that I'm married to an honorable man. But we were talking about the Montrose boy. His father is pretty high up in management at the hat factory.'

'She's not out with his father,' Claude points out.

'All I know,' Babe says, 'is that he wrote a good editorial about Emmett Till for the school paper.'

Despite Emmett Till's great-uncle's courageous identification of two white men, a jury of twelve other white men acquits them of murder. The jurors deliberate for only sixty-seven minutes. According to one of them, they would have been faster if they had not stopped to drink pop.

Before, Babe could not get enough of the good news. Now she is addicted to the bad. When she finds out that Emmett Till's father did not die in France fighting for the American proposition that all men are created equal but was executed by the U.S. Army in Italy for raping two women and killing a third, she is devastated. The father's crimes do not justify the son's fate, but they somehow sully the cause. Or maybe the glee of the southern press in reporting the story does that.

When a grand jury refuses to indict the two white men for kidnapping, she ties up the newspapers and magazines she has been saving, carries them to the garbage can beside the garage, lights a match, and drops it in. The edges of the magazine on top catch fire and begin to curl. The movement makes the pages seem suddenly alive. The embers go out. She strikes another match and drops it in. The edges come to life again, then die. She is useless. She cannot even start a fire. She begins taking matches from the box, one after the other, striking them, dropping them in. The papers catch in one place, another, a third. The flames lick the late-autumn dusk. She leans over the can, feeling the heat on her face. Her tears sizzle in the fire. She is mourning the boy, but she is also grieving for her own life. Claude is mended, and she is, in some way she does not understand, broken.

Even before Claude turns in to the driveway, he sees a ribbon of smoke curling into the blue twilight. He cannot imagine what Babe could be burning. He has already taken care of the leaves. Still, the idea that she is cleaning house is

338

encouraging. He does not give a damn about the house, but he does about her. Action is a good sign. He was hopeful about her obsession with the Emmett Till case, but since the men were acquitted, she has been taking it hard.

He stops the car in the driveway and sits watching her. There is something wrong with the way she is leaning over the garbage can. She is too close. If the flames leap any higher, they will singe her hair.

He gets out of the car and starts toward her. As he gets closer, he sees into the can. The flames lick at the leggy woman on the cover of *JET*. The effect is of a religious painting of a sinner burning in hell.

He lifts his eyes from the flaming trash can to Babe. Her hair falls forward lankly. Beneath one of his old flannel shirts, her body is hunched into a question mark of despair. Tears run down her face. Perhaps it's the soot, but her skin looks gray in the gathering twilight. When did the girl he fell in love with, the wife he came home to, the woman who put up with his tortured nights and silent days and shattered mirrors, become an old lady?

He waits for the feeling of disgust, but his heart surprises him. It folds over in pity. A sudden rush of tenderness overtakes him. He makes a resolution. It is not much of a sacrifice. She will never even know about it. But in his helplessness, it is all he can offer. Next time Eloise Amison comes into the teachers' room, leans over his chair, and rests on his shoulders those tits that send the entire male population of the school into a hormone-thumping frenzy, he will get up and move away.

'I could have put them out for the trash men,' he says, and puts his arm around her to draw her back from the flames.

March 1956

'What did Dr Flanner say?' Claude asks as soon as he walks in that evening.

'He says I'm a healthy girl. Except for a minor ailment he calls housewife's syndrome.'

'It sounds like dishpan hands.'

'According to him, it can be cured by gardening or needlepoint or painting by numbers. He says he's dying to try the last himself, but he doesn't have the time.'

He goes to the cabinet to pour himself a drink. She already has one sitting on the counter. He knows what will happen if he agrees with the doctor.

She comes back to the subject when they sit down to dinner. During her *Cordon Bleu* period, they ate in the dining room. Now they are back in the kitchen.

'Before you switched and started going to Morris, what did Dr Flanner call you?' she asks as she passes him the peas.

'What do you mean?'

'Your name. Did he call you Claude or Mr Huggins?'

'I don't remember. What difference does it make?'

'None, I suppose, but I couldn't help noticing. I call him Dr Flanner. He calls King Gooding, who went in after me, Mr Gooding. But he calls me Babe.'

'So?'

'You don't see anything funny about that?'

'King Gooding is president of a bank. And Flanner was just being friendly.'

'No, he was being patronizing. He also told me to put on my clothes, like a good girl.'

'I'd rather he say that than tell you to take them off.' He grins. He is trying. That only makes it worse.

'And that business about taking up gardening or needlepoint or painting by numbers.'

'What's wrong with that?'

He reaches for the wine bottle and refills his glass.

'Thank you,' she says.

He refills hers.

'Anyway, I do garden,' she insists. 'After a fashion. I put in geraniums and impatiens every spring.'

'And you do a beautiful job.'

'Now you're patronizing me too.'

'It was a joke.'

'Needlepoint and coloring books for grown-ups. Talk about useless pursuits.'

'Then find something useful.'

'Like what? The South Downs Ladies' Historical Society? They wouldn't have me even if I wanted to join. They won't have Millie either, not since she married Al. Only Grace passes their test of social and racial purity. God, I hate this town.'

'Now it's the town's fault.' He stands and starts out of the kitchen. She is surprised. They have had far worse exchanges than this, she has been far more maudlin, and he has not left the room. A moment later, he returns carrying the evening paper open to an inside page and hands it to her.

'What's this?'

'You want to do something useful? The Montgomery bus boycott. You went to pieces over Emmett Till. Another woman refused to give up her seat on a bus.'

'You're sending me to Alabama?'

'Read the article. There are demonstrations all over the country. In Boston, seventy-five legislators walked out of committee meetings in sympathy with the strike. I bet there are offices and fund-raising organizations in western Massachusetts.'

'You think they'd want a white woman?'

'Is this the girl who talked her way into the Western Union office? Those legislators are white. The Boston NAACP is the most integrated branch in the country.'

'How do you know something like that?'

'I'm a schoolteacher. It's my job to know arcane facts that are of no discernible use to anyone.'

She picks up the paper and reads the article. A paragraph about one of the rallies stops her. An interracial audience laughed and wept and cheered. She tries to remember when she has laughed and wept and cheered all at once. During the war, of course.

November 1957

Babe planned to tell Claude first, but on her way home from the NAACP office that afternoon, she runs into Millie in the supermarket and cannot resist.

'You're looking at the new fund-raiser for the regional branch of the NAACP. No more volunteer work. As of today, I'm gainfully employed.'

Millie looks up from the cartons of milk she's loading into her basket. 'You mean they're going to pay you?'

'Don't sound so shocked. I'm raising money for a good cause, not selling my body.'

'It's just that volunteer work is one thing. We all do it. But a paying job . . .' Her voice drifts off. There is something wrong here, but she cannot put her finger on it. 'What does Claude say?'

'He doesn't know yet.'

Millie's eyes widen. 'You took a job without asking him?'

'I'm thirty-seven years old. I don't need a note from my husband to take a job.'

'But what if he minds?'

'Why would he mind having me doing something useful and getting a paycheck in the bargain?'

'All I know is, from the very beginning, even before Al started the business, when he was still working for his uncle, he said no wife of his was going to work.'

Babe grins and puts a container of cream for Claude's coffee in her basket. 'Then isn't it lucky I'm not married to Al. Not that I don't love him,' she adds as she wheels away.

As soon as she rounds the corner into another aisle, she stops smiling. She cannot be angry at Millie for being herself. But she is.

'I ran into Millie in the market,' she tells Claude after she breaks the news. 'According to her, even before Al was a success, he said no wife of his was going to work.'

'Then isn't it lucky you didn't marry Al.'

She has to laugh. 'That's what I told her.'

'Want to go out to dinner to celebrate?'

'Only if you do.'

'Should I open a bottle of champagne?'

'Neither of us even likes champagne.'

'Then how do you want to celebrate?'

She grins. A mirror image of the expression inches across his face. They leave a trail of shoes and shirts and trousers and underwear from the kitchen to the bedroom.

Afterward they lie, still tangled together, sweaty, gleeful, feeling strangely young. An image of Eloise Amison flashes through his mind. He does not even like large-breasted women, but he cannot help himself.

'Auden said it best,' he murmurs into her hair.

'What did Auden say best?' she asks his chest.

'"Any marriage, happy or unhappy, is infinitely more interesting than any romance, however passionate." I forget the rest, but it's something about marriage being the creation of time and will.'

'We just got lucky,' she says.

'That too,' he agrees.

CHAPTER 17

GRACE

June 1954

Grace is just finishing setting the table when Morris gets home. He puts his hat and bulky black doctor's bag on the top shelf of the front hall closet. When she first knew him, that bag worked on her like the Miltowns some of the women she knows are beginning to take. Every time she thought of Charlie and decided she could not go through with it, Morris would turn up with that bag in his hand, and she would feel a calm settling over her. The bag was tangible proof of his goodness. He was a man who cured the ailing, tended the dying, and caused pain only in the interest of healing. Now it is just a black leather bag.

He comes into the dining room and kisses her on the cheek.

She does not pull away. She does not even notice. He might be holding a door open for her or passing the salt.

'Something smells good.'

'Pot roast.'

'I'm a lucky man.'

The comment is like the door held open or the salt passed. He has a litany of similar phrases. They ought to put you in mass production. How did I get so lucky? You and Amy are the best thing that ever happened to me. They are not lies, more like slogans or ads on the radio. She tunes those out too.

He takes this week's issue of *Time* from the hall table, where she has left it for him, and goes into the sunporch. She does not pay much attention to that either. He is an easy man to live with. Affable. Appreciative. Unobtrusive.

She goes into the kitchen to slice the pot roast. All in all, it is not a bad arrangement, she thinks, as she takes the heavy iron pot from the oven. Amy has a male presence in the house, and all the magazines and books say that's important. She does not want to think of the trouble fatherless girls can get up to. The situation is better for her too. She prefers being married to being a widow. No more having to be grateful to other women's husbands for picking her up before and driving her home after parties, where no one wants her in the first place, because who wants an extra woman. No more having to rely on Claude or Al to mix the drinks before dinner or start the outdoor grill on a Sunday afternoon. No more having to listen to other women going on about their husbands or, worse still, stopping in the middle of a story because they realize she does not have one. Things could be worse. So why has the pot roast gone wavy through the shimmer of tears?

Mac has made up his mind. He is going to stay away from them. He has had enough of being the husband's buddy, the faithful hanger-on. He has had enough of watching her and having to watch himself.

The phone on his desk rings.

'I'm sorry to bother you at your office,' she says.

She has never called him here before. 'It's no bother.'

'But I have to talk to you before Morris gets home.' Her voice is low and throaty, more intimate over the phone than in person. 'His birthday is next week. I thought I'd give him a surprise dinner on Saturday. The usual suspects, but I wanted to make sure you could make it.'

He tells himself not to read anything into the statement. She probably said the same thing to the rest of the crowd when she called each of them. But he cannot help himself.

'I'll be there,' he says.

Autumn 1955

Amy stands in front of the mirror in the second-floor girls' room, tugging on her bangs. She could kill her mother for making her get her hair cut at Diamond's. Her mother insists it's the best hair salon in town. Sure it is, if you're a hundred years old. She tugs at her bangs again, but they won't get any longer. She could kill her mother and commit hari-kari herself. Her first week in senior high school, and she looks like Mamie Eisenhower. That's what Janice called her this morning. Mamie Amy. For the rest of her life, she'll be known as Mamie Amy.

She takes half of her ponytail in each hand, pulls apart to tighten the elastic, and goes on frowning at herself in the mirror. Smile, grown-ups are always telling her. The other day, some man on the street she did not even know said it. Smile, he called out to her. A pretty girl like you should smile. She smiles at her reflection in the mirror. The stupid grin makes her look like a clown. She goes back to frowning and turns up the collar of her blouse. Her mother doesn't let her leave the house with her collar turned up – she says it's cheap – but her mother doesn't know what she does once she gets to school. Even Miss Amison wears her collar up, and she's a teacher. She wears a small scarf tied inside the collar and leaves the top three buttons of her blouse open. When she leans over, you can see white flesh spilling over the top of her bra.

Amy turns sideways to the mirror and pushes out her chest. She still has an A-cup profile. It's pathetic.

Karen comes out of the stall and stands next to her at the sink, washing her hands. It's mean to think it, but Karen makes her feel better. Karen has no profile at all. She wears a double-A and doesn't even need that.

Amy gives another tug to her bangs, and they go out into the hall and head for Room 211, where the newspaper staff meets. She knows she'll never make the paper, but her mother encouraged her to go out for it. Your father was a wonderful reporter, she said. If he had lived, there's no telling how far he would have gone. She doesn't pay much attention to her mother, but Aunt Babe told her she should try out for the paper too.

When she gets to the door, she almost turns around to leave. There must be fifteen sophomores in the room, all boys.

Eddie Montrose, the editor-in-chief, is sitting – no, lounging – on the teacher's desk at the front of the room. A cigarette dangles from his full lips. They're not allowed to smoke in school, but it's after school, and the classroom has become the newspaper office. Still, the cigarette dangles from his lips, unlit. Gilly Jackson, the managing editor, is passing out mimeographed sheets of paper.

'Take a sheet,' Eddie says. 'That has the bare facts of the story. Then grab a desk. When I give the word, start writing. Time counts. If you want to be a newspaperman' – he glances at Amy and Karen – 'or gal,' he adds, as if the idea is a joke, 'you have to learn to write fast. But keep it accurate. You've got twenty minutes.' He looks down at his watch. 'Go.'

Amy knows she has done something wrong, because she finishes in fifteen. She does not hand in her story. People will think she's showing off, or know she did it wrong. She keeps reading it over, trying to figure out her mistake. All she finds is a missing comma and a spelling error. She waits until two boys have walked to the front of the room and given Gilly their stories. She stands, keeps her head down as she goes, and hands in hers.

Three days later the list of the four sophomores who made the paper is posted on the bulletin board outside the principal's office. Her name comes last, after three sophomore boys. She wonders if it's a mistake.

Her first job on the paper is typing the stories the other reporters write. Except for the two other girls, one for each year, they're all boys, so they don't know how to type. Eddie Montrose is the only one who types his own stories. That's because he writes them right on the typewriter. He sits at a desk, with a pencil behind his ear and an unlit cigarette hanging from his mouth, typing with two fingers. He hits the keys so hard sometimes she thinks he's going to hurt the machine, or himself. When Miss Amison, who teaches English and is the faculty adviser, comes in, he does not take the cigarette out of his mouth, and she does not tell him to. All she does is lean over his desk. That slows down the typing.

One afternoon at the end of her first month on

the paper, she is typing a story about the previous Saturday's football game, when she realizes she is alone in the office with Eddie Montrose. Her finger hits the *D* instead of the *C*. After she makes three more mistakes in the same line, she pulls the paper out, crumples it, throws it in the waste-basket, and puts in a fresh sheet. She starts to type again, makes four mistakes in the first two lines, and takes the paper out. As she reaches for a fresh sheet, she notices that the other typewriter has stopped.

'You know the rule about baseball players,' he says.

She cannot believe he's talking to her, but no one else is in the room.

'What?' she asks without turning around.

'If one guy fumbles, there'll be a run of fumbles. Slow down, squirt, or we'll run out of paper.'

She cannot believe he called her squirt. He makes up nicknames for most of the boys on the paper, but not for the girls. On the other hand, maybe he doesn't know her name.

Then he does it again. She has finished typing the piece, and he has taken that and the story he was writing and put them in a manila folder, and she is putting on her coat, when he says, 'Want a ride, squirt?'

She sits in the front seat, clutching her books to her chest, staring through the windshield as the flaming trees slide by, racking her brain for something to say. Her mind is blank as a washed blackboard. She looks down at the books on the seat between them, but she has nothing to say about chemistry or the history text Uncle Claude assigns for senior year, and she has never read *For Whom the Bell Tolls.*

He glances over and sees her staring at the books.

'You like Hemingway?'

She shrugs. She has never read Hemingway.

'What about poetry? Wait, don't tell me. I bet you like Emily Dickinson.'

She does like Emily Dickinson, but she can tell from the way he says it that she's not supposed to.

'Yeah, I figured. Girls always do. Eliot's my man. At least the poetry is. The guy's something else. That phony English gentleman stuff makes me sick. T.S., Mr Eliot, I say to that.'

He looks over at her again and laughs. She knows he is waiting for a response, but she doesn't know what it is supposed to be. She manages a smile.

'You don't know what T.S. means, do you?'

'Aren't they his initials?'

'Yeah, but that's the joke. They also stand for tough shit.'

'Oh, sure,' she says.

'Oh, sure,' he mimics, then does the most amazing thing. He reaches over and tugs her ponytail.

He asks her where she lives, she tells him, and for the rest of the ride she doesn't have to talk, because he is telling her about how Ernest Hemingway started out on a newspaper, and drove an ambulance in World War I, and covered the Spanish Civil War and World War II, and now that there's no war he shoots big game in Africa.

'My father was a newspaper reporter. Before he died in the war.'

'My father's a manager at the hat factory.' He shakes his head at the oncoming traffic. 'Talk about dullsville. If I ever end up like that, I'll kill myself.'

She isn't sure what to say to that. She doesn't want to insult his father, but she doesn't want him to think she disagrees with him.

He pulls up in front of her house. She cannot stand for this to be over. She cannot wait to get away. The strain is too much.

'Thanks,' she says, and starts to open the door.

'Listen, squirt,' he says. 'Want to go to the flicks Saturday night?'

Her heart flops over.

'Okay,' she says.

Then he does it again. He reaches over and tugs her ponytail.

She says nothing to her mother that night or the next. She is afraid her mother won't let her go. She has gone to the movies twice before with boys, but they were her own age and didn't drive. She wonders if she should lie and say she's going with Karen. But then how will she explain to him that she wants to meet him at the movie? Finally, she brings up the subject while her mother is washing the dinner dishes and she's drying.

'Eddie Montrose asked me to go to the movies Saturday night.'

Her mother turns from the dishes to her. 'He's a senior, isn't he?'

She knew it.

'Yeah, but really responsible. He's the editor of the newspaper.'

Her mother smiles. 'As if I didn't know.'

'What do you mean?'

'I mean you haven't stopped talking about him since you made the newspaper. What are you going to wear?'

She can go!

'It's only Thursday,' she says, though she knows exactly what she is going to wear. Her pink sweater set and her gray pleated skirt. The only decision she hasn't made is whether to keep her hair loose or put it in a ponytail. Loose seems better for a date, but she keeps remembering how he tugged her ponytail.

Her mother puts the last pot in the rack but goes on standing at the sink, staring out the window, though it's dark and she can't see anything but her own reflection.

'I remember what I wore on my first date with your father.'

'What?' She doesn't really care, but she wants to be nice, because her mother is letting her go.

And she wants to keep her mother thinking about what she wore a hundred years ago, not what she, Amy, is going to wear Saturday night. She does not want her mother messing around with her and Eddie Montrose. She wants to keep this for herself.

Her mother is still going on about her father. She cannot imagine her father, no matter how many stories her mother tells her. Sometimes she thinks if he were alive, he would love her so much. Sometimes she thinks he would see through her good-girl front to the mean, selfish, sneaky person she really is. And sometimes she thinks he would see through the mean, selfish, sneaky person to the real her.

When the bell rings that Saturday night and she opens the door to find Eddie Montrose standing in the vestibule, she is surprised. Is this the same Eddie Montrose she knows from school, the one who stars in the movies she runs in her head before she falls asleep every night? She never noticed his eyebrows before. They run straight across his forehead without a break. She's not saying he isn't handsome. She just never noticed them before.

He steps into the front hall. She is relieved that she does not have to drag him in, because her mother would never let her go off with some strange boy she hadn't met. She introduces him to her mother, and Morris, and Uncle Mac, who is here again this weekend. It's like running the gauntlet before they can get away.

In the car, she is even more nervous than she was when he drove her home from school. She keeps thinking of what her mother told her. When you get to the movie, don't jump out of the car. Wait for him to come around and open your door. That shows he respects you. Amy doesn't think it shows he respects her. She thinks it shows she's a spaz who can't open her own door. But when he gets out of the car, she goes on sitting in the passenger seat while he walks around to her side. It takes forever.

In front of the movie, she spends another forever reading the poster, just about memorizing the poster, because she can't bear to watch him buying the tickets. She feels funny about his spending money on her.

She can barely follow the movie with him sitting beside her. Spencer Tracy is supposed to have one arm, because he lost the other in the war. It's kind of like Uncle Claude's fingers, except no one ever mentions Uncle Claude's fingers, but in the movie everyone keeps making fun of Spencer Tracy's missing arm. When he beats up one of the villains with what Eddie leans over and says is judo, everyone in the audience cheers, even Eddie, so she cheers too. Then the audience settles down again, and Eddie reaches an arm around her shoulders. She stops breathing. She does not start again until they leave the theater.

After the movie, they go to the Hut, where everyone goes after the movies, unless they go to

Caputo's for pizza, and because he orders coffee and pound cake, she does too, though she usually has an Awful Awful. It's a huge glass full of ice cream, milk, whipped cream, chocolate or vanilla flavoring, and God knows what else, and if you drink three in a row, which she has never been able to do, you get your name up on a board.

'I don't get how people can drink those things,' he says as a tray full of them goes by.

'Me neither,' she says, and is glad her name is not up on the board.

When he pulls up in front of the house, she gets ready to wait until he climbs out and comes around the car to open her door. She wouldn't put it past her mother to be sitting in the window seat in her bedroom, watching. But instead of getting out, he turns toward her and reaches over as if he is going to tug her ponytail, only she has left her hair down tonight. He changes course, takes her scarf in his hand, and pulls it toward him.

'Come over here, squirt.'

She scuttles along the front seat after her scarf.

His breath smells of cigarettes. She tries not to mind. How can she mind? She's kissing Eddie Montrose. But when she kisses him in her bed before she falls asleep every night, he doesn't smell of anything. At night in her bed, he doesn't stick his tongue in her mouth either. She's heard of that, but she's never had anyone do it to her. She starts to pull away, but he won't let her. He takes his tongue out long enough to whisper relax, then sticks it back in. She just hopes she doesn't choke. After a while, she begins to get used to it. After a while, it doesn't even seem so bad, as long as she doesn't think about the cigarette smell. She wonders how long this is supposed to go on. She's getting kind of bored, but she doesn't want to hurt his feelings. And she doesn't want him not to like her.

She opens her eyes to try to get a glimpse of the clock on the dashboard. All she sees is his face, all squinched up against hers, with that line of eyebrows. She closes her eyes again. A minute later, she thinks he has his hand on her chest. She can't be sure, because she's wearing a coat. Then he begins pressing, and she's sure. This isn't like the scenes she puts herself to sleep with either. In those, he slips his hand inside her bra, smooth as silk. Now he's mashing around. She doesn't know why. It would make sense if she were Miss Amison, but you can't feel an A-cup through a coat and twin sweater set. When he stops kissing her for a minute, she says she has to go in.

He doesn't say anything. He just gets out of the car. She sits waiting for him to come around to her side. It takes even longer than it did at the movies. He's silent on the walk up the path. He is angry at her. She never should have said she had to go in. But she does. She has a curfew. She can't say that. She does not want to remind him she's only a sophomore.

They reach the door and stand in the glare of the overhead light that burns white and cold as ice. She looks up at him, then away. His lips are swollen and he has pink lipstick smeared on his chin. She wonders if she is supposed to tell him.

'Well, thanks,' she says.

The swollen lips move. 'Want to go out next Saturday, squirt?'

He is not angry at her. He likes her.

They are a couple. She is Eddie Montrose's girl-friend. She has a boyfriend who is a senior. No one calls her Mamie Amy or makes fun of her anymore. Every Saturday night, they go to the movies. A couple of times a week, after they finish working at the newspaper, he drives her home from school. Sometimes she would rather walk with Karen, but she does not say that. No girl in her right mind would want to walk with another girl when she could drive home with a boyfriend, a boyfriend who is a senior, and the editor of the paper, and has a car. Only some-times they don't drive home. Sometimes they drive out to a road beyond the pond and park. A funny thing begins to happen. The more they do in the car, the less she runs the movies in her head before she goes to sleep. She tries to, because she misses them, but no matter how tight she closes her eyes and imagines, she can't summon that romantic Eddie.

February 1956

Grace feels like a girl again. But feeling like a girl when you're a thirty-six-year-old woman with a husband and daughter is dangerous. It is also thrilling.

She lies listening to the sound of Morris's breathing in the other bed and the hush of the snow-shrouded night beyond the windows. Now and then tire chains clank in the silence.

She cannot sleep. She does not want to sleep when she can keep running the scene in her head.

She was in the kitchen, making another pot of coffee, because Al and Claude and Mac needed coffee before they got behind the wheel to drive home.

'Can you use any help?'

She did not turn when she heard his voice.

'Now you made me lose count.'

'You're up to six spoons.'

So he had been standing there watching her for a while.

She turned to face him. He was not leaning against the counter with his hands in his pockets or his arms crossed at his chest, pretending ease, as he usually did when he stood watching her. He was not even trying to hide the tension. Or was she projecting her own quickening of senses onto him?

The murmur of Morris telling a joke and Millie's

purr of laughter were faint whispers in the distant living room. The only sound in the kitchen was the soft whir of the electric clock over the stove, the hum of her life running out.

They stood that way for a moment, then, as if the dance had been choreographed, as if they had been rehearsing it for years, they moved together at the same instant. He bent to her, and she lifted her face to him, and somehow the synchronization erased any qualms. This was right. The dizziness in her head told her that, and the tightening in her stomach, and the contraction in her groin. She felt his erection against her. It was not only right, it was inevitable.

She heard the familiar creak of the floorboards between the front hall and dining room. They let go of each other and stepped back.

'I thought you might need help,' Morris said as he came into the kitchen. His big smiling face was innocent as a child's. His voice did not hold a whisper of suspicion.

A car clanks by in the street below.

They had both had a lot to drink. Everyone always did at these dinners. She wonders if Mac is regretting it. She imagines him lying in his boyhood bed in his parents' house, wrestling with his conscience, chastising himself for wrecking what he thinks is a marriage.

Two feet away, Morris exhales noisily, like a baby blowing bubbles of saliva.

She turns her head on the pillow. The room is

dark. She can barely make out his shape. Except for the sound of his breathing, he could be a heap of blankets or a pile of laundry. His being there, his lying in a separate bed, his oblivious sleep infuriate her. It is all his fault. If he were a real husband, she would not be falling into other men's arms just because they reach for her. He deserves whatever he gets.

The next morning as she is making breakfast, she remembers the lists Millie made years ago at the beginning of the war, reasons for following Pete to camp, reasons against it. She cannot put her pros and cons on a legal pad, but she does not have to. They do battle in her head. She is a married woman. She is a nice woman. Think of Amy. What if she is found out? What if she gets pregnant? And a thousand other terrors. The column in favor is shorter. I deserve some happiness.

After breakfast, as she and Morris sit at the table with their last cups of coffee, reading the Sunday paper, she reaches over without thinking and picks up a piece of toast Amy has left on her plate. As she starts to take a bite, she notices the thick slather of butter and jam. She puts the toast back on the plate.

Mac calls that afternoon. Amy answers the phone. 'It's Uncle Mac,' she says. Morris puts down the Sunday paper, gets up out of the big chair in the sunporch, and goes to the phone.

He does not call again on Monday. She is relieved. And she is forlorn. She stands in the front hall and the kitchen and the bedroom staring at the phone, willing it to ring.

Tuesday is Valentine's Day. St Hallmark's Day, Babe calls it, as she does Mother's Day and Father's Day. But Babe is a cynic. Mac is not. Surely he will call today. But he has not called by the time Morris gets home that evening.

He stands on the mat at the back door, taking off his galoshes, then crosses the kitchen to her and kisses her on the cheek. The gesture infuriates her. Doesn't he know what she is contemplating? Can't he sense it?

When he returns from putting his hat and coat and doctor's bag in the hall closet, he is carrying a small package wrapped in silver paper stamped with red hearts. He holds it out to her.

She puts down the spatula and takes it from him.

He starts to sing. He rarely sings. He is unlike Charlie in that respect too.

'I can't give you anything but love, baby.'

He goes on crooning as she unties the ribbon, peels off the paper, and snaps open the small velvet jeweler's box.

'Diamond bracelets Woolworth's doesn't sell, baby.'

The blue-white diamond earrings wink up at her.

Damn it to hell, she thinks.

'Thank you,' she says. 'They're beautiful.'

March 1956

When Mac calls again, she tells him she cannot do this to Morris. He does not argue with her. A week later, she changes her mind and calls him. No, you were right, he tells her. We can't do this to Morris. A few days later he calls, just to see how she is, he says. She tells him she is fine and gets off the phone. They ride up and down on their consciences as if on a seesaw. But as the winter drags on, her scruples freeze over. She finds herself thinking about Mac when she should be paying attention to her husband, or worrying about her daughter, or listening to what someone is saying. Twice she slips and calls Morris Mac. He does not notice. Maybe that is what persuades her.

The next time Mac calls, the seesaw is in perfect equilibrium. Neither of them mentions Morris. He says he has to see her. She says she wants to see him.

'I think I'll go into Boston to shop tomorrow,' she tells Morris at dinner. 'Nothing fits since I've lost weight. And Diamond's doesn't have a thing.' She warns herself to stop. She is making too many excuses.

'You're not going to be in Cambridge, are you?'

She stops with her fork halfway to her mouth. Mac's hospital is in Boston, but his apartment is in Cambridge.

'I don't think so. Why?'

'Nothing, really. I thought if you were, you could pick up some shirts for me at J. Squeeze.' It is what he calls J. Press.

She tells him she'll be happy to.

King has put on his clothes again and is sitting in the consultation room on the other side of the desk from Dr Flanner.

'EKG is normal,' the doctor says. 'Blood pressure is fine. Your heart sounds strong. I'd say you're in good shape for a man your age. No traces of that earlier incident. You could put on a few pounds. Otherwise, keep doing what you're doing, and I'll expect an invitation to your centennial birthday celebration.'

King thinks about it on the way to his car. He went for the checkup because Dorothy kept pleading with him to go. She has lost a son. She fears losing a husband, especially since his heart attack. But he does not give a damn about his EKG, or his blood pressure, or his heart. His clean bill of health is an obscenity. What right does he have to a clean bill of health at sixty-eight when Charlie died at twenty-six?

Grace draws the tube of Peaches 'n' Cream over one side of her upper lip, then the other, then across her lower. Her hand is steady as a surgeon's. Her cold-bloodedness shocks her.

The phone rings. Her hand freezes. It is Mac, with a case of the scruples she does not have. She picks up the receiver.

'Mrs Banks,' she hears Naomi say, and exhales in giddy relief.

'Yes?'

'I'm at Mrs Gooding's.'

'Is anything wrong?'

'I think you'd better get over here.'

'The doctor gave him a clean bill of health,' Dorothy says as soon as Grace walks in the door. 'Just yesterday. And then this morning . . . at breakfast . . .' She begins to cry again.

She repeats the phrases to everyone who comes to pay respects, and by noon the house is full. King was an important man. Dorothy has many women friends. 'A clean bill of health,' she keeps saying. 'And then this morning . . .'

The clean bill of health, Grace thinks, is what killed him. The prospect of all those years ahead without Charlie, all those years of his own life piling up when Charlie's was snuffed out before he even got started. That was what stopped King's heart.

Amy does not know why she does it. She knows it's wrong. She doesn't even want to do it. If her father could see her, he would know how bad she is.

The monitor from the vice principal's office comes into the newspaper staff meeting and says she has a note for Amy Gooding. Amy can't think of anything she has done wrong, except when she goes parking with Eddie, and the vice principal would not write a note about that. She takes the note and unfolds it.

Your mother called to say your grandfather passed away. She wants you to come home right after school.

Amy stands staring down at the words, trying to figure out what she feels. Nothing. She supposes she's sorry, but that's because it's sad to think of anyone dying. When Karen's dog died, she and Karen both cried buckets. But now she isn't even tearing up. Maybe if it was her father, she would be crying, but she was too little to understand when he died. Or maybe she is just a bad person. Only a bad person could not feel terrible about her own grandfather dying.

She must be staring at the note for a long time, because Eddie asks what's up.

She does not want to tell him. She does not want to tell anybody. Why do these things keep happening to her? There must be something wrong with her. She folds the note in half again, sticks it in her pocket, and says nothing is up.

After the meeting, he asks if she feels like driving

around. She puts her hand in her skirt pocket. The note is still there. She'll have to tell her mother she never got it.

'Sure,' she says.

This time when he takes her hand and tries to put it on the bulge in his corduroys, she doesn't pull it away. It's not so terrible. It's just a lump. Then he unzips his fly, and suddenly it's in her hand, all hot and sweaty, and it is terrible. She tries to yank her hand away, but he has her wrist and is moving her hand back and forth. She doesn't know how he can do so many things at once. One of his hands is moving hers up and down, and the other is in her blouse, and his tongue is in her mouth. She closes her eyes. She does not want to see his thing. On the back of her eyelids she sees her grandfather lying in a coffin. She is sorry now she wasn't nicer to him.

He begins reaching under her skirt. This is where she always clamps her legs together, only now she doesn't. She is tired of fighting him. She just wants him to like her.

He takes his tongue out of her mouth and his lips away for long enough to say something. It isn't I'm crazy about you. It isn't I love you. It's don't worry, I have something.

He lets go of her wrist. She takes her hand away. She wants to wipe it on her skirt, but she doesn't want to hurt his feelings. Her eyes are still closed. She does not want to see it. She does not want to see what he's doing. She is half sitting, half

369

sprawled on the front seat. The armrest on the door is digging into her neck. He has pushed up her skirt and pulled down her pants. The air is cold on her skin. Her grandfather must be cold too. Once, when she was little, her grandmother went all over the house looking for her, and when she found her reading in her grandfather's den, her grandmother said she was just like her father, but her grandfather said no she wasn't.

He is climbing on top of her. She opens her eyes in time to see his face getting closer. He is holding his thing in his hand. He begins pushing it against her. She has a feeling this is not the way it's supposed to be, but she does not know how it is supposed to be.

'Open your legs,' he says. He sounds angry again, but he can't be angry. She's letting him do what he has been trying to do all winter.

One leg is crushed against the back of the seat. She moves the one that's on the floor. He's pushing harder now, but he still can't get in. She doesn't see how he's ever going to. He grabs her other leg, the one that's crushed against the back of the seat, and pulls it up so her foot is pointing toward the roof. Her hips tilt after it. He shoves himself in. The pain goes off like a small explosion. She lets out a yelp. He doesn't seem to hear her, but how could he above the noise he's making. He sounds the way Frankie Hart does when he hits the finish line in a race and stands bent over with his hands on his knees, panting like a dog.

It doesn't hurt as much now, but she still wishes it would be over. Then it must be, because he groans, and stops thrusting, and flops down on her.

She wonders if she's supposed to say something. She waits for him to. She looks past him out the window. A cold mottled moon is rising in the darkening sky. She thinks of her father lying in the cold ground. She imagines her grandfather being lowered into the dirt beside him.

He sits up and twists away from her. His hands are in front of him, and she can't see what he's doing, but he must be doing something, because his head is down as if he's concentrating. He rolls down the window and throws something into the woods. Then she hears the sound of a zipper. He turns back to her. His lips are swollen, but they're not set in the sullen line. He opens his mouth. She wonders if this is when he tells her he loves her.

'You'll like it better next time,' he says.

This time the weather does not mock them. A steel-gray sky stretches above the cemetery. The wind works them over like a sparring partner. Patches of snow strew the ground, dirty as old rags.

From time to time, Grace glances at her daughter, who stands between Dorothy and her. Her thick black hair hangs around her face like a shroud. Her creamy skin is mottled from the wind. Her dark eyes are red and raw, as if she has been crying for days. Grace is surprised. Amy was not any closer to King than she was. But he left his mark on them. King is the reason she sleeps alone, untouched and aching.

Something makes her turn her head away from Amy. Her eyes meet Mac's. He has been watching her. She looks away before she can read anything in his face. No, before he can read anything in hers.

The minister is talking about King, only he calls him Charles. Like Charlie. She will never forgive King for the advice he gave her years ago. But she is grateful to him now, for helping her make up her mind.

'I was surprised Mac came home for the funeral,' Morris says in the car on the way home.

Grace does not answer.

'He says he's staying for a few days. I think King's death has him worried about his parents.'

She still does not speak.

'I invited him for dinner tomorrow night.'

Her head swivels to him. 'You didn't!'

He glances over at her, and she reads the surprise in his face, then feels the blood rising in her own.

'I just don't think we ought to be giving dinner parties the day after King's funeral,' she says evenly. 'He was Amy's grandfather.'

He turns back to the road and slams on the brakes just in time to keep from hitting the car in front of them.

'Mac isn't exactly a dinner party,' he says. For the rest of the way home, he keeps his eyes on the road.

She has to head him off, but she cannot imagine how. If he were in Boston, she could telephone him, but if she calls him in South Downs, his mother is likely to answer. Her only hope is to track him down in town. He always turns up at the drugstore at some point when he's in town. She'll find him if she has to spend the entire day loitering on Broad Street.

She does not have to spend the entire day. She walks by the drugstore, peers in, sees he is not there, and heads for Diamond's. When she comes out twenty minutes later, he is driving past the front entrance of the store. He sees her, pulls the car to the curb, and leans over to the passenger side to roll down the window.

She bends until her face is on a level with the car. 'I have to see you,' she says.

'I know. Get in.'

'No, that's not what I mean.' But suddenly she wonders if it is. It would be so easy to open the door, get in, and drive away with him. 'I mean I have to see you to tell you I can't see you.'

'That doesn't make sense.'

'You know it does.'

'Get in the car, Gracie, and we'll talk about it.'

'There's nothing to talk about. It's wrong, and we both know it.'

'It's not wrong. I love you.'

She shakes her head. Her hair swings in front of her face, blotting him out for a moment. If only it were that easy.

'You don't love me.'

'Don't tell me what I feel.'

He has never spoken to her so harshly. That should make it easier. It doesn't.

'Get in the car, please.'

She starts to shake her head no again, then notices two women from the ladies' historical society staring at them from across the street. She reaches for the handle, opens the door, and gets in. As he pulls out into the stream of traffic, a horn shrieks.

'Ever hear of looking, buddy?' the driver shouts.

Neither of them speaks until they have left the downtown area and are on a road out of town.

'Where are we going?' she asks. When did it become we? She went looking for him to tell him she could not see him. Now they are driving off into the countryside together. This is not turning out as she planned.

'Somewhere we can be alone.'

'No!' Her voice shrieks like the horn of the car he cut off.

'To talk. I just want to talk to you.'

'There's nothing to talk about,' she says again. 'It's over.'

He swerves onto the shoulder of the road, cuts the engine, and turns to her. She presses herself against the door until the handle digs into her back. He reaches for her hand. For a moment it lies cradled in his on the seat between them. It would be so easy to leave it there. She pulls it away.

'Don't you see?' she says. 'King's death was a sign.'

'King's death was a physical occurrence. His heart stopped. It has no moral significance. Death never does.' His mouth twists into a grimace as he says it, and she knows he is thinking of his time in the Pacific.

Her hand begins to lift of its own will. She wants to touch his arm, to caress his cheek, to feel his mouth in her palm. She wants to comfort him and be comforted by him. She makes her hand into a fist and jams it into her pocket.

'All right, it wasn't a sign,' she admits. 'But it made me see things clearly. We can't do this. It's not right.'

'It's right for us.' His mouth caresses the words. She closes her eyes. She cannot look at his mouth. She opens her eyes, and when she speaks, she does not caress the words. She spits them out like stones.

'But not for other people.' She clenches her fist tighter until her nails are digging into her skin. 'We can't do this to Charlie.'

She sees the expression on his face and realizes what she has said. 'I mean Morris.'

He turns away from her and starts the car. This

time he looks in the side mirror before he pulls out, though there is little traffic.

'No, you mean Charlie.'

On the road back to town, he does not have to glance at her to know she is crying. He doesn't care. He is too angry at her. He is too disgusted with himself. When Morris asked if he minded, he should have said yes, he minded. Yes, he was mad as hell. But he didn't. He deserves what he gets, or rather what he will not get.

She was dry-eyed at the funeral, but she cried in the car with Mac, and in the weeks that follow, she finds herself tearing up at nothing. One night she lies in bed crying so bitterly that she cannot stifle the noise.

'What's wrong?' Morris's words float across the no-man's-land between the beds.

'Nothing.' Another sob escapes. 'I'm fine, really.'

She hears his mattress sigh as he gets up, then feels hers shift as he sits on the side of the bed.

'This isn't about King,' he says.

There is something in his voice she has not heard before. Not sympathy. He has always been sympathetic. This is deeper, less facile, more wary, the voice of the human being beneath the cartoon husband.

He lifts the covers and gets into bed beside her. Her body freezes. He is going to console her, but she does not want his consolation, not for the loss of Mac. She knows now it is a loss.

He rubs away the tears with his thumb and smooths her hair back from her face. She waits for one of the anodyne phrases. There's nothing to cry about. Everything is all right. I'll take care of you. But he does not say anything. She waits for the kiss-off kiss. But he goes on stroking her hair. A moment later, his hand moves to her shoulder. He slides off the strap of her nightgown and peels down the top.

She is so surprised that she takes a moment to realize what he is doing. When she does, she is embarrassed. I don't need your pity, she wants to scream. But she does need it. The intimacy shames her but not her body. It presses itself against him. It clings to him. It opens itself to this man who is infinitely gentle, perfectly proficient, and entirely without physical passion.

Afterward he lies stroking her damp hair back from her face again.

'I don't know what I'd do if I lost you,' he whispers.

A little while later, he gets out of her bed and goes back to his. The next day, neither of them mentions the incident. But after that, every few months, he comes to her bed. She never stops him. She closes her eyes. Usually she thinks of Charlie. Occasionally she thinks of Mac.

CHAPTER 18

MILLIE

Autumn 1955

The odd part of it, Millie will realize when she calms down, is that she is not surprised. She always knew she had it coming one way or another.

She has set the day aside to tackle the children's closets. A cleaning woman comes in three times a week, but you cannot trust a cleaning woman to know what should be kept, what should be thrown out, and what should never have been there in the first place.

She starts in the girls' room. Jack is more of a pack rat, but two of them mean twice the clutter. By eleven-thirty she has filled three large trash bags with outgrown clothes, forgotten toys, and junk they have carried home from birthday parties and family outings and school. She thinks back to her own childhood room. Strange how much less they had of everything before the war.

When she has finished arranging things – and God help her if she puts Betsy's possessions on Susan's side or vice versa – she takes the box of trash bags and makes her way to Jack's room, though Al does not think she should be cleaning out his closet.

'He's almost thirteen,' he said when she told him at breakfast that today was her closet day. 'He's old enough to clean out his own closet.'

'I don't mind doing it.'

'I wasn't worried about you. I was thinking of him. He deserves a little privacy.'

'I'm cleaning his closet, not bursting into the bathroom when he's in the shower.' She stopped doing that a year ago, when he went berserk one night.

'What are you going to do if you find copies of *Playboy* or something like that?'

'I don't know. What do you think I should do?'

'Stay out of his closet.'

If he has copies of *Playboy*, he has found a better hiding place for them. She finds nothing but old sneakers, forsaken balls, bats, and skates, and boxes of half-finished plane, tank, and ship models. The ones he completed are displayed around the room.

It takes a while for her to work her way to the box in the back, all the way on the side. Even before she pulls it out, she knows what it is. She has always known. When the teacher called home and asked for Mrs Swallow, she knew. And when he got into fights, she knew. And when he came home asking if he was Jewish, she knew.

She drags the box out of the closet and opens

the flaps. He is not usually neat – what boy is neat? – but the contents are in perfect order, the letters on one side, the pictures on the other, the sketches spread carefully beneath them.

She lifts out several photos and begins going through them. Pete in his new uniform, staring into the camera of a professional photographer; Pete in training camp; Pete in England. She knows them by heart. Yet the years have made them unfamiliar.

She reaches into the box again and takes out another handful. These are from before the war. In them, he plays ball, horses around with the guys, and graduates from high school. One of the photos stops her. Jack has put a picture of himself in with those of Pete, as if he is trying to go backward in time to find a way into Pete's life. The tears blur her vision. She blinks to put the picture back in focus. It is not of Jack. It is of a young Pete, so young that he is closer in age to Jack than to the man he would have been now, than to her. He is wearing Jack's wide-apart blue eyes and square face and unruly cowlick. She imagines Jack looking at it as if looking into a mirror.

She begins putting the photos back in the box, but another one catches her eye. In this one, Pete stands at the edge of the pond with a bunch of girls in bathing caps and boys in those old-fashioned swimming suits with knitted tops like pieces of chest armor. Grace is there, but not with Charlie. She can't find Babe. She searches for herself. The picture must have been taken during one of the times Pete took up with another girl.

Suddenly her face jumps out at her. She did not recognize herself because the strap of the bathing cap pushes her cheeks up and out of shape. Only it is more than that. She did not recognize herself because she cannot remember being that girl. She cannot remember believing that despite her mother's death, and her father's, the world would still hand her happiness, as long as she had Pete.

The face in the photograph goes blurry through a new rush of tears. She is not crying for his death, though for a year after it she cried herself to sleep every night. After she married Al, she took her tears where he could not see them. He was always wondering why she spent so much time in the shower. But gradually she stopped crying in the shower, and over the sink, and when she went to check on Jack in the middle of the night. Gradually, she stopped grieving. The fact shames her, but she cannot help herself. She had a few months with Pete. She has been married to Al for almost ten years. For ten years they have eaten meals together, and gone to the movies together, and decided to buy this or not buy that together; they have made love, and had arguments, and raised children; she has seen his hair begin to recede, and he has pretended not to see her stretch marks. She cannot remember being married to Pete any more than she can remember being that girl who trusted the world to hand her happiness. She cannot imagine not being married to Al.

Jack spots the smoke halfway down the block. As he gets closer, he sees the sooty plume rising from Uncle Claude's yard. He looks up the driveway. Aunt Babe is standing over a garbage can. She is staring down into it, and the flames are licking up at her, and he knows, as he stands there, that this is not the way a normal person burns leaves or household trash or newspapers. He thinks of going to see if she's okay. His mom is always saying Aunt Babe needs help. He stands waiting. If she looks up, he'll go. She does not look up. He starts walking again.

His mother is in the kitchen with the electric mixer going. He hopes it's brownies. He drops his books on the table as he goes past and crosses to where she's standing at the counter. As she turns off the mixer, he starts to dip his finger in. She usually tells him to wash his hands first, but sometimes she doesn't notice.

She doesn't tell him to wash. She just pushes his hand away.

'I thought we agreed it's wrong to take things that don't belong to you,' she says without looking up from the mixing bowl.

He doesn't know what she's talking about. Brownies don't belong to anyone. She makes them for him, his sisters, and his dad.

'I only wanted a lick.'

She puts the spoon down and steps back so she is facing him with a few feet of kitchen between them. 'I'm not talking about brownie dough.'

'I didn't swipe anything.' He thinks of the Snickers bar, but how could she know about that? He didn't get caught at the store.

'I cleaned out your closet today.' She stops, as if she is waiting for him to say something.

He looks down at his feet. She did not even notice the mud on his sneakers. The realization scares him.

'I found a box there that doesn't belong to you.'

He drags his eyes up from the floor. 'I just wanted to look at the stuff.'

'You should have asked me.'

Sure, a voice in his head shouts, and you would have said no. But he knows better than to talk back to her now.

'Those were my letters and my pictures,' she goes on, and he does not recognize the voice. It is hard as steel, with none of the lilt she uses to charm the birds out of the trees. 'My letters and my pictures, and you stole them.' It is the voice of a drill sergeant in the movies or a coach at school telling you he is not going to take any more guff. 'You stole them and you hid them from me.'

They go on standing that way, as she stares at him with hard, unforgiving eyes he has never seen, and he wonders what to do. Suddenly he knows. He feels his own fury rising until his chest heaves with it. He wants to hit her. He wants to start swinging at her the way he did at Billy Craig the time they had the big fight. He is tall enough to. He could really hurt her if he wanted. His hands have balled into fists. He hides them behind him, but he cannot hold back the rage.

'You stole them from me,' he yells. 'He's my father, and you stole him from me and hid him. You took away my father.'

His hands are still balled behind him. His fists tremble with the urge to pummel her. He feels himself taking a step forward. He sees his knuckle connect with her nose. The blood spurts out and runs down her face. She staggers from the force of his hand.

He closes his eyes, then opens them. She is still standing there. He takes several steps back, bumps into one of the kitchen chairs, and sits down hard. His breath is coming in shallow gasps. His fists hang at his sides. He forces them open, but he cannot look up at her. He is terrified at how close he came to hitting her.

March 1956

Millie is surprised when Jack says he wants to go to King Gooding's funeral.

'For Amy,' he explains.

It is not a lie. He is going partly for Amy, but he is also going for himself. His dad doesn't – didn't – like King Gooding, and a lot of people were afraid of him, but he always felt as if he and

King Gooding were almost friends. King gave him that dollar, and asked if he was young Pete Swallow, and when he said he wasn't sure, called him on it, so that he had to stand up and say, yes, I'm Pete Swallow. He owes King Gooding more than a dollar.

He was too little to go to the cemetery that day, so they left him in the car, but he remembers getting up on his knees in the backseat to watch what was going on. He saw the big wooden box, just like the one the men are lowering into the ground now, but then there was a flag on the box, because King Gooding's son died in the war, just like Jack's father, Pete Swallow. The hero.

He looks from the hole in the ground to the stone next to it.

CHARLES HENRY GOODING, JR.
1918–1944

What he can't figure out is why Charles Henry Gooding, Jr., is buried here, and his father, Peter John Swallow – Peter John Swallow, Sr., if you count him – is buried in France. He knows not to ask his mother, but he cannot stop thinking about it. If his father were buried here, he could visit him. He could ride his bike out after school, sit on the grass, and shoot the breeze with his real dad.

Millie stands staring across the open grave at Grace, Amy, and Dorothy. Amy looks up, sees she is being watched, and drops her reddened eyes again, but not before Millie catches the wild, trapped look in them. It makes her, perversely, even lovelier. She is still in high school, and talking about college, but Millie cannot help thinking the sooner Grace marries her off to some nice boy, the better off she'll be. Otherwise, she has a feeling Amy is in for a hard time. So is Grace.

She looks from Amy to her grandmother. Dorothy's eyes are red too. Millie does not know why she is surprised. She thought of King as an old man. Old men are supposed to die, though during the war the arithmetic was reversed. But King was not an old man to his wife. And now he is gone, and she is alone. She pictures Dorothy rattling around that big beautiful house on her own, no husband, no son, nothing but silence as loud as a shriek. The prospect is terrifying. It makes her hang on to Al's arm as they make their way down the path and out of the cemetery. Not until she is in the car does the thought come to her. She wonders if Dorothy is going to sell the house.

November 1957

Millie drives by the house daily, sometimes more than once a day. She does not bother Dorothy, merely cruises by slowly, admiring the half-timbered façade with the brick chimney, the mullioned windows, the shrubs that encircle the house like a demure skirt. A large wound in the trunk of one of the two tall oaks on either side of the path has been painted black, and Al thinks they may have to have it cut down. She is hoping they can save it. She likes the symmetry.

She is itching to get inside the house and start measuring, though Al does not want her to until they have closed on it, and she does not want to appear to be rushing Dorothy. It's bad enough the poor woman lost her husband. Now she's giving up her house. Before the war, she probably would have held on to the place, but times are changing. Widows and retirees are selling their big, expensive-to-heat, hard-to-keep-up houses and moving to Florida or Arizona, where they live on scratchy long-distance telephone calls and vanishing memories.

One day as Millie drives by, she sees Dorothy standing on the lawn, talking to a man in overalls and a heavy work jacket with KYLE'S TREE CARE AND SURGERY written across the back. Millie is embarrassed to be caught casing the joint, as Al calls her drives by, but Dorothy waves, and Millie stops to say hello. Dorothy asks if she'd like to come inside and have another look around the house. Millie says she would like to very much.

The two of them move through the house in tandem, Dorothy sometimes leading the way, sometimes stepping back to let Millie enter a room ahead of her. Millie is looking at the house, but Dorothy is taking a tour of her life. They go into

387

King's study, which still smells of his cigars. 'How I hated that smell,' Dorothy says, and turns away, but not before Millie sees the tears welling up. They stand in the archway to the dining room, where Naomi's mother and then Naomi served them a thousand dinners. She opens the door, and they lean out into the screened-in porch, where Dorothy tells her she once came home early from a ladies' historical society meeting and found Charlie and Mac and a bunch of other boys smoking. The wistfulness in her voice is like a wrench twisting Millie's insides.

'I hope you'll be as happy here as we were,' she says as she walks Millie to the door.

For the rest of the afternoon, as she picks up the dry cleaning, takes Al's brogues to the shoemaker, goes to the supermarket, and has a prescription for Susan's cough filled at the new drugstore chain next to the supermarket – she feels guilty because she should go downtown to Swallow's, but this is so much more convenient – she keeps imagining how happy they are going to be in that house.

By the time she loads her groceries into the car and starts home, it is getting dark, and she has to turn on her headlights. As she passes Babe's house, they sweep over the front yard and silhouette Babe climbing out of the car. She wonders when Babe gets her marketing done, and her dry cleaning picked up, and Claude's shoes to the shoemaker. Poor Claude. Babe says that sometimes, when he gets home first, he puts the potatoes in to bake or lights the burner under leftover stew. Al would never do that. But poor Babe too. She pretends to love her job, but if Claude were more of a go-getter like Al, Babe would not have to work.

Millie is past the house when she glances in the rearview mirror and sees a figure coming down the driveway. There is no reason Jack should not be there, but she cannot help wondering why he is. She backs up the car.

'Need a lift, young man?'

He looks startled, but that could be the headlights.

'What were you doing there?' she asks when he climbs in.

'Nothing,' he says, and slides down lower in the seat.

'Nothing?'

'I wanted to ask Uncle Claude some questions.'

'About what?' She has heard him ask Claude about the war, just as he asks Al, but once or twice when he didn't know she was listening, he asked about Pete.

He skulks down in the seat another couple of inches. 'My history project.'

'I thought you had Mr Dickerson for history.'

'Yeah, that's the problem. He's not as good as Uncle Claude. That's why I need help.'

It's a perfectly logical answer, but she cannot get over the feeling that he is up to something, and that Babe and Claude are keeping it from her.

★ ★ ★

Millie is ashamed of herself. After all she has been through – losing her parents, losing Pete – she should not be going to pieces about losing a house. She should be counting her blessings. No woman in her right mind would be sitting on a closed toilet with the mascara running down her cheeks and a wad of wet tissues in her hand, grieving for a house that was never hers. But it is not only the lost house, it is the lost happiness. When Dorothy walked her through a few days ago, filling the house with her memories, Millie could not help peopling the rooms with Al and the children and her. She stood in the living room and saw the Christmas tree in front of the mullioned windows. She looked up the staircase from the front hall and saw first Betsy, then Susan, coming down it in a white dress. Both times she married in a suit, and there had been no staircase, only her aunt's living room with Pete and a judge's chambers with Al. She stood in the center of King's cigar-reeking den, stripped it of the heavy leather furniture and big mahogany desk, and put in a couch made for wear and tear and a twenty-four-inch television. She saw all five of them eating popcorn, toasting marshmallows in the fireplace, laughing, talking, teasing. The house would be restitution. The house would give her back everything she keeps losing. But now she has lost the house too.

There is a knock on the door. 'Mil,' Al says, 'are you okay?'

'I'm fine.' She stands and begins to wash her face.

He opens the door a crack.

'You sure?'

She turns her dripping face to him and manages a smile. 'Of course I'm sure.'

'It's only a house,' he says, but she can tell. He is disappointed too. He loved the house. And he loved the idea of living in King Gooding's house.

Al sits on the side of the bed, listening to his wife crying in the bathroom, and makes up his mind. This time he is not going to let them get away with it.

Dorothy said she was terribly sorry, but she had a better offer. When he pointed out that she had already accepted his, she admitted she had but said he had not put down a deposit and she had not signed anything. If a Jew tried to get away with a double deal like that, they'd call him every name in the book. He offered to top the new bid. Now he was angry. He wanted to live in King Gooding's house because Millie loved it, and because it was beautiful, and because it would make King Gooding turn over in his grave and his good Christian neighbors mad as hell. He wondered if they had really found her another buyer or merely persuaded her not to sell to him.

He can imagine the scene. Did it happen last night, or did she need a few days to get up the courage to tell him? He can even guess the players. Cox, who lives across the street from her and runs the bank now that King is gone. Swain of Swain,

Swain, and Dobbins, Attorneys-at-Law. Fearing, who came close to being indicted for some insurance hanky-panky, but at least he is not a Jew. He sees the three men, solid citizens, good Christians, walking up her path through the autumnal dusk, their feet crunching the acorns from the oak that isn't sick. She is surprised to find them there, but she invites them in and offers them a drink, and they accept, because this is, after all, a neighborly call. He can imagine the conversation too. They talk about property values, and the neighborhood going down, and – here is the kicker – what King would have wanted. And so this morning she called him and said she was terribly sorry but she had a better offer. Her voice was thin and a little embarrassed. He had to give her that.

Millie is still in the bathroom, crying. He is damned if he'll let them get away with this. He will not say anything to her yet. He is not sure he can pull it off. And he knows his wife. She will swear secrecy, but in a moment of weakness or excitement, she will let something slip to Grace or Babe, and that will be the end of it.

He gets up, goes to the door, and opens it a crack. 'It's only a house,' he says. But he knows it is more than that, for him as well as for her.

BOOK VI

1962–1964

CHAPTER 19

BABE

May 1962

Babe arrives at the restaurant before Claude. They drove in to Boston together this morning, but when he went off to the state teachers' meeting, he warned her he might be late to dinner. She does not mind being first. She just wants to get off her feet and order a drink. She spent the morning at the Boston NAACP office and the afternoon shopping with Grace and Amy for Amy's trousseau. The word strikes her as a hoary nineteenth-century anachronism, but Grace loves it. She is also a pushover for any song that has the words *young* and *love* in it. 'Younger Than Springtime.' 'Hello, Young Lovers.' 'Too Young.' Sometimes Babe envies Grace her starry-eyed innocence; sometimes she wonders if Grace has ever really been married. How can she still work herself up to such a pitch about engagements and weddings and happily-ever-afters?

She crosses the plush carpet of the entrance hall, gives the maître d' her name, and says they have a reservation. He consults his book, finds the name, looks up, and tells her Mr Huggins is not here yet.

'That's all right,' she begins, but he has already moved on to a couple behind her. She glances around for a place to sit, but there are no chairs, only lots of gilt mirrors and overblown flower arrangements.

When Babe decided she would drive in to Boston with Claude, he said they ought to splurge on a celebratory dinner.

'What are we celebrating?' she asked.

'My not getting the principal's job.'

The fact that he can joke about it does not make her feel less guilty. 'That's my fault.'

'You helped,' he admitted. 'Rabble-rouser, pinko, and a hyphenated term beginning with a word I won't use and ending in lover are just a few of the more endearing names you're called around town. But I like to think I had something to do with it.'

'I'm sorry.'

'I'm not. I'd like the extra money, though we're doing all right with both our salaries. But let's face it, I'd be lousy at the job, not to mention miserable in it. The way things are now, every so often – not regularly, I admit, but every so often – a smart kid with a curious mind rears his head in that crowd of juvenile delinquents I'm supposed to be turning into useful members of society. And, believe it or not, I still get a thrill out of it. But in the principal's office, all I'd be doing is disciplining the juvenile delinquents and listening to teachers' gripes.'

She is not sure whether she envies his equilibrium or disapproves of it. In his place, she could not resist going after the job, even if she knew she would be miserable once she got it.

A man comes in and gives the maître d' his name. The maître d' tells him he is the first to arrive and shows him to a table.

She stands shifting from foot to foot, gazing into the dining room. Groups of twos and fours and sixes sit eating, drinking, smoking, talking. Here and there a lone man waits for a companion. She wants to know why she cannot sit at a table waiting for Claude.

She approaches the maître d' again and tells him she would like to wait for Mr Huggins at the table. He apologizes and says the table is not yet ready, though beyond his brilliantined head, she sees several empty ones scattered around the room.

A moment later Claude arrives, and the maître d' shows them to a table, pulls out her chair for her, and says he hopes she enjoys her dinner.

'That's an about-face,' she murmurs to Claude, and tells him about having to cool her heels in the entrance area while everyone else was being seated. 'I know I'm not exactly a fashion plate. I spent the afternoon watching Grace spend unconscionable sums of money for clothes I can't believe Amy will ever wear. But I didn't think I looked that down-at-the-heels.'

'You look fine. It has nothing to do with that. He just can't seat a lone woman.'

'Why on earth not?'

'Because the assumption is that a woman alone in a place like this is a hooker.'

'You're not serious?'

'Dead serious. You can't really blame him.'

'Want to bet?'

'He's trying to run a business, and there are laws against soliciting.'

She leans back in the chair, looks around the room, and brings her gaze back to him.

'You know what I ought to do? I ought to take everything I've learned at the NAACP and put it to work getting women into fancy restaurants. And everywhere else they're not wanted.'

CHAPTER 20

GRACE

May 1962

Later Amy will blame her mother, but how can it be Grace's fault? She did not force Amy to do anything. She did not even express disapproval. Perhaps her face showed concern, but what mother's would not when her daughter comes home from school three weeks before the wedding and says she is going to call it off?

Grace does not mind the embarrassment of sending out the cancelation cards; or the bother of returning the gifts; or the waste of all that money for a wedding dress Amy will not wear, food no one will eat, and music that will not be played. Well, she minds, but what really upsets her, what terrifies her, is that Amy is making a mistake she will regret for the rest of her life. Roger is a wonderful catch, as the term goes, though Grace would never use it. Good-looking but not too handsome, which is always dangerous; considerate; well mannered; from a solid family; headed toward a good future. He is about to graduate from Yale Law School. More to the point, because Grace is not a fool – she, of all people, knows the difference between appearance and reality – he adores Amy, and not in a brotherly way. He is also an anchor for her. The first time Amy brought him home, Grace felt as if she had navigated the vessel that was her daughter's life through rough seas and finally steered her into a safe harbor.

'Did you have a fight?' she asks now.

They are sitting in the window seat of Grace's bedroom, the same room where they clung together and cried after Grace returned from her wedding trip. Morris is at a meeting of the county medical association.

Amy hugs herself and shakes her head.

'Then what?'

'I just don't think I can go through with it.'

Grace lunges for the lifeline. Amy did not say she cannot go through with it. She said she doesn't *think* she can go through with it.

'Oh, sweetheart, everyone has pre-wedding jitters.'

Amy looks up from behind the curtain of hair. Her face is white and drawn. Three angry red pimples deface her usually flawless skin. 'You call spending every night for the past two weeks crying in a bathroom stall jitters? Every time someone comes in, I have to flush the toilet so they won't hear me.'

'That's exactly what I call it.'

'If everybody has them, how come the two other

girls in Northrup House who are getting married after graduation don't spend their nights sitting in the bathroom crying?'

'What other girls do or don't do is beside the point. Only one thing matters. Do you love Roger? I know he loves you, but do you love him?'

Amy drops her head and the curtain of hair shrouds her face again. 'Sometimes I think I do. But other times I know I don't love him the way other girls love their fiancés.'

Grace wishes she would stop talking about other girls.

'Not because there's anything wrong with him.' She fingers the pimples. 'Because there's something wrong with me.'

Now Grace understands. The problem is not jitters, or Roger, or other girls; it is Amy. It is the two of them. They are a blighted family of widows and orphans and mental hospitals and broken engagements.

Grace takes Amy's hand from her face. 'There's nothing wrong with you.'

'There is, but that's the funny part. When I met Roger, I thought he could fix it.'

Hope beats its puny wings in Grace's chest. Morris could not make them whole, but Roger is not Morris. She reaches an arm around Amy's shoulders. 'There's nothing wrong with you,' she repeats, 'nothing that marriage to a wonderful boy like Roger won't fix.'

Amy's doubt is no match for her mother's

certainty. It carries her to the front door when Roger shows up later that evening, though she told him not to; and through the days to the wedding; and into the moment she slips her hand through Morris's arm to walk down the aisle in the white organdy dress embroidered with tiny roses and forget-me-nots that won't go to waste after all.

CHAPTER 21

MILLIE

May 1962

Millie sits in what was once King Gooding's den. During the commercials, she cannot help glancing around the room, admiring what she has made of it. The newly installed French windows open into the garden and bring the outdoors inside. The wicker chairs and sofas seem to float in the space. Their chintz-upholstered cushions are light as clouds. She worried that the big television would ruin the English-country-house aura of the room, but when she closes the doors of the tall oak armoire, no one even knows it's there. The doors are open now, and the television is tuned to *Perry Mason,* and she and Al sit on one sofa while Betsy and Susan sprawl on the other, twined together, supple as kittens. Now that each has a room of her own, they rarely squabble.

It's only a house, Al said, when he thought they had lost it. There are other houses, Grace assured her. A house does not solve problems or bring happiness, Babe warned, and looked as if she was about to say more but didn't.

Millie tried to believe them. She went to look at other houses. Some were bigger, some more architecturally impressive, but none was right. Even if the engineer's reports on those houses vouched for roofs and foundations and plumbing, those houses struck her as flimsy. Only this house withstood the test. Since she was a little girl, before her mother went into the hospital, before her father drove into a tree, the big house at the end of the block, the Gooding house, was solid. That was why she was heartbroken when they lost it. And that was why Al got it for her.

The idea was simple, he told her after he pulled it off. Anyone could have thought of it. She disagrees. She is not saying Jews are more clever. More devious, she now knows is how other people put it. But she does believe you have to have oppression bred in your bones to find ways around or under or through it.

At first he worried his lawyer would not go for the idea. There was no reason to assume George Givens was not a card-carrying anti-Semite. The lunch club in Boston where he could not take Al as he did his other clients, and the course where he played golf, and the hotels where he and his wife vacationed were all restricted. But there is no accounting for people's flashes of generosity or gratuitous acts of cruelty. The war was full of them. Al heard of soldiers defiling enemy bodies, then turning around to shelter a mangy stray dog. Aboard ship, he saw men bully other men for no reason other than the scent of weakness, then risk their lives to pick up a lifeboat full of strangers. The cousin his uncle brought over after the war said the camps were full of small atrocities and minute acts of kindness, though he does not elaborate, and Al has never asked him to. Perhaps the really surprising fact is that Al is surprised when George Givens agrees to the plan. Where did he get the idea that anyone, even an anti-Semitic lawyer, if he is an anti-Semite, is of a piece? Or maybe Givens just wants to hold on to him as a client.

Whatever the reason, Givens takes the money Al lends him without interest, buys the house from Dorothy Gooding, then turns it over to Al as payment for the loan. Millie is over the moon. The expression comes to her from out of the blue. Then she remembers how she knows it. Pete used it in his letters from England. The house has opened her even to that.

When Jack took one of the old photographs of Pete from the box he had found and put it on the dresser in his room here, she did not protest. She even bought a frame for it. Sometimes, when she goes into Jack's room for one reason or another, though now that he is away at school she has fewer reasons to do that, she stands in front of the photograph staring at it. She is glad it's there. If it weren't, she would not remember what Pete looked like.

She glances from the girls to Al again and

suddenly remembers sitting on the steps of that cramped apartment over the garage where she and Jack lived at the end of the war. I can do this, she thought then. It may not be love, but it's right. And now it is love. The change, the growth, strikes her as at once an inevitable outcome and an outrageous stroke of good luck.

The phone rings and both girls spring for it. Susan gets there first, but it must be someone they both know, because they hold the receiver between them, each putting an ear to it, and launch into a duet of talking, giggling, and whispering.

Millie stretches her legs along the sofa and kneads Al's thigh. He does not take his eyes from the television screen but winds one hand around her foot.

'That was Jack,' Betsy says after they hang up.

'Why didn't you let me talk to him?'

'He said he was in a hurry. He just wanted to let you know he's coming home for the weekend.'

'Is he bringing that girl again?'

'*That* girl.' Al winks at his daughters. 'Unless a girl is descended from the founding fathers on one side, robber barons on the other, and is a glamour-puss herself, she's not good enough for your brother.'

'I'm glad I'm such a source of amusement to you all. Did he say he's bringing her or not?'

'All he said,' Betsy tells her, 'is that he's coming home because he wants to talk to you about something.'

'Maybe he wants to talk to you about *that* girl,' Susan says, and grins at her father.

On Friday afternoon, Millie drives to the railroad depot to meet Jack's train. She stands leaning against the hood of the station wagon under a sky so clear it looks like tinted glass, feeling the lemony sunshine on her face. She hopes he is not bringing the girl. She certainly hopes the girl is not what he wants to talk about. He is much too young to be getting serious. He still has two more years of college.

He steps down from the train, stands for a moment combing the platform, spots her, and starts toward her. Even his walk is like Pete's. For years she tried to persuade herself he was imitating Al, but Al springs while Pete loped. As Jack lopes toward her now, she remembers driving up to Dartmouth with Al last year to pick him up at the end of the term. The friends he introduced them to called him Pete. So did the girl he brought home a few months ago. At home, he is still Jack. She did not mention the split personality to him or to Al.

When he reaches the car, he bends to kiss her on the cheek, and for a moment that passes so quickly she cannot catch it, Pete is stooping to her, and a pain she thought she was immune to goes off like a flashbulb, then dies.

She hands him the keys. He takes them, tosses his suitcase in the back, and gets in behind the wheel. He puts the key in the ignition but does not turn it. All around them, cars are pulling out of the parking area, but he goes on sitting there. Finally, he turns to her.

'I might as well get this over with,' he begins. 'Before we get home. This has nothing to do with Dad or Betsy or Susan. Especially not with Dad. I'm grateful to him. I don't want to hurt him. But this is about me. About my real father and me.'

'Dad is your real father. He raised you.'

'You know what I mean. If you want to help me, that's okay. If you don't, I'm still going to do it.'

She waits. He can call himself Pete, but she will not let him change Baum back to Swallow. She will not let him wound Al.

'I'm going to bring his body home from France.'

She is surprised at the feeling of relief that washes over her. This is less than she feared.

'I've already started the paperwork,' he goes on. 'Uncle Claude is helping. Before you get angry at him, I'm the one who's doing it. I went to him a couple of years ago, and he said if I still wanted to do it when I turned eighteen, he would help, but before that it was up to you.'

Just as the rush of relief surprised her, so does the feeling of gratitude. For all their differences, she can trust Claude and Babe. She is glad he turned to them, though she cannot help wishing he had come to her.

'You never asked me.'

'What would you have said if I did?'

408

She does not answer.

'You wouldn't even talk about it. I remember once when I was little and Aunt Grace brought home Uncle Charlie's body, she said something about bringing home my father. You shut her up as if she'd said a dirty word in front of the children.'

'That's not fair.'

He shrugs. The callousness of the gesture is like a slap in the face, that he can hurt her this way and then shrug.

'I'm not saying you didn't have your reasons. You probably thought you were doing what was best for me. But you weren't. So now I'm going to do it whether you like it or not. I don't mean that harshly, just as a fact. I'm going to do this no matter what anyone says.'

'It's that important to you?'

'Apparently.'

Apparently. Where is this cruelty coming from? All the same, she is not an unreasonable woman. She knows when to yield.

'Then we'll do it together,' she says.

The more she thinks about the idea on the way home, the more she warms to it. Maybe Jack's reinterment of Pete's body will let him finally bury the past.

CHAPTER 22

August 1964

The early-morning sky stretches like a soiled gray sheet beyond the window, but even the oppressive weather cannot sour Babe's spirits. Her optimism feels indecent. She should not be cheerful on the day of a funeral, but she cannot help herself. Maybe the cliché is true. That is why it's a cliché. Time heals. She is glad Jack insisted on bringing his father's body home. They will lay more than Pete to rest today.

When she comes downstairs, she finds Claude sitting at the table with a mug of coffee and the morning paper. His cotton robe has fallen open. He is wearing nothing under it. Neither of them sleeps in anything. His penis lies innocent and defenseless. She wonders if it's the male mindset. If she were sitting exposed at the kitchen table, she would know it.

The sight of him distracts her, so her eyes take a moment to focus on the newspaper. She can read the headline from halfway across the room.

TWO TORPEDO VESSELS
BELIEVED SUNK IN
GULF OF TONKIN

She will not let the news intrude. She flees to the quotidian.

'I left your navy-blue suit in the bathroom,' she says, as she goes to the refrigerator to take out the orange juice, butter, and jam. 'The steam from the shower will get rid of the wrinkles. I hope. I forgot to take it to the cleaner.'

He does not ask her why she is worrying about a wrinkled suit when they are going to a funeral. He knows the defense of the everyday.

The fog has not burned off by the time they reach the cemetery. It hangs like a curtain from the sky and steams up from the ground. At Charlie's reburial, the weather jeered at them. At King's funeral, it assaulted them. Now it is in cahoots with them. A soft landing, a misty fade-out.

Several cars are parked along the narrow dirt road that runs beside the graveyard. Grace, Morris, and Amy sit in one of them, the engine still running to keep the air conditioner going.

Claude turns off the ignition. His car has no air-conditioning. Babe watches as Amy opens the door and climbs out of the backseat. She is wearing dark glasses, though the sun does not pierce the murky sky. Her long print dress makes her look as if she has just climbed down from a

411

covered wagon. Babe can imagine how the outfit goes over with Grace. But the dress is the least of it. Eleven months after Amy went through with the big wedding, she walked out of the marriage. Her mother was heartbroken.

'At least she was the one who left,' Grace said to Millie and Babe after the divorce. Her face brightened. 'Come to think of it, she's always the one who leaves. Eddie Montrose; that boy from Harvard her freshman year; the one from Dartmouth she almost got pinned to; the French professor, and I don't have to tell you he had me worried.'

Babe thought, but did not say, because she did not want to undermine whatever consolation Grace could find, that perhaps Amy leaves first so she cannot be left.

Amy makes her way through the gate into the cemetery, the thin cotton dress swaying as she walks. Charlie's grave is three rows in. She stands at the foot of it, studying the headstone, though there is little enough to read. She looks from the headstone to the grave. It is covered with deep-green ivy – no rusty dying leaves, no errant outgrowths. Grace pays to have the grave tended. She also drives out weekly to see that she is getting her money's worth. King taught her that much. Amy screws up her face as if she is trying to concentrate. Babe watches her and knows she is struggling to conjure a father out of the morning mist.

Grace gets out of the car, walks through the gate, and crosses to stand beside her daughter. At first, Babe thinks from the way Amy lists that she is going to walk away, but she doesn't. They stand at Charlie's grave, not touching but bound.

The others begin getting out of their cars. Millie, Al, and the two girls; Morris; Pete's parents and Mac; Babe and Claude. They straggle through the gate.

The open grave lies two rows over from Charlie's. Suspended above it, the coffin gleams in the milky morning. They arrange themselves around it. Mrs Swallow is flanked by her husband and remaining son. Mac stands rubbing one wrist with the thumb of his other hand. His expression is distracted, the gesture unconscious. The scar has begun to fade. Babe senses that, though with the exception of the few times she has run into him on the street when he has come home to visit his parents, she seldom sees him anymore. He stopped accepting their invitations around the time King Gooding died, and gradually they stopped asking him. A few years ago, she heard he was going to marry, but no report of a wedding followed the rumor.

Naomi has come too. She stands beside her son, who has traveled up from New York for the funeral. He was a baby when Pete died, but there is a connection among Amy, Jack, and Frankie. When their fathers went off to fight, some of them to

413

die, and their mothers sought the comfort their children did not yet know how to give, the children found solace among themselves. They still do. Though they rarely see one another, they stay in touch.

Naomi's face is solemn, but the way she clings to Frankie's arm gives her away. She is hanging on the future. A few months ago, Frankie graduated from law school.

Morris comes up the gravel walk, stops beside Grace, and puts his hand on her elbow, as husbands do to wives at gravesides. For a moment, she looks as if she is going to take a step away, but she remains where she is.

Millie and Al stand beside the open grave. As Millie reaches to draw in the two girls, her heel sinks into the soft earth, and she goes over on one ankle. Al grabs her arm to steady her.

She is wearing a black linen suit and a black pillbox hat. She reminds Babe of someone, but it takes a moment to figure out who. Millie is dressed like Jackie Kennedy at JFK's funeral the previous November, except that she is not wearing a mantilla. Millie would not wear a mantilla – it is too Catholic – but the impression is pure Jackie. Babe does not want to make too much of it. Half the women in America are trying to look like Jackie Kennedy. But she cannot get over the feeling that there is more to it than that. Millie gave in to Jack about bringing the body home, but she will not risk falling into that abyss of loss again. She has agreed to grieve for Pete, but she will make her grief public, national, historic. Anything but personal.

The minister takes his place beside them. Al says something to him, and he steps back. Jack is still missing.

He told Millie he would meet them at the cemetery. He also said he had a surprise. Millie is sure it is a girl. She is always sure it's a girl.

'At Pete's reburial?' Babe asked when Millie told her the day before.

'That just shows how serious it is. He wants her here for this.'

The minister looks at his watch. Mac stares at the suspended coffin. Mr Swallow moves his hat from one hand to the other and back. He is the only man with a hat. Since the late president took the oath of office bareheaded on a frigid January day, only old men wear hats. They are a nation of old men who wear hats and hatless young men dying before their time. The thought, Babe knows, is a little wild. She is on edge. She is eager to get this over with. They all are.

Beside her, Claude puts his hand in his pocket, then takes it out. He no longer tries to hide it. She no longer notices the missing fingers.

A car pulls up. They turn as a single entity. A man and woman get out, but the woman is old, and the man is not Jack. He is carrying flowers for someone else's grave.

The minister looks at his watch again. The others

415

look at one another or away. They cannot be annoyed at Jack. Jack is why they are here.

'I hope nothing's wrong,' Grace says in an undertone.

'He probably hit traffic,' Al murmurs.

'Where is he coming from?' the minister asks.

'College,' Al says. 'New Hampshire.'

Another car pulls up. There is only one person in it. Through the windshield, Babe recognizes the shape of Jack's head and the width of his shoulders. During the war, she used to say she could never be a plane spotter, because she could not tell the silhouette of one plane from another, but Claude insisted all she had to do was pay attention. You know it's me coming down the street from a block away, he said, just by the shape of my body and the way I move. If you get to know the different planes, you'll be able to recognize them too. It was a man's argument, off the mark for a woman. She has no interest in the shape of planes. She cares about the contours of people.

Jack gets out of the car. From where they are standing, only his head is visible. The car hides his body. He bends and reaches back in the car. Through the window, Babe sees him pick up something off the seat, but she cannot tell what it is. He straightens, closes the door, and lifts the hand that is holding the object. He puts on the hat. Her breath catches in her chest. She does not have to be trained to spot military silhouettes to recognize the service cap.

416

He starts toward the gate. He is a moving image, coming more sharply into focus with each step. The peak of the hat casts a shadow over the top half of his face, like a masked bandit stealing his own future. The fitted green jacket stiffens the easy sway of his shoulders. The collar of the khaki shirt and the dark tie seem to be strangling him. The heavy black shoes transform his customary lope into a march. No, the shoes do not do that; *they* have done that. Millie with her secrets; the movies with their ersatz heroism; the comic books with their bang, boom, swat, splat; Claude with his missing fingers that take on an aura of mysterious glamour, because he never talks about how he lost them but everyone wonders and imagines and admires; herself with her shameful nostalgia for a life lived with her heart in her mouth, but lived.

He is standing in front of them now. The morning mist is starting to burn off. A streak of sunlight sears a hole in the soiled white sky, hits the infantry insignia on his collar, and glances off it like quicksilver.

'Oh, shit,' Amy murmurs.

The coffin with what is left of Pete's body disappears into the grave and hits the ground with the same dull thud Babe remembers from the other funerals, but now there is a difference, because now no one knows what to say. It is too late for condolences for Pete; too soon – never, they pray

– for Jack. They climb back into their cars for the drive to Millie and Al's.

As Claude pulls up in front of the house, Babe notices Grace and Amy standing in the driveway. They are cantilevered toward each other, and she does not have to hear them to know they are arguing. They face off, a long-haired, bizarrely dressed waif against a meticulously turned-out woman in a buttoned-up linen suit and straw hat. A girl who has left a trail of men in her wake against a one-man woman who has never forgiven her second husband for – for what? Babe wonders. For marrying her? A daughter struggling and afraid to break free of her mother against a mother desperate to hold on to her daughter. Amy has worked so hard to be the opposite of Grace that she has ended up her mirror image, left to right, right to left, but identical.

Babe goes into the house and heads for the kitchen to see if Millie needs help. She is standing at the counter, frozen in place. Only the tears streaming down her face move.

'Just don't tell me I brought it on myself,' she says when she sees Babe.

'I wasn't going to.'

Grace appears at the back door in time to hear the exchange. 'You did what you thought was best.' Her voice is gentle, though her face is still flushed from the argument with Amy.

'You both did,' Babe tells them.

Millie takes a handkerchief from the pocket of

her black suit and mops her eyes. 'Go into the living room. Please. I'll be all right in a minute.'

Grace catches Babe's eye and nods toward the door.

Babe is surprised. She thought Millie wanted both of them to go inside, but now she understands. She means Babe, the wife who has never been a widow, the woman who is childless but has never had a child break her heart. The lucky one, they think, should go away and leave the two of them to their grief.

She turns and starts through the dining room. Beyond the French doors, a swirl of tie-dyed color and a stain of dark green that almost fades into the trees catch her eye. Jack and Amy are sitting at the round wrought-iron table. A fine rain, more like a mist, has begun to fall, but the big umbrella over the table shelters them. What do they say to each other, these two children who have grown up on rumors of the fathers they never knew?

As she stands watching them, she senses Al crossing behind her. He goes into the kitchen, and a moment later Grace comes out. Even she, who shares the heartache of lost husbands and damaged children, cannot console Millie now. But Babe hears the rise and fall of Al's voice in the kitchen and Millie's answering it in a practiced duet, and recognizes not a song of solace – if anything happens to Jack, there will be no solace – but the refrain of Millie's fierce will.

Grace goes past Babe to the other set of French

doors, opens them, and steps out into the garden. She stands hesitant, her body leaning almost imperceptibly toward her daughter, then away. Amy goes on talking to Jack. Her mother might as well be invisible.

Grace starts across the yard, oblivious of the drizzle, or pretending to be. A moment later, another figure comes out of the French doors to the sunporch and follows her. Mac is carrying an open umbrella. As he catches up to her and reaches out to shelter her with it, she turns back to him, and Babe sees her face. It has collapsed into jarring, disjointed pieces, a cubist portrait of desolation and fear.

Mac's lips begin to move. Babe thinks Grace is going to bolt, but she stands listening. He goes on for some time, and as he does, she begins to put her face together. By the time they turn back to the house, it is a mask of perfect composure. They start across the yard, side by side, in step with each other, but the umbrella is large, and they are careful to keep several inches of damp daylight between them. The space, Babe thinks, is a lament for what might have been.

Babe turns back to Amy and Jack just as Claude comes up behind her and puts his left arm around her shoulders.

'Were we ever that young?' she asks.

'Before the war.'

The soreness in his voice takes her back.

After the war, they wrote and promised and

420

prayed. *After the war* we'll do this or that or another thing. *After the war* we'll be together. *After the war* we'll be happy. *After the war* we'll be safe. In all their dreaming of *after the war,* they never dreamed there is no after to war.

She reaches up and covers his hand with hers and, as she does, another thought crosses her mind. She knows the question is foolish, but she cannot help herself.

'Would you have married me if there were no war?'

She waits for his answer, though she is sure he will tell her what she wants to hear.

He surprises her.

'If there were no war?' he repeats. 'Imagine.'